HEDGING DEATH

A Judge Avery Lassiter Novel

Stacey Jernigan

2022 White Bird Publications, LLC

Copyright © 2022 by Stacey Jernigan
Cover design by E. Kusch

Published in the United States
by White Bird Publications, LLC, Austin, Texas
www.whitebirdpublications.com

ISBN 978-1-63363-581-4
eBook ISBN 978-1-63363-582-1
Library of Congress Control Number: 2022932777

PRINTED IN THE UNITED STATES OF AMERICA

Dedication

This novel is dedicated to all the judges, attorneys, United States Marshals, and law enforcement officers who every day work hard doing their jobs—being guardians of the American justice system and the Rule of Law—and, of course, to my dear family.

Author's Note

Because I am a sitting United States judge, and I am also married to a police officer, I feel compelled, at the outset, to clarify certain points regarding this novel.

First, **with the exception of the Prologue herein** (which describes real-life events that happened July 7, 2016, in Dallas, Texas) the following is a work of fiction. While some of the characters and events beyond the Prologue may be loosely based on actual persons and events, and some of the places (in my home state of Texas and in various other faraway spots) are certainly very real, the human characters in this novel are absolutely fictional. Judge Avery Lassiter, the main character in this novel, is not me.

Second, one should not assume that any statement or opinion expressed or implied by any characters in this novel are necessarily mine or are somehow a reflection on how I might rule on any particular issue in any case in the future.

HEDGING
DEATH

Judge Avery Lassiter Novel

White Bird
Publications

*"The arc of the moral universe is long,
but it bends toward justice."*
                              —**Theodore Parker**

Prologue

July 7, 2016, Dallas, Texas—End of Watch

Shots fired. Officers down.

Sometimes weapon fire is not easily recognizable to an untrained ear. Rapid gunfire can sound like fireworks, vehicles backfiring, or noises from nearby construction sites. Given the time of year, many in the dense crowd thought that the artillery barrage might have been bottle rockets or other pyrotechnics, left over from a recent Fourth of July celebration. Others had little doubt about what they were hearing.

Judge Avery Lassiter sat up in bed, bleary-eyed, watching the television news coverage that night. As the saying goes, "if it bleeds, it leads." Thus, there was non-stop streaming of the horrific events as they unfolded. The news cameras kept panning to cops on the streets of downtown—just near Avery's courthouse. Avery recognized no one so far. She kept noticing the same dazed look in all of the cops' eyes—a look she had seen before—that so-called "thousand-yard stare" of detachment and numbness. She told herself that most of them who lived would eventually be okay. The extremity of the moment would be followed by the recognition of being alive in the moment. That's how these things usually worked. The brothers and sisters in blue were nothing, if not resilient. However, the survivors would be forever haunted by those who didn't live through this night.

July 7, 2016 was a hot day in Dallas, Texas. It was a Thursday. Since the preceding Monday had been Independence Day, the streets of Downtown Dallas were less congested than usual. Many people had taken a week-long holiday. The only thing atypical about this sultry summer day was that, in the evening, a rally had been organized by a group known as the Next Generation Action Network to protest the recent killings of two Black men, Alton Sterling and Philando Castile, by police officers in Louisiana and Minnesota, respectively. The rally that night in Dallas was one of several being held simultaneously across the United States.

The starting time for the event was 7:00 p.m. Central Daylight Time—about an hour and a half before sunset. The location for the beginning of the rally would be the Belo Gardens, directly across from the Earle Cabell Federal Building. Around 800 protesters attended the rally, and around 100 police officers were assigned to work the event, providing contingent crowd control and traffic diversion in the surrounding areas. The protesters would march a short route, mostly along Main Street.

The protest was peaceful—actually, a model of the way free expression and the right of assembly should ideally work in a democratic society. Some protesters brought their children with them—it was summertime after all. The law enforcement presence was deferential and affable with the crowd. There was no trouble of any sort at first. In fact, the rally was in some ways patriotic—partly because of the time of the year. There was a mood of mutual respect and calm in the atmosphere. The organizer of the demonstration was an ordained minister. Attendees were mostly friendly, dignified, and somber as they lit candles, uttered doleful chants, and sang hymns. The Dallas Police Department had, for many years, maintained a relatively positive rapport with the citizens in the community. Momentarily, things turned a little frightening, when approximately twenty to thirty open-carry gun-rights activists joined the protest, some wearing gas masks, bulletproof vests, and fatigues—in addition to carrying rifles. While this caused some tension, the activists caused no trouble. They were mostly ignored. They eventually went on their way, distancing themselves from the crowd.

Just before 9:00 p.m., as the cloudless sky grew dark, graced with an incandescent crescent moon, "shit turned real," as Officer Max Lassiter was prone to say.

The demonstrators had walked from the Belo Gardens down Main Street, in a westerly direction, towards Dallas's Romanesque-style sandstone "Old Red" Courthouse. A few in the crowd posed for pictures there. The burnt sienna and gray-trimmed courthouse, with its rusticated marble accents, was built in 1892. It stood majestically, in stark contrast to the modern glass and steel structures of the city, with its stunning clock tower, castle-like turrets, spires, arches, and terracotta winged, spiny-backed serpents perched on the top. Children sometimes remarked that the courthouse looked like a gingerbread castle with its puffy, whimsical features. Some children that night pointed toward the bell tower with its shimmering light, wondering if they saw two ghostly apparitions watching over the sea of people. They shouted, "Look! It's the ghosts of Bonnie and Clyde!" These were children of a local criminal defense lawyer. The children had slightly confused the details of their father's scary bedtime stories regarding the ghosts of Bonnie and Clyde—who were allegedly seen, from time to time, roaming Dallas landmarks. In 1934, the infamous Clyde Barrow's corpse had been lain out for public viewing prior to his funeral at the nearby Belo Mansion (now the Dallas Lawyers' headquarters, which was formerly a funeral home). He'd been shot and killed in an ambush in Louisiana. For years since, there had been folklore that Clyde Barrow's spectral image stalked, back and forth, haunting that nearby facility—which was actually a few blocks northeast of the march.

As the crowd of demonstrators U-turned easterly at Old Red, sauntering slowly up Main Street, twenty-five-year-old Micah Xavier Johnson, a former U.S. Army Reservist, dressed in a tan body armor vest and other tactical clothing, and equipped with two handguns, an assault rifle, and vast amounts of ammunition, parked his mother's black sports utility vehicle that he had driven downtown. He parked it illegally, southbound on Lamar Street, between Main and Elm Streets, beside El Centro College. Johnson had been shadowing the march, driving from street to street, until this particular moment. The young man was approximately one block from the unsuspecting crowd. He left the hazard lights flashing on the vehicle and cautiously emerged from the car. Johnson took a few steps out of the darkness and onto the spongey asphalt of Lamar Street. He was somewhat of an imposing figure, with a tall, muscular physique, bristling black facial hair, and brown hollow eyes. He paused for a protracted moment, balefully gazing back and forth over the crowd, and then began a vicious ambush—rapidly firing a Izhmash-Saiga 5.45mm rifle (a variation on the AK 174 semi-automatic) into a parked police car and at a group of police officers who were strolling with the demonstrators. Johnson's bullets were disturbingly accurate, hitting several officers and a civilian. It was initially difficult to discern how many police officers and citizens were down in the chaos. The scene was one of bedlam as most in the massive crowd of people frantically scattered in all directions.

As the shots rang out, echoing like cannon fire through the canyons of Downtown Dallas, it had a disorienting effect. It was almost impossible to tell the direction from which the torrent of bullets was coming—much less whom was being targeted. Was the carnage random, or was it only the police who were under attack? Were there multiple perpetrators and, if so, were they perhaps those open-carry guns rights activists who had marched by earlier? Was it one or more high-positioned snipers? Perhaps the children of the defense lawyer had, in fact, truly seen figures up in Old Red's bell tower after all. People in the crowd bolted for their lives as the shots continued. Parents crouched behind cars with children. Some in the crowd simply stood frozen in bewilderment, paralyzed by fear. Injured victims were thrown into parked police cars and were hurried to nearby hospitals.

The shooter, Micah Johnson, was not finished with his ambush. With what was described as the fierce look of a predator, he swept around facing the opposite direction and ran northward up Lamar Street, wildly peppering shots into the glass doors of one of the entrances of El Centro College. Two campus police officers behind the glass doors were injured. More than four dozen students and instructors were still present on campus, just finishing up summer school classes at this late hour.

The gunman continued working his way up Lamar Street, passing his own vehicle, eventually creeping up on a Dallas Transit police officer, fatally shooting him from behind, as the officer peered around a concrete pillar. Micah Johnson robotically continued to fire his gun as he shifted, turned, and zigzagged up the campus sidewalk—almost as though he were racing through an imaginary minefield. One of the injured El Centro campus police officers heroically managed to rise to his feet. The campus officer ran out onto Lamar Street, saw the fallen Transit officer, and attempted to help him. As he did, the shooter rounded the corner at Elm Street, continuing to blast shots into the glass windows of El Centro. Johnson eventually ducked inside the college, just as the instructors and frantic students were managing to evacuate from another end of campus. He then went into a stairwell to apparently hide or rest up for another phase of his murderous rampage. Johnson had a student access card that had allowed him entry onto the campus. He had seemingly planned every detail of his mission quite well.

At some point in his spree, Johnson was injured and began spurting a stream of his own blood on the sidewalks outside of El Centro. About fifteen minutes after the first shooting spree had paused, the second of the two injured El Centro campus police officers saw Johnson's blood trail and followed it to find Johnson, lying in a supine position, in an El Centro stairwell. Upon seeing the officer, Johnson vaulted to his feet—obviously not seriously injured, and apparently, feeling rested and reinvigorated enough to begin another phase of battle. A spectacular shootout ensued. At some point, the beleaguered campus police officer—fighting alone against a better armed, well-prepared executioner— was forced to retreat, and Johnson ran into a second-floor library.

Then Johnson perched himself in a north-facing window and resumed his massacre, shooting at police officers down below on Elm Street. He struck and killed a fifty-five-year-old Dallas Police Sergeant at that point, who was climbing out of his patrol car by a 7-11 convenience store. He also struck and injured another DART police officer working at the West End rail station.

Downtown Dallas was a horrific, turbulent crime scene for more than five hours—with an active shooter still at large. All Dallas Police Department officers were called to duty by 10:00 p.m. United States Marshal task force officers were brought to the scene as well and were roaming the streets in full tactical gear. All businesses and buildings were on lockdown, with innocents sheltering inside, as helicopters swirled around the bloody scene.

Police investigators eventually determined that Micah Johnson had moved into an alcove toward the center of El Centro's campus, away from all windows. But the police did not have a clear view of him. The next step was for SWAT officers to enter the building—it was believed, at this point, that Johnson was the only person inside. Subsequently, in the early hours of July 8, there ensued a lengthy standoff between the shooter and SWAT officers, during which at least 200 rounds of ammunition were fired. During the confrontation, Johnson was described as savoring every moment, showing a mixture of bravado, arrogance, and shamelessness as he laughed at police, sang songs, and asked how many people he had killed so far.

The Dallas Police Chief eventually made a bold decision, to send in a remote-controlled robot with a pound of C-4 explosives attached to it. The robot was sent down a hallway inside the college toward Johnson where it was then detonated. Johnson was killed instantly. It was the first time that a robot had been used in U.S. law enforcement history to put down a perpetrator in this type of context.

Later, in a dark hallway inside El Centro, police discovered that the shooter had scrawled "RB" in his own blood in two places on the wall. The meaning remains unknown to this day. "Righteous blood"? Some speculated that perhaps Johnson was attempting to write "RBG"—for the red, black, and green flag, also known as the Pan-African flag. The red, black, and green flag was later discovered on Johnson's social media page. Or maybe, others speculated, "Rosebud" (a throwback to the dying words of a character in the Hollywood film *Citizen Kane*)? Various theories would later abound on Internet blogs—some plausible and some ridiculous. There were other cryptic markings on the wall that have never been identified. As far as investigators could determine, Johnson (who lived with his mother) was not affiliated with any group. He was a lone wolf. Another lone wolf who chose a path of violence.

During negotiations, the shooter told police negotiators that he had placed explosives in various spots around Downtown Dallas. The shooter warned, "The end is coming." Thus, the nightmare continued for hours after Micah Johnson's death. No bombs were ever found, but a search for bombs was carried out throughout the night and into the next day, and the city was on edge until the threat was thoroughly investigated. Downtown Dallas was a blockaded crime scene, blanketed in a chilling, funereal atmosphere, for several days.

In the end, twelve police officers were shot by Micah Johnson (eight Dallas Police Department Officers and four DART officers). *Twelve were shot*—was that merely a coincidence or by design, since "twelve" is a slang term for police? Five officers died. "End of watch," as the police family says.

The nightmare, of course, would never completely end for the friends and loved ones of the fallen. In addition to the officers, two innocent civilians were injured but recovered—one was a mother who was shot while shielding her terrified children. The fallen were sons, daughters, spouses, parents, brothers, sisters, friends. They were individuals positively impacting their communities—regularly accomplishing amazing but unnoticed personal feats. Those who knew them well described them as selfless heroes who had no desire to be acknowledged or recognized. One fallen officer had served three tours of duty in Iraq as a Naval officer and was awarded several medals for his valor. Another officer had served in the Army and was said to have frequently purchased meals for homeless people when he was out on patrol. Another had played semi-professional football and people described him as a big guy with a bigger heart. Yet another was active in his church, where he handed out stickers to children as they departed from Sunday School—he had postponed a family vacation by one day to work at the rally, grinning sheepishly when his colleagues teased him about his unfailing work ethic. Decent, quiet heroes, one and all.

Inside Micah Johnson's home, Dallas Police found metal piping, chemicals, and instructions for making a bomb. It appeared that he had been practicing explosive detonations, and they were large enough to create mass devastation. Also found in his home were ballistic vests, rifles, ammunition, and a personal journal of combat tactics—including a tactic called "shoot and move," designed to confuse police. Johnson had no criminal history. He had served in the U.S. Army Reserve for six years (achieving the rank of private first class) and had completed an eight-month tour in Afghanistan. Police were convinced that he had bigger plans.

Was he mentally ill, with perhaps post-traumatic stress disorder, or just an angry, evil soul? A lunatic or a hater? Horrible events demand answers. But does it really matter? Johnson managed, in one night, to forever alter the lives of a dozen innocent victims and their loved ones. Like November 1963, Dallas's happy, positive image was again besmirched by the acts of a killer.

Avery's beloved Cavalier King Charles Spaniel, Baxter, was by her side snoring loudly. He was her constant companion—they had been through so much together. Usually, his slobbery snores had a soporific effect on her, but not on this night. Avery's phone did not stop beeping with texts and calls. All of her colleagues at the courthouse wanted to know what was really happening. Did Max know? Was Max involved?

Avery stayed awake, afraid of going to sleep. Afraid for the kids. She had to be ready. She had to practice in her mind how she would handle things—just in case. That's what one must do when you are married to a cop. You practice in your mind. Everything is for the greater good. If a cop dies in the line of work, so be it. They die for the greater good.

Chapter One

Three Years Later (July 2019)— "Pseudocide" is Painless.

Faked deaths. Also known as "staged deaths." Evanescing
without a trace.

"Yes, feigning one's own death is a 'thing,'" Avery was
explaining to Julia one Saturday afternoon while the two of
them rinsed and diced vegetables for a salad. Avery was
apprising Julia as to why her father would be away from
home for an indeterminate length of time, while next
coaching Julia through preparation of Baba Jo's favorite
recipe for meaty, cheesy manicotti.

"No, silly, your dad is not faking his own death! Oh my
gosh, Julia!"

Julia looked back at her mother with a kittenish half
smile.

Max Lassiter was taking an extended trip down to
Mexico to investigate what was believed to be a pretend
death of a man named Cade Graham, a well-known wealthy
playboy and high-flying, Dallas hedge fund manager.

Graham was the founder and CEO of Dallas-based Ranger Capital, a multibillion-dollar conglomerate, which managed not just hedge funds but private equity funds, CDOs, CLOs, REITs, life settlements, and all manner of complicated financial products. This investigation was part of Max's new post-retirement gig—working as an investigator for Premier Mutual Life Insurance Company.

Max had "escaped the confinement of the police department" and retired a couple of years ago—not long after the July 2016 police massacre. He had started this "strange new endeavor," as Avery called it, last January. He now referred to himself as a professional "finder." And he was referring to this Mexico assignment of his as "Operation Hedge Hog." His investigative assignments always had some catchy code name. Just like with the corporate transactional lawyers Avery used to work with at her old law firm. It appears one could not ever use actual names for their projects—whether there were legitimate confidentiality concerns or not. "Project Orion," "Juno," "Calypso"—there was never any rhyme or reason to them. At least "Operation Hedge Hog" had a meaningful tie to Cade Graham's profession.

"Why do people fake their own deaths, Mom?"

"Well, it happens often enough that there is even an official term for it: 'pseudocide.'"

"I have never heard of that word."

"I hadn't either until your dad started this. Anyway, why, you ask, would a person execute such a hoax? Honey, I could spend all day answering that question. There have been plenty of reasons people have orchestrated their own deaths throughout history. People who engage in this come from all walks of life—from ordinary, everyday people, to egomaniacs, eccentrics, to well-known authors, to women escaping domestic abuse (a *donna fugata*, as they say in Italian), to corporate titans, to hedge fund managers, to former Nazis. Most often, though, they are middle class, middle aged, heterosexual white males with families."

"You've just described Dad!"

"Yes, I suppose I have."

"But why, Mom? Why do people do something so weird?"

"It's usually about escaping some undesirable situation, sweetie. But I would say it is most often about money—such as someone falling into financial distress and trying to escape the consequences. Conversely, sometimes someone has had the good fortune of coming into a lot of money—like an inheritance or winning the lottery—and is trying to escape a spouse or family or friends seeking a share. This is sad, but I have even heard of young people with significant amounts of student loan debt faking their deaths to get out of the burden of having to pay it."[1]

"You mean like if Heath did it, because he chose to attend such an expensive private college and has such huge student loans now, Mom?"

"Not funny, Julia!"

"Can you get arrested for faking your own death?"

"Well, faking your death—just basically going missing off the grid—is not by itself a crime. Technically, a person can go missing if he or she chooses. You know, just check out of life, so to speak. But most of the time, a fraud is going to be committed somehow in the process, or the person is going to end up committing some other crime as part of faking his death."

"Like how?"

"Well, a 'pseudocide' usually starts with a person leaving random evidence to mislead people into thinking that he or she is dead, but there is usually no corpse (for obvious reasons). Sometimes, the evidence that they leave to mislead people ends up being fraudulently created and so that fraudulent evidence can be a crime. Sometimes, the

---

[1] *See generally* Elizabeth Greenwood, Playing Dead: A Journey Through the World of Death Fraud (Simon & Schuster 2016).

death-faker will next assume the identity of an actual dead person with similar vital statistics and age. That would also be a crime."

"Oh yeah, I've seen that in a TV show before."

"Ha! I bet you have. And insurance fraud is very high on the list of reasons that people are known to fake their deaths—that is, as part of an attempt to fraudulently collect life insurance policy proceeds. And that's why your father is getting involved in the alleged death of this fellow, Cade Graham."

"I'm not sure I get what you mean, Mom."

"Let's see. I assume you know what life insurance is, or no?"

Julia raised her right eyebrow and shrugged her shoulders. Julia had never been very childlike—always an old soul—so much so that sometimes Avery forgot that she was a child and didn't already know some basic things that adults know.

"Okay, I'll explain. I pay premiums every month for a life insurance policy, so that if I die before you are grown up, a pot of money will be paid out by the insurance company that will support you, since if I am dead, I am not around making money anymore to support you. Just like car insurance is for the situation when you are in a car wreck, life insurance is for when someone dies—there will be money to pay out to people who depended upon that person."

"You're being so morbid, Mom."

"No, not really. The concept of life insurance came into existence a couple of hundred years ago. It's generally quite a good thing that can give parents peace of mind for their families. But, like any other commercial enterprise in life, there are always going to be dishonest people who figure out a way to exploit the system. There are many documented cases, from the very beginning of the industry, of schemes where people have faked their deaths, or the deaths of friends and loved ones, to receive life insurance money."

"How do people do it usually?"

"Well people are sometimes good at it and people are often terrible at it. According to your father, people most often fake a water accident—a drowning or falling off a boat far out in the ocean from the shore. Presumably, the perpetrators believe that drowning out at sea provides a plausible reason for the absence of a body. These cases are almost always suspicious, especially if the person has been in legal or financial trouble. In a drowning, a body will typically wash up, usually in the first few days. So, if there's a drowning and no corpse ever appears, it's very suspicious in the eyes of law enforcement. Of course, sometimes people just leave a suicide note and disappear—causing suspicion about whether foul play was involved."

"The character Juliet from *Romeo and Juliet* faked her death, Mom!"

"Yes, Julia. At least, initially. That didn't work out very well, did it? And some people think Elvis and Michael Jackson might have faked their own deaths."

"Huh?"

"Oh, never mind. Before your time, sweetie. Anyway, it is really very hard to get away with faking your death. People think they are geniuses at staying hidden, but they leave breadcrumbs everywhere. Digital footprints. Technology has been an absolute gamechanger when it comes to ferreting out missing people—well, at least missing adults. A person really must completely do away with all technology and go completely off the grid. That's why the U.S. Marshals almost always find their fugitives because people can't stay off their phones or computers or avoid ATMs or credit cards or video cameras."

"I bet I could disappear, Mom."

"Oh please. You can't stay off your phone for five minutes."

In fact, Julia had just put down her vegetable peeler and was doing internet searches on her phone. She had just *Googled* Cade Graham's name and saw plenty of pictures of him—mostly standing with beautiful and extremely young women in exotic locations. He looked fifty-something and had slicked back, collar-length, silver hair, a tanned complexion, sparkling green eyes, and fluorescently glowing white teeth.

"I found pictures of Cade Graham, Mom. He apparently wears nothing but black turtlenecks. And only hangs out with girls who look barely older than me."

"Lovely. Anyway, there is a creepy, underground market out there with resources to help a person orchestrate a fake death. For example, you can obtain a fake death certificate through these underground markets. Mexico is one place where people have been known to easily get a fake death certificate. It's usually accomplished through people who work for the government providing the documents that people need. It might cost you $150 to get a fake death certificate. Then the person just arranges for it to be filed with the U.S. Embassy down there. 'John Doe was killed in a car wreck while vacationing in Mexico.' There are also certain countries where there are corrupt morgues, where the operators take in dead homeless people and keep them on ice until someone comes around and wants to buy a body to pass it off as himself."

"That's so disgusting!"

"Yep, it is all right."

"So, what's the deal with Cade Graham? Why do Dad and the insurance company think that he faked his own death?"

"Oh, Mr. Graham is, or was, a real piece of work. A real hedonistic, narcissistic playboy. He has—or had—fashion model or actress girlfriends on almost every continent, it seems. As you noticed from your internet search, they all look disturbingly young. And he seems, over time, to have developed a reputation as being a hustler working the bottom rungs of Wall Street. A ton of people hate him, don't trust him, and can't figure out how on earth he manages to make so much money in both good times and bad times. Other people think he's magic and will write him a blank check to invest money with him any time he asks. He supposedly went vacationing in Mexico recently and died in a fiery, single-car crash. But the facts just don't all add up."

"How so?"

"Well, not only is Mexico not Cade Graham's type of vacation hot spot—he is more the French Riviera, Marbella, or Amalfi Coast type—but there was recently a lot of strange activity in some of his hedge funds—a lot of money disappearing. People were suing him, and the Feds were investigating him for all sorts of things. His world was crumbling around him. All kinds of problems were mounting up."

"Well, was his body not in the car that crashed or something?"

"Funny you should ask. He rented a car and apparently crashed into a bridge embankment. There was a fiery explosion. Supposedly, nothing was left of Cade Graham but bone fragments. The life insurance company was naturally suspicious—a lot of people are suspicious—but the life insurance company was especially, since there was a very large policy on Mr. Graham that was taken out only a few months ago. So, your dad's new boss sent him and some forensic experts down to look at the car. As it turns out, there were unusual things, like his skull remains were down in the floorboard and the teeth did not match Cade Graham's dental records. Long story short, it turned out to be the remains of an old Mexican man stolen from a nearby mausoleum, not Cade Graham's, and the inside of the car had been set on fire—it did not catch on fire from the crash. Now your dad is on the hunt for Cade Graham down in Mexico."

"Operation Hedgehog. You think he'll find him?"

"Don't know. We'll see, sweetie. Cade Graham could very well be half-way around the world by now."

"Well at least if Dad does not find him, maybe he'll get to work in some fishing down in Mexico while he is there.

He seems to like to do that."

"Your dad likes to fish on the Caribbean side of Mexico. Cade Graham apparently died—or fake died—near Cabo San Lucas on the Pacific Ocean side."

"If they can't find him, Mom, what will happen to his life insurance money?"

"Hmm. I don't know the answer to that. I mean the life insurance company is not going to want to pay it out for sure. But I've never asked your dad who the beneficiary is on his policy that might be trying to collect on it. That's an interesting question. He was not married, but he supposedly had a couple of illegitimate children."

"Oh, Mom, I just thought of another faked death. Richard Braden, right?"

"Julia, stop! We don't ever talk about the Braden boys in this house. Not ever. End of conversation."

Chapter Two

Hidalgo, Mexico—Mission Creep from Operation Hedgehog.

Summer can be hard on old men. "*El Verano puede ser dificil para los hombres viejos.*" Max Lassiter's Spanish language skills were not very good, but they were getting better. He thought this was the correct translation for what the mumbling old man shuffling by him just uttered. The old man was right. Max Lassiter's father had died of a heart attack in his front yard on an airless, scorching July day just like this one. Max himself had a heart attack on a hot day on the job awhile back—not long after the July 7, 2016, Dallas police massacre. It had prompted his early retirement from the police department. If this current endeavor could be called "retirement." Anyway, Max figured the old man was probably a paid lookout for the *Huachicoleros*. The old man probably figured Max was a lookout, too.

Max took a sip of his almost empty bottle of Pacifico as he sat in the driver's seat of his borrowed, dusty black Isuzu trooper. The Mexican beer tasted like ethanol or nail polish remover or some other chemical that one should not ingest, but it was the only thing around to drink. Max opened his vehicle door and fed the remains of his lunch to a stray dog that was sniffing at a pothole a few feet away. A part of Max wanted to stay in his vehicle and ignore what was starting to rapidly unfold around him. Maybe he was too old for this. Another part of him wanted to head back to Texas and abandon this side-mission he had undertaken. But, of course, he could do neither.

It was happening again. And this time Max was there to witness it. The intelligence information he had gotten from some of his law enforcement resources had proven correct—they said this was the spot and date that the *Huachicoleros* would hit next, and it had just happened. There had been another breach of a gasoline pipeline in rural Mexico. Fuel was spewing out of a puncture in the pipeline with a vengeance and force of a hot-springs geyser. There had been an epidemic throughout Mexico in recent months of bandits—the *Huachicoleros*—digging up gasoline pipelines in desolate areas, and puncturing those pipelines with high-powered drills, then installing taps to siphon off the gasoline and sell it on the black market. *Chupaductos* (pipeline suckers) is what some folks called them. This time, it was a pipeline in the central-eastern state of Hidalgo, connected to a nearby refinery operated by PEMEX. The *Huachicoleros* were branching out from their usual region of stealing in the so-called Red Triangle of Puebla.

Max Lassiter was perspiring heavily as he looked on at a distance with binoculars. For hours he had been slumped down in his vehicle in a parking lot of the dilapidated Santa Veracruz Church—a sad jewel of yesteryear, with its parishioners having long since abandoned it when mining in the area had ceased. Max had gotten a tip from one of his DEA buddies who was tracking some drug cartel activity in this region that something big might be going down in this location today. Max observed a bizarre, festive atmosphere evolving down around the punctured pipeline. Two hundred or more nearby villagers had swarmed the site with plastic jugs and pails. Word had gotten out, far and wide, that there was once again free fuel for the taking. Last time it happened in this region, on Mother's Day, the gasoline bandits had even brought some free appliances for many lucky villagers to take back home—to curry favor and buy silence.

In addition to rural villagers, there were masked men, armed with AR-15 rifles, with large tanker trucks, that were siphoning off fuel to transport away to unknown places. The masked men generously allowed villagers to take a pail of gasoline here and there. It was a *quid pro quo* of sorts to the villagers. "Don't tell anyone who we are, and you'll get your piece of this." But no one would dare tell who the masked men were—with or without the chance for free gasoline. The gasoline bandits were in control. *Ellos estaban en control del territorio.* The ongoing fuel theft racket was costing PEMEX, and some of their U.S. joint venture partners, billions of dollars each year. The Mexican government was allegedly determined to crack down on the problem. But they claimed to have no idea what criminal actors were behind it all. In months past, it had been a criminal gang (*El Bukanas*) tied to the *Zetas* cartel that were believed to be the gas thieves. But there were different unidentified actors now. DEA had some interesting theories, but they were getting no cooperation from Mexican authorities.

There was a contingent of Mexican military personnel and *Policia Estatal* on the current scene, but they were doing nothing to stop the spectacle that was unfolding. They would occasionally shout instructions to the crowd, but their commands were wholly ignored. The law enforcement officers did not even attempt to confront the masked men. The crowd slowly turned from boisterous and excited to aggressive. Villagers were elbowing and pushing at each other. Suddenly, somewhere in the melee, there was a spark and the fuel pouring out of the pipeline ignited making an enormous blast. Instantly, before anyone had processed what was happening, flames and plumes of smoke billowed into the air. People were engulfed in flames, running, gasping, and screaming. In a blink of an eye, the chaos of the fuel pipe pilfering had transformed into an astonishing panorama of maimed, bleeding, and burned bodies everywhere. Some nearby children playing stickball were calling out for help, after one of the boys fell to the ground struck by flying, burning debris.

Max Lassiter slammed down his binoculars. "Holy mother of God! This cannot be happening!"

He had a choice to make. Every neuron in his body was firing up and ready to charge into action. Did he go into rescue and recovery mode? *Or did he keep searching for Marcus Braden (aka Smith) in the chaos*—because he was absolutely certain that Marcus was there somewhere in the bedlam.

Max had no doubt whatsoever that Marcus had breached this pipeline, just like he breached the last three in other parts of Mexico. This was Marcus Braden Smith's latest criminal enterprise. At least one of them. Rumors had been circulating on the streets for months that a "blond gringo" going by the name of "Enos" had cozied up to certain of the Mexican drug cartels, because of the gringo's savvy with bitcoin and his ability to launder dirty money through opaque bank accounts in tax havens around the world. Max was certain that "Enos" was Marcus Braden Smith. He had no doubt that the substantial sum of wealth that Marcus managed to amass from the Karl Lee kidnapping two years earlier was not enough to keep him satisfied. And sitting anonymously on a white sandy beach in a Mexican coastal town, drinking cerveza, likely bored Marcus after a while. Max Lassiter's instincts told him that Marcus was probably up near the tanker trucks. Marcus had probably been supervising the masked men.

"Dammit!" Max wailed. He knew there was no real choice. People were burning and dying in the inferno all around the pipeline. Max would have to let Marcus Braden Smith, the man who killed two federal judges and countless innocent bystanders—and tried to kill Max's wife—quietly slip free again.

Max grabbed for his push-to-talk on the passenger seat. "Dave, are you seeing this shit storm from where you are?"

Dave Carrillo was a retired Deputy U.S. Marshal who was also working down in Mexico for Premier Mutual. Dave was parked on an elevated spot about a half-mile away and copied that he did. "Oh yeah. I see it all right. Max Lassiter, you are a shit magnet for sure, I tell you."

"I'm going in. I think our mission is aborted for today. But use your best judgment on whether to reposition and try to follow some of the *Huachicoleros* with the drone at this point."

"Well, Max, we are way outside of our field instructions either way, huh?"

Max threw down his push-to-talk and exited his vehicle. He bolted toward the chaos, pulling and directing the bloody, lacerated, and burned victims away from the smoke, flames, and searing heat. Through the sulfurous haze, Max managed to see an old white Toyota T100 pickup truck speed rapidly away from the tanker trucks, creating a cloudy dust storm in its wake. He could not see the persons inside, but he knew in his gut Marcus Braden Smith was in there. Slipping away to wherever he was hanging out these days in Mexico—apparently sometimes Baja, sometimes Yucatan, now Central Mexico. It was almost as though Max, and he had a cat and mouse game going on at this point— did Marcus know Max was onto him?

A few hours later, Avery Lassiter sat in her chambers, during recess from a trial. She was catching up on the daily news headlines on her desktop computer. To her horror, there were pictures cropping up all over the international news and social media of a terrible scene currently developing in Hidalgo, Mexico. There were videos of people on a smoldering scorched landscape, screaming for help and running for their lives, some burned or engulfed in flames. There were forensic technicians carrying burned bodies out on stretchers. Helicopters were evacuating victims from the apocalyptic scene. A horrific human tragedy was unfolding. Dozens, including children, were presumed dead.

Avery wondered where Max was right now and if he knew what was happening. Her instincts told her that he was probably right there in the middle of it—even though there would be absolutely no reason for him to be. And, of course, he was.

Chapter Three

The Mother of All Ponzi Schemes? BASA, Inc.

Judge Lassiter was interrupted from the news stories regarding the tragedy unfolding in the Mexican desert by her law clerk. Millicent told her that it sounded like the lawyers in her courtroom were getting noisy and irascible during the recess. Perhaps the judge should go into the courtroom and calm them down (or, alternatively, "beat them into submission"—a joke by Millicent, but a very tempting proposition nonetheless).

Judge Lassiter was in the middle of a trial that she described as involving "the mother of all Ponzi schemes." It involved a company known as BASA, Inc. Avery told Millicent that she wondered if the litigants involved in the BASA trial had started out their dispute with the old "1, 2, 3, 4, I declare a thumb war" children's game. Then things had probably escalated to arm wrestling. Then maybe a fistfight. Ultimately, since having a duel at sunrise with pistols in some dewy, quiet field was not an option, one of the parties likely threatened to sue the other. Then it was "game on."

"Phase 1" of the BASA lawsuit brought the filing of claims, counterclaims, third-party claims, cross claims, as well as the assertion of every affirmative defense ever recognized in a statute or the common law. The old "throw it all against the wall and see what sticks" litigation strategy. Every week seemed to bring a new request by someone for a TRO or preliminary injunctions.

"Phase 2" ramped up with motions to dismiss, motions for sanctions, and motions to disqualify opposing counsel for all sorts of alleged conflicts of interest and other improprieties.

Then "Phase 3" exploded with discovery fights, motions for protective order, motions to quash subpoenas, arguments about redacted documents, arguments about vague privilege logs, and motions to compel production. In that phase, there had been an especially entertaining dispute involving the spoliation of evidence on a computer hard drive—supposedly one of the key witnesses had deleted thousands of files off her laptop computer and then downloaded thousands of pictures of cats onto the computer hard drive, to ensure that the deleted files were covered over and could never be retrieved. The hearing on that matter took a couple of days of forensic expert testimony to explain what exactly had happened and, of course, everyone got to see lots of cat pictures.

Then "Phase 4" brought motions for summary judgments, motions to file documents under seal, motions to exceed page limits on briefing, motions to file sur-replies, motions *in limine*, and *Daubert* expert-disqualification motions.

Avery said that, if this case had a theme song, it would be Richard Wagner's *Flight of the Valkyries*, complete with a backdrop of *Apocalypse Now* and Huey chopper crews soaring through the sky, preparing for battle in an ominous precursor of bloody destruction. This was the classic case of

Rambo litigants who liked to fight more than win. And a "win" was only a win if the other side died (literally or figuratively). Just like in the *Game of Thrones*—you either win or die. The litigants all had lawyers who had win-at-all-costs in their DNA and seemed perfectly happy to play the toxic game that their clients wanted them to play. Elihu Root once said, "About half of the practice of a decent lawyer is telling clients that they are damned fools and should stop." Unfortunately, these lawyers had either never heard that pearl of wisdom, or simply did not care about being decent. To Avery, it felt like time-wasting, passive aggressive, chest-pounding. It was utterly useless nonsense, disguised as litigation strategy.

Currently, in Avery's oak-paneled, dimly lit, portrait-lined courtroom, there were hundreds of banker boxes lining the side walls, containing unknown documents that the lawyers must have thought should be always easily accessible. There were more laptops, iPads, hotspots, cords, chargers, power strips, and gadgets in the courtroom than in a big-box electronics store. The billable hours were astonishingly high, and the billing rates of the lawyers were astronomical—the blended rate of all the lawyers in the courtroom each day was more than $1,200 per hour. Judge Lassiter and her law clerk Millicent—both of whom, like the lawyers, were working around the clock (but for government paychecks)—were physically and mentally exhausted.

But the lawyers seemed indefatigable. The courtroom was their natural habitat, and it seemed as though they never wanted to leave it. Avery, in exasperation, had eventually sent the parties to mediation before one of the wisest, most respected retired judges in the country. But there was no settlement. You cannot persuade people who do not want to be persuaded. The mediator had later reported to Avery that the parties were like "a bunch of pugnacious, mean honey badgers without an economically rational bone in their bodies" and that "they would rather die than settle." Then the best-of-the-best, kind old Judge Hall, Avery's bowtie-wearing colleague down the hall, even graciously presided over an eve-of-trial settlement conference with them. He said that he tended to agree with the "honey badger" comment, adding that there should be "a pox on all of their houses." Strong words from the kindest man to ever don a robe.

So here they were now in "Phase 5" of the litigation that was styled as *Chapter 11 Trustee of BASA, Inc. v. Toro Capital, et al.* It was a bench trial that had, so far, gone on for ten excruciating days (for eight hours each day—or 480 minutes each day, as Judge Lassiter liked to say), and it was nowhere close to being finished. Every document that was offered into evidence was objected to. Every sentence spoken by every witness was alleged to be hearsay or otherwise inadmissible. Every lawyer wanted to take every witness on *voir dire* at multiple points during his or her testimony, and then argued "lack of foundation" and moved to strike everything that the witness had said. And every objection that was sustained was met with the predictable request to make an "offer of proof." The lawyers and parties were completely tone deaf as to how they sounded to the court. Either that or they just did not care. Damn the torpedoes, full steam ahead. It was all wonderfully exhilarating to them. Like the smell of napalm in the morning.

At this pace, the lawyers would be hard-pressed to finish the trial by Thanksgiving. And, of course, numerous post-trial motions and appeals would follow. Maybe a good, juicy motion for writ of mandamus would be pursued at some point along the way before the trial was finished, if someone got especially irritated about a ruling during the trial. Meanwhile there was a simultaneous insurance coverage lawsuit underway, because all of the lawyers involved believed that BASA had liability insurance policies that should pay for every dime of damages that might ultimately be awarded, and, naturally, the insurance companies wholly disagreed. Miles to go before anyone slept.

So, what was all this fighting for?

Avery had spent an hour that morning trying to explain the answer to this question in simple terms to her three brilliant (but very green) summer intern law students. To the interns, it seemed to be all about girlfriends, golf trips, and gambling. There had, indeed, been a lot of testimony regarding these subjects. But it was not quite that simple.

First, the interns wanted to know what exactly was a "Ponzi" scheme?

Avery swiftly went into her professorial mode. She loved it when she had a group of intellectually curious interns. Blank, unvarnished slates, eager to learn. Not jaded like Avery felt she had become. Avery had an especially talented group of interns this summer.

"A Ponzi scheme, kiddos, is a type of fraud in which people are lured into making an investment by being promised ridiculously high rates of return on their money, with little or no risk of losing it. Maybe they are promised insane rates of return like fifty percent in forty-five days or one hundred percent in ninety days."

"Wow. That alone is pretty ridiculous."

"Yep. The term 'Ponzi scheme' is named after a swindler named Charles Ponzi, an Italian-American businessman in Boston who orchestrated an infamous fraud scheme back in 1919, supposedly involving international postal coupons—which people were led to believe they could buy at a steep discount. So, Rule #1, is ridiculously high rates of return are promised in a Ponzi scheme. But Rule #2 is that the arranger of any Ponzi scheme typically represents to investors that they are investing in some type of unique product or service—maybe precious metals, stocks, bonds, private equity funds, or some other commercial enterprise. But, in realty, they are not."

Millicent chimed in. "We have seen Ponzi schemes where people were asked to invest in crazy, farfetched things like rare pink diamonds, gold dust from Africa, 'coiled hair

10 struck gold stellas' (which were rare old gold coins), and bottled water supposedly infused with special minerals mined from a secret location in the Holy Land. But, as Judge was saying a Ponzi scheme only involves the perpetrator taking people's money and pooling it with other people's money, and mostly using it for his own personal purposes—usually a lavish lifestyle."

"Like girlfriends, golfing, and gambling," one intern chimed in.

"Bingo," Judge Lassiter replied, "and so much more."

"Yep, we have seen Ponzi fraudsters in this court spend the money on Lamborghinis, McLarens, Rolls Royces, private jets, yachts, houses in the Hamptons, Costa Rica, Lake Como, or Malta. We've pretty much seen it all."

"Millicent is correct. Sad but true. But, most important to making it all work—what I would call Rule #3—is that the Ponzi scheme mastermind will, for a while, pay handsome returns to the early investors by raising money from later investors. This is like what is sometimes referred to as a pyramid scheme—both types of schemes involve using new investors' funds to pay the earlier investors. It may work great for a very long time. You may have heard about Bernie Madoff or Allen Stanford in law school, as examples of this, right?"

The student interns nodded affirmatively.

Millicent chimed in again. "It becomes kind of Jonesy." Avery looked baffled by this term. "I mean, people will hear from early investors—maybe friends at church, or neighbors, or golfing buddies—that they are making tons of money. So more and more new investors are lured in and invest. But the Ponzi scheme eventually implodes when the stream of new investors dries up and there's no more money to keep paying people. The people who invest at the tail end of a Ponzi scheme are typically the big losers—unless a receivership or bankruptcy case is filed early enough to hopefully sort it all out—hopefully figuring out a way to recapture and redistribute funds in a fair way."

Avery now understood the "Jonesy" term.

Millicent, while dismantling and restyling her messy chestnut hair bun, further chimed in to help. "So, recapping, students, the classic feature of any Ponzi scheme is a guaranteed promise of ridiculously high returns on your money with supposedly no risk. But another hallmark of a Ponzi scheme is an investment that has not been registered with the Securities and Exchange Commission. We forgot to mention that one. Also, Judge, it seems like these masterminds of Ponzi schemes always act like their investment strategies are way too complicated to explain to mere mortals, and the investors are usually never allowed to view official paperwork for their investments. And, of course, the investors always have difficulty when trying to remove their money."

"Well said, Millicent. I think you'd make a much better law school professor than me."

One of Avery's interns, Sarah, a tall, thin, beautiful young woman, with long bouncy blond ringlets, who had been an aspiring Olympic skater as a teenager and had a depth of empathy like few aspiring lawyers Avery had ever seen, looked perplexed. "Judge, why in the world do people fall for this kind of thing?" Sarah looked like tears welled in her eyes.

Another intern, Spence, who was more hardened and seasoned than Sarah—having worked as a CPA several years before law school—rubbed his thumb and fingers together and said, "Cheddar."

Avery then was the one who looked perplexed. Millicent chimed in and told Avery that Spence's hand gesture was the "universal hand gesture for money."

"Also, FOMO," Millicent added.

"Huh?" Avery looked confused once again.

"That means 'fear of missing out' in millennial-speak, Judge," Millicent answered.

"Oh, well yes. Fear of missing out—fear that your golf buddy or neighbor or colleague is going to get rich from this fabulous opportunity and you are not. Anyway, Sarah, your question is a great one. Perhaps only a psychologist or God could really answer your question. I'm sure some psychology professors or grad students somewhere are researching it as we speak. Why do so many people fall for these Ponzi schemes? I sure don't know. People want to believe. They happily and gullibly drink the Kool-Aid."

"Huh?" Now all the millennials were the ones looking perplexed, looking strangely at Avery.

"Oh, good grief. Just do a *Google* search of Jim Jones and Guyana and my Kool-Aid reference will be obvious. Creepy, but obvious. We all need to stop talking in metaphors that date us, I suppose."

Avery could see Spence furiously doing *Google* searches on his phone, trying to keep up.

Avery continued. "Seriously, you will find, kids, a disturbing fact of life in our courts is that we see, again and again, that folks want to believe that people who present themselves as knowledgeable, trustworthy, and charming are just that. Just like people want to believe that a certain politician is different. Or that the palm reader or psychic is truly gifted enough to tell them their futures. Or that aliens are all going to land and take over our planet. We even seem to have phases in our society where there is a 'Ponzimonium'—an outbreak of Ponzi schemes."

"So, what is the Ponzi scheme about in this BASA, Inc. trial, Judge?" Sarah asked.

"Well, I don't know if you ever read about a young woman out in the Silicon Valley named Elizabeth Holmes and the Theranos debacle, but this was something that appears to be remarkably similar to that situation. I'm sure you can find stories on the Internet or podcasts about Theranos."

"May I continue, Judge?" Millicent chimed in with verve.

"Sure, go ahead. You explain things better than me."

"So, in our case, there was a charming, handsome

fellow named Dmitry Basayev, an immigrant from Chechnya, behind the Ponzi scheme, and he ultimately created his company called BASA, with investors' help. Basayev came to the United States in his early twenties to study at the University of Rochester, then went to Emory University for grad school. He studied computer science and microbiology. Supposedly a star student. Also did research at the CDC. You have probably heard of these various bacteria that have cropped up around the world that are resistant to some of the usual antibiotics, such as the drug-resistant Staph infection called "MRSA." There are drug-resistant germs that contaminate medical tools—catheters and breathing tubes and the like. Dmitry Basayev represented that he had invented some revolutionary protocol that would be remarkably effective in killing these drug-resistant germs, and—most importantly—Basayev had a fail-safe and efficient way of dispersal that was supposedly going to be game-changing for the healthcare industry. Judge, explain the technology as best you can—I don't understand it."

"Well, supposedly it was essentially an ultraviolet light-infused, germ-killing mechanism. Basayev certainly isn't the only one to get a patent on or experiment with the idea of such a system. But he was telling parties that he had mastered the concept like no one else had. His system supposedly coupled ultraviolet technology with some superior air purification technique that no one else had created. Some cutting-edge technology, supposedly. And he had a patent pending on the technology that he said was superior to others in the industry."

"So, Dmitry Basayev goes to some of his buddies from his college days that are now with investment banks, hedge funds, and private equity firms, hoping to get them to drum up some investors for him," Millicent added, trying to hurry the story along.

"Like the investment firm Toro Capital—the main defendant?" Spence queried.

"Yes. Then Basayev's buddies, in turn, introduced him to their bosses and some of their client-investors, who all ended up thinking that Basayev is a visionary—that his ideas have the potential to create a very innovative company in the infectious disease space. Their investors took a fly on it, not knowing anything. They were convinced that this would be something that would change the world. But it was either a total fraud—something that Basayev completely fabricated—or, alternatively, perhaps an idea that Basayev had not yet fully developed. The debate is still raging about which is the case. I mean, maybe Basayev just totally over-sold the idea and the progress that he had made on it."

Avery stepped over to the Keurig machine to make her third cup of coffee. "So, the big mystery is whether Basayev was sort of a 'fake it 'til you make it' kind of guy, as the expression goes, or a total fraudster? That is the big lingering question everyone still has."

"So does the bankruptcy trustee that has been appointed over BASA, Inc.'s affairs think it was nothing but a big fraud?" Sarah asked.

"Yes. That's the theory of his case, all right. He's very strident in his beliefs. In any event, over a billion U.S. dollars were put into BASA, Inc. Not only did individual investors put large sums of money in, via hedge funds and private equity funds, but pension funds, institutional investors, and even some labor unions were among the major investors. In fact, if this were not all complicated enough, some Union bosses have been charged with accepting bribes from one of the hedge funds involved, in exchange for moving funds of the union over into the hedge fund that then later invested the funds into BASA. It's pretty ugly."

Avery sipped her hazelnut coffee.

"Who are the other defendants being sued besides Toro Capital? I'm not sure I am following the theory of the case and who all the bankruptcy trustee is suing?"

"Well, Toro Capital was able to raise so much

investment capital for BASA that it was given a lot of power with BASA and was able to pick some of the seats on the board of directors. It recruited some highflyers such as some retired Senators to be on the BASA board to give the company some credibility or *gravitas*. The Trustee and BASA, Inc.'s investors now think that Toro Capital and BASA, Inc.'s board of directors should have known what was going on and should themselves be financially accountable for the investors' losses. So these are the primary targets being sued."

"How could Toro and these sophisticated board members have been asleep at the switch?"

"Well, it's not as though Basayev took the money and ran. Basayev hired friends from his grad school days to come to work for him—microbiologists, virologists, pathologists, engineers, and other technical staff. He supposedly had a large lab with state-of-the-art technology in a secluded, well-guarded warehouse just south of Dallas. Basayev paid himself and all his friends very large salaries. They all were allegedly working around the clock on perfecting the disinfectants and the dispersion system, but it was all very secretive. Basayev went on golfing trips and so-called road shows to meet with different investment bankers and hedge fund managers, doing interviews, raising more and more money. But it seems that he was always 'just a few months away'—or a few clinical trials away—from rolling out his product."

"People wanted to believe that this handsome, young, educated man, with his charming Eastern European accent, was going to eventually make them all multimillionaires with his cutting-edge invention that they helped fund," Millicent chimed.

"Exactly. Eventually his extravagant claims of a revolutionizing product were exposed for the fraud—or at least the exaggeration—that they were. The bankruptcy trustee and investors in our case are adamant that it was nothing more than a billion-dollar Ponzi scheme. A fantasy created by Dmitry Basayev. Interestingly, a secluded warehouse that allegedly had housed Basayev's state-of-the-art lab was discovered, shortly after the bankruptcy case was filed, and it had been completely cleared out—empty— although it did appear that at one time there might have been some research activities going on there. Anyway, some of the early investors in BASA got paid—allegedly from licensing deals that Dmitry Basayev represented he had negotiated with certain foreign, third-world governments. But it appears that the early investors were only getting paid with the later investors' money."

"The story of our lives here. Other people's money. And how people sometimes use it as their own, thinking no one will be the wiser."

"Anyway," Avery continued, "whether a total fraud or mere exaggeration, it is starting to seem increasingly clear, from what we are hearing in the courtroom, that the product and the dispersion system were never fully developed— much less sold or licensed. So BASA, Inc. filed a Chapter 11 bankruptcy case in March 2017, and here we are, more than two years later, with everybody suing everybody."

"Judge Lassiter says this case is a lawyer's dream."

"Are we going to get to see Dmitry Basayev testify?" Sarah chimed in.

"Afraid not. He has mysteriously gone missing, just like his lab. He and his team of geniuses seemed to have dropped off the face of the earth. Who knows? Maybe they are all enjoying the good life on some remote island."

"Who is the mysterious hat-wearing woman always sitting in the back of the courtroom?" one intern asked.

"I'm pretty sure it is Dr. Astrid Nilsson."

"Who is that?"

"She is a Nobel Prize winning scientist who used to teach at Emory University and work at the CDC. I don't think she does anymore. She developed the reputation there as a bit of a heretic. Anyway, I suspect she may be called as an expert witness at some point or perhaps she is just an interested observer. But she is herself a molecular biologist who specializes in infectious diseases."

"Was she involved with the company somehow? Was she perhaps a professor of Dmitry Basayev's? I don't remember seeing her name on anybody's witness list."

"I don't know. I guess time will tell."

"She looks so mysterious and strange and private. I never would have guessed she was a scientist of some sort. She looks more like some actress from a film noir. Judge, how do you know who she is?"

"You kids don't know who she is because you are too young. *Google* her sometime but make sure it is *after* the trial is over—just in case she ends up being involved in all of this somehow. She was quite the media darling a decade or so ago when she won the Nobel Prize. But she comes across as a little looney. If she takes the stand at some point, we are probably all in for a real show."

Annalise, Judge Lassiter's judicial assistant, popped her head in the door. "Judge, you told me to tell you when it has been twenty minutes. It has been twenty-two."

"Okay. Recess is over. Let's go back to hear more bickering. Interns, you can sit behind Millicent. Do what she says. If she needs research or copies of documents, or even coffee, please oblige. She drinks it black."

"Black, like my soul." Millicent could be so dramatic.

Avery rolled her eyes and popped two aspirin in her mouth, gulping them down with water as she zipped up her robe.

"Judge, do you have a headache?" Annalise asked with concern.

"No. I'm just preparing for the inevitable."

Chapter Four:

What if the Ponzi Scheme Wasn't Really a Ponzi Scheme, But Something Far More Bizarre?

"All rise!"

Judge Lassiter's court reporter, David, had a booming baritone voice that filled the courtroom and sounded like James Earl Jones when he uttered the court cry. Avery loved it. It was a nice way to enter the courtroom. Not only was David's voice imposing but so was his physical appearance. Avery felt extraordinarily safe with David in the courtroom. Usually, court security officers do not sit in the courtrooms that handle federal civil matters, unless something problematic is anticipated, or unless something troublesome arises at some point during the proceedings. David, an Army veteran, was the kind of man who looked like he could easily handle any n'er-do-well that might decide to cause trouble in the courtroom. But Avery didn't really worry much about trouble in the courtroom these days. Sure, "Richard Braden" had sent her a book, *The Hitchhiker's Guide to the Galaxy*, awhile back, with a cryptic note inside suggesting that he was still alive, watching her, and would eventually come and harm her. Avery had also later received an anonymous note at home, post-marked from Malta, with various forty-two riddles. And sure, at every forty-two milestone since receiving these communications—the forty-two-hour mark, the forty-two-day mark, the forty-two-week mark—she worried a little extra. And the Marshals Service and court security officers, whom she eventually told about the Richard Braden mailings from Malta, were never relaxed in their vigilance. But Avery had serious doubts about whether the "Richard Braden" mailings were genuine or part of a sick hoax that someone else had orchestrated. Moreover, Avery knew that there were quiet, ongoing efforts on the part of the Marshals Service, with the help of INTERPOL, to track down Richard Braden if he was truly still alive—in Malta (where his mailings originated) or wherever. They would find him. He would eventually leave breadcrumbs. Meanwhile, Avery regularly told her family, that she "refused to let the Braden brothers live rent-free in her head." She would win any psychological games in which the Braden Brothers tried to engage her.

"Please be seated," Avery said in a quiet voice, as she sat in her big cushy brown leather chair behind the bench. Avery rubbed her eyes and put on her Tiffany reading glasses. The fluorescent lighting in the courtroom seemed especially bright and harsh to Avery today.

As Avery started to ask whether there were any housekeeping matters before resuming witness testimony, a lawyer whom Millicent and the interns had nicknamed "Muttonchop Man" started to approach the lawyers' podium. Muttonchop Man, whose real name was Harvey O'Malley, was a curmudgeonly, wrinkled old lawyer who sported nineteenth century style facial hair—with broad sideburns that resembled a piece of chopped mutton, extending downward in a squared off fashion, along his lower jaw lines. Muttonchop Man had some paperwork in his large, pink, fumbling hands that he asked if he could hand up to the bench. Avery gave him permission.

As Muttonchop Man approached, wearing a baggy funereal suit, Avery got a sniff of his strong aftershave lotion—it smelled like what she remembered of her late grandfather's Old Spice. What Muttonchop Man had handed Avery was a motion to abate the trial—indefinitely— because of some "newly discovered, significant evidence" that allegedly might change every party's view of the entire BASA case.

This was a new one. In fact, this was perhaps the one and only legal maneuver that no one had attempted so far in this case—the old "newly discovered evidence" excuse. Avery was naturally more than a little skeptical. This case was fast becoming the Apollo 13 of lawsuits—a new problem popped up, it seemed, every hour.

"Okay. I am going to remain calm and assume that this abatement motion is presented in good faith and that all of the lawyers in the courtroom have seen this motion and are aware of whatever this newly discovered evidence is?" Avery flipped through the document. "Uh, actually I don't see a certificate of conference on here to indicate that you have conferred with any of the other lawyers."

Muttonchop Man hesitated and began his usual awkward throat-clearing before speaking. "Well, Your Honor, this has all been happening at warp speed. And, as you know, my client is only involved at the periphery of this litigation."

The latter part of what he said was true. Muttonchop Man was at the periphery. He represented a couple of east coast labor unions that had invested some of their members' funds in the hedge fund Toro Capital which had, in turn, invested in BASA. Muttonchop Man's clients arguably did not have direct standing to ask for any relief in this particular lawsuit—although Avery was certainly sympathetic to the collateral damage that his clients had suffered. Two leaders of his labor union clients had now been indicted for taking bribes from Toro Capital, and now the new leadership of the unions had instructed Muttonchop Man "to make things right" and somehow get the union's money back. But were things really happening at warp speed? It didn't seem like it to Avery. Things seemed to be moving far too slowly from her perspective. But Avery decided to indulge Muttonchop Man for a bit.

Muttonchop Man's argument was quite interesting. Apparently as Muttonchop Man had been sitting through trial, he had been reviewing some of the bank account statements for a BASA operating account that were admitted into evidence. While reviewing those, he noticed some "unusual cash transfer activity" in the weeks leading up to BASA's bankruptcy filing.

Avery tried to remain calm. "Okay. Let's be real. Isn't there always unusual cash transfer activity with bankrupt companies leading up to a filing?" Avery waited with an indifferent expression. "I mean, has there ever been a bankruptcy case in the history of the world where there wasn't unusual activity leading up to the filing of the case? This better be good, counsel."

"Your Honor, BASA, for some unknown reason, was transferring huge amounts of money to the DRI-MED Helicopter Company in the eight to ten weeks before BASA filed bankruptcy. Why would a company engaged in a mere Ponzi scheme be doing that? DRI-MED Helicopter Company is a publicly held NYSE-listed company that provides choppers for offshore oil drilling platforms as well as for emergency medical evacuations."

"Yes, I am well-aware of who they are. DRI-MED Helicopter Company has actually been in a bankruptcy case itself in recent months in Judge Hall's court down the hall."

Avery knew her former law partner, Ward Scott, had come out of retirement to represent DRI-MED Helicopter in its Chapter 11 case. She had purposely distanced herself from having any discussions with Judge Hall or Ward about the case. She literally had no idea what was going on in that case.

"So, I was thinking to myself." Muttonchop Man slowly stroked his huge reddish-gray sideburns. "Why would BASA—which, again, was allegedly masterminding a Ponzi scheme, while telling folks it was developing a disinfectant and dispersal system for super germs—be sending large amounts of money to a helicopter company? Was Dmitry Basayev somehow connected to DRI-MED Helicopter Company? Nope. Not according to any information that I have been able to detect."

"So, did you look through all of the public filings in the DRI-MED Helicopter bankruptcy case? That might shed some light, don't you think?"

"Great minds think alike, Judge. Yes, as a matter of fact I did, Your Honor. And, low and behold, I found an interesting-sounding contract that was disclosed in DRI-MED Helicopter Company's bankruptcy paperwork. The contract was described as 'Project Grotto' and was said to be between DRI-MED Helicopter Company and an entity called 'DB Biocontainment, LLC.' And I also saw in some of DRI-MED Helicopter's recent income statements that DRI-MED had received large amounts of revenue associated with some sort of 'biocontainment project— Grotto' in the exact same dollar amounts as the cash transfers from BASA, Inc. to DRI-MED. Last but not least, I did a corporate records search and found out that DB Biocontainment, LLC is a Delaware limited liability company, and its sole managing member is—guess who?"

"We are all waiting with bated breath, Mr. O'Malley."

"Dmitry Basayev. Also, DB Biocontainment, LLC just so happens to use the exact same business address as BASA, Inc."

"Hmmm. So, you are saying that Dmitry Basayev had a side business of some sort—DB Biocontainment, LLC— and it may have had a contract with the DRI-MED Helicopter Company? And Dmitry Basayev may have commingled funds of BASA, Inc. with that side business?"

"Yes, Your Honor."

"I admit that this is all interesting, and I'm not sure where it might lead. Maybe a fraudulent transfer lawsuit is in the future against DB Biocontainment or DRI-MED? But is that really grounds for abating and continuing this trial? I mean can't all the lawyers in this case walk and chew gum at the same time? I mean no disrespect by that. Just a silly expression. But can't you all investigate these newly discovered facts and meanwhile this trial goes forward? You have armies of lawyers and financial advisors working on this case. There would seem to be no lack of resources to throw at this."

A lawyer suddenly jumped up whom Avery's law clerk and interns nicknamed "The Robot." "Your Honor, may I interject?"

His real name was Austin Chertoff. The Robot had a master thespian, eloquent voice.

"You asked Mr. O'Malley if he had communicated with the other lawyers in the courtroom about this so-called newly discovered evidence and he conveniently sidestepped your question. I would like you to know that this is the first that I have heard of any of this."

The Robot was a frighteningly perfect, statute-quoting, blond crewcut wearing lawyer—part man and part machine. He was straight-backed with a soldier-like stature and always wore an American flag pin on his lapel. Avery's intern Spence referred to the Robot as "smoother than a fresh jar of Skippy." Avery noticed that the Robot had just discreetly popped into his mouth some military grade, caffeine-infused chewing gum that he was well known to use as an energy booster. Supposedly the gum more efficiently and rapidly dispersed caffeine into one's mouth tissues than coffee or cola, plus it did not require bathroom breaks as often as ingesting a liquid.

"I ask. I implore you. Is there a reason that Mr. O'Malley could not have picked up the phone or perhaps even visited with us in the hallway about this?" The Robot stood at attention with a half-warm and half-fierce smile and spoke his words with a breezy, imperious tone. The Robot was on a roll during this ten-day trial. He was representing BASA's Chapter 11 Trustee, who was, of course, the plaintiff suing Toro Capital and the former directors of BASA for millions of dollars. The Robot did not want anything to derail him at this point. He no doubt thought that victory was within his grasp. It usually was.

"How about that, Mutton-er... Mr. O'Malley?" Avery was mortified that she had almost slipped up and called Harvey O'Malley by her law clerk's nickname.

"Your Honor, this has been a whirlwind of information flying at us. We've been drinking from a fire hose, trying to process all this information. And, I haven't even gotten to the weirdest part."

Millicent noisily grabbed a sheet of notebook paper and wrote on it with a black felt tip marker, "Oh no, he said it! Judge is about to come unglued! Everybody take cover!" Millicent shoved the sheet of paper in front of the interns. The interns looked quizzically back at Millicent. Millicent then wrote, "Judge hates it when lawyers say, 'they've been drinking from a firehose.' They all say it ALL the time."

Judge Lassiter darted a curt look over at Millicent, shook her head, and let out an audible sigh. She then looked back at Mr. O'Malley. "I'm listening. This better knock my socks off."

"I did some public records searches for DB Biocontainment, LLC. Boy was there some interesting stuff that turned up."

"Go on."

"Turns out that the company owns the following assets encumbered with liens: some ambulances described as 'ambulatory mini-biocontainment units'; a private cargo plane that is described as having medical equipment and a specially designed biohazard unit on board; and a ground lease, fixtures, and equipment at a certain real property location in Ellis County, Texas that *formerly served as the*

*site of the U.S. government's so-called super conducting
super collider project."*

Avery's jaw dropped. "What? You said the super
conducting super collider project? Do you mean that old
atom smasher project that lost its federal funding back in the
1990's?"

"Yes! Ellis County, Texas. That's the one, Your
Honor."

Avery sighed loudly. "Okay. Let me test my memory
here. You all told me previously during this case that there
was an old converted, secluded warehouse south of Dallas
that BASA, Inc. was supposedly using for its research
facility. Then you all told me that the warehouse was, in fact,
empty. Abandoned. Are you now telling me that this
property—the former super collider property—where DB
Biocontainment apparently has a ground lease, is something
altogether different or near that warehouse or what?"

"So, it would appear, yes. The abandoned warehouse is
a couple of miles away from the former super conducting
super collider project. Both are in Ellis County."

"Holy cow. Show me your paperwork. Do you have
multiple copies of all of this for the other lawyers here?"

"A few. Yes."

Muttonchop Man turned to his pale, pencil-thin, red-
haired paralegal who, with catlike swiftness, darted to some
banker boxes stacked up against the courtroom wall and
dutifully retrieved several copies of black-bound notebooks,
thick with paper and colorful tabs placed throughout. The
paralegal had been in the courtroom many days and
normally wore her hair in a tight matronly bun, but today the
woman wore her hair down. It cascaded down her back, long
and wavy, like mermaid hair. The paralegal sashayed around
the courtroom in a skin-tight chartreuse colored suit, her
high heels clicking on the marble checkered floor, passing
out the notebooks. Everyone eagerly devoured the contents.
It was as though today was the woman's big moment in the
spotlight. After she made the rounds passing out the

notebooks to all of the lawyers, she sat down with a satisfied look on her face. The only sound in the courtroom at that point was the noise of flipping paper.

Judge Lassiter finally spoke. "Well, you weren't exaggerating when you said you discovered something weird. Weird seems like an understatement really. What on Earth could this all mean?"

"I don't know, Judge. But I'm thinking that Dmitry Basayev was up to something other than a Ponzi scheme. It appears that a whole lot of BASA, Inc. money (or I guess I should say my clients' and other investors' money) may have been diverted to whatever this company DB Biocontainment, LLC was or maybe still is doing."

At that point Avery noticed the mysterious Dr. Astrid Nilsson getting up and quickly walking out of the back of the courtroom. The courtroom door loudly slammed behind her, causing everyone to jump, turn, and glance. Then all eyes turned back and stared at Avery.

"Okay. We're just going to cool breeze this one for a few days."

Muttonchop Man looked at Avery with a confused look in his eyes. Avery realized that she had momentarily slipped into cop jargon—being married to someone in law enforcement for years tends to do that to a person.

"Uh, what I meant was, I am going to give all of the lawyers and parties here seventy-two hours to digest all of this. We will come back on Thursday at 11:00 a.m. and have a status conference and decide what we are going to do."

Avery realized at that moment that she had not said anything to, nor heard anything from, the defendants' lawyers all morning. The defendant Toro Capital was represented by a larger-than-life lawyer that folks in the legal community nicknamed the Whale (Edgar Wesson). The two, former board of director members of BASA, Inc. that were being sued, Dr. Fred Merryman and former Senator Ed Cotton, were represented by two wiry, bald fellows who almost looked like identical twins (and they were even both named Paul—Paul Thompson and Paul Gray). The "twin Pauls," as Millicent referred to them, who were rather bland and milquetoasty, were completely overshadowed in their role as defense counsel by the Whale—always deferring to anything he said. The Whale and the Robot had gone toe-to-toe against each another many times in their careers—often in rather epic legal battles—and they could not have been more different. Each was brilliant and effective in his own way. The Whale was a very tall and heavy attorney who was like a junkyard dog. He had long, slicked-backed ink-black hair, a gray and black beard, and droopy, sad brown eyes. He was disheveled and always reeking of cigarette smoke. He wore his Harvard college ring on his right middle finger—believed by all to be a subliminal gesture to his adversaries. The Whale was most often on the plaintiffs' side—being the natural-born aggressor that he was. In this trial, he was not only on the defense side, but had been uncharacteristically quiet and reserved so far, presumably hoping that the Robot somehow could not meet his burden of proof.

"Messrs. Wesson, Thompson, and Gray, what say you? I should have asked your thoughts before announcing we would adjourn for seventy-two hours. Do you have anything to add? Any light to shed on these odd facts that we have just heard about from Mr. O'Malley?"

The Whale stood, his droopy face looking as inscrutable as always. "I am afraid I have nothing to add, Your Honor. We agree to this break for now." The twin Pauls looked at Judge Lassiter with their owlish eyes and nodded in unison.

"All right. I will see you all on Thursday."

Avery slammed her gavel hard against her bench.

"All rise," bellowed David in his baritone voice.

Avery, Millicent, and the interns quietly slipped out of the courtroom and went back into chambers.

"Oh my God, Judge! This is crazy! What do you think is going on here?"

Before taking off her robe, without answering, Avery walked over to one of the numerous whiteboards in her chambers, picked up a black marker, and began writing on it:

"All you really need to know for the moment is that the universe is a lot more complicated than you might think, even if you start from a position of thinking it's pretty damn complicated in the first place."

Avery quietly walked back to her closet and hung up her robe.

The interns looked at Millicent puzzlingly.

"*Hitchhiker's Guide*. The Judge is kind of funny about that book. And Ernest Hemingway, too. She quotes them at random times. Get used to it.

Chapter Five

Two and a Half Years Earlier (Flashback, Late February 2017)—Prudhoe Bay, Alaska.

It was mid-winter. The sky looked leaden and gray on this late February morning, as though snow would soon be falling again. It was thirteen degrees Fahrenheit—average for the North Slope this time of year. However, just a week earlier it had been forty-two degrees Fahrenheit. The climate swings lately were getting stranger and stranger in this remote part of the Arctic. Some days it was amazingly mild. Then back to ten or twenty degrees below zero.

Meanwhile, caribou quietly roamed the tundra. And several transient maintenance workers from Texas, who had been deployed to the Trans-Alaska Pipeline in the Prudhoe Bay Oil Field to perform cleaning work, with corrosion-detecting pig equipment, were busily trying to finish their tasks before bad weather or darkness required retreating to their lodges at Deadhorse. There is only about four-and-a-half hours of daylight at this isolated area in late February.

But the maintenance work could not wait until a more convenient time. The workers were employed by Tex-Core, a large pipeline operator, and one of the joint venture partners on the pipeline.

At the Fairweather Deadhorse Medical Clinic, a few miles away, several workers who had recently been working at the processing facilities adjacent to the pipeline, had become ill with something unusual and hard to diagnose. The oil field workers began arriving at the clinic the preceding week with high fever, body aches, a general malaise, respiratory distress, and uncontrollable vomiting and diarrhea. Auxiliary health care was provided to this clinic by Tex-Core as well as the Prudhoe Bay Fire Department. The healthcare workers had soon become alarmed by the severity and gruesomeness of the workers' symptoms and the inability to effectively treat them with some of the usual antibiotics and drugs. Some were slipping into organ failure, and the dreaded cytokine storm that sometimes occurs with bad viruses (an overreaction of the body's immune system) and were even manifesting a very strange additional symptom: the irises of their eyes were teeming with some sort of pathogen and were actually changing colors—usually to a light blue. These workers were all generally healthy, fit men in their thirties and fourties. The higher-ups at Tex-Core eventually dispatched a small team of investigators to bring back blood samples for testing. Dr. Astrid Nilsson, a Nobel Prize winning microbiologist, recently retired from the CDC, was standing by in an underground BSL-4 lab facility in the lower forty-eight, waiting to put her expertise to work.

Dr. Nilsson had, for several years, been studying the subject of zombie pathogens in the melting permafrost. Could this be what was triggering the strange illness? This was Dr. Nilsson's working theory. Across the Earth's permafrost—the perennial frozen ground which covers an area twice the size of the United States—there are tens of thousands of human bodies (as well as wildlife) that were buried at death and, unlike in warmer climates, decomposition never set in. The human and animal corpses were preserved in the frozen soil. Some of these humans died of ravaging diseases such as smallpox. There are many bodies buried in the permafrost in both Scandinavia and Alaska of people who died of the widespread 1918 Spanish flu. Many scientists (including Dr. Nilsson) had spent much of their careers asking, what would happen if modern humans were suddenly exposed to deadly bacteria and viruses that have been dormant for hundreds or even thousands of years? Climate change and the melting permafrost had accelerated that discussion.

Maybe we were about to find out. That's what Dr. Nilsson thought. Maybe the soils melting around Prudhoe Bay were releasing ancient viruses and bacteria that, having lain dormant, were springing back to life. It was not an absurd theory. Dr. Nilsson had just published an article that was gaining attention in more conventional medical circles. In August 2016, in a remote corner of the Siberian tundra called the Yamal Peninsula in the Arctic Circle, it was widely reported that a twelve-year-old boy died and at least twenty people were hospitalized after being infected by anthrax. The working theory was that, more than seventy-five years ago, a reindeer infected with anthrax died and its frozen carcass became trapped under a layer of frozen soil. The reindeer stayed there until a heatwave in the summer of 2016, when the permafrost it was trapped in, thawed. The reindeer corpse was then exposed and released infectious anthrax into nearby water and soil, and then into the food supply. More than 2,000 reindeer grazing nearby became infected, which then led to a small number of human cases. Similarly, scientists in recent years discovered fragments of RNA from the 1918 Spanish flu in corpses buried in mass graves in the Alaskan tundra.

Dr. Nilsson had used startling words in her published paper that received mixed reactions: "As a result of the permafrost melting, deadly infections from centuries ago may come back, especially near the graveyards where the victims of these infections were laid to rest. Dormant viruses and bacteria may become the source for future outbreaks of disease unlike anything the world has ever seen."

Even before Dr. Nilsson's test results were back, Tex-Core had assembled a sort of infectious-disease SWAT team in the Prudhoe Bay Oil Field, staffed by a little-known company that was based in Ellis County, Texas—DB Biocontainment, LLC—to head off what they feared could fast become an epidemic. While this area of Alaska's North Slope is very isolated and sparsely populated, certain of the oil field workers frequently visited the general store and a local pub in Deadhorse—possibly exposing some of the locals. And several of the workers brought spouses with them, some of whom had returned home by now. They traveled on a bus down the Dalton Highway to Fairbanks, and then took a commercial airline home. Finally, a few of the oil field workers returned home and later manifested the same symptoms (high fever, body aches, respiratory distress, and uncontrollable vomiting and diarrhea). Thus, family and friends and countless others might have been exposed by this point.

Only two things could be said with certainty at this juncture. The illness seemed to be drug resistant. And early reports from the SWAT team deployed by DB Biocontainment, communicated only to Tex-Core officials, were indicating that the illness bore a striking resemblance to the 1918 Spanish flu (H1N1)—the strain of influenza that, over about an eighteen-month period, swept the globe and killed somewhere between fifty and one hundred million people. However, this version of influenza affecting the Prudhoe Bay oil workers seemed like a far more severe, mutated form of it. And, of course, it had the strange feature of changing the color of the victim's irises to light blue. What was happening in Prudhoe Bay seemed to involve a frighteningly more aggressive form of the illness.

A private cargo plane, with a specially designed

biohazard unit inside, arrived at the Deadhorse Airport early one March morning. It was unmarked on the outside—just a navy-blue body with no distinguishing marks. Upon its arrival, workers emerged wearing astronaut-like protective clothing. Head-to-toe body suits with powered air-purifying respirators attached, aprons, and gloves. They greeted an ambulance on the tarmac and methodically wheeled several patients to the aircraft and up a motorized, conveyor belt through the doorway. The aircraft was a fully equipped, traveling infectious disease unit designed to deal with biosafety level-4 pathogens. The plane quickly departed and headed for the Dallas South Port Airport. From there, the patients would be transported by ambulance to a remote underground facility in Ellis County, Texas.

Chapter Six

Another Day in Paradise.

Today, Avery was enjoying a much-needed break from the BASA trial, while Muttonchop Man, the Robot, the Whale, the Twin Pauls, and the dozens of other lawyers involved in the BASA case were, no doubt, rabidly churning out billable hours, trying to unravel the mystery of what was going on with the mysterious entity DB Biocontainment, LLC and the Ellis County, Texas underground property.

Avery could only imagine what life was like at the various law firms during this trial—and particularly after this new development. Avery shuddered a bit as she remembered her early career days at her old law firm, Madison, Spencer & Collins, recalling what it was like when something big like this was underway. She remembered the whirlwind of people buzzing through the firm hallways, and conference rooms filled with boxes and papers stacked high. There would be late nights with pizza, barbeque, or Chinese food catered to the office, to sustain the toiling lawyers during fourteen-plus hour days. She remembered the feeling of wanting to go home to at least take a shower but having too much to do for that luxury. She even remembered one corporate merger on which she had worked, where a whole floor of her firm's downtown Dallas office was dedicated to the storage of boxes of documents that needed to be reviewed in connection with a government antitrust investigation. The firm paid for a masseuse to come to the office every night and give fifteen-minute chair massages to associates, so that they would have the stamina to keep reviewing documents into the wee hours. Avery wondered if the poor associates working for the Robot and Whale were treated to that same sort of incentive. The perquisites were probably much better by now. Thirty-minute chair massages maybe? Free Dallas Mavericks or Cowboys tickets to the lawyers who reviewed the most boxes?

Avery came in to work on this BASA-free day at a somewhat more leisurely hour than she usually did, stopping along the way to get some breakfast tacos and pastries for the crew at work. As she walked through the ground floor lobby of the courthouse, to mail a letter before heading up to her chambers, she could hear music blasting from the downstairs courthouse convenience store at an outrageously high volume. The song was *Let It Whip!* by the Dazz Band, circa 1982. It hardly created a dignified atmosphere for this temple of justice.

Avery said hello to one of the court security officers after she tossed her letter in the mail chute and asked if he thought it might be appropriate to suggest that the young cashier in the convenience store turn down her music. He chuckled a bit. "It's been a crazy morning already, Judge. Some jogger found a dead body in the park across the street around 5:30 this morning, and we have been running around getting video recordings from all of the cameras on the perimeter of the building, trying to help the Dallas police with their investigation."

"Oh, no! I didn't even notice anything amiss as I drove

in. Don't know how I missed the hoopla. Any clue who the victim was or the circumstances?"

"I think it may have been a homeless fellow, but that's just my guess since they sometimes sleep in the park overnight. But I doubt it was heat stroke or other natural causes since the police have draped the area in crime scene tape and are wanting to see video recordings. It's outside my bailiwick, so I haven't asked too many questions."

"Gosh, that's just terrible. Please keep me posted if you learn anything you can share, Gus."

"Will do. And I will go talk to the disco queen in the snack store."

"Thanks." Avery winked at him.

Avery took the elevator up to chambers, balancing her coffee and treats. When she walked into chambers, she greeted Annalise, Millicent and the interns, and asked if they had heard about the dead body found in the park across the street. They had not but had seen some police activity when they came in and wondered why.

"Gus said it could have been a homeless guy, but he had a hunch there might be foul play of some sort."

"Maybe one of the courthouse ghosts got loose and wandered over there and killed the poor guy." Millicent grinned devilishly.

Annalise looked annoyed. "Our sweet Millicent has been regaling the interns this morning with all of the courthouse ghost stories. It's not been a very productive day so far."

"What brought this on? Did one of you interns stay late last night and hear the whispers in the corridors outside our chambers? Or footsteps in the old ceremonial courtroom that's above our chambers? Did the doors lock on you? The lights flicker? If you stay too late in this courthouse it's bound to happen."

Sarah the sensitive intern looked genuinely concerned. "Judge, I thought this was all a joke that the law clerks in the building were playing on us interns, but now that you are saying all of these things I am totally creeped out!"

"Oh, Sarah. These stories are silly. But just take my advice and do not dare go anywhere near the criminal holding cells upstairs late at night. A lot of people have said you can sometimes smell cheap perfume and burning hair up there. It is probably the spirits of former inmates who were killed in the electric chair and their heartbroken girlfriends they left behind."

"Judge! You're as bad as Millicent!" Annalise seemed scared herself.

"I know. I guess I really shouldn't have mentioned, even obliquely, that Texas used to execute people with the electric chair, huh?"

Sarah looked horrified.

"Hey, just be glad you are not interning at the San Antonio Federal Courthouse. It sits where the north wall of the Alamo was. Imagine what they see there late at night. Judge King's courtroom sits right on top of the spot where William B. Travis was shot and killed."

"Okay." Millicent interjected, unfazed. "The honest truth. One hundred percent. Footsteps can regularly be heard in the upstairs courtroom late at night when no one is in that courtroom. I swear I have heard them enough times that I will never work up here late at night alone again. And even sometimes during the day, the doors to Judge Lassiter's courtroom have sometimes opened on their own and have locked on their own a few times as well. And the lights sometimes dim during court for no apparent reason. And there have been three times in three different cases since I have been here that a witness on the witness stand has randomly said that she feels something like a person tugging on her shirt. It's always been when a woman is testifying that it happens. There would have been absolutely no way for those witnesses to have known about the previous episodes of this happening. And one of the court security officers has told me that surveillance cameras filming in the courthouse late at night have caught images of an apparition—a woman in a white flowing chiffon dress—walking around the hallways."

"For God's sake, stop! I have something to talk with Judge Lassiter about alone now. Would you kids please go back to your offices and get some work done!" Everybody obeyed Annalise immediately. They always did. Avery always said that Annalise wore dignity like a second skin. She was skilled in soft force. She had a generally tranquil demeanor and a chic maternal presence. But when she uttered a simple command, to disobey it would be like shaming Sister Mary Angelica Humilitas by giggling during holy communion.

As the kids scurried to their desks in the library, Annalise began talking in hushed tones. "Judge, I know I worry too much, but I need you to listen to a voicemail we received overnight and tell me if it conjures up any concern."

"Ugh. Your look worries me."

"There are no words on the voicemail. No message. At least no message in English. At one point I thought I might have heard some faint words in another language. Anyway, it is likely just a wrong number from a butt dial—forgive me for saying that. But you know what I mean—when someone's cell phone in his back pocket accidentally dials a number and the person doesn't realize it and goes on about his business?"

Avery tried not to snicker. Of course, she knew what Annalise meant. Annalise was so proper and reserved.

"Anyway, let me just play it for you. Maybe it's nothing."

Avery, put her load down. She had learned not to ever discount Annalise's instincts. They were as good as anyone's Avery knew.

"Go ahead and play it."

"Okay. First, before you ask, no there is no caller ID information. The caller information comes in as 'UNKNOWN.'"

Annalise played the message. As Annalise foretold,

there were no discernable voices—at least none speaking English. For the first few moments, all one could hear was the sound of what seemed like waves lapping, wind gusts, some seagulls, boat horns. Then there were noises that sounded like a large vehicle, maybe a city bus, stopping and starting. After about three minutes, some church bells started chiming, playing strains of *Nearer My God to Thee*. Avery then could hear meows of cats in the background. Then some footsteps and a male voice saying what sounded like "*bongu*."

"Oh my God. This is going to sound crazy, but I think I know where that call is coming from. Malta. St. Julian's, Malta. I'm almost sure of it. There is a hotel there where our family stayed. It's right on the bay—Balluta Bay—between St. Julian's and Sliema, Malta. There is this beautiful neogothic-style Roman Catholic Church that chimes portions of *Nearer My God to Thee* every fifteen minutes. It's gorgeous. It's a Carmelite Church—The Parish Church of Our Lady of Mount Carmel. There is a bus stop right in front of it. And there is a feral cat colony there between the hotel and church along the promenade on the beach. And '*bongu*' is 'good morning' in Maltese!"

Avery was almost out of breath.

"Hasn't Richard Braden sent you mail from Malta in the past?"

"What time did the call come in, Annalise?"

Annalise sighed. "Would you believe 11:42 pm?"

Annalise and Avery stared at each other in silence.

"What are we going to do about this?" Annalise said, breaking the awkward silence.

"We are going to pretend like it didn't happen for now."

"What? Are you kidding me, Judge? After all that has happened to you? Do I need to remind you that less than three years ago you were lying in a hospital bed for two weeks in Austin after Richard Braden's brothers tried to kill you? After they succeeded in killing many wonderful lawyers who used to appear in this courthouse? How could you possibly take any chances with this?"

"Annalise, please." Avery looked ashamed. "Please, I haven't forgotten. I'll, of course, never forget. But let me talk to Max first before we report this. I just want to think this through with him. And that's assuming I can track him down. Will you call Max's boss, Joe Meno at Premier Mutual, while I am in court and see if he's heard from him lately? Max's cell phone hasn't been in range apparently for a few days. I haven't heard from him for almost a week."

"Okay. Will do."

Annalise continued to give Avery a concerned, disapproving look.

"Annalise, please don't look at me like that. It will be okay. I promise. I'll talk to Max. By the way, were there any other phone messages this morning?"

Annalise could not believe Avery was so casually changing the subject. But, unbeknownst to Annalise, Avery was still very much fixated on the voicemail. Her gut told her it presaged more worrisome things to come.

"Well. the Young Women's Lawyers Association called to see if you are attending their wine and cheese pairing event tonight. You never RSVP'd."

Avery sighed. "Will you call and politely decline for me? Tell them I'm lactose intolerant or something. Does lactose intolerant even apply to cheese?"

"Well, even if it does, you aren't wine intolerant, Judge."

"Okay. Point made. I guess I should go. Could you please call them with my belated RSVP?"

"Will do. Oops, look at the time, Judge." Annalise glanced at her watch. "Grab your robe. Remember, you set an emergency hearing for that billionaire Southern Belle lady."

"Ugh. How could I forget? Somebody, shoot me. Just aim true and make it as painless as possible."

"Judge!"

"Sorry. Bad choice of words."

Chapter Seven

The Accidental Witness.

"In Texas, women seem to think the higher the hair, the closer to God."

Avery recalled those amusing words, often uttered by her late mother, as she intently observed the woman currently on her witness stand. If those words were true, then this witness, with her blond, puffy bouffant (sealed not to move with ample amounts of Aquanet) was surely well on her way to the pearly gates of the Lord's celestial city.

Avery had scheduled an emergency hearing on her first day off from the BASA trial. The hearing scheduled was on a motion to quash a subpoena in a case unrelated to BASA. The case was a real Greek tragedy—Texas style. It involved a formerly wealthy Dallas widow, Constance Malloy. A classic riches-to-rags story. Billionaire one day. Bankrupt the next. It happens more often than the average person might think.

Constance Malloy, the recipient of the unwanted

subpoena, was in her own Chapter 7 personal bankruptcy case. Although obviously very distraught, she was one of those perpetually perky types, bedecked in glittery jewelry, colorful nails, a citrus green Prada lunch frock, and a matching Prada handbag that Avery knew was worth several months' salary for most working folks. Perhaps not the smartest wardrobe ensemble for a woman coming before a federal court seeking bankruptcy relief. Avery had a nagging feeling that this Southern Belle-of-a-woman did not appreciate the gravity of the moment. She was on the precipice of absolute ruin. Her story, like so many folks who daily entered Avery's courtroom, was yet another example of how, at any moment, the bottom can drop out of any of our lives. Things can change for the worse very quickly. Two years ago, this woman was probably putting her name on the waiting list at the Chanel store in Highland Park Village, eager to receive the designer's newest $25,000 handbag of the season. Now she was considering donating plasma for extra income.

"I am very nervous, Judge Lassiter. But I knew I had to show up today and tell my story and ask you to put a stop to this insanity."

"We appreciate you being here. I know that coming downtown to testify in a court hearing is never fun for anyone. Take your time. Drink some water and tell us if you need a break."

"You know, Judge, the court security guards wouldn't let me bring in my vanilla latte. I had to throw the entire thing down the drain in the women's restroom. I had hardly taken two sips."

"I'm very sorry about that. We do have a lot of rules in the courthouse. I know not everyone likes them. There is a pitcher of fresh water for you there on the stand."

"Is it tap water?"

"Yes." Avery almost felt the need to apologize for not having San Pellegrino or Topo Chico.

"Did you hear about the horrible accident on the

freeway, Judge? A truck of those miniature horses overturned. There were miniature horses everywhere. I mean they were scattering all over the place. I nearly hit one. That would have been my luck."

"Yes, Ma'am. I heard that the police had to shut down a mile of highway for quite a while. Very bizarre. And, sadly, I heard that a couple of the miniature horses were struck and killed by motorists."

"Oh no!"

Suddenly a cellphone of one of the lawyers in the courtroom began ringing. The ringtone was the song *Enter Sandman* by Metallica. The offending lawyer, Artie Mannheim—a "superdork," to use Millicent's term for him—was a pale, thin, clumsy man with a protruding forehead and prominent Adam's apple. Mannheium grabbed his phone with embarrassment and stuttered out profuse apologies for his *faux pas*. The day just kept getting weirder by the minute.

The hearing scheduled that day originated from a bankruptcy trustee's motion to compel a deposition of this glittery, nervous woman and, of course, her motion to quash the subpoena relating to that. Constance Malloy was well-known in the Dallas fete set. The widow had gone from "old money" to "no money" in a fairly short time period. Naturally, it all seemed rather curious. The bankruptcy trustee's request was hardly unreasonable or controversial— he was certainly entitled to investigate the financial affairs of a person who had filed for personal bankruptcy, to better understand her assets, liabilities, and financial condition. It is fairly normal. But Mrs. Malloy was vehemently objecting—she had no intention of willingly sitting for a deposition. She thought it all seemed humiliating and undignified. This bankruptcy case that she had filed was "not her fault." The lawyers had recommended it— practically forced it on her, she said. And she had been the victim of the "lowest forms of charlatans and con men."

It seems that Mrs. Malloy's dearly departed husband—

the late Mr. Marvin Malloy—was a successful businessman and titan in the energy business. He had been a business partner with two other fellows named Mr. Jarvis and Mr. Holly. The three business partners held extensive real estate holdings and a jet leasing business, in addition to oil and gas interests. Mr. Malloy unexpectedly died in a tragic hunting accident in Argentina a few years back. His obituary reported that Mr. Malloy had a net worth of over one billion dollars at the time of his death. Thereafter his widow, Mrs. Malloy, took over his interests. Not long after she did, the tripartite partnership fell apart. There were numerous lawsuits between the former partners. There were IRS audits. Things got very nasty. The numerous lawsuits between the former partners resulted in Mr. Holly obtaining a $200 million judgment against Mr. Malloy's estate, Mrs. Malloy, and their various business entities. Eventually, Mr. Holly formed a special purpose company that he called Lex Talionis, LLC, created for the sole purpose of pursuing Mrs. Malloy to the ends of the Earth for payment of the $200 million judgment.

Lex Talionis was relentless. It seized bank accounts of Mrs. Malloy. It seized a yacht. It put liens on her vast real property holdings. It went so far as to purchase from a bank the mortgage covering the widow-Malloy's luxurious, 18,000 square foot mansion on Turtle Creek in Dallas. Then Holly/Lex Talionis engaged in a legal maneuver that Judge Lassiter had seen all-too-frequently in her years of handling legal feuds and financial debacles. Holly/Lex Talionis declared the mortgage on Mrs. Malloy's mansion to be in default for silly technical reasons and exercised Holly/Lex Talionis's option to begin foreclosure and to have a receiver appointed, *ex-parte*, to take possession and control of the mansion's contents. The receiver that Holly/Lex Talionis hired was a down-and-out Dallas lawyer, Rex Marsh, who was a college fraternity brother of Mr. Malloy's. Rex Marsh had long been on the "outs" with the Malloys, after their son broke up with his daughter on the day before her debut at the

Dallas Symphony Orchestra League's debutante Presentation Ball. And a few years later, as if to rub salt in the wound, on the day of the Cattle Baron's Ball, the annual fundraiser auction for which Mrs. Malloy was chair, Rex Marsh, as receiver for Holly/Lex Talionis, took control of the Turtle Creek mansion and had a sheriff deputy escort Mrs. Malloy off the premises—with dozens of neighbors and reporters watching and snapping pictures. Within hours of his appointment as receiver, Mr. Marsh evicted Mrs. Malloy from her home and thereafter improperly removed almost every item in it—including the dress and jewelry that she planned to wear to the Cattle Baron's Ball that night. This is what had prompted Mrs. Malloy to file bankruptcy— after a short stay in rehab that she badly needed after the whole trauma.

It was an exhausting hour of testimony for everyone, including "Coco Chanel," Mrs. Malloy's ten-pound, rhinestone-collared Shih Tzu dog, that Avery had allowed Mrs. Malloy to bring in as an emotional support animal. After all, if Avery's dogs could sometimes attend court, why shouldn't Avery allow Coco Chanel? It seemed therapeutic for Mrs. Malloy.

As Mrs. Malloy was concluding her testimony and was about to leave the witness box, she suddenly shrieked "What was that?"

Avery, the lawyers and other spectators stared at Mrs. Malloy in silence?

"Are you okay Mrs. Malloy?"

"Judge, I could swear I felt something like a person tugging on my sleeve just now. It was eerie. I felt a cool breeze at the same time, like it was pushing me to stay seated here."

Millicent and the law interns sat with large eyes looking frozen.

Avery shrugged and acted unaffected. "Maybe it was Coco Chanel tugging at you, possibly? And we have such a drafty courtroom."

Mrs. Malloy got up and crossed back over to sit by her lawyer at counsel's table. It was all very awkward, and she looked very flustered.

Avery ended up ruling that, unfortunately, Mrs. Malloy would need to cooperate with the bankruptcy trustee and sit for a deposition and produce various documents that the trustee was seeking. Mrs. Malloy didn't seem to understand. But Judge Lassiter tried to explain that the trustee had to do his due diligence as part of her case. Mrs. Malloy broke down in tears. As she awkwardly sobbed next to her lawyer, her false eyelashes began falling off and streaming down her cheeks, looking rather creepy like spider legs. Coco Chanel pawed at her face, apparently thinking that the eyelashes were alive. It was all a very unpleasant scene.

After court, Avery did her usual debriefing with her law clerk and interns. Of course, all they wanted to talk about was the moment Mrs. Malloy said she felt something tugging at her sleeve. Avery ignored that banter.

"Have you kids ever heard of the Ernest Hemingway famous quote from the book *The Sun Also Rises* where one of the characters asks Lady Brett Ashley's drunken and broke Scottish fiancé *'how did you go bankrupt?'*"

There were blank stares.

"He answered, *'Two ways. Gradually then suddenly.'*"

After a pregnant pause, Millicent told the interns, "Remember I told you, the judge is always quoting Hemingway, even when you least expect it. Get used to it."

Sarah, the empathetic law intern, interrupted the silence. "Well, I think it was sad how naïve and clueless Mrs. Malloy seemed. And her lawyer, Mr. Metallica or Mannheim or whatever his name was, just sat there like a weasel in a tie the whole time. Didn't seem to be helping her at all, if you ask me. Do you think he even explained any of the basic process to Mrs. Malloy?"

The other intern, Spence spoke up. "Judge, my law school professor says that we have bankruptcy courts so people won't kill each other over debt. But he also says these courts are also kind of like the land of broken promises."

Millicent added her two cents. "Funny, but my old law school professor used to say that these courts decide the 'order in which a person can screw his creditors.'"

Avery bristled. "I suppose these are all apt comments to some extent. It's a tough place. You cannot get through most days without feeling like getting mad or crying. In fact, if I ever get where I stop feeling some emotion on days like today, it will be time for me to quit. Hopefully, most judges can always see a little bit of themselves or their family members in the faces of the parties who appear before them. That's part of the 'mercy' side of judging. Anyway, today's testimony described the classic reversal of fortune that we hear about so often in our courts. This area of law is not for the faint of heart."

Annalise popped her head in Avery's office. "Max's boss, Joe Meno, has tracked down Max. He's going to be calling you any minute."

"Okay. Everybody out."

Chapter Eight

It's Complicated.

Avery always said that Max Lassiter was a complicated and exhausting man. And his powers of recuperation were astounding. He had been injured on the job so many times she lost count. But, two years ago, Max was in a hospital bed, having suffered a heart attack while chasing a twenty-three-year-old armed robber. That *Dirty Harry*-like moment resulted in two stents being inserted into Max's heart. He had cheated death that day by about twelve minutes according to his doctor. After a short medical leave, Max returned to work, but things never felt quite the same. Part of it was the heart attack and feeling less than the man he was before. But part of it was losing friends and colleagues in the July 7, 2016 massacre just a few months earlier. Some things are hard to shake. "Seven-seven" is what they all called it. He would never completely shake "seven-seven."

So, Max retired—turned in his badge and put away his guns and handcuffs. Spent most of his days fishing or trolling on the internet. But he was too restless to stay retired. Why are men so frequently that way? Now Max was working on foreign soil as a contractor for Premier Insurance. He was one of their professional "finders." Premier often hired retired law enforcement officers for investigative work. Max had always been a man who kept some distance between himself and others. Now this was more than ever the case. Possibly the perfect job for him. There were very few people who knew exactly what Max was doing down in Mexico. Not even Avery. Unbeknownst to Avery, a retired U.S. Marshal who was down in Mexico with Max—a fellow named Dave Carrillo—was also a contractor with Premier and referred to Max's current gig as the "Max Lassiter Vengeance Tour." But it was growing much more complicated than that each day.

Avery's cell phone rang at 11 a.m.

"Good grief, Max. Where are you? Are you okay? I haven't heard from you for a week now!"

Max sighed and paused a bit. "Actually, right now I am at about Latitude 25.51 degrees and Longitude 99.37 degrees, sitting in a bar across from Dave Carrillo—another guy that Premier has assigned to my project along with me. He's retired from the U.S. Marshals Service. FYI, Dave knows a lot of the same people we do from the good old days of your Marshals security detail and the Braden brothers investigation."

Avery heard very little after the words "I am sitting in a bar."

"You are sitting in a bar at 11:00 a.m., or whatever time it is there?"

"We're in the same time zone as you."

"Really, Max? That's a tough gig you have going on down there!"

"I'm sorry. I'm really tired. It has been a rough, few days." As Max said those words, he looked at his arms, bruised from the Hidalgo rescue incident. "I've had some unexpected things get me sidetracked. I've pretty much been travelling all over the country, and I have been in some remote spots in Hidalgo where I had spotty cell phone reception."

"Hidalgo? Why on Earth have you been in Hidalgo? I thought Cade Graham was supposedly killed—or was fake killed I should say—near Cabo San Lucas? Hidalgo must be over 1,000 miles from Cabo! I only know that because Hidalgo has been in the news a lot recently because of that pipeline explosion earlier this week."

"Yeah." A long awkward silence followed.

"Yeah? Hello?"

"Well, I guess you could say that this situation with Cade Graham has gotten way more complicated than Premier originally thought. It's far stranger, as it turns out, than simply an apparent faked death."

"How so?"

"Well, where do I begin."

Dave Carrillo looked up at Max, rolled his eyes, and took another sip of Pacifico. Max returned the look with the Italian salute.

"Avery, let me bounce a couple of questions off of you relating to some of what we are investigating down here. Some insurance-related questions."

"Okay. And, by the way, the kids and I are just fine, Max, in case you were wondering but just forgot to ask."

"Oh God. I'm sorry, Avery. I texted Julia earlier today before this call. She updated me on just about every subject imaginable. Including lots of stories about Baxter Squared."

"Baxter Squared" was Max's nickname for the two new Cavalier King Charles Spaniel puppies that Avery recently adopted, Jake and Finley. Sadly, sweet old Baxter, the family's previous Cavalier King Charles Spaniel, died last year of congestive heart failure, close to the same time that Max had his heart attack. Sad coincidence.

"It's okay, Max. Really. It's just disconcerting that you can go a week without checking in. When you do, you say you have been in Hidalgo, which is not only a thousand miles from where you are supposed to be but also at the center of an international human tragedy right now. I'm still trying to process that one. But I'm glad you texted with Julia. Did she tell you about Finley getting stuck in the doggie door the other day?"

"Yes. Y'all are feeding him too much."

"Well, anyway, go on and ask me your insurance questions. You probably don't want to be arguing with your wife and talking about doggie doors when you're sitting in a Mexican bar across the table from Dave what's-his-name. By the way, is Dave married?"

"It's Carrillo, and no he's not." Dave looked at Max perplexed. Max shrugged.

"Okay, Avery, again, I am very, very sorry about being out of touch."

"Apology accepted. Now, Max, really. Go back to your insurance questions." Avery was trying to prolong the moment when she had to tell Max about the mysterious phone message left the night before.

"Have you ever heard of the life insurance *settlement* business?"

"Sure. I have had a couple of disputes involving life insurance settlement companies in my court."

"Well, let me see if I can explain something that Premier discovered that was going on with Cade Graham and maybe you can fill in the gaps if you think I am not understanding this all correctly."

"I'm all ears."

"As I understand it, there is a so-called secondary market for life insurance policies, where some companies are basically in the business of buying individuals' life insurance policies for cash if, say, a person needs the money or doesn't feel like he needs the protection of life insurance anymore. It's usually older people—seniors—who have had their policies in place for a very long time."

"Yes, that's correct. And the term used for that is a 'life settlement transaction,' even though that may sound like an ambiguous term for what is going on. You may have seen the TV commercials for this industry. Moms and pops with grown up kids who feel like they don't need their policies anymore. So, they can sell their policies for a cash payment—at a discounted amount below the face value of the life insurance policy. The company that buys the life insurance policy continues to pay the premiums on the policy. And then when the person dies, the purchasing company gets to collect the life insurance benefit—in other words, the entire face amount of the policy."

"Yep, I have seen those creepy TV commercials."

"And to be clear, the life insurance policy may very well have a cash surrender value that the insured person could ask to receive from the insurance company, but maybe that value is not so great. But, in contrast, these so-called life insurance settlement companies will pay these individuals quite a bit more than the cash surrender value. So, I guess it can be a good deal for everyone concerned. The elderly person who doesn't have a need for the policy gets a good cash 'settlement,' and the life settlement company pays the premiums on the policy after buying the policy and gets to receive the full, face value of the policy when the original policy owner dies."

"I have to say, I can barely believe this is legal, Avery. It sounds like these companies are basically betting money on the prospect of people dying quickly so they don't have to invest in paying a lot of premiums but get to collect a big, fast cash profit. Sounds like a recipe for disaster to me."

"Well, I know what you mean, Max. It's always seemed a little creepy to me, too. But actually, there was a U.S. Supreme Court decision more than a century ago in which the Court held that a life insurance policy is private property than can be transferred at the will of the policy owner.[2] I guess you could say that Court decision sort of paved the way for this sort of thing—although the industry didn't

---

[2] *Grigsby v. Russell*, 222 U.S. 149 (1911).

really get going until the AIDS epidemic in the 1980s."

"What in the hell does AIDS have to do with any of this? And, please, Avery, give me the short version of whatever the answer is. You're starting to lose me by talking about Supreme Court cases."

Dave Carrillo burst out laughing and spit out some of his beer. He was trying not to eavesdrop too much on Max's conversation, but it was getting impossible not to.

"Hey, you started this discussion, Max, by saying you wanted me to answer some questions about life insurance. I'm just answering your questions. I think your words were that you wanted me to 'fill in some gaps in your knowledge.'"

"Okay. You're right. Back to AIDS."

"Anyway, this is really creepy, but the 1980s, when AIDS was a new disease and practically always a death sentence, is really when the practice started up of selling— or settling—life insurance policies. Terminally ill AIDS victims would sell their life insurance policies to get cash to pay for their medicine. Sadly, these policies were quick payoffs in that situation, because the policy owner would usually die in a couple of years or less, after selling the policy. These are referred to as viatical settlements where the policy holder is terminally ill. But the more common situation is where the policy holder is a senior—over age sixty-five—and not terminally ill."

"Again, I just can't believe this shit is legal. Some greedy, tie-wearing weasel lawyer probably invented this."

"Why does everyone keep referring to lawyers as tie-wearing weasels today?"

"What?"

"Oh nothing. Max, I doubt a lawyer invented the life insurance settlement business. Actually, I have no idea. Maybe a lawyer did create the whole idea. But I do know that law makers, both in Washington and at the state level, have certainly investigated this industry on occasion. And truthfully, the insurance policy holders typically end up getting a lot more cash than they otherwise would from the cash surrender value that the insurance company itself would pay. So, again, I guess it's not unreasonable to think of this as a win-win type of transaction. And there is some regulation of the industry. I am by no means an expert at all, but I recall that there are some restrictions on what you can and can't do."

"Okay, stop there. I want to hear about the restrictions."

"Well, let's see. There's a concept that you must have an 'insurable interest' in the subject matter of any insurance policy. So, for example, you cannot be the original purchaser of a life insurance policy *on a stranger* or some other random person with whom you don't have any kind of a relationship."

"Like, I could not go out and take out an original life insurance policy on my next-door neighbor."

"Exactly. Also, you cannot enter one of these life settlement transactions at the very same time that a policy is issued. In other words, you can generally only purchase another person's life insurance policy *after* it has legitimately been in place for several years."

"Aha! So, *there is* a line you can cross where it's not legal! Told you, Dave."

"Sure. But, again Max, I am not an expert on this. Max, what in the world is going on with Cade Graham and life insurance settlements? Why all these odd questions? I thought you were going down to Mexico just to investigate his apparent pseudocide."

"Well, as I understand it, Cade Graham, Mr. Hedge Fund Genius, created a specific hedge fund at his company, Ranger Capital, that was purchasing life insurance policies. He drummed up dozens of investors to contribute money for his 'life settlements hedge fund,' and, through a broker, the fund acquired more than 5,000 policies having over one billion dollars of face value."

"Okay. I understand. I have certainly heard of hedge funds getting involved in the life insurance settlements business. It is not in and of itself problematic, Max."

"Well, as it turns out, Graham, in connection with buying up these life insurance policies, was using a supposed 'expert' who was inputting life expectancy data that suggested that the people selling the policies would die much sooner than they were, based on actuarial tables. The result was the hedge fund was not collecting funds on the policies as expected. It was a frigging disaster. The *Wall Street Journal* wrote an expose on it and reported policy holders were living two and three times beyond projections."

"Oh, how terrible. People were living longer than expected," Avery said sarcastically.

"I'm telling you. I don't know how in the world this is legal. It certainly doesn't feel legal—or at least not moral or ethical."

"Okay. Well, go on. I've got to hear the rest of this."

"Anyway, for a couple of years, the hedge fund was paying about $1 million per month just on the premiums on these 5,000 life insurance policies and collecting nothing, zippo, because basically no one was dying. The hedge fund eventually ran out of cash. Graham was losing his shirt on this business—or rather his investors were. People were getting really pissed off at Graham. The SEC was investigating him. The situation was becoming untenable. Cade was having to cover the cost of maintaining this fund from other resources. He was robbing from Peter to pay Paul in his hedge fund empire—by borrowing from unrelated hedge funds in the Ranger Capital empire, he managed to pay the premiums on the life insurance policies."

"Okay. Well, you and everyone else in Dallas knew that Graham was on the financial precipice. This was just one of many reasons that he was, I guess. Right? Oh, wait, don't tell me. Do you think Cade Graham started putting hits out on people that had the life insurance policies owned by his hedge fund, so that some of these policies would start paying off? He's hiding out in Mexico and playing dead while ordering hits on people? Good God, I feel guilty just suggesting something so terrible. I'm going to be struck by lightning any moment."

"It's actually not a bad guess, Avery. But no. For some reason, Premier—which was the issuer on a lot of these policies—started noticing that Graham's hedge fund had recently started buying up a lot of policies on people who were American citizens now living in Mexico. These were middle class folks who had retired in Mexico. Mostly on the Yucatan Peninsula near Cancun, Cozumel, and Playa del Carmen. Nice weather. Low cost of living. And there is a nice senior living community down there called *Isla Valladolid* where many of these ex-pats retired. *Isla Valladolid* has extremely nice, posh independent living condos, assisted living facilities, and a nursing home for the residents when they start to eventually need that type of care. All high-rises overlooking the ocean."

"Sounds like a place I might like to live someday."

"Uh, better hold that thought. I don't think you'll feel that way when I'm finished with my story."

Dave Carrillo chimed in from across the table. "Tell her the part about the REIT. Ask her what the hell a REIT is." Dave had now abandoned any reservations he might have had about eavesdropping. Realizing this, Max put his phone on speaker.

"Oh yeah, Dave wants me to tell you that a REIT—which I understand means a 'real estate investment trust'—happens to own this bougie *Isla Valladolid* property, and the REIT is minority-owned by Graham and majority-owned by some Mexican nationals who have close ties to one of the big drug cartels. The *Oscuro* Cartel. And then this Mexican-cartel controlled REIT leases the property to another entity—an operator/tenant—that Graham mostly owns and controls through offshore companies."

"Welcome to the world of structured corporate finance, Max—well except for the drug cartel part. Lots of interconnecting relationships and frequently offshore companies. That's interesting, but let's get to the really good stuff, Max. I feel you're building to a punch line here."

"Oh, you bet your life there's one. Anyway, strangely, soon after Graham started buying life insurance policies on lots of the folks down at *Isla Valladolid*, the liquidity problems of Graham's life insurance fund significantly reversed. Why? Because people down at *Isla Valladolid* *started dying more frequently* in comparison to folks on the other life insurance policies that the fund had earlier purchased. Many of the policies on the *Isla Valladolid* folks had not been in place very long either—which makes me think back to one of the restrictions you mentioned earlier. In other words, it wasn't like all these ex-pats had life insurance in place for twenty years and then decided to sell it when their kids grew up. A lot of the policies were recently purchased. Anyway, Premier had begun to grow suspicious about what might be going on, shortly before Cade Graham's untimely demise. They have me looking into all of this shit, as well as trying to track down Cade Graham."

"Holy cow." Avery sat in stupefied silence for a moment. "Okay, well, I have to say this. Now that you have mentioned stuff about a drug cartel, and a bunch of people dying, I am starting to get a little worried. But why, again, were you in Hidalgo this week? Hidalgo is nowhere near the Yucatan Peninsula and it's also nowhere near Cabo. Were you taking the scenic route from Cabo across the Mexican desert or what?"

"You might say I was." There was another awkward silence.

Dave Carrillo suddenly choked violently on the peanuts he had just popped into his mouth.

"What's wrong with Dave?"

"He's fine. He just got something caught in his throat."

"Okay, well, this would normally be the point where I'd go into a lightning round of questions with you, but I'll stop with the interrogation. I have a very strange feeling about all of this, Max, but I'll assume this is one of those 'need to know basis' situations. I'll just stay tuned to see where this all goes. Any idea how much longer you are going to be down there?"

"Uh-oh. You just asked me another question, Avery."

"It's in my nature. My DNA. I can't help myself."

"Your DNA, or the curse of your profession? Anyway, I'm unfortunately going to answer you with a non-answer. I really have no idea where this is all going or how long it will take. I'm sorry. You and the kids try to have a nice summer without me, Okay?"

"Very funny. Okay, unrelated, there is something I need to tell you. It's the whole reason I reached out to your boss to track you down. I'm dreading telling you, but here goes. It may be nothing, but I got a weird voice mail message at the office at 11:42 last night. The caller ID showed unknown caller. And there was nothing but background noise on the voice mail, like it was a butt dial. But here's the catch. I'm pretty sure the call originated from Malta."

"Wait a second. Did you say 11:42?"

"Yeah."

"Hmmm. What are the odds?"

"You tell me, Max. Should I tell the Marshals?"

"Why don't you back up first and tell me why it is that you happen to think the call originated from Malta."

"Why don't I just make a recording of the call and send it to you by text. You can listen and tell me what you think. I want you to tell me if you recognize the same noises that I think I do in the background, without me influencing you with what I think I heard. I've got to run into court in a few minutes. I'll send you the recording in five minutes. Please call me back later, would you? I'm really trying to keep a cool head on this. I need your perspective."

"Of course, I will. Now you've got me a little worried."

"Maybe it's nothing. A wrong number. And promise me you won't share anything about this with Dave. I don't want him to call any of his old Marshal buddies unless you and I decide that it's probably necessary."

Avery and Max hung up. Max looked across the table

at Dave Carrillo who had now started on his second beer. "Shit. We may need to go to Malta sooner than we thought, Dave."

"You mean there's going to be mission creep on our mission creep?"

"Yep."

"Never been to Malta. I hear it's nice."

"Blue calm waters. Great fishing."

Chapter Nine

Retired Deputy U.S. Marshal Dave Carrillo (a.k.a. the "Swiss Army Knife").

Dave Carrillo was a retired Deputy U.S. Marshal who, similarly to Max, could not stay retired very long. It was the curse of law enforcement. The families of these men will tell them that they have bruised and bled enough for their fellow man and it's okay to give it a rest, but it's hard for them to see it that way. A person cannot easily deescalate from years of constant adrenalin rushes. Ernest Hemingway once wrote, *There is no hunting like the hunting of man, and those who have hunted armed men long enough and liked it, never care for anything else thereafter*. Dave Carrillo and Max Lassiter both bore truth to that Hemingway insight. Most people don't understand this very much. Some people think it sounds somewhat barbaric. But those who live with these types of men know that the protector instinct resides strongly within them.

Dave had enjoyed a long and interesting life and a

storied career. He could wax for hours about the colorful experiences that had made him a legend within the U.S. Marshals Service. The stories got better and better, the more cerveza or, preferably, Macallan Scotch that he drank.

Dave had grown up in Gunnison, Colorado with a life that revolved around fly-fishing, hunting, skiing, and working as a white-water rafting guide on the Taylor River during his summers. Smart as a whip, he had left his family's ranch at the base of Tenderfoot Mountain at age eighteen to attend the Colorado School of Mines to study nuclear science and engineering. To the surprise of many people who knew him, he left there after three years (while making straight A's, saying he was bored) and next joined the United States Marines. He thereafter fought in various theaters during Desert Storm and several other ancillary combat missions. He put out oil field fires in Kuwait. He trained law enforcement personnel in Nigeria, teaching them strategies to fight Boko Haram. He also developed a specialty niche directing reconnaissance drones for missions, from Pakistan to Yemen, and from Algeria to Somalia. He eventually left the Marines and joined the Marshals Service. There, he soon developed the nickname "the Swiss Army Knife," because he could do absolutely anything and everything with ease. He was called upon to do whatever task was necessary—big, small, unusual, or impossible. He mostly worked on fugitive task forces over the years, especially focusing on international fugitive extractions from difficult places. He was then deployed for a few years in WITSEC (witness protection security). He was even posted as a guard down in Antarctica for a while (where there is, of course, not much need for law enforcement, since mostly only scientists and researchers reside there, but the U.S. Marshals are dispatched there to provide some semblance of law and order, just in case). He was a devastatingly handsome, tall bachelor. He was divorced—he was a good catch, to be sure, but there were not many women who could tolerate his restless and peripatetic lifestyle. Sadly, men like Dave—

while interesting and fascinating—don't always make the best spouses.

Retirement from the Marshals Service is generally mandatory at age fifty-seven. But Dave Carrillo had retired a few years shy of that, at fifty-four. After years of commendations for amazing, successful missions capturing drug kingpins, sex traffickers, and others on America's Most Wanted list, he was assigned one day to an absolutely demoralizing security protection detail of an ill-tempered and arrogant judge that wore him down. It stripped him of his manhood, he joked. So, he called it quits.

Dave called the judge-protectee who ended his career the "Dragon Lady"—specifically, "Judge Amelia F'ing Ramsey, the Dragon Lady." Her middle name was actually Fiona. But Dave preferred to suggest that the "F" stood for something else. The judge was a megalomaniac with delusions of grandeur.

Judge Amelia F'ing Ramsey wore nothing but gray pant suits, white starched Oxford shirts, and comfortable, black Clarks shoes. Every single day of her life. It's been said that the average person makes 35,000 decisions per day (starting with breakfast, what to wear, whether to take an umbrella to work, *etc.*). Judge Amelia F'ing Ramsey believed in cutting down on the decision-making process in life wherever possible, to avoid wasting brain power on the trivial things in life—like one's wardrobe.

She had piercing, icy blue eyes—the only color in her otherwise drab, solitary life. She worked like a machine, and with great efficiency. She worked when she wanted and on what she wanted. She wrote her own rules, and no one knew what those rules were. They just knew that they better not ask too many questions or there surely would be repercussions. Opacity was her hallmark. Transparency was for the weak. Everyone was on a "need to know" basis with her, and they simply did not need to know anything about her. To her credit, she somehow got away with writing her own rules and keeping people out of her business—she was oddly proprietary, in a profession that is supposed to be about the public. She was in complete control of her own identity. People were afraid to challenge her, assuming (probably correctly) that resistance was futile. To her, there were two kinds of people in this world: those willing to drop everything and do anything she asked of them for nothing in return, and those whom she resented. She, frankly, was not even fond of the former type of person—she just recognized that she had an occasional use for them. She certainly never reciprocated their courtesies.

Judge Amelia F'ing Ramsey was rigid. Inflexible. Tone deaf. A bureaucratic box-checker with the personality of a hall monitor. She did not have a creative bone in her body—except when it came to feigning elaborate, false humility when it suited her. She did not want to hear anyone's opinion, unless it was one praising her. God forbid you ever talk over her or interrupt one of her lengthy bloviations about herself and her work. She was a narcissist in a category like no other. She had a greatly inflated sense of self. She loved titles, awards, validation, and flattery. She thought she was above all others and deserved to be constantly praised. The truth was that she was not the big deal that she thought she was. But she had no awareness of this fact. She was a mere trial court judge. And she was rather one-dimensional really. She could work on only one case or project at a time—albeit extremely well. Most people do not have that luxury or, frankly, would not want to live that way. She did. She could toil in sequestered confinement for weeks or months at a time. She enjoyed fixating on Sisyphean tasks. She valued knowledge over wisdom. Discipline over creativity. Convolution over simplicity. To her, every lawsuit was like a chess game. She had no connection to humanity or empathy for anyone's plight or suffering. She did not have time for that. Kindness and mercy were not in her repertoire. She only cared about statutes. The people in front of her may as well have been characters in a book. And she trusted no one. She thought that everyone was involved in a complex and devious scheme to undermine her.

Judge Amelia F'ing Ramsey was not liked by her colleagues, much less the parties who had the misfortune of being in her court. Thus, it was no surprise when she received a heinous death threat (which was left in a red envelope, on top of a shopping bag full of excrement, on her front porch). Every judge receives a death threat, sooner or later. In fact, it was a surprise that Judge Amelia F'ing Ramsey did not get them more frequently.

When Judge Amelia F'ing Ramsey got her death threat and the bag full of dung, poor Dave had the bad luck of being the one assigned to handle her protective detail. It was not an assignment that anyone would relish. The judge had gone overboard demanding that the Marshals Service assign her "the best, no slackers." They sent her the best—over-qualified as Dave was.

Deputy Dave Carrillo, "the best," soon found himself, and the team of other fine deputies assigned to Judge Amelia F'ing Ramsey's house, reduced from extraordinary man hunters to hen-pecked man servants. They felt like vassals in the judge's medieval torture chamber. And Dave was not one inclined to genuflect to advance his career—especially for the likes of Judge Amelia F'ing Ramsey. The man had a backbone of steel. The judge didn't like Dave's "arrogant" attitude. She didn't like the ground rules that Dave set for her, and *vice versa*. She yelled at Dave for wearing a firearm inside her house, insisting that he leave it outside. He refused, of course. She requested that he and he alone (not any of the other Deputy Marshals) walk her demon dog with her every day at the precise same time (her dog was a deaf Bassett Hound named General Sherman). Dave refused her request, telling Judge Amelie F'ing Ramsey that having predictable habits and patterns, like walking a dog at the exact same time every day, was not a smart idea. She requested that Dave's Deputies bathe General Sherman in her outdoor carriage house. Dave, of course, drew the line on that one. She demanded Dave pick up her dry cleaning of gray suits and white Oxford shirts every Friday, promptly at 3:00 p.m., so she could get the "early bird" ten percent discount. She called Dave "Deputy Corleone" and asked him if his family was in the mafia. She asked him why he was so slow to answer her phone calls whenever he did not happen to answer on the first ring. She was smarmy and condescending to him. Reptilian. Dave literally saw the head of a dragon when he looked at her.

Finally, one morning, Dave suffered all that he could take. After all, he was a man with a strong sense of dignity— not the spineless invertebrate she ,wanted all people around her to be. He was a man accustomed to speaking truth to power, and he usually got away with it. When Judge Amelia F'ing Ramsey greeted him at her backdoor that morning, with her customary scowl, and asked him to make her a pot of coffee, and make it snappy, and also directed him to "take out the trash as soon as possible," Dave put his Ray-Ban sunglasses back on, walked over to the trash can, grabbed it by the handles, and turned it upside down, dumping all of her trash on the Turkish silk rug in her kitchen that she constantly told him not to step on.

Judge Amelia F'ing Ramsey stared in horror at Dave for a few moments. It was a stare-down of epic proportions, except that Dave had the advantage, because he was wearing his Ray-Bans. Finally, Dave said in almost a whisper, "Surely you should have realized, Judge Amelia FUCKING Ramsey, that the chances of me making your coffee and taking out your trash this morning were between slim and none, and slim just left the building."

Dave's words hung in the air as the judge continued to stare at him with her icy blue eyes. No one had ever dared to confront Judge Amelia F'ing Ramsey so brazenly. Dave then walked over to the judge's $75,000 ebony lacquer Ezio Belotti kitchen table, slammed his Marshal credentials on it, and walked out of her house. That was it. With that, a legendary career had ended.

Dave Carrillo notified the other Deputies outside the

Dragon Lady's house what he had just done. They stared at him in shock and disbelief. He then called his Chief immediately. He told his Chief that he was heading to the office in his G-ride to turn in the vehicle, retire, and collect his things. He would fill out whatever paperwork his boss needed him to complete. When he walked into the Marshals office that day, word had gotten out, and Dave Carrillo received a standing ovation from his colleagues. At least that's the way Dave tells the story.

Ironically, the day after that incident, the sender of the death threat was identified and arrested. It was a neighbor of Judge Amelia F'ing Ramsey's, who was sick and tired of General Sherman, the judge's Basset Hound, defecating on his lawn.

Chapter Ten

DB Biocontainment, LLC and the Ellis County Tunnels.

There once was a U.S. federally funded research project known as the "super conducting super collider." It was supposed to be the largest, tubular "particle accelerator complex" in the world. It was being constructed deep beneath the ground, in the mid-1980s, under the rolling prairie southeast of Dallas, in Ellis County.

Ellis County is about one hour north of the infamous Branch Davidian complex in Waco. There, the late cult leader David Koresh and his Branch Davidian commune went up in flames in 1993 (not one of Texas's—or the ATF's—finer moments). The completed super collider was intended to allow scientists to accelerate particles to very high kinetic energy levels, let them impact into one another, and then study the aftermath or byproducts of these collisions to learn more about the structure of the subatomic world and the laws of nature. Nearly two billion dollars was spent on the project by the U.S. government and another

$400,000,000 was contributed by the State of Texas. Then Congress abruptly stopped funding the project in 1993 when it was around twenty percent complete. No known connection to the Branch Davidian debacle, other than timing.

At the time of the defunding, the underground tunnel was fourteen point six miles long, with seventeen shafts to the surface. To some, it seemed uncomfortably like the Viet Cong's Cu-Chi tunnels, only this was being designed for scientific advancement, not warfare. After the defunding, the property was deeded to Ellis County, Texas, which then tried to sell it for many years. The property was finally sold to a famous entrepreneur and trucking magnate in 2006. It thereafter changed hands many times. Finally, in early 2015, an anonymous buyer purchased it (an offshore company with some vague name—Ellis Acquisition One, Ltd.) and leased it to a party named DB Biocontainment, LLC.

No one in the area had heard of Ellis Acquisition or of DB Biocontainment. In fact, no one around paid much attention to what was happening with the property during all those years after the demise of the physics project. Most folks believed a local chemical manufacturer occupied the premises.

Dmitry Basayev, through DB Biocontainment and its investors, quietly reformed the property. He reformed it to a new scientific purpose. A multi-unit underground hospital and BSL-4 research laboratory. It was his own Noah's ark, of sorts. Basayev would perfect his superbug disinfectant system and related products there. The BASA, Inc. disinfection system invention was very real—not the fiction of a Ponzi scheme. It was, in essence, a state-of-the-art disinfection infrastructure—initially contemplated for healthcare facilities, but eventually hoped to go into any number of public spaces. It included such features as ceiling and wall panels that emanated UV light, an air purification ventilation system, a collection of i-Robot type roving machines that constantly disinfected floor surfaces with a combination of laser and environmentally friendly chemical products, bio-booths to scan people entering and exiting from facilities, and a cleaning system for catheters and medical tools that had superior qualities to any other products on the market.

Basayev also intended that his underground facility would be used to treat patients with strange viruses or bacterial infections, that were not welcome anywhere else, in a safe, secluded, cement and steel encased subterranean environment, where they could be treated with minimal risk (taking advantage of the BASA disinfectant system in the process). He would experiment with anti-viral medications and vaccines there. He would conduct robust clinical trials that were required by the FDA and other regulatory authorities to bring his products to market. It was really the perfect location for his secret plans. As far as the BSL-4 facility, the only thing remotely comparable to it was a room nicknamed the Slammer at an Army research lab in Maryland and certain Doctors Without Borders facilities, all of which were much less grand in scale.

The underground project was completed by early 2016. Basayev and his team nicknamed it the Grotto. It was like a horizontal, tubular, missile silo. First, at the southern-most end of the tunnel, there was an isolated, communicable infectious disease unit. It was located at the remotest back part of the tunnel, with a separate entrance and exit through one of the seventeen shafts to the surface. It was a fully equipped negative pressure isolation ward designed to deal with biosafety level-4 pathogens. Resident in this isolated, quarantined patient unit were patients in very bad shape with lethal infectious diseases—patients with very "high viral load" and sepsis syndrome, leading to severe diarrhea and organ failure. The patients at this stage were inserted with breathing tubes, put on dialysis, and were usually undergoing platelet transfusions. Often, various other experimental treatments were being implemented—many not FDA-approved. This was referred to as Chamber 1 or, by its nickname, the "Wildfire Chamber" (a reference to the secret, microorganism-securing underground facility in the book *The Andromeda Strain*).

Second, there was a dedicated clinical laboratory next to the quarantine unit, just down the tunnel, for analyzing blood and bodily fluids from patients in the Wildfire Chamber, by simply taking samples down the tunnel without having to go into any separate environments. Everything in theory was all self-contained, and all patients and high-risk pathogens were contained. There were staff nurses, physicians, clinical pathologists, virologists, laboratory technical staff, and environmental services. There was a constant buzz of people, studying symptoms, modes of transmission, and treatment options. This was referred to as Laboratory 1 and nicknamed the Wildfire Laboratory.

There was also a center unit, within the isolation unit, made of stainless steel and other highly durable materials, for contaminated waste to be brought and decontaminated with harsh chlorine bleach solutions and then burned—not sent through pipes and drains into the other areas of the tunnel or the public water system. This was referred to as the Decontamination Pit.

Further down, there was another sterilization unit for personnel to shower and bring their own laundry before entering and exiting the facility each and every day—with, once again, egress through an exclusive shaft to the surface for this portion of the tunnel. This was sarcastically referred to as the Spa.

Still further down was another unit for patients who were not suffering from any type of communicable disease but were having an adverse reaction after exposure to the BASA experimental super-germ disinfectant system. The culprit for these adverse reactions seemed to be the UV light exposure that was part of the decontamination system (in ceiling and wall panels). It was still being adjusted to determine the optimal UV sterilization levels and some patients were unfortunately experiencing skin cancer and other adverse reactions. This was referred to as Chamber-2 or the Nebula Chamber.

And yet further down at the other end of the tunnel from all the previously described units were laboratories and offices devoted to other research endeavors—mostly research aimed at perfecting the disinfectant system, but other research pertaining to pathogens and drugs. This was Laboratory-2 or the Nebula Laboratory.

Finally, at the very opposite end of the tunnel, far away from the patients and laboratory units, there were fully furnished living quarters, lavished with fine architectural details, vaulted ceilings, glass tiles, chandeliers, amply stocked kitchens, bar facilities with fine wines and liquors, and recreational amenities, for those who chose to stay onsite 24/7—including Dmitry Basayev, Dr. Astrid Nilsson, and a few other scientists. Also, Dmitry Basayev's elderly father, Arkady Basayev, a retired international journalist of some notoriety, having covered decades of conflicts between Chechen rebels and the Russians, and having exposed numerous scandals and atrocities over the years, lived there, having recently immigrated from Grozny, Chechnya.

The Grotto was an amazing subterranean secret vault, of sorts, devoted to health care innovation. Patients were being observed. Research was being conducted. New and old therapies tried. All out-of-plain-sight. Signage at the surface entrance shafts to the tunnel, and all about the surface nearby, signaled the usual "KEEP OUT," "DANGER," "NO TRESPASSING," and "HAZARDOUS SUBSTANCES IN USE" warnings. Most nearby residents believed that the new owner of the facility was a private company engaged in some sort of government subsidized scientific research, similar to what had originally been intended for the super conducting super collider, and really did not have much curiosity regarding the comings and goings and activity at the tunnel. And, as for the medical and scientific personnel working there, no one involved was asking the source of the funding for the facility. It had to be enormously expensive to run and maintain all of this. Most every scientist involved was earning six figures. The capital expenditures that had been undertaken were enormous. But Dmitry Basayev was a genius. People trusted him. The scientists in the tunnel were going to save the world.

Meanwhile, who were the patients who consented to treatment in this unconventional underground facility? Consent might be too broad a term. There was a random assortment of patients in the Wildfire Chamber—most of whom were unconscious and not capable of consenting to anything. If they survived, they would be eternally grateful for being brought back from the brink. If they did not, no one would be the wiser and they would have made their contribution to medical science, in Basayev's estimation. For the greater good.

In early March 2017, a group of oil field workers were brought in from Prudhoe Bay to the facility by DB aircraft. And since late Fall 2017, a steady stream of elderly patients from the Yucatan Peninsula down in Mexico had been arriving—some for the Wildfire Chamber 1 and some for the Nebula Chamber 2.

Chapter Eleven

The Braden Brothers (n.k.a. "Enos" and Rasmus Aavik).

It had been more than three-and-a-half years since Judge Lassiter's former law clerk, the notorious Matthew Braden "Smith," had gone out in an elaborately planned, maniacal blaze of glory in an Austin, Texas hotel conference room—killing numerous innocent victims (mostly lawyers) in the process. His twin brother and cohort in crime, Marcus Braden "Smith," who had killed two judges and more than a dozen other innocents himself, in a related crime spree spanning from New Jersey to Dallas, had not been seen or heard of since the Austin tragedy. Marcus was believed to have headed west from Austin, with lots of money, slipping across the Rio Grande border into Mexico. He had apparently managed to somehow disappear into oblivion. This much was true.

Marcus Braden thought that he would forever outsmart and elude any law enforcement officers who might still be looking for him. After all, in his mind, they were all idiots, and he was brilliant. He had outwitted law enforcement agencies many times before. His newest persona was "Enos," a "blond gringo" who had cozied up to certain of the most dangerous Mexican drug lords—most notably, those in the up-and-coming *Los Chupas* cartel—because of his savvy with bitcoin and ability to invest and launder the cartel's money through opaque bank accounts around the world. *Los Chupas* interchangeably referred to him as "Enos" and "the CFO." They were strange bedfellows indeed. A kid from New Jersey with spikey bleached blond hair (he had long ago abandoned his dreadlocks) hooking up with drug traffickers, *Huachicoleros*, and *sicarios*. He sometimes hung out in a barren, interior region of Mexico in Hidalgo these days, but also sometimes in a lavish, remote villa in Baja California and, still other times, in Yucatan. "Enos" had slowly gained significant trust from *Los Chupas's* leaders. While he had initially attracted their interest because of his savvy with hiding money, and access to international bank accounts, he had proven himself capable of so much more. He had ways of growing the cartel's financial accounts in a manner that they could not begin to comprehend. Additionally, it had been Enos's idea to move in on the gas pipeline sucking business. It had infuriated the *Zetas* and some of the other gangs when *Los Chupas* started in on this endeavor. A couple of the gangs thought that they had a monopoly on this enterprise. But *Los Chupas* was fast developing a reputation as a group of *hombres* that should not be crossed. You had to co-exist with them, it seemed. They had *sicarios* who were brutal and protected their growing turf. The *sicarios* were not just killers who executed revenge killings or taught someone a lesson now and then. They were apparently being hired for all sorts of strange, unconventional hits. Many in both the law enforcement community as well as the organized crime world were not at all sure what all the *Los Chupas sicarios* were pursuing. *Los Chupas* was a strange new breed of Mexican gang. And Enos was just another part of its strangeness. Normally the

Zetas were not afraid of anyone. *Los Chupas* was a whole different factor in a new equation. And even if he felt invincible, the enigmatic Enos always traveled with his own entourage—his own version of Praetorian Guard it seemed. This entourage included an odd teenaged boy nicknamed *Monaguillo* which means "altar boy."

Then there was the case of Richard Braden—the brother who faked his own death. Irony for sure, given that Max Lassiter's current line of work revolved around investigating and becoming an expert on people like Cade Graham who fake their own deaths. Richard Braden was now known as Rasmus Aavik and had, for many years now, been living a private life on the island nation of Malta, telling anyone he met that he was a sailor from Estonia, sharing stories of sailing in regattas around the world. He had mastered an Estonian accent quite well.

Malta is only seventeen miles by nine, and it sits somewhat isolated in the middle of the Mediterranean Sea, about half-way between the toe of the boot of Italy (in a southwesterly direction) and Tunisia (due east of it). Malta is small and rugged. It is graced with calm blue bays (some with harbors full of sail boats and yachts) and curvy hilly roads. It has steep, vertical cliffs of golden hued limestone. It is partly beautiful and partly third-worldly. There are various forms of fortification all about the island (watchtowers, fortresses, and thick stone walls) and a few castles and beautiful churches (the High Baroque styled St. John's Co-Cathedral being the most famous). These are vestiges of centuries past, when Malta was a sought-after prize of many empires because of its strategic location in the Mediterranean. Malta was frequently under attack—during, first, the Crusades and, later, during World War II. In the year 1530, the Order of the Knights of St. John (noblemen from the most important families in Europe) were sent to the island, with the mission of protecting Europe and the Catholic Church from Muslim invaders (specifically, the Turks of the Ottoman Empire). They fortified the island with amazingly thick stone walls and watch towers. The Knights and Maltese (with a population of only a few thousand back then) were later able to withstand an epic onslaught from 40,000 attackers from the Ottoman Empire, during the so-called Great Siege at Malta in 1565. The Knights had considered this a critical battle to keep the Muslims from having a stepping-stone to retake parts of Europe as they had centuries before. Later, during World War II, the Maltese were besieged again and bombed heavily by Axis powers (by this point in time, Malta was under the rule of the United Kingdom which continued until 1962).

Despite its history of standing its ground and keeping people out, Malta is now a place where a person can rather easily worm himself in and disappear forever. Malta is part of the Schengen Treaty of countries and, thus, if one flies there from anywhere in the European Union or other Schengen Treaty countries (which one nearly must), no one checks for a passport upon one's arrival. It is also an easy, short boat ride from the porous borders of places such as Tunisia and Libya.

Malta, while beautiful, exotic, and an all-around lovely place, is a haven for a variety of criminal financial activity and other at least questionable practices (the government has considered officially backing Bitcoin in recent times). Gambling (there are casinos there) and the mafia are now ubiquitous.

Richard Braden (n.k.a. Rasmus Aavik) had arrived in Malta before Matthew and Marcus Braden had ever stepped foot in Texas. He had read books, as a child living in a Catholic orphanage, about the Knights of St. John and the Great Siege at Malta, and the place had captivated his imagination. He moved to a spot called St. Julian's Bay, overlooking the tranquil blue Mediterranean. He moved there shortly after the State of New Jersey reported him as having died, in the year 2002, from a Staph infection—this had been a report fictitiously created by the young Richard Braden, who very early became a skillful cyber-criminal.

Still somewhat young when he arrived, Richard managed to endear himself to the staff at a beautiful gothic style church facing the bay there— The Parish Church of Our Lady of Mount Carmel—with an imposing bell tower that chimed portions of *Nearer My God to Thee* every fifteen minutes. There was a feral cat colony right by the church along the promenade on the beach which Richard helped maintain for many years. There was an easily accessible ferry in St. Julian's Bay that could take one to the historic capital of Malta, Valletta.

Valletta fascinated the young Richard Braden when he first arrived, with its narrow, cobblestone streets and amazing high views of the island's cities and fortresses. He eventually bought a Vespa so that he could ride around the island and explore. As a young man, he eventually left the Church that had taken him in and took on the identity of Rasmus Aavik. He was able to get a job at the Bank of Valletta, rising from clerk to teller to account manager in time. He managed to pose well as an Estonian ex-pat and learned the Maltese way of life quite well.

Everyone speaks both English and Maltese in Malta. Maltese is difficult (it is a Semitic language written in Latin script, derived from an Arabic dialect that first appeared during the Ninth Century Muslim conquest of Sicily), but Richard, like his two brothers, was highly intelligent so he had no problem mastering the language. Eventually, Richard purchased a quaint small sidewalk café which he named *Deheb Qumar*, serving mostly Italian and Sicilian cuisine, but also a few local specialties like rabbit and garlic octopus. He adorned the walls of his café with posters and memorabilia from movies like *The Godfather, Good Fellas*, and *Scarface*. Frank Sinatra tunes were always playing softly in the background. There were cigarette vending machines and a small bar in the front of the café, and several video cameras hidden in random spots around the café. Richard (Rasmus) drove a cobalt blue Land Rover Defender that, every day, he parked in front of the cafe. Most days,

Richard (Rasmus) sat at the bar, taking notes, with a pencil in an old-style ledger pad with carbon paper, seemingly adding up figures and occasionally handing pieces of paper to men who would randomly walk in. He led a discreet but interesting life. Restauranteur. Bookie. Money launderer. Financier. Investor. And, of course, former Estonian sailor.

Chapter Twelve

The Secret World of Cade Graham.

Cade Graham had led a rather charmed life for his fifty-plus years, until his troubles of the past two years. He grew up in the exclusive Highland Park enclave in Dallas, Texas. He was the only child of a workaholic heart surgeon and an alcoholic mother, and the grandson of a storied East Texas oil wildcatter—the latter of whom had mostly raised him. He was tall, well-built, and handsome, with a confident Texas swagger. He still looked rather boyish in middle age. He went to Princeton for undergraduate studies, played football for the Tigers, and was president of the exclusive Cottage Eating Club, as had been his father and grandfather before him. After graduation, he worked several years at the New York Stock Exchange, then earned an MBA from Wharton, and went from there to Bear Stearns on Madison Avenue. He eventually came home to his native Dallas after the Bear Stearns implosion. Once back in Dallas, he started working in private equity and, ultimately, the largely unregulated hedge fund industry. Both private equity and hedge funds thrived in the freewheeling business culture of Big D—a perfect fit for Graham. He also liked that it was still a male dominated world. He liked the gambling and risk-taking that are inherent with hedging and distressed investing. Perhaps it was something in his DNA or a learned trait from his wildcatter grandfather.

After a few years of feeling like he was working round-the-clock, making other people fabulously wealthy (Graham was a mere millionaire while his bosses were billionaires), he decided to form his own company—Ranger Capital. Graham had weathered the capital markets crash of 2008 quite well, despite losing big in mortgage securitization at Bear Stearns. He almost always came out on top in his life. It astounded everyone who knew him. Even as his colleagues were licking their wounds in 2008 and ratcheting themselves down to a more pedestrian lifestyle, Graham had acquired a mansion on Strait Lane in Dallas with a sixteen-car garage full of Lamborghinis, Ferraris, McLarens, and Aston Martins. He also owned a villa overlooking Lake Como in Italy, an apartment in Paris in the Eight District, on the Right Bank (a.k.a. "VIII arrondissement" or *huitieme*), and a small, moated Norman country home near Lisieux, where he enjoyed boar hunting. He played golf with celebrities and politicians. He gave to all the right charities. He had young girlfriends everywhere and allegedly had a couple of illegitimate children whose existence and identity were closely guarded secrets. But he was mostly a loner. A prosperous and hedonistic—and hardworking—loner. Tabloids and internet gossip blogs described him as a Gatsby-like enigma. He had sensibly and cannily never given an interview to any of the usual high-finance media outlets. Among other things, it was impossible to accurately approximate the fortune he had amassed.

But times had, for once, finally turned hard for the

ordinarily Teflon-coated Cade Graham a few years back. His boyish brown hair had turned silver, and his sun-kissed smooth skin had grown weathered. In recent years, Graham's Ranger Capital had specialized in the "SPAC" and "de-SPACing" segment of the capital markets, where investors essentially give an investment manager a blank check to create a special purpose acquisition company ("SPAC"), that will then go out and find a company with which to merge ("de-SPAC"). Among the vehicles that Ranger Capital ended up using these blank checks for were: (1) a fund that invested in life insurance policy settlements; (2) REITs that owned real estate on which hospitals, medical buildings, senior living communities, and rehab facilities were built—which were then leased at lucrative prices to tenant operators; (3) funds that lent money for medical research and development projects; and (4) funds that invested in pharmaceutical companies. In other words, Graham essentially just used the SPAC blank checks for whatever he wanted and whenever he wanted, until he found good companies with which to de-SPAC. In any event, the REITS and the pharmaceutical companies had performed fabulously well. But the life insurance settlement fund was an unmitigated disaster, as was the fund that had been investing in medical R&D.

The medical R&D fund was especially bothersome to Graham. One of Graham's illegitimate sons had gone to Emory University (on his dime) and majored in Biology before going to Harvard for an MBA to follow in his father's footsteps in the world of high finance. While at Emory, he had worked as a research assistant for a grad student there named Dmitry Basayev. Basayev was supposedly a genius who was now on the verge of coming out with revolutionary break throughs in the areas of infectious diseases and state-of-the-art protocols to destroy super bugs. Graham's son introduced him to Basayev. While Graham had long ago learned that great ideas were a dime a dozen, Basayev's extravagant claims about revolutionizing the medical care world in general seemed to have legs. The young, handsome Chechen immigrant had the kind of hubris and charisma that Graham liked.

Graham, at the urging of his illegitimate son, invested several million dollars in early 2015 in a project of Basayev's known as DB Biocontainment, LLC. Graham not only made large loans to DB Biocontainment, LLC, but he also created an offshore company that would buy the aforementioned land in Ellis County, Texas and lease the land to DB Biocontainment, LLC, as tenant. The land would be used as an unconventional, state-of-the-art, underground research facility. Graham made this investment not only at the encouragement of his illegitimate son, but also at the encouragement of another hedge fund, Toro Capital (which had been formed by several of Graham's old buddies from Bear Stearns). Toro Capital had invested heavily in another one of Basayev's companies called BASA, Inc., which was supposedly working on the ultraviolet and air purification disinfectant system that would effectively destroy super germs in medical facilities and public spaces like no other product on the market. Toro Capital had a track record of investing its clients' money extremely well. So, Graham felt optimistic about Dmitry Basayev. Of course, by late March 2017, BASA, Inc. was in a Chapter 11 case and, thereafter, was accused of orchestrating a massive Ponzi scheme. And Toro Capital was later sued for its role in funding the alleged Ponzi scheme.

Luckily, at least for Graham, he did not buy much debt in BASA—and what little debt he did purchase he had hedged by buying credit default swaps. A credit default swap, or "CDS," is similar to insurance for people who loan money or invest in debt. A debt holder who buys a CDS is guaranteed by the CDS issuer that if the CDS-covered debt goes into default, the CDS issuer will buy the debt from the debt holder for the full amount (face value) of the debt. Thus, the CDS issuer was left "holding the bag," so to speak, on the BASA, Inc. debt that Graham had owned. It had become a very common thing, over the last few years, for Cade Graham to leave others holding the bag.

Graham seemingly disappeared off the face of the earth a few months after the BASA, Inc. bankruptcy case was initiated. He had allegedly sold his palatial mansion on Strait Lane and all the fancy cars inside of it in 2018—the mansion had been vacant ever since—and county deed records indicated it was now owned by an offshore entity whose beneficial owner was unknown. Later, by summer 2019, there were press releases indicating that Graham had been killed in a fiery car crash near Cabo San Lucas, while vacationing. Premier Mutual was convinced that Graham had faked his death. Not just because of the two million dollar life insurance policy that then became payable to his illegitimate son. That kind of money was chump change to Graham. It was Graham's life insurance settlement business that was troubling Premier Mutual. Premier Mutual was convinced that Cade Graham had a massive fraud going on—perhaps even something ghastly—involving Graham's hedge fund that was buying up policies of folks down at the *Isla Valladolid* retirement community.

The insurance company, Premier Mutual, was trying to put the pieces together. Thus far it had determined that a great number of life insurance policies that were recently purchased by Graham's hedge fund were policies that had been owned by ex-pats in Yucatan. Why the sudden surge of business from elderly U.S. ex-pats down there? And they weren't just people generally in the Yucatan Peninsula area. They were all residents at the posh *Isla Valladolid* property. Premier had undertaken a significant amount of undercover investigation with the help of lawyers and former law enforcement agents and discovered that *Isla Valladolid* happened to be owned by a REIT in which Cade Graham (through offshore companies) had a significant minority interest, which REIT then leased the property back to a *tenant* that Cade Graham also owned and controlled. Meanwhile, in further performing due diligence, Premier

Mutual happened to learn that the majority owners of the REIT that were co-owners (indirectly) with Graham on *Isla Valladolid* were various Mexican nationals who had close ties to the *Oscuro* drug cartel.

This is where Premier Mutual's due diligence—which had taken months to assemble—had turned troublesome. Unlike the numerous other life insurance policies that the Graham hedge fund had invested in over the past several years, the life insurance policies for the *Isla Valladolid* residents had provided very rapid payoffs. In other words, the folks on the *Isla Valladolid* policies *died much quicker* than had historically happened on Graham's purchased policies—usually in less than two years. Cause of death on all these folks? Many reportedly died of *natural causes* or *infectious disease*—with nothing more specific than this on their Mexican death certificates. This, in and of itself, perhaps was not that strange. Tens of thousands of elderly people die every year of infectious diseases. Some of the folks died on site. Others were transported back to the U.S., via flights out of Cancun airport, for treatment in the U.S. at their request.

Premier Mutual was getting very little cooperation from Mexican authorities in investigating any of this, even though, from Premier's perspective, there were more red flags popping up than in a Chinese Communist Party military parade. Thus, Premier had put together a team of retired U.S. law enforcement officers to do some discreet digging for them. Among them: Max Lassiter and Dave Carrillo, both of whom had already developed significant expertise and connections because of other investigative and surveillance projects that they had undertaken in recent months.

Chapter Thirteen

Isla Valladolid: Flashback, Fall of 2016.

Inside the front office of the *Isla Valladolid*, the office
manager, Barbara Bella Torres, whom coworkers and
residents nicknamed "Malibu Barbie," buzzed around at
breakneck speed. Bella was tall and thin, with a silky brown
complexion and platinum bleached blond hair that was
always neatly styled with a bouncy, preppy flip. She had
emotive green eyes that were actually beautiful brown eyes,
when she was not wearing her opaque color-tinted contact
lenses. Her fingernails were long and pointy, always freshly
painted candy apple red (to match her dermal-filled plump
shiny lips), and her wrists were adorned with David Yurman
cable bracelets. She wore colorful tight-knit dresses, which
snuggly hugged her plastic surgery-enhanced curves. She
wore strappy Jimmy Choo high-heeled shoes. She always
had a phone headset atop her bouncy blond mane. She
frequently went back and forth to conversations on the
headset and in-person conversations with coworkers,

residents, or guests. She was a multitasking hub of constant activity. Everyone who had anything to do with the *Isla Valladolid* property knew her well, and she knew them even better. She was the gatekeeper whom no one could get past without saying the magic words. She was flirtatious with all men, but none of them dared flirt back. She was the girlfriend of the head of the *Oscuro* drug cartel, Mateo Guerrero. She drove a turquoise-colored Porsche 911, with the top always down.

At 2:00 p.m., on a balmy Fall afternoon, Phil and Denise Davis from Katy, Texas arrived at the property for a tour and meeting with Malibu Barbie. They were interested in moving into the community. They had sold their house in Texas and were staying nearby in a rental property. The Davises were in their early sixties. Phil had recently retired from a job as a land man for an energy company based near Houston, and Denise was a retired kindergarten teacher. They had friends from their church who had moved down to the property a year ago and they raved about the amenities and quality of life. The cost of living was so much lower in Yucatan than in the U.S. One could hire maids, cooks, and other service providers there for a fraction of the cost to which they were accustomed. And *Isla Valladolid* was luxurious. There were three pools, tennis courts, walking trails, a dog park, on-site restaurants, salons, a movie theatre, and two 18-hole golf courses.

The Davises had already toured *Isla Valladolid* several times. At this point, they were ready to discuss available units and prices.

The structural design of this continuing care retirement community seemed like pure genius. People typically moved into the property during their early-to-mid-sixties, while hopefully still healthy. During the initial phase of their inhabitance at the property, they would buy a condo in the first high rise facility called "*The Mayan*," that was a property full of independent living units. *The Mayan* units had high end craftsmanship quality finish outs: granite and quartz counter tops, hardwood and travertine tile floors, subzero refrigerators and other state of the art appliances, smart home features, high ceilings, media rooms, master suites with spa-like baths, and large windows and balconies overlooking glistening white beaches and the turquoise Caribbean Sea.

During the second phase of residents' stays at *Isla Valladolid*, they would move into a condo in a high-rise facility called "*El Merida*," which was an Assisted Living complex. It was still very high end, but the units were designed for elderly residents who were starting to have mobility difficulties and were in need of occasional visits from care providers. The units at *El Merida* had features such as ramps, wider hallways, hand railings, and simpler kitchens, since care providers frequently cooked or brought in meals.

Phase three was the skilled nursing home facility called "*Todos Santos*," for when residents became mostly bed ridden and needed round-the-clock care. It was a white plaster walled, concrete tile-roofed bungalow type facility, surrounded in plush greenery, with a five-star rating, and excellent medical care and rehabilitation facilities. Most expats who were accustomed to U.S. healthcare standards were pleasantly surprised at the quality of care available.

The cost of entry, while somewhat affordable, was not cheap. A person or couple wanting to move in (typically at Phase One, into *The Mayan* independent living condos) had to put down an "Initial Entry Deposit" of between $200,000-$500,000, and then had monthly rent ranging from $1,000-$2,000 per month thereafter (depending on the size of their condo and increasing as they scaled up to assisted living and then nursing home assistance). Many folks had equity in their homes in the U.S. They would sell their homes and be able to pay the Initial Entry Deposit from the sales proceeds they realized from their homes. However, other more middle-income folks might not have that much equity or other available resources to pay the Initial Entry Deposit. At this point, Malibu Barbie was able to quickly squelch any concerns.

The Davises were an example of hardworking folks who had decent retirement benefits, but a modest home in Texas, that did not yield much equity, after putting three children through private universities. In situations like this, Malibu Barbie would ask whether one or both of the couple by chance had existing life insurance policies. If so, were they willing to sell their policies for cash? At that point, the couple would get a quick lesson in life insurance settlement transactions. If a couple had one or more life insurance policies, perhaps a company associated with one of the owners of *Isla Valladolid* (Cade Graham) might be willing to purchase their policies with enough cash so that they would have funds to pay the Initial Entry Deposit. It frequently sounded like a win-win solution. Many couples, such as the Davises, would do the transaction—securing their spot at *Isla Valladolid* so that they could live happily ever after in the Yucatan sun.

But what about those couples that did not have life insurance? Malibu Barbie would quickly put these folks' minds at ease as well. "Many people, she would explain, might have life insurance policies through a former employer, or that they otherwise obtained at some point in their lives, long ago, and had forgotten. She would offer to do a "background search" for them and see if there was any existing policy out there, by scrubbing "various public data bases." Malibu Barbie would ask the couples to sign various paperwork that was allegedly intended to give her authority to perform record searches for possible life insurance policies. In fact, the paperwork would be an application for a new life insurance policy. In relatively short order, Malibu Barbie would typically come back with "good news," notifying the couples that she found a policy in existence for one or both—about which they were invariably shocked but delighted to learn. Maybe $100,000 on each the husband and wife. Maybe $200,000 each. Maybe more. Usually, the wife was the beneficiary on the husband's alleged policy and vice versa. At that point, Malibu Barbie would inform the couple that one of *Isla Valladolid*'s owners (a reference to Cade Graham) could make arrangements for the purchase of their policies if they were interested. And the purchase proceeds might just be enough (or close to enough) to fund the Initial Entrance Deposit. It was like manna from heaven. Found money. It was often what sealed the deal for new residents.

Chapter Fourteen

Back to Present Day—Another Missing Cow Case.

Avery was walking into her chambers on Wednesday morning, juggling her coffee and multiple bags and books, on the day after she had spoken with Max and Dave Carrillo. The next day, Thursday, the BASA people would be back in court—most likely with some more, Richter scale-shattering information—and she couldn't help but be distracted, wondering what she might be hearing from them.

"Kids, for crying out loud, please don't ever wear a Metallica t-shirt and flip flops to work. Never!"

Avery made this pronouncement between sips of coffee as she walked in the door and greeted Millicent and the interns.

"Uh, that was random," Millicent said with a confused look on her face.

"No, Millicent, it wasn't random. I actually just saw Judge Davis's law clerk out in the elevator lobby on this floor in a Metallica t-shirt and flip flops. For God's sake.

The kid went to Yale. Does he think it doesn't matter how he dresses?"

"Actually, Judge, he dresses like that a lot. Like all the time. I think Judge Davis is pretty laid back about it. And the law clerk—I think his name is Andrew—paces out in the lobby a lot, on his cell phone. He says he pretty much works on his cell phone."

"What is he, a salesman? How does a law clerk work on his or her cell phone?"

"Judge, you can pretty much do everything on your phone. I can do research and even write orders for you on my phone."

"Good God. Is it so bad to sit at a desk like a civilized human being? I don't understand you kids. How do you concentrate and deeply think while pacing and staring at a tiny little phone screen?"

Avery dropped her load on her desk, grabbed her robe, and zipped it up in a huff. The interns and Millicent stared at her.

"Kids, all I am saying is dress and act like a lawyer. I don't care if you were Order of the Coif, Editor-in-Chief of your law review, or number one in your law school class. Dress and act like a lawyer. A grown up. A dignified human being. That's the end of my rant. Let's go into court."

Millicent looked at the interns and shrugged, cracking a grin, trying not to laugh. She motioned for them to follow her into court.

Today Avery had a hearing set in one of her "missing cow cases." If a person is a judge for long enough in Texas, sooner or later he or she has a few missing cow cases. The stories are all exactly the same. Ranchers or Urban Cowboy wannabes buy a bunch of cattle. They take out bank loans to pay for the purchase and upkeep of the cattle until the cattle can be fattened and sold for profit. But unfortunately, there is often a default on the loan. There are suddenly several missed payments. Then the friendly but worried banker decides to go out and inspect his cow-collateral. But, to his shock, the cows are gone—or at least mostly gone. Then the litigation begins. Some are alleged to be "deads" (that is, cows that were ravaged by some illness or injury and succumbed). Some supposedly wander off to unknown pastures. Some are stolen by bands of cattle thieves (does this really still happen?). The rancher is inevitably accused of conversion or something worse. Millicent always sighs, whenever she and the judge take a recess from one of these hearings, and says to the interns, "This is all so *No Country for Old Men*." Her comment is apropos. There were always dusty boots, bolo ties, and big belt buckles in the courtroom on these days. All of the rancher lawyers reminded Avery of dear old Dean John F. Sutton, Jr. from her University of Texas Law School days—Avery's first professor to drill into her head the importance of specific facts in deciding the outcome of any lawsuit (*facts matter; evidence matters; facts don't cease to exist just because you ignore them*). And the torrent of cow clichés that always went along with one of these days in court never failed to disappoint. "How do you count missing cows, Your Honor? With a cow-culator, of course!" "How do you avoid having cows disappear, Your Honor? You need more cow bell." "Your Honor, my opposing counsel may sound persuasive, but he is all hat and no cattle." "Your Honor, the documents they produced in discovery are so heavily redacted it's like looking at a black cow eating licorice at midnight." Avery called it bovine bonanza. Millicent called it heifer hell.

When Avery finished cow court, she grabbed her phone and saw she had received a text message from Max. "Holy cow, Annalise. Max has texted me from Mexico."

"Ugh, Judge. *Et tu*? If I hear another corny cow cliché, I think I am going to go mad. Get it, Judge? Mad cow disease?"

"*Et tu*, Annalise?"

Avery slipped into her office with a wan smile, texting Max back that she could talk now if he was still free. She figured Max was ready to talk about the strange phone voice mail from the other night, and she couldn't wait to hear if he also thought it originated from Malta. Maybe her imagination was getting the best of her.

Avery waited for what seemed like an eternity. No response. Max must have gotten sidetracked.

Avery walked over to one of her white boards in her chambers and with a blue marker wrote, "God grant me serenity. Give us all peace in our mind, body, soul, and spirit."

She then started flipping through the cow evidence notebooks on her desk. Millicent popped her head in the door. "Judge I am about to walk over to Chef Wang for lunch. Would you like me to get you some *moo* goo gai pan? Get it?"

"Argh! Stop it! No more bull!"

Chapter Fifteen

*Enos. onion and a Meeting at Hussong's Cantina, Baja
California (Flashback, Fall of 2017).*

For a few months, in 2016 and into early 2017, Cade
Graham's life generally—and specifically, arrangements at
Isla Valladolid—seemed to be going quite well. Graham's
financial missteps seemed to have been curbed a bit. His
beautiful, bougie, Yucatan retirement community was
ninety percent occupied with residents who all timely paid
their rent. Thus, the tenant-operator of *Isla Valladolid*
(which was, of course, a company owned and controlled by
Cade Graham) was able to timely pay its monthly rent to the
REIT (the landlord/trust that owned the underlying
property). Cade Graham's majority co-owners in the REIT
(the *Oscuro* Mexican crime cartel) were partially pleased.
However, it is never good enough to only partially please a
Mexican crime cartel.

How in the world did a Dallas, Highland Park-bred, Ivy League educated, white privileged male—with all of his enormous wealth, beautiful girlfriends, and continental panache—ever get entangled with a Mexican crime cartel? How did *Oscuro* become the majority owners of the *Isla Valladolid* REIT?

It started innocently enough. Cade Graham had become entangled in some nasty litigation with some major players in the credit default swap (CDS) industry. Graham had been accused of misrepresentations, bad faith, and outright fraud in some cases. After a couple of years of this, no one in the CDS industry would deal with Graham or his various hedge funds anymore. He had become *persona non grata*. Radioactive. Fallen from grace. None of the usual CDS issuers would touch any of Graham's deals. This was problematic. It is difficult to operate hedge funds without the ability to acquire credit default swaps or have similar products in place, now and then. Graham's illegitimate son once again entered the picture.

The illegitimate son went by the name of Ethan Alves. Cade Graham had a contractual arrangement with Ethan and his mother, Marisol Alves, such that Graham would provide generous monetary support to Ethan and Ethan's mother, a former Brazilian model, but Ethan could never use Graham's last name. As it turned out, Ethan had a friend from Harvard Business School from an affluent family in Mexico City that had an investment firm that catered to wealthy Mexican nationals. According to Ethan, that friend owed Ethan some favors, as a result of past trading tips that Ethan had sent his way. Ethan bet Cade that he could arrange for some of his friend's cash-rich Mexican clients to enter into a credit default swap transaction with Cade *in connection with buying the BASA debt*. In fact, young Ethan had made it happen. Thus, Cade Graham originally got involved with Dmitry Basayev (and DB Biocontainment, LLC and BASA, Inc.) at the urging of Ethan—first, due to Ethan's connection to Dmitry Basayev from their days at

Emory University together and, second, because Ethan sweetened the deal by finding some wealthy Mexican investors to provide credit default swaps in connection with his father's loans to BASA.

The problem now was that those wealthy Mexican investors—primarily friends and associates of Senor Mateo Guerrero, the leader of the *Oscuro* crime cartel—had lost their shirts on the BASA credit default swaps. And now Senor Mateo Guerrero and all his investing *amigos* from the cartel were out for blood from Graham—literally and figuratively. Under immense pressure, Graham satisfied his blood debt to the *Oscuro* cartel by giving them a majority interest in the REIT that owned and served as the landlord of *Isla Valladolid*.

That arrangement satisfied *Oscuro* for a few months. But, eventually, the *Oscuro* cartel was not making as much money from the *Isla Valladolid* operation as it felt it should. Senor Guerrero and other cartel leaders demanded a face-to-face meeting with Cade on their turf, in Mexico City. The meeting happened in the swanky offices of Ethan Alves's friend's high-rise office. The cartel's lawyers and accountants previewed to Graham, before the meeting, that they wanted a higher rate of return on their investment, and that they hoped he would come up with some effective strategies. Thus, feeling enormous duress, Cade figured out a way to once again make a deal with the devil.

He offered to let the cartel buy into his life insurance settlements hedge fund with extremely good terms. The cartel subsequently invested U.S. $10,000,000 dollars. With the extra funds, the hedge fund could offer to buy life insurance policies for more future residents at *Isla Valladolid*, so that they could get the occupancy at the property up to one hundred percent. Moreover, the cartel could start earning money on the life insurance settlement hedge fund as residents eventually died.

This worked out nicely for a while. But the cartel leaders eventually were, once again, not quite copacetic with things. The life insurance settlement hedge fund was not providing an adequate return on their $10,000,000 investment. Bluntly put, people were not dying at the rate predicted by the actuaries.

Graham became desperate. He was accustomed to dealing with disgruntled investors from time to time, but nothing compared to his demanding, new cartel clients. His boyish toothy white grin and sinuous sense of style did not garner the same patient reception with *Oscuro* that it had always seemed to generate with the country club set back home. He knew that these guys were ruthless and would literally start cutting off body parts if they did not see the financial results that they expected soon.

Graham could always trust himself to come up with clever solutions, but, this time, his usually quick mind was barren of ideas. One day, when sitting in an airport bar, he remembered a story he had heard a while back about another hedge fund manager, Sam Israel, who faked his own death, when he was facing criminal fraud charges. Israel did not get away with the hoax. As Graham recalled, Israel had a girlfriend assisting him in the hoax—he figured the girlfriend probably screwed things up for him. Graham was of the general view that women always screwed things up. Misogyny was among Graham's many qualities. Graham also vaguely recalled another guy who faked his own death in a plane crash but was later captured. The more bourbon that Graham drank, the more he began to like this macabre idea of faking his own death. He figured he was smarter than those other fools and could successfully pull it off. He had enough money stashed away in Cayman and Isle of Man bank accounts that he could easily start a new life. Maybe it was time to exit stage left and live anonymously in some new place. Perhaps the Cook Islands.

Graham carefully did his research. He learned that there were consultants who would, for about $30,000, make you disappear. These were known as invisibility or disappearance services. One could also essentially buy do-it-yourself death kits, where you could order fake death certificates and make arrangements with black market morgues, and even funeral parlors who would do a fake wake for you if you wanted. The Philippines seemed to be the epicenter for pseudocide services like this. But Graham had no appetite for going to the Philippines. Besides, that would not make any sense. He had no reason to be in the Philippines. On the other hand, people knew he had investments in Mexico—at least the people that he wanted to believe he was dead—and, thus, there would be no reason for folks to be suspicious if he suddenly died in Mexico.

After a few weeks of more research and soul-searching, Graham decided to go with a disappearance service in Mexico. In his research, Graham learned about certain disappearance services that could be found on the Dark Web with all communications occurring through ProtonMail (an encrypted email program). Graham had a personal laptop that was loaded with "TOR" anonymity software and which, thus far, he had dedicated solely to his occasional Dark Web and ProtonMail communications that were necessitated with the *Oscuro* cartel folks. Graham had learned of a site on the Dark Web called Enos.onion. It looked like whomever was behind Enos.onion was into every black market imaginable: hit men for hire; hackers for hire; blackmail through "deep fakes"; bitcoin exchanges; offshore shell company formation; laundering funds through management of offshore accounts; shady investment opportunities; insider trading tips; sex trafficking; and disappearance services. Basically, any illicit thing that one could think of could be arranged through Enos.onion. And the site looked surprisingly sophisticated, unlike a lot of the other options out there. No misspellings; no propaganda concerning government-insurrection or end-of-the-world; and none of the other tell-tale signs of so many of the bush-league fraudsters on the Dark Web.

Cade Graham and "Enos" (*i.e.,* Marcus Braden) met one afternoon in Ensenada, Baja California after communicating through Enos.onion. They planned a meeting at Hussong's Cantina on Ruiz Avenue. It would be noisy and crowded with margarita-drinking tourists and they could blend in unnoticed.

Graham walked into Hussong's at 2:00 p.m., on an early fall day, as instructed. The place was packed, as Enos said it would be. A Mariachi band was playing loudly, the bar was cramped with day drinkers and others who did not seem to realize that summer had ended. The rectangular, four-walled cantina was full-to-capacity. Graham scanned the room for a thirty-ish-year-old white male, with blond spiked hair in a Jimi Hendrix T-shirt. He saw him in the back, left corner of the room, near an exit door. Graham chuckled to himself about how cliché this seating choice was. Graham made his way through the crowd. He managed to blend, even in Ralph Lauren Chalmers Crocodile loafers, Kiton trousers, and a Piaget watch. It helped that he had acquired from a street vendor, before walking in, a *Xolos de Caliente* hoodie and a *Rosarito-Ensenada* baseball cap.

Graham walked up to Enos's table and stretched out his hand and said, "Enos? I'm St. Jude." St. Jude was the fictitious name that Graham had used in communicating with Enos on the Dark Web. Enos did not hold out his hand in return but pointed to the wooden chair across from him, gesturing Graham to sit.

"St. Jude—as in the patron saint of lost or desperate causes?"

"You're Catholic, huh? Didn't see that one coming."

"Oh, you'd be surprised."

Graham noticed that Enos was wearing an eight-pointed cross around his neck, the symbol of Malta and the Order of St. John, and silently wondered why this odd man might have chosen that fashion statement.

With no further introductory small talk, Enos said, "Why do you want people to think you are dead?"

"Well, that was quick. Aren't you going to offer to buy me a drink first?"

"Well, I don't think they have any Blanton's Bourbon here. I figure that's probably your alcoholic beverage of choice. Isn't that what Princeton men drink?" Enos had noticed Graham's Princeton college ring on his right ring finger. Perhaps he would not have been so keen to observe it, were it not for the fact that "Enos" had grown up in a Catholic orphanage not far from Princeton.

Graham was more than a little surprised by this Dark Web criminal's apparent savvy. "Does it really matter why I want to fake my death? Why would you ask? I thought I was hiring a hit man, basically, not a therapist."

"Hey, I get bored. I just like to get to know who I'm dealing with. And you want me to do this the right way, don't you?"

The truth was that Enos, in fact, really did not need to know too much about his pseudocide clientele to properly provide disappearance services to them. But Enos smelled opportunity here. "St. Jude" was not the typical down-and-out schmuck who wanted his wife and kids to think he was dead.

"Let me order a drink first. I'll have what you're having, Enos."

"*Casa Dragones Joven Tequila.*"

"Not bad."

"Enos" and "St. Jude" spent a few hours together that day. The longer they spent, the more Cade Graham drank, and the more details Enos extracted from him. Graham told him about *Isla Valladolid* and about the ill-begotten joint venture with the *Oscuro* cartel on the REIT that owned the property. He told him about the life insurance settlements business in which he recently let *Oscuro* participate. He shared how the *Oscuro* leadership did not think they were getting a high enough return on their investment. Graham also shared that his hedge fund business, overall, was not making much money. Interest rates were ridiculously low. His life insurance settlements hedge fund had zero cash flow because people weren't dying soon enough. His R&D funds were upside down because all of its research projects were on a slow track—delayed clinical trials and slow regulatory approvals—with no development of marketable, revenue-producing products on the near-term horizon.

Graham even let Enos in on a little secret that almost nobody knew: Graham controlled an offshore company that owned the former super collider in rural Texas.

"Have you ever heard of that, Enos? It's an underground science project. It was supposed to be an atom smasher. A fifty-mile enclosed subterranean ring. But now that I have invested in it, it's like fucking Wildfire from *The Andromeda Strain*. My scientists are working to revolutionize the healthcare sector if I can just hang on long enough to see it happen. They're inventing germ killing technology and vaccines and shit like you wouldn't believe. If I could just wait things out a little longer, I'll be making so much money on that project, with all their cutting-edge R&D, that I would gladly deed over one hundred percent of that whole damn *Isla Valladolid* property to *Oscuro*. Hell, I'd hand over the whole life insurance settlements hedge fund, too."

The more Braden heard, the more he realized that he had struck gold with this random contact. Although Graham never shared his true name, Braden was no dummy. He figured out the moment that he saw Graham that he was a guy with a polished assuredness and *savoir faire* that came from serious money. Braden further determined, within several minutes, that he was staring across the table from a former titan of Wall Street—a now terrified hedge fund manager—who had made the dreadful mistake of marrying up with some highflyers in the Mexican mob. What Graham did not know was that Enos—Marcus Braden—had his own connections to a different up-and-coming cartel, *Los Chupas*. And Enos knew a hell of a lot more about the *Oscuro* cartel than Graham did—despite Graham's having taken $10,000,000 of *Oscuro*'s money.

"I have a proposition for you, St. Jude. I'm happy to

make you look dead. It will all be perfect. You can pay me $30,000, fly away to whatever exotic place you want, and *Oscuro* will never be the wiser. I am very good at what I do. There's no one better. None of my clients has ever complained or been busted. But I suggest something different for you, other than just disappearing."

By this point, Graham had drunk far too many tequila shots. He stared at Marcus bleary-eyed. "You have a better plan for me? God, you have no idea who you are dealing with. But go ahead, Enos, or whatever your name is. Tell me your alternative plan. I'm dying to hear it."

Enos paused a few moments and surveyed the room. "So, I have been doing this death market stuff for quite a while. But you probably figured out from my website that I am into a lot of other stuff, too."

"A lot of illegal shit."

"Are you judging me? A hedge fund manager, who's in bed with a Mexican crime cartel, and has under-aged girlfriends all over the world is judging *me*?"

"You say that like it's a bad thing—being a hedge fund manager. Do you think 'hedge fund manager' is a pejorative term, you little shit? We make the world go around. We make free enterprise possible. We make the creative ideas in men's brains become reality by matching them with the money to make things happen. And do you resent my track record with beautiful women, Enos? Do you maybe have a problem relating to women?"

Enos stared back at Cade Graham utterly undeterred. "I noticed you skipped right over the part about being in bed with a Mexican crime cartel."

Graham smirked as he had another shot, but he realized that he had perhaps spoken a little too freely that afternoon. Had he even mentioned his young girlfriends to Enos? Why would Enos make that comment? Graham certainly did not remember having had such a conversation.

"Let me lay this all out. Just like you, St. Jude, I make a shitload of money. And, trust me, very little of it is generated from my invisibility services these days. You might say I am a master hedger, just like you are."

"Really?" Graham rolled his eyes. "I highly doubt that."

"Hear me out. You've wasted this much time with me. It won't hurt you to spend a little more."

Enos poured Graham another shot.

"St. Jude, it occurs to me that you have actually been a particularly good hedger—at least where this Dmitry Basayev fellow you've told me about is concerned. For example, you mentioned how you insisted on having credit default swaps in place in connection with the millions of dollars that you loaned to now bankrupt BASA. Thus, you actually managed to not lose your ass on your BASA debt, unlike Toro Capital, which apparently didn't have the good sense to hedge like you. Now Toro is owed millions of dollars and is being sued over its role with BASA. Toro's investors are pulling out right and left and it's probably going to have to dissolve. You aren't being sued, St. Jude, on that one. Sure, you fucked up royally and got your credit default swaps from a Mexican crime cartel, and that created a whole other set of problems for you, but you don't seem to be up to your neck in trouble in the U.S. to the same extent Toro Capital is. By the way, where did you say BASA filed its Chapter 11 bankruptcy case?"

"Dallas. Why the hell do you care?"

"You have got to be shitting me!" Enos burst out in laughter.

"Why would I be shitting you about something like that?" Graham's head was starting to throb, and he was starting to want this afternoon to end.

"Anyway, you also told me, St. Jude, that you have acquired shares in every pharmaceutical and technology company that is likely to get the rights to BASA's disinfectant system and to DB Biocontainment's vaccines and therapies—assuming all of those products come to fruition. That was a smart hedging move for sure—you are covering all your bases there, St. Jude. Meanwhile, you really do seem to have a cash cow going from the rents that your REIT is earning on *Isla Valladolid* and some of your other properties. The way I see it, your only problems, buddy, are the slow-paying life insurance settlements and, I suppose, the length of time it is taking to get the disinfectant and vaccines that Basayev is working on completed and to market. And, of course, the fact that *Oscuro* is breathing down your neck. What if I have a solution to all of this that doesn't involve faking your death?"

"Who the hell are you, Enos?" Graham slammed down another shot of tequila.

"I'm your Huckleberry, St. Jude. Your new business partner. The one who is going to save your ass from the boiling ocean that it's in."

Graham stared at Enos for a few moments in silence. Enos broke the silence.

"St, Jude, I don't understand why a guy like you would act like a rat abandoning a sinking ship. You're not on the Titanic, dude. You have just hit a little rough water."

"Tell me what you are thinking, Enos."

During the next few hours, Enos was the one doing most of the talking. He shared many of the details of his own business ventures—only those in which he had been engaged after his move to Mexico, of course. His pseudocide services. His hitman services. His Bitcoin acumen and mastery of hacking into the blockchain.

"Do you remember that infamous hack of a Japanese bitcoin exchange site a few years ago, St. Jude? Remember the wild swings in Bitcoin prices after that? I bet you never dreamed that a loner down in Mexico had a little hand in that. I bet I pocketed more money in connection with that little trick than you probably earned in the wild days leading up to the 2008 financial collapse."

"You have got to be shitting me?"

"Nope."

Enos went on to explain his eventual partnership with

Los Chupas and how he encouraged their debut into the gasoline pipeline puncturing business to compete with the *Zetas*. In repayment, *Los Chupas* eventually started entrusting Enos with investing and laundering their drug money. He had become the *Los Chupas* CFO. Enos laundered money through businesses and accounts as far away as Malta, Guernsey, and the Cook Islands.

"Malta? I guess that explains your necklace. Did you get that as a gift for opening a bank account with the Bank of Valletta or something? Where are you going with all of this, Enos?"

"St. Jude—patron saint of desperate cases and lost causes—when your legitimate hedging wasn't getting you the results you wanted, what did you do? You entered the dark side, by partnering up with *Oscuro*. Then when that became a fucking disaster, you came to me, wanting to fake your death. But it sounds like you have not thought through at all the next phase of your life—if you do fake your death. I present to you now a *Tertia Optio*."

"Third option. Go ahead. I'm listening." Graham stared at Enos intently. Graham was impaired from too much tequila but alert enough to realize that Enos seemed prodigiously eloquent and learned. To Graham, it just didn't seem to add up. Was this a set up?

"So, there are, it seems to me, a couple of ways for *Oscuro* to get a good return on its investment. First, through BASA. You said earlier that *Oscuro* holds large amounts of debt that is owed by BASA—thanks to that shitty little credit default swap transaction they did with you. How can that debt get a good return when BASA is now in Chapter 11? Sounds like BASA would have to have a giant upswing in value to solve *Oscuro's* problem. The best way for BASA to recover its lost value is if it quickly finishes its disinfectant system and takes it to market. I see an opportunity to capitalize on the fact that everyone in the world, at this point, thinks BASA is a fucking Ponzi scheme, except you. So, speeding up BASA's development of its disinfectant system is the key to getting value paid out to BASA's debt holders, including *Oscuro*. Hold that thought for a moment, St. Jude."

"I'm having trouble holding my bladder right now, much less my train of thought, but go on."

"The second way for *Oscuro* to get a good return on its money is for your life insurance settlements business to start paying off which, of course, requires people to die faster than currently they are."

"No shit, Sherlock. What are you saying?"

"Well, there is an obvious way here to kill two birds with one stone—to speed up the research and development on the disinfectant product, and get it to market, *and* also increase profitability on the life settlements business. There is an overlapping solution, you could say. Ideally, it would involve Dmitry Basayev's cooperation. It will be a little harder without his cooperation."

Cade had, by this point, become too inebriated to have a meaningful conversation. He was lucid enough to be somewhat frightened—assuming he was following Enos's train of thought. Enos could perceive this. He grinned and stood up.

"Tell you what. Meet me here the same time next Friday, St. Jude. 2:00 p.m. I'll have my formal proposition— my grand solution for your problems—all mapped out for you. You can accept my grand solution and compensation terms for the proposal, or I'll just arrange to fake your death for the $30,000, as we originally discussed. I have a car waiting outside for me. My driver can take you back to wherever you are staying if you'd like a ride."

"You have a driver? Oh, of course you do. You're a fucking hedge fund manager like me."

Enos stood waiting with a blank expression.

"No, Enos, I'm good. I have my own driver waiting. I guess I will see you next Friday."

With that, Marcus Braden (a.k.a. Enos) walked out of the cantina, where a young well-dressed teenaged boy was holding the door for him, and an entourage of *Los Chupas* foot soldiers and an armored Town Car were waiting to escort him away.

Chapter Sixteen

A Brother-to-Brother Chat (Flashback, Also Fall of 2017).

Marcus returned to his villa outside Rosarito, Mexico and began his nightly trolling of the internet. On this night, he did searches for Cade Graham. He knew that was who "St. Jude" was. He figured it out soon into their long meeting. His internet searches confirmed it. He found countless pictures of him. The paparazzi loved Graham. Moreover, Braden found some articles in the financial press about Graham's forays into the healthcare sector and the recent troubles he was confronting with angry investors, the SEC, and his disputes with rating agencies regarding various comments and positions they had taken regarding companies in Graham's vast business empire. Nowhere could Marcus find any reference to Graham's investments in the DB Biocontainment underground facility or in *Isla Valladolid*—and certainly no hint of an association with *Oscuro*. Marcus grinned thinking about how Graham had kept all this information secret with his byzantine web of offshore companies. And now Marcus had insider information, so to speak, about Graham's widespread endeavors. He liked having insider information. That was his *modus operandi* in life. His stock in trade.

Before Braden closed his laptop for the evening, he decided to do a search on the PACER website for the BASA Chapter 11 case and the lawsuit within that case involving Toro Capital. As his search query turned up the case, he burst into almost uncontrollable laughter. "This is too fucking good to be true."

Realizing it was 4:00 a.m. in Malta, he grabbed his phone and texted his brother.

"Bro, are you by chance awake? Got a great story for you."

To Marcus's surprise, he got a quick reply. "I'm always awake. I work my ass off, and you know it. Got bets to collect and a café to run, among other things. [Wink emoji.] What's up?"

"Met an American today. Filthy rich. Hedge fund guy. Going to start doing some business with him. Turns out he has been involved from the fringes with a company involved in a bankruptcy case in front of our favorite bitch judge. What are the fucking odds?"

"No shit? LMAO."

"Made me wonder if you've been in contact with the Honorless Avery Lassiter lately? Can't let her get complacent. LOL."

"Actually, it's been a while since I've contacted our dear judge. Been busy. Maybe, I'll send her a bottle of *Latitud 42* wine. I ordered some of that for my cafe the other day and thought of her."

"Or maybe send her a bowl of petunias. Get it?"

"Of course. 'Oh no, not again!'"

"What the fuck does that falling bowl of petunias shit mean anyway?"

"I don't know. The book is weird. I can't believe she likes it."

"Probably her kids got her into it. Little Heath and little Julia. I always thought we should have gone after them. Maybe we should hack little Julia's laptop or something fun like that."

"Whatever. But, come to think of it, the two-year anniversary of dear Judge Lassiter's near-death experience in Austin is coming up soon—November is right around the corner. Maybe that would be a good excuse to check in with her."

"Oh yeah. Copy that. I'll come up with something to rattle her."

"Sounds good. And I'll let you in on the details about my new American hedge fund client soon. It's gonna be fun."

A few weeks later, in mid-November 2017, Judge Lassiter was opening her daily mail at her kitchen table. There were a few cards for her birthday and the usual bills and junk mail. As she looked at the return addresses on each piece of mail, she suddenly gasped. There was a burnt orange envelope with a return address from Valletta, Malta. Avery sat in silence for a few moments, and then stood up, went to one of her kitchen drawers, and pulled out some latex gloves and a letter opener.

Inside the burnt orange envelope was a tissue-thin white sheet of stationery. Written on it were:

> *Jackie Robinson.*
> *Bill Clinton.*
> *Street on which Grand Central Station and*
> *United Nations building, NY, NY are*
> *located.*
> *Your parking space number at the*
> *courthouse, transposed.*
> *Location of the famous surrealist's Andre*
> *Breton's apartment in Paris.*

North Latitude of Chicago.
Happy Birthday. Still watching all your
paths!

Avery knew immediately what this seemingly cryptic message meant. Jackie Robinson famously wore the number 42 on his jersey. Bill Clinton was the 42nd president. Grand Central Station and the UN building are both on 42nd Street in New York. And Avery's parking space in the courthouse was twenty-four—the reverse of forty-two. Andre Breton famously lived at 42 Rue Fontaine in Paris. Chicago lies at latitude forty-two degrees.

One or maybe both of the Bradens was still out there, still taunting her. Would she ever be free of them? And how? What was the endgame?

Chapter Seventeen

The Dark Web (Flashback, Spring 2019).

"So, what is this so-called 'Dark Web' that apparently you have become an expert on? Is it really some subterranean 'other' internet? Can anybody access it? If so, how? And why is it called 'dark'? Is everything about it seedy and sinister?"

Avery was pestering Max with rapid-fire questions one afternoon, while she made a fruit pizza for Heath, who was home from grad school. Max sat at their kitchen table maneuvering multiple laptop computers. It was shortly after Max started his new gig with Premier Mutual, which was a few months after his retirement. Max had purchased two new laptops for his new investigative role. A normal one and one solely dedicated to Dark Web research.

Max sighed. "Have I ever told you that you ask a lot of questions, Judge Lassiter?"

"I believe you have, perhaps more than once." Avery smiled and coyly batted her eyes. '

"Why don't you just ask Alexa all your questions, Mom?" Heath had popped into the kitchen and filled up a water bottle. "I hear you asking poor Alexa something forty-two times a day. Alexa is your new favorite interrogation victim. You're abusing your artificial intelligence robot. She's like your virtual law clerk."

"Well Alexa doesn't complain about it one bit, Heath. She loves it when I ask her questions. Anyway, Max, tell me about the Dark Web. I want to know all about it."

"Y'all are so weird." Heath walked out of the kitchen.

"Let me try to explain this simply, Your Honor. The Dark Web is actually a collection of websites, not a separate internet unto itself. It's still part of the World Wide Web. But it is not accessible in the same way that the average person is familiar with. Rather, at least in theory, it is cloaked with anonymity."

Avery stopped working on her pizza and stared at Max with a look that said, continue. He knew the look well.

"To understand it, think of the normal internet and all the regular websites that you visit as the 'Surface Web.'"

"Okay."

"On the 'Surface Web,' all the websites are indexed and have links so that they are reachable and turn up when internet searches are launched with commercial search engines such as *Google*, *Bing*, or *Foxfire*. So, say you want to look up fruit pizza recipes. You, of course, go to *Google* and type in 'fruit pizza recipes' and you get lists and lists of websites that you can click onto if you want. But then there is, within this same World Wide Web, a vast so-called 'Deep Web,' which is simply the collection of all the websites on the web that are not reachable by doing a search on the conventional, commercial search engines like *Google*."

"Max, you said '*Deep* Web' just now, not '*Dark* Web.'"

"I meant to say Deep Web. Just keep listening."

"Okay, but just so I am clear, Max, these sites in the Deep Web are not set up with indexes and links, so to speak, to be searchable?"

"Correct. So, this Deep Web is not in and of itself sinister. It is basically just unindexed websites. Period. And there are a huge number of unindexed websites that include mundane content like government data bases, registration-required web forums, and research websites. Hardly scandalous stuff."

"Okay. Got it. So, the World Wide Web is the surface web. And then there is the unindexed portion of it called the Deep Web. But how do you get to the websites on the Deep Web if they are not indexed?"

Avery had finished her pizza, covered it with foil, and stuck it in the refrigerator for now. She picked up her fat Cavalier, Finley, and sat at the kitchen table. The other dog, Jake, immediately jumped up on her lap as well.

"Well, you have to know the domain name to get on a site on the Deep Web. Like 'CavalierKingCharlesSociety.org' or whatever."

"Gotcha. Go on. I'm digging this."

Max rolled his eyes. "Well so then you get to the actual '*Dark Web*,' which is a subset of the '*Deep Web*.' Not only are the sites on the 'Dark Web' not accessible with the usual search engines like *Google*—in other words, one must know the domain name to ever hit upon them—but, different from the Deep Web, the IP addresses of the servers that run these Dark Web sites are masked. They're anonymous. Thus, people typically cannot determine where these sites are hosted or by whom. And, likewise, even the users who happen to visit the websites can remain anonymous. This anonymity all happens, at both ends, through special so-called anonymity software. In other words, you cannot access these websites on the Dark Web with standard internet browsers."

"You mean, not through *Google* or whatever."

"Correct. You need something like TOR—which is an

acronym for 'the onion router.'"

"I have heard of TOR. I didn't realize it was an acronym for anything."

Avery got up and got the dogs duck feet treats. Finley and Jake loved duck feet just like dear old Baxter did.

"Yep. TOR is by far the most well-known of all the kinds of anonymity software. The 'onion' metaphor is a reference to how the software encrypts web traffic from a user to a particular site in layers upon layers (like an onion) and redirects this traffic around the world through randomly-chosen intermediate computers, each of which removes a single layer of encryption before bouncing the data on to the next computer in the network."

"Ugh. Complicated. So, I guess you are telling me that the idea behind this process is to prevent anyone – even a person who controls one of those computers in the encrypted chain–from matching the traffic's origin with its destination?"

"Yep. And then there is also anonymity software that separately is just designed to protect the anonymity of the host (the most common software of that ilk is called I2P)."

"So, let me see if I've got all this. When a person goes to an internet site using the TOR software, the site he or she visits cannot easily see the person's IP address. And the person, in turn, cannot identify the location of the website's server."

"Correct."

"Are the .com or .net addresses the same as what is on the conventional web?"

"No. Websites on the Dark Web often have a web address that ends in the domain suffix ".onion" as opposed to ".com" or ".net.""

"What legitimate reason would people have to set up a website this way? Are there any legitimate reasons or are they all criminal?"

"Of course, there are some legitimate reasons. Maybe a person has genuine privacy concerns. Journalists have been known to communicate with anonymous sources through sites set up this way on the Dark Web. There are also political discussion forums and whistle blower safe sites. Ironically, the TOR software and network was originally developed by the U.S. Department of Defense. Right now, TOR is a nonprofit run by volunteers, but it is funded by the likes of the National Science Foundation. So, it's not inherently a bad thing."

"But, often, these Dark Websites are about criminal activity, right?"

"Yep. Drug sales, sales of stolen property, hit men for hire, hackers for hire, bitcoin laundering, insider securities trading, sex trafficking, child porn, blackmail through deep fakes, terrorism. Basically, any illicit or depraved thing you can think of, and then some."

"What are y'all talking about now?" Julia burst into the kitchen. "What's a deep fake?"

"What—you knew what everything was that your dad just named except for a deep fake? Good God. What have we done to our children, Max? They hear too much bad stuff in this household. We have *got* to stop talking about work so much."

Avery used to say when she was pregnant, back when she was a lawyer representing oil and gas clients and crusty old bankers and the like, that she was afraid her babies were going to come out of her womb chomping on cigars and yelling and cursing. She had, of course been joking about what types of behavior they might be detecting in boardrooms and conference rooms while she was carrying them. But now she and Max were talking about the Dark Web in their kitchen. The place that kids should feel most warm and loved.

"Dad, what's a deep fake?"

"End of discussion, Max. Julia, do you want some fruit pizza?"

"No, I want to hear more about the Dark Web, Dad."

"Oh my God. I just want my children to be normal."

"What's normal?" Julia grinned.

Avery looked back at sweet Julia. Indeed, what was normal? Their family had not known normal for a long time it seemed.

Chapter Eighteen

Serendipity—Max Lassiter's Off-the-Books Investigation Intersects with Premier Mutual's New Investigation (Flashback, January 2019).

Premier Mutual's size and earnings place it in the Fortune 500. Its earnings were divided between life, casualty, and property operations and mutual funds. Joe Meno was the head of Premier's private investigations department. Meno was a retired U.S. Air Force Lieutenant Colonel, a former big-city police officer, and a former U.S. Marshal. Premier frequently hired retired law enforcement officers to lead their security and investigation units. Sometimes they, in turn, contracted out specific investigative jobs to former law enforcement officers.

It was Joe Meno who was contacted by Premier's Chief Compliance Officer one January afternoon, after certain personnel at Premier began observing that something seemed very amiss with regard to certain life insurance policies that Premier Mutual had been required to pay off, in the last several months, that were held by the Cade Graham life settlements hedge fund. Was it just strangely coincidental that so many of the people who were the subjects of these policies and had recently died were residents at the *Isla Valladolid* retirement community, and just so happened to have sold their policies to the Cade Graham hedge fund to pay for their entry deposit at *Isla Valladolid*? Why were there so many deaths in such a short period of time? Something felt very wrong with all of this. It was a statistical anomaly. Maybe it was all on the up-and-up. But that seemed highly doubtful. The company hoped that Meno might put together a team that could investigate and determine whether there was any reason to suspect foul play.

Joe Meno could hardly believe what he was hearing. The serendipity of it all. Meno had been long-time friends with Max Lassiter from their days serving on the Dallas Police Department together. Meno knew that Max had been down to the Yucatan a couple of times recently—telling his family that he was going on deep sea fishing trips—but was really sleuthing around on his own, trying to track down the elusive Marcus Braden. For years, Braden had seemed to be totally underground. Invisible. There was evidence that he had been in Mexico, but not much more than that was officially known. Max had been relentless (unbeknownst to Avery) since his retirement in January 2017, running his own private manhunt for Braden—scouring the internet and becoming proficient with Dark Web research tricks. Max texted with a small group of former law enforcement guys regularly, including Meno, sometimes sharing information that he learned, asking for people's thoughts about theories Max had, and sometimes asking if people had contacts with this or that agency in Mexico with whom Max could perhaps visit. Max had obtained surveillance camera pictures of Marcus Braden from the Four Seasons Hotel in Austin, Texas, that captured the horrific incident in November 2015. Braden had been running around naked that day in the Four

Seasons conference center—trying to distract the Marshals working security. The pictures of his actual face were not bad but were not that great either. Max had obtained a far better picture—a mug shot from the Austin Police Department, since Marcus had been arrested that day and had been detained, before getting released seventy-two hours later. Max also had some pictures from the Camden, New Jersey federal courthouse where Marcus had once worked as a janitor, as well as some pictures that were confiscated by the FBI during its raid and search of Matt Braden's desktop computer from the brothers' house on Pluto Lane in Austin. Max created a gallery of all of these photos and uploaded them into various facial recognition applications including TinEye and Vigilant Solutions, that make photo images searchable against social media, CCTV cameras, doorbell cameras, *etc.* Max even had a couple of friends in the DEA working in Mexico with connections to CNI (*Centro Nacional de Inteligencia*), who tapped into its own facial recognition platform to see if any photos resembling Marcus Braden ever popped up.

Eventually, a fellow with blond, spikey hair, approximately thirty years old, who looked as though he might be Caucasian—although it was hard to tell in the grainy photos—kept popping up as a possible match to Marcus Braden's photos. He had shown up in a dozen or so CCTV photos. These photos were captured from parking garages, restaurants, and other spots in the Ensenada and Rosarito areas of Baja. More recently, on the opposite side of Mexico in Yucatan, the image had appeared on several surveillance videos, including a couple from *Isla Valladolid*. Max initially had doubts whether both sets of photo-hits could be Marcus—since they showed up on opposite sides of the country. But Max struck gold one day when one of his photos captured the spikey-haired blond guy getting into a black Lincoln Town Car, and Max could see the license plate. This was in front of Hussong's Cantina in Ensenada. Then several weeks later, a photo of the spikey-haired blond guy popped up on a *Isla Valladolid* camera. Once again, that photo showed him getting in and out of a black Lincoln Town Car—the exact same make and model of car, but with a different license plate as the car that was outside of Hussong's. Max then went to the section of the Vigilant Solutions platform that stores geolocation data regarding license plates captured from LPR (license plate readers) services—services used by law enforcement agencies and asset recovery firms. He obtained various hits for the cars in various locations. Searching records in Mexico's equivalent of the Department of Motor Vehicles, Max discovered that both vehicles were owned by the same individual, Nicolas Samaniego. When Max shared all of this with one of his friends at DEA, the friend nearly "shit a brick," in Max's colorful words. Nicolas Samaniego was a leader in an up-and-coming cartel known as *Los Chupas* that was making its mark across Mexico and making a lot of enemies within the ranks of other more established cartels. Moreover, some of the spots at which the Lincoln Town Cars had been geo-tagged were known haunts and watering holes for *Los Chupas* foot soldiers. Max's DEA buddy told him that DEA and local Mexican authorities had been monitoring a site on the Dark Web called Enos.onion. They thought it might be a hub for *Los Chupas*. And word on the street was that there was a blond gringo with blond spikey hair that had a prominent role in *Los Chupas*. Further rumors were that the blond gringo was spearheading *Los Chupas*'s foray into the gasoline pipeline puncturing business. Many of the pictures of the blond spikey-haired man showed a young, well-dressed teenaged boy by his side. Max's DEA agent friend's intelligence suggested the kid was someone nicknamed *Monaguillo*, which means "altar boy" in Spanish.

So, for several months now, Max had a working theory that Marcus was entangled now with *Los Chupas*. He had spent countless hours (unbeknownst to Avery) scouring every news article that he could find regarding *Las Chupas*. He had visited with buddies in law enforcement in Texas,

California, Arizona and within Mexico to tap their knowledge about the cartel. He occasionally went to the Enos.onion website to see if he could develop any clues whether Marcus might be the one behind it. If Marcus was the person behind Enos.onion, he was involved in some very bad shit. The website was horrific. But Marcus, unfortunately, was not stupid enough to put any pictures on there or other personal information from which he or anyone else might be identified. Max had spent a large part of the latter years of his career busting criminals who were amazingly brazen and stupid—posting pictures of themselves on websites or other social media with guns, drugs, or cash in front of, perhaps, an easily-recognizable motel or night club, or next to a car with a visible license plate. Max had laughed with his buddies about how the female police detectives could send suspects a friend-invite on their social media accounts, and they would almost always accept—no questions asked. It was easy to solve a lot of crimes these days by simply sitting at one's computer and scouring social media. But it was not going to ever be that easy with Marcus and *Los Chupas*. Max felt like he had probably become the world's leading expert on *Los Chupas*. But it hadn't yet led him to Marcus Braden.

Meno called Max on a Friday afternoon and asked him if he was interested in possibly taking on some contract work for Premier Mutual that would involve some cross-border intelligence gathering.

"Max, are you sitting down?"

"Why? What's up?"

"You are not going to believe what Premier wants me to do—put together a team to look into possible linkage between the alleged death of Cade Graham and a big-time fraud on Premier. There's some possibility that there may even be a Mexican drug cartel involved. I hope you are in the mood to go to Mexico on my team."

"I'm all ears."

Chapter Nineteen

Tertia Optio (Flashback, Fall 2017).

One week after the original meeting at Hussong's between "Enos" and "St. Jude," they were back there again, at the same table in the back near the exit door, drinking the same brand of tequila. "St. Jude" originally declined any alcohol. He fully intended to stay sober this time during his interactions with "Enos." But thirty minutes into their meeting, he succumbed and poured himself a glass of the *Casa Dragones* that "Enos" had already ordered.

The cantina was once again noisy and crowded. There were no mariachis this week. Instead, a rather amateur Eighties rock band was belting out Van Halen and Bon Jovi tunes. Their screechy distortion was loud and grating. Cade Graham stared into his glass of clear liquid. He was remembering his late grandfather's words that "every flood begins with a single raindrop." He felt like he was drowning in a flood, all right. He had made a deal with the devil known as *Oscuro,* and now he was considering going double or nothing and doing a deal with a different devil.

"Are you ready for me to lay out my plan, St. Jude?"

"Your so-called grand solution? Sure. I can't wait."

Braden could tell that he had Graham exactly where he wanted him—feeling like a frog in a pot of boiling water, unable to get out or to avoid the inevitable.

"We can do my plan in gradual phases, or more aggressively. Your choice. But I think you probably have enough time to appease the *Oscuro* boys where we can do this in measured, unhurried steps. That'll probably make you feel more comfortable. Get you used to it all."

"What do you mean? Get me used to what? Spell it out, Enos."

"Phase One would be the life insurance settlements business. We will get it to profitability and then some."

"And how is that going to happen?"

"Subtly. Discreetly. We'll do hits on select residents at *Isla Valladolid* who sold their life insurance policies to your hedge fund to pay for their entrance fees. We will do it in a way not to arouse suspicions. All of the deaths will look like they were the result of natural causes, and we can also do a few accidents offsite. That will generate a welcome stream of cash flow—finally—to get *Oscuro* off your ass for a bit."

As Graham sat there speechless, two beautiful and scantily clad young women walked near their table and giggled as they took selfies in front of a bull pinata. Enos observed Graham looking them up and down. Enos thought it was amusing how Graham's face could transform so quickly from reflecting shock and horror at the notion of executing hits on old people, to showing his lascivious side at the sight of two teenaged girls.

"St. Jude, pay attention! We've got some serious business to discuss. That *Lolita* complex may finally catch up with you and get you in more trouble than this *Oscuro* shit if you don't start reigning it in."

Graham gave Enos a strange look. Why would Enos say that to him? What did he know?

"Next, Phase Two will be a little more complicated and will require Dmitry Basayev's cooperation. Phase Two will be introducing an infection into the environment at *Isla Valladolid*. Probably just at the nursing home portion of the property—*Tudos Santos*—not the other two facilities. Phase Two will not raise any eyebrows. Old people get deathly sick from viral and bacterial infections all the time. Simultaneously with introducing the infection at the property, you will introduce the disinfectant system that Basayev is working on. If the disinfection system works, fantastic. Basayev will have a success track record—in other words, more clinical setting trials, so to speak—so that he will get a bit closer to bringing the disinfection product to market. If not, oh well, that's okay. Basayev is still learning and perfecting the product, and he will get a batch of new clinical trial data based on the trial usage of the system at *Isla Valladolid*. And, as folks die from the infection that we introduce into the environment, at least you are collecting on the life insurance policy settlements. It's the ultimate hedging strategy, don't you think, St. Jude? Win-win."

Graham could hardly believe what he was hearing. Enos sounded like a mad man. A violent, ruthless, mad man. Of course, what should Graham have expected? He had seen the panoply of criminal activity on the Enos.onion dark web site. Graham wanted to bolt out of Hussong's. But he realized that he was likely in too deep at this point, with all the information he carelessly shared with Enos at their last meeting. Caught between the devil and the deep blue sea.

"What if I say no and that you are a fucking monster, Enos? You told me at the end of our last meeting that, if I choose to reject your grand solution, I could do the $30,000 pseudocide transaction and our relationship would be over. I may have been drunk off my ass, but I do remember that much."

"Are you worried that I won't keep my word, Cade Graham?"

Graham's face turned ashen. How in the hell did he

know his real name? Graham knew for certain he had not shared it with Enos. He never would have made that mistake—drunk or not.

"Are you worried that maybe I will hurt you or your illegitimate son Ethan Alves? Or Ethan's mother Marisol Alves? She is hot, by the way. Smoking hot. Kind of looks like a young Bianca Jagger, back in her heyday."

"Son of a bitch."

"Oh, come on, Cade. Do you even give a shit about Ethan and Marisol? Are you worried I will tell *Oscuro* something about you that they don't already know, like about the Texas supercollider site and all the opportunity there that you left *Oscuro* out of?"

"You are a fucking lunatic."

"Says the pedophile hedgie with ironclad scruples."

The two men stared at each other for several moments in silence. Enos had the kind of eyes that remained so fixed on his subject that no move could escape them. It was unnerving to Cade. He felt utterly trapped.

"Cade Graham, I'm just trying to help you. Remember? I'm your Huckleberry. And I've got a hell of a plan if you'll only recognize it. You can take your moral high ground— Mr. International Hedge Fund King—but I know all about the corporate rape you've gotten away with over the years, not to mention your raping of pretty, young teenagers. How old was Marisol when Ethan was born? Sixteen? It's the ultimate hypocrisy for someone with your track record to express moral indignation about what I am suggesting. My plan is for the greater good—when you think about it."

"The greater good? How do you figure that?"

"Some people are expendable, Cade."

"Expendable? Expendable? You're going to have to elaborate on that."

"I'll be blunt and tell you what other people don't have the candor or the courage to say. *Some lives mean more than others.* It's that simple, really."

"What are you saying? You're going to have to spell it

out."

"The folks at *Isla Valladolid* don't have that much longer to live and breathe on this planet—at least not in a meaningful way. They are old. And their deaths will not be in vain if medical science is advanced in the process of terminating them."

"Words of wisdom from a hit man."

"History is full of hit men, Cade, that, if you were honest, you would have to admit made the world a better place."

"And history is full of violent opportunists, too."

Enos gave Graham a cold, deadly stare that made him shudder. Graham kept sipping his tequila. Enos continued.

"Army snipers are heralded as heroes by some—but they are hitmen. War heroes—they are generally hit men. Police officers—hit men. I would say that every death that I personally have ever caused or arranged has, frankly, made the world a better place in one way or another."

"Your view of yourself is pretty damned elevated, Enos."

"I once had a brother that died for the greater good. He was essentially a suicide bomber. Unfortunately, he didn't get his job completely done. That sometimes happens. But that's a story for another day. Anyway, think about the Enola Gay and Truman's decision to drop the A-Bomb on Hiroshima. It was all for the greater good. You know Truman said he had no problem sleeping at night over all those 100,000 or so deaths in Japan. So why do you fret over a bunch of eighty-somethings' accelerated demise?"

"You have just compared yourself to war heroes and to a former U.S. president. Amazing. Anyone else you want to compare yourself to, Enos? Maybe Gandhi? Jesus?"

The two of them again sat in silence a few moments as the band took a break and some tourists sat down at a table nearby. Marcus observed that Graham was breathing heavily and was bouncing his right knee almost as though it was spasming.

"'Self-righteousness is easy and cheap.' Who said that, Cade? Damn, I hate it when I can't remember something like that. That's going to drive me crazy all day I bet."

"Enos, shut the hell up and tell me how would you accomplish these deaths? These deaths that you think would happen for the greater good?"

"Like I said, randomly at first. There could be some deaths on the property at *Isla Valladolid* that would look like natural causes. Some others could be by staged accidents offsite when the residents take day excursions. You know how those retirement communities are. The residents are always going to museums and nature hikes and shit like that."

"How do you kill someone and make it look like a natural death? Have you done that kind of thing before?"

Enos burst out laughing. "I'm a fucking hit man, Cade. Do you think I do the deed only in some gruesome or grisly fashion? With an electric saw, an assault rifle, or a car bomb? How cliché Hollywood! Have you ever heard of the blue men deaths in New York City in the 1940's?"

"No, Enos. I haven't. Forgive my ignorance."

"Well, let's just say that sodium nitrite is very easy to obtain, and it looks and tastes exactly like table salt. But if you ingest too much sodium nitrite, you become violently ill with what looks like either food poisoning or carbon monoxide poisoning (depending on how much you ingest). If you ingest way too much, your skin starts turning sky blue. A toxic dose is only about three grains. That's what happened to a bunch of homeless men in New York City who were found dead and were all the color blue. They all happened to eat oatmeal at a soup kitchen in which a cook had mistakenly put sodium nitrite in the oatmeal. The sodium nitrite was on site at the soup kitchen to cure meat."[3]

---

[3] Berton Roueche, *The Case of the Eleven Blue Men,* THE NEW YORKER (May 28, 1948).

"What are you saying?"

"Cade, you know what I am saying. Why are you playing dumb? Anyway, there are so many ways to do this. Snorkeling accidents when the old folks go out on one of their regular excursions. A car accident. A Segway mishap. Perhaps a hairdryer dropped in a bathtub. Maybe I could even put a Typhoid Mary in one of the restaurants at *Isla Valladolid*. Maybe a fake nurse goes on site with syringes full of some cyanide or some other sort of poison. Maybe some warm water gets accidently poured on rat poison or pesticides used at the property, creating phosphine gas, which will cause respiratory failure, if you do it just right at the right spot. And the beauty of all of this is that, down here, it's not like you have forensic experts and police detectives crawling all over the scene investigating, or medical examiners conducting autopsies. Even if someone suspects foul play, forget about it. No one's going to get around to investigating."

"All for the greater good."

"Now, you're getting it, Cade. You're a quick study, being a Princeton man and all. What do you say? Are you ready to start making some real money and, in the process, contributing to the advancement of science?"

"Enos, you have no idea what Dmitry Basayev's disinfectant system entails or what all would be involved in getting it up and going at *Isla Valladolid*. It would involve a major capital investment and there would be weeks of disruptive construction, such as installing ceiling and wall panels with ultraviolet light systems. There is also an air purification system that would have to be built into existing ventilation systems that incorporates robotics technology. There would need to be bio-scanning booths set up at entry and exit points around the property and personnel would have to be trained in how to maintain and use the booths. It cannot all happen overnight. And for the usage of the system at *Isla Valladolid* to qualify as a clinical trial for FDA purposes, or to get a CE mark in the European markets, there are all sorts of record keeping and shit that you have to do to build evidence of clinical safety and effectiveness. Clinical studies must be overseen by doctors and clinical investigators and conducted under the review of an independent review board. Basayev isn't going to be able to tell the regulatory agencies, 'Hey, we tried this system out for a while down in Mexico at a nursing home and it all worked great' and get credit for that as a qualifying clinical trial."

"Cade, if you arrange through Dmitry Basayev to get the system up and running at *Isla Valladolid*, I promise I can get you whatever documentation you need to prove there was oversite and monitoring and that regulatory approvals were obtained down here."

"Just tell you what type of fraudulent or forged document that Basayev needs, and you can deliver it, huh?"

"Yep. Pretty much."

"What if I say no to all of this, Enos? What if I don't want to do business with you at all—not even the pseudocide at this point?"

"Aw, Cade buddy. Are you reneging on our deal? I thought this was going to be an either-or thing, not neither. Either you liked my *Tertia Optio* or we did your pseudocide. Now you are trying to drop me like your prom date on the day before the prom."

"Enos, at this point I'll pay you the $30,000 for doing nothing, except pretending that you never met me."

Enos shook his head and sighed. "St. Jude, just one week ago you were melting down in an existential crisis. The way I see it, you *need* me."

"I need you? I need you?"

"Tell you what. I have a little present for you, Cade. I somehow knew in my gut that you might feel morally torn by my proposition. Well, I wasn't sure if you would be torn or not. As I said earlier, given your track record, the thought of you having much of a moral compass seemed a bit unlikely. But I thought there was some decent chance that you might feel a little ambivalent."

"What are you saying? Stop with the damn riddles."

"Like I said, I have a special present for you. A gift. Today at 5:00 p.m."

Graham looked at his watch. It was 4:55 p.m. He started looking around the cantina to see if anything looked amiss. Nothing but happy tourists drinking themselves into oblivion.

Enos continued. "A group of your tenants at *The Mayan* facility of *Isla Valladolid* were going on a day trip today to visit *Chichen Itza*, then were going for an early happy hour and dinner at a cantina, a few miles from *Isla Valladolid*. I read about it on *Isla Valladolid's* Facebook page a few days ago. It just so happens that somebody tampered with the saltshakers at the cantina. Yes, you guessed it, Cade. The salt was replaced with sodium nitrite. So, depending on how many of your tenants decide to salt up their meals tonight, we may have a few dearly departed residents in a few hours."

Graham looked at his watch. It was 4:56 p.m.

Enos began quietly singing as he twirled his drink. "Hey Jude, don't be afraid. You were made to, go out and get her. The minute you let her under your skin, then you begin, to make it better... And anytime you feel the pain, hey Jude, refrain. Don't carry the world upon your shoulders... I always liked that song. My mother used to sing it to me when I was little. But then she killed herself. Anyway, too late to turn back now, Cade. The game has begun. Just sit back and wait. It won't be long now."

Twenty-four hours later, Graham was lying in a lounge chair on the beach facing the Pacific Ocean, at Cabo's Sunset Beach Hotel. He had been nursing a bad hangover all day. At 5:00 p.m., Graham's cell phone rang. The caller I.D. showed a number that Graham did not recognize. He hesitated but answered the phone.

"Who's this?"

"Don't be so jumpy, Cade. It's your Huckleberry. I know you are probably on pins and needles waiting to hear about your gift."

Graham sat up and looked around, as though he was afraid someone was going to overhear the conversation.

"Well. Do you want to take a guess? Go ahead, guess."

"Tell me, Enos. Tell me what happened!"

"Four dead, and another in the *Galena Hospital,* and his prognosis does not sound very good. Newspapers are already reporting a bad outbreak of food poisoning occurred at that popular little cantina and the place has been shut down by the health department. Pity. What do you think that payoff for four or five residents will be? I figure that they each had at least a $200,000 or a $250,000 face amount life insurance policy, don't you think? So, $1 million, or maybe $1,250,000? That ought to get *Oscuro* off your ass for a while."

And, with that, a flood had begun. Actually, the first fateful raindrop fell when Cade had negotiated the credit default swaps with *Oscuro*. God damn Ethan. Ethan had never been anything but trouble for Graham. Now, there was nothing Cade could do to make it all subside. Enos was going to be a bigger problem for Cade than *Oscuro*.

Chapter Twenty

For the Greater Good (Flashback, Spring of 2018).

It has been said that there is no honor among thieves.

  Los Chupas was quickly developing a reputation throughout Mexico of having in its midst extraordinary, mercenary hit men who would do anything for quick cash. *Sicarios*. The *sicarios* had done many dirty deeds, occasionally killing high profile businessmen, government officials, *policia*, and the families of those people as well. They also, of course, were taking a large market share of the *Huachicoleros* business. *Los Chupas* had greatly angered the *Zetas* over their entre into the gasoline pipeline puncturing business. *Los Chupas* had partly accomplished their success in this area by developing cozier relationships with governmental officials than the *Zetas* had. But *Los Chupas* was gradually becoming an effective, strategic hedger, just like some of their cartel competition, branching out into more and more enterprises. Certainly, they had by Spring of 2018, a few months after the meeting in the Fall of

2017 between Enos and Graham. So, while the *Oscuro* cartel had its foothold in *Isla Valladolid*, through its majority interest in the REIT that owned the real property (and, thus, was essentially *Isla Valladolid's* landlord collecting rent from the residents), and while *Oscuro* was also hedging that REIT investment, through its $10,000,000 investment in Graham's life insurance settlements fund that owned the life insurance policies on *Isla Valladolid's* residents, *Los Chupas*—unbeknownst to *Oscuro*—had, through Enos/Marcus Braden, managed to get in on the action at *Isla Valladolid* too, so to speak. Soon *Los Chupas* would get crossways with *Oscuro,* just as it had already with the *Zetas*.

Between October 2017, after his meetings with Cade at *Hussong's*, and March 2018, Enos and his *Los Chupas sicarios* carried out numerous hits on unfortunate residents at *Isla Valladolid,* to speed up payouts on the life insurance settlements. First, there was the sodium nitrite episode at the cantina, killing five residents. Another resident had been the victim of an unfortunate mishap (drowning) while snorkeling. Two more residents were involved in a deadly traffic incident, while sightseeing on Segways. Enos was charging Cade a fee of a mere $10,000 per hit—a bargain he told Cade. Of course, Enos was playing the long game with Cade, so he thought of these early hits as something like a "loss leader." Eventually the more complicated hits would be commenced, as part of Enos's Phase II of his grand hedging scheme. The Phase II hits would be charged a higher fee, since they were more "value-adding" to Cade Graham's hedge empire than the earlier ones—to use Enos's words.

Phase II was multifaceted. It involved, first, installing Dmitry Basayev's disinfection infrastructure (UV panels, air purification ventilation systems, robotic equipment, bio-booths, and other cleaning protocols) throughout *Todos Santos*—the nursing home portion of *Isla Valladolid.* Then, infection would be introduced at the same facility. Adding infection would be challenging. Some residents would succumb to the infection, resulting in more life insurance payouts. Others would, hopefully, stay healthy, proving the efficacy of the disinfection system (and giving BASA the much-needed clinical trial data it needed—which Enos would make sure was forthcoming with forged documentation). Some residents would become very ill but not quickly die, and Basayev could experiment on these patients with some of his various drug therapies that were still in R&D stages back at The Grotto. Again, this would give Basayev the much-needed human clinical trials for some of his therapies that were still in development stage. Phase II, of course, involved the cooperation of Basayev. Cade argued with Enos that obtaining Basayev's cooperation would probably be impossible. But Enos had an answer for that, too.

Cade barely had a direct relationship with Dmitry Basayev—his son Ethan Alves was the one that had the relationship with Basayev, from their overlapping time at Emory University. Thus Cade, at the coaxing of Enos, decided that he had no choice but to bring Ethan into the loop. Enos urged Cade not to panic. This would all look like a wholly legitimate opportunity. Obviously, Cade, as the control person of the tenant/operator of *Isla Valladolid*, could consent to the installation of the disinfection system at the property and could finesse obtaining any consents from the REIT/landlord. Meanwhile, Enos would prepare paperwork, purportedly from various Mexican governmental agencies, permitting installation of the disinfection system and clinical test trials of the system and various drug therapies at the nursing home facility. The paperwork would all be in Spanish, of course, but Enos would provide translated versions and have a Mexican lawyer available to answer any questions that Basayev might have about the legitimacy of it all. Enos would also prepare paperwork purporting to be consents from the residents agreeing to be part of the clinical trials.

Enos would get a facilitator fee for all of this

$1,000,000 which would be paid half in cash (monthly installments) and half with a portion of Cade Graham's equity ownership in the offshore company that owned The Grotto.

Chapter Twenty-One

The Grotto Meeting (Flashback, Spring 2018).

In the Spring of 2018, Ethan Alves, at the request of the father whom he idolized, set up a meeting at The Grotto among himself, Graham, Basayev, and Dr. Astrid Nilsson. Enos would be joined in by conference call—being introduced as a consultant. At this point, in Spring 2018, it was roughly one year since BASA, Inc. had filed its Chapter 11 case in Dallas. Dmitry Basayev had gone underground, literally and figuratively, a few weeks after the case had been filed. He was not simply dodging the angry investors in that case. He was literally scared for his life. Dmitry still figured that if he worked hard and put his nose to the grindstone and got his disinfectant systems up and running soon, he could make everyone happy. In time, the court and all of the investors would know that BASA was not a Ponzi scheme and that he was not a crook. He may have over-promised and under-delivered; but he would get this product completed, the clinical trials executed, and bring it to market.

Meanwhile he was working equally hard on his other therapies and vaccines being developed under the DB Biocontainment, LLC moniker. In particular, he and Dr. Nilsson had identified the Prudhoe Bay, Alaska disease to, in fact, be a mutated, highly deadly version of the H1N1 virus that experts believed the Spanish Flu had been. The two of them were convinced that the Prudhoe Bay virus was a bomb buried in the permafrost that would inevitably go off and be catastrophic. And now, after more than a year, they had created an antiviral that seemed to prevent the virus from multiplying in the body.

Given Dmitry's desperate and anxious state of mind these days, the conversation with him was going to go much more easily than Graham might have imagined.

The stated purpose of the meeting was to discuss a possible clinical trial opportunity for both the BASA, Inc. disinfecting system as well as some of Basayev's developmental drug therapies and vaccines. It was all top secret. No one other than the participants must know of the meeting. The purpose had obviously piqued Dmitry's interest. The meeting was scheduled for the conference center at the Grotto in Ellis County. Ethan Alves and Cade Graham had visited the facility before, since Graham, of course, owned the real property through a REIT. But that had been many months ago, well before it became a world-class virology lab.

The meeting was scheduled for 9:00 p.m. on a warm March evening. Cade and Ethan were told to go to the nearby warehouse in Ellis County that BASA had used as its business address and, in fact, had at one time used as a research lab. They should arrange to have a car service drop them off there. Then a car arranged by Dmitry would pick them up and drive them to the underground facility.

When Ethan and Cade arrived at the warehouse, everything went according to plan. A navy-blue SUV waited in the warehouse parking lot when they arrived with a small, elderly man wearing a Burberry driver's cap at the wheel.

The driver rolled down the passenger side front window and shouted in a thick eastern European accent, "Tell me your names, please, gentlemen."

"Cade Graham. Ethan Alves." Ethan replied.

"Please get in."

As the two of them climbed into the back seat of the SUV, the driver turned around and reached out his hand to both Cade and Ethan, introducing himself as Arkady Basayev.

"So, you are related to Dmitry?"

"I am his father. I came to America to retire, and my son has already put me to work for him. I can't get a break."

"Are you also a scientist?"

The old man laughed. "Oh, no, no, no. My son got his mother's brains. I was only a journalist. For many years. And I was not very popular with either the Russian government or the Chechens during my career. I am quite glad to be very far away from them now. I am now just Dmitry's errand boy. And I am okay with that at this stage of my life. He is doing important work."

"So, do you live down in The Grotto along with Dmitry?"

"Yes. It is an unconventional way to live. But it is quite comfortable. The living quarters allow Dmitry to work almost 24/7, and I can assure you he does. So, you are two of his investors I hear?"

"Yes, something like that. We have invested in The Grotto and Dmitry's activities and raised money from other investors."

"Well, be good to my boy. He is not going to sell his soul for profits. Don't put pressure on him. I assume that's what you are here to do. To put pressure on him so that you can make more money faster. He is a brilliant scientist. He must have time to get things right."

For the remainder of the drive, the men sat in silence. It was a short distance to The Grotto.

The surface above the facility was quiet and

nondescript. It seemed like a contradiction. It was just a field of bluebonnets surrounded by farm and ranch land. A few signs warned that it was private property and trespassers should stay away. But against this pastoral scene were occasional steel and glass domes—seventeen of them in all—containing elevators that could take entrants down the various shafts accessing the underground.

Upon their arrival, Cade and Ethan were escorted to one of the enclosed, steel domes with a sign reading "Conference Center." At the point of entry, there was a bio-booth at which visitors were required to enter and stand momentarily while different bodily functions were scanned and measured. Then once a green light appeared overhead, the visitors were instructed to board an elevator that would take them down to the tunnel. The elevator trip was swift. It was difficult for a visitor to determine the depth of the subterranean journey—the elevator buttons and lighting had no indicators. Cade was trying to remember during the ride down how far underground the tunnel had been burrowed. That detail had not seemed important to him at the time he began his funding of The Grotto.

The elevator doors opened, and Cade and Ethan were surprised to see Dmitry waiting for them. Ethan and Dmitry hugged like old friends. Dmitry was a tall, handsome man with thick, tousled brown hair, angular cheek bones, a sharp jaw full of stubbles, and large, light blue, serious eyes. He wore a white silk shirt and black trousers. He had a gentle demeanor. He looked a little older than Cade remembered and his face a little pallid. Perhaps he really was working 24/7 as his father had indicated, and that had aged him. Cade also didn't remember him having such vivid, piercing blue eyes.

"Welcome, gentlemen. I trust everything worked out smoothly for your trip here?" Dmitry spoke in a soft, velvety voice still heavily accented with his native Chechen.

"Yes. We enjoyed meeting your father, Arkady."

Arkady had apparently temporarily slipped away.

Dmitry sensed that both Ethan and Cade were studying his face and thought that they may have noticed his blue eyes. "Are you wondering if I have started wearing colored contact lenses?"

Both Ethan and Cade did not know how to respond.

"I am not that vain. I am afraid that I fell victim to a certain virus that we have been studying here. The virus has the strange tendency to change the color of one's irises to this light blue. Luckily, I survived the illness, but my eyes did not change back. We don't know if they ever will. I have decided I sort of like them though. Anyway, would you like to look around tonight while you are here or go straight to business? I will warn you that if you want to take a tour, you will probably need to plan to stay overnight, because there are many protocols that need to be followed when travelling through the various units here—for both your own safety and the integrity of our labs. It takes a fair amount of time to travel the lengthy corridors and then to go through the decontamination process. And the infectious disease unit—the unit we call Wildfire—is off limits to all but a few. I can, of course, show you some pictures and invite in some of the personnel who work there, if you desire."

"Actually, let's go straight to business. We have a consultant standing by in Mexico to participate by phone in our meeting and we want to be respectful of his time. If we have time when our meeting is finished, maybe we will look at the Nebula lab and some of the other facilities that don't require the lengthy protocols."

"Very well. Follow me to the conference facilities."

Cade and Ethan looked around in amazement as Dmitry led them through a long hallway lined with thick, smooth stone, arched vaulted ceilings, marble columns, chandeliers, and travertine floors. Fine art was displayed sporadically along the walls, with brass plates below each piece with words that appeared to be Cyrillic. Dmitry quickly explained, "My father brought these pieces with him from Chechnya. They were painted by an artist friend who, along with his family, was murdered by the Russians. My father wrote extensively about the Chechnya purges and its victims including this artist. My father's writings gained international attention and won him a Pulitzer Prize. One of the artist's few surviving family members gave all of these pieces to my father, in gratitude for his exposing the atrocities." The pieces were all very dark, portraying dreary and melancholy figures.

From time to time, as they walked along the corridor, Dmitry would point to doors, noting they led to living quarters, kitchens, bars, and recreational amenities. When they at last reached a large state of the art conference room, Dr. Astrid Nilsson was there to greet them. She said very little. She merely held out her hand and pointed them to the beverage bar, inviting them to help themselves. She then pointed to the conference phone in the middle of a black marble conference table and told them that they could call their consultant in Mexico, adding quickly that there were security features, so they did not need to worry about unwanted listeners. Cade dialed up Enos, introducing him to Dmitry and Dr. Nilsson as their consultant in Mexico City, "Enos Francisco."

The meeting began with Cade sharing the fact that he was the controlling owner, with some silent Mexican investors, of a large, luxury retirement community called *Isla Valladolid*, in Yucatan. He invited both Dmitry and Nilsson to come and visit the property to see what a lovely and state-of-the-art concept it was for aging residents seeking quality opportunities not available in the U.S. Then came the hard sell. Cade, Ethan, and the Mexican investors all desired to create an opportunity for Dmitry and his team to perform clinical trials of their disinfection system and maybe some of their other therapies and products down at *Isla Valladolid*. Cade and Ethan elaborated that the Mexican investors had some motivations besides just desiring to advance medical science. Specifically, the Mexican investors had been involved behind the scenes with BASA.

Ethan had negotiated credit default swaps with these Mexican investors relating to Cade's loans to BASA. Thus, these Mexican investors became the actual holders of Cade's BASA, Inc. debt when BASA, Inç. went into default on the debt and filed Chapter 11. The Mexican investors wanted to see BASA succeed with its disinfection system, so that maybe their debt could be finally paid off. They figured they had nothing to lose by allowing clinical trials at *Isla Valladolid,* and perhaps everything to gain. Of course, unbeknownst to Basayev and Nilsson, only part of this story was true. Yes, there were Mexican investors who held BASA, Inc. debt who would like to see BASA succeed. But those Mexican investors: (a) just happened to be a Mexican crime cartel; and (b) also had no awareness about this strategy to implement clinical trials at *Isla Valladolid*. This was all the brainchild of Enos. And, of course, unbeknownst to Cade, Enos was not a lone wolf but, rather part of a rival cartel, *Los Chupas*.

Graham's life was getting more and more complicated. But his initial trepidation, moral consternation, and outright fear that he had felt when he first met Enos had transformed into something far different now. He was actually somewhat invigorated feeling like he might have a path out of his financial trap. He might not need to fake his own death and fade into anonymity after all. He was feeling a little more in control these days, although, in fact, he was not. Enos and *Oscuro* were in control. But Graham felt like Enos's plan was going to keep *Oscuro* at bay, and that they might just all hit a homerun with the Basayev products.

After a few weeks of on-again off-again discussions, Cade and Ethan sealed the deal, regarding getting the disinfection system and all of its protocols installed and implemented at *Isla Valladolid*. Dmitry and Nilsson agreed to the plan. They even had further discussions that if this went well, Cade had other properties in his healthcare portfolio that might also be available for clinical trials.

Dmitry put Nilsson in charge of the project. She could

handle the logistics of the installation of the disinfection protocols at *Isla Valladolid* as well as decide which therapies and anti-virals they might suggest for trials there. Dmitry was not much of a businessman—he was a charming salesman and a scientist. At this point he just wanted to be in his underground lab. Dr. Nilsson had vast experience with clinical trials and the approval process and what not. She would be the point person on this.

This all set up nicely—exactly how Enos and Ethan knew that it must. Ethan knew Dmitry well, but his father really did not. Ethan knew—and had told Enos—that Dmitry would never agree to purposely introducing infection at the *Isla Valladolid* nursing home. Dmitry was, at bottom, a very ethical person. "Do no harm," and all of that. Experimenting with his disinfection system and introducing therapies in which he strongly believed was one thing. But purposely infecting humans was way over the line. Dr. Nilsson was an altogether different breed, and Ethan knew it from his days hearing her lecture at Emory. She was a person who, without a doubt, could be sold on the concept of pursuing "the greater good" to advance medical science. Emory had fired Dr. Nilsson for some of her heretical statements and stances that had embarrassed the university. She would have no problem exposing elderly people who had serious pre-existing health conditions—practically on death's doorstep anyway—to deadly infections, with the hopes of using their experiences and reactions with therapies or antivirals, to find cures that would benefit humankind. When Ethan and Enos approached her outside of Dmitry's presence about the concept of introducing infection to some of the nursing home population at *Isla Valladolid*, the conversation went very smoothly. Nilsson was extremely receptive to the idea. She knew just the one that she would like to introduce—the mutated H1N1 virus from the permafrost. This would all be very discrete. Only a handful of people would know what was happening—she, Ethan, Cade, and Enos. *A quiet team that was going to dramatically advance the cause of healthcare by light years in a short time.* They would perfect their antiviral for the permafrost flu, as she called it, before it had spread with abandon all over the world—which she believed was an eventuality. They referred to the plan as Project Ember.

One other person knew about Project Ember: Arkady Basayev. He was a man who could never quite "turn off" the award-winning, investigative journalism instincts he had honed over the years. He had never trusted Nilsson. And he absolutely did not trust Dmitry's financial backers to have medical science and human lives anywhere on their list of priorities. Arkady had secretly recorded the initial March 2018 meeting in The Grotto conference room and had recorded several phone conferences that took place there subsequently involving Nilsson, Cade, Ethan, and Enos. Arkady's only problem was figuring out what to tell Dmitry and when.

A few weeks after the Grotto meeting with Ethan and Cade, Dmitry wandered down to Laboratory-2 at 4:00 in the morning as he often did. He had grabbed a cup of coffee in the kitchen on the way and realized from the turned-on Keurig machine that someone had just made a cup a moment or so before. Probably Dr. Nilsson. As Dmitry walked into Laboratory-2, he indeed saw Dr. Nilsson across the way at her usual spot, staring into a test tube and taking occasional notes. Dmitry studied Dr. Nilsson's face with part admiration and part anxiety. She had been his mentor since his earliest days at Emory. Just a year before he started there, she had won a Nobel Prize for her research regarding CRISPR sequences in bacterial genomes and antiviral defense mechanisms. Sadly, only a few years later, her reputation had tarnished from one of brilliant visionary to heretic because of some of her radical ideas regarding how to push CRISPR research to very far boundaries—beyond simply editing genes to make organisms virus-resistant, but experimentation with neural and brain organoids and similar technologies with human subjects, before such technologies were peer-reviewed and "ready for prime time." She was unceremoniously terminated and escorted from the Emory campus when word leaked that she had been experimenting with trying to manipulate human brain tissue in her lab with her graduate students. But she wore the mantle of heretic somewhat cheerfully. She was unrepentant for her tendency to push the envelope. She felt that many of her colleagues were cowards to spend so much time on decoding and recoding genomes in bacteria, plants, mice, and other mammals, and not stepping things up to human applications. Their caution had the effect of blinding them to all of the human suffering in the world and dedicating their power to change it. How could they be so spineless?

It has been said that nearly all great scientists are perceived to be heretics at some point in their careers—quacks or crazies—only to be proven right in time. Galileo, Darwin, Einstein and countless other geniuses were, of course, ridiculed by the orthodox scientific community. Cast out into the wilderness and even persecuted. The old "first they think you're crazy; then they fight you; then you change the world" mantra that has been voiced by geniuses and fraudsters alike. This was a frequent theme of Dr. Nilsson's lectures to her students and colleagues. She sometimes compared her own plight, after being fired, to a Hungarian doctor named Ignaz Semmelweis. He was baffled in the mid-nineteenth century by the fact that the death rate for women giving birth at his hospital was much higher than it was for midwife-assisted births in the same community. When he espoused a theory that doctors were killing women by failing to adhere to basic hygiene—for example, by not washing their hands in between dissecting corpses and delivering their babies—he was vilified, driven to alcoholism, and eventually committed to an insane asylum, where he died. It was at a time when doctors resisted the idea of antiseptic hygiene. Decades later, germ theory emerged with scientists like Louis Pasteur and Semmelweis is now considered the father of antiseptic treatment.

Another favorite example of hers was Barry Marshall, the Australian medical researcher who in the 1980s suggested that stomach ulcers might be caused by bacteria, not stress and spicy food. He theorized that antibiotics might be used to treat ulcers, and his theory was dismissed by mainstream science, and he was barred from experimenting on humans. Undeterred, Marshall infected himself by drinking a brew of the bacteria Helicobacter pylori, then, after becoming ill, cured himself with antibiotics and ultimately proved his theory that ulcers can be caused by bacteria. While his theory was not readily accepted, it ultimately won him the Nobel prize in 2005.

Dr. Nilsson operated on the margins, to be sure. She was atypical in comparison to so many other scientists, in that she was not anti-religious or an atheist. Dmitry had observed that she started every morning in her lab with the Lord's Prayer. When Dmitry once questioned her about her faith, she said little except that the prayer reminded her that she was part of a larger process. She said she could never lose sight that everything she did was for the greater good. God's greater good. Today's failures would lead to tomorrow's victories.

Dmitry worried plenty in recent months that he was being taken advantage of by financial promoters and charlatans. He knew his investors only cared about profits and this sometimes diminished his passion. But, on further thought, he knew Dr. Nilsson would not let the financial promoters control their grand plans or the ultimate outcome. Yes, there was a business side to all of this. And there were occasionally ethical quandaries to navigate. But this was all secondary. DB Biocontainment was going to change the world. It would all be worth it.

Chapter Twenty-Two

The Implementation of Phase II and Project Ember (Flashback, Spring and Summer of 2018).

After a short planning phase, the BASA disinfection system was up and running at the *Tudos Santos* nursing home facility and in other common areas at *Isla Valladolid*. A group of contractors and engineers from the Ellis County facility swept in and had the ultraviolet panels, air purification ventilation systems, robotic equipment, bio booths, and cleaning systems in place in a matter of days.

Malibu Barbie was not at all happy when the contractors and engineers showed up. She was a control freak, yet no one had told her anything. That was a huge mistake. Malibu Barbie preferred to be in charge of anything and everything at *Isla Valladolid*. Most infuriating to her was the annoying, cocky blond spikey haired man who seemed to be the boss of all the contractors. He had come around the property a few times before, acting like he was interested in it for one of his parents, getting information about the amenities and activities at the property, and asking to see available units and whatnot. Now he was supervising the installation of this disinfection system. What was all of that about? Malibu Barbie planned to report it all to her boyfriend, Mateo Guerrero, who ran the *Oscuro* cartel. He had placed her in her position at *Isla Valladolid* to make sure nothing went on without his knowledge.

Once the disinfection system was in place, the next stage of Phase II commenced. "Project Ember": the introduction of the permafrost virus into the nursing home. The "hit men" for this task were contractor "attendants" and "nurses aids" at the facility. The facility regularly used an outside service to shuttle in this type of staff. The Project Ember team were trained for two essential tasks. First, as to one test group ("Test Group A"), they would administer injections of what they were told was a therapy agent that would enhance the residents' immune systems. In fact, the injections were doses of the flu-like virus extracted from the patients that had been evacuated from Prudhoe Bay. Second, the attendants and nurses' aids would monitor certain vital signs and body fluids of all other patients in the nursing home ("Test Group B"), to both: (a) detect any signs of the permafrost flu that might show up in them; and (b) generally monitor for any adverse reactions that might occur in residents, after implementation of the disinfectant system.

Finally, when any of the nursing home residents became sick (whether it be the "Test Group A" residents injected with the Prudhoe Bay virus or the "Test Group B" residents—from either a spread of the Prudhoe Bay virus or from adverse reactions to the disinfection system), they were evacuated and transported to The Grotto in Texas. There, the patients were guinea pigs for the Dmitry Basayev team's experiments with antivirals and other therapies. It was a win-win, at least from the perspective of Enos, Ethan, Cade, and Nilsson. If Dmitry's team cured the infected patients with his anti-virals, then these therapies were one step closer to being proven effective and approved by regulators for marketing. Meanwhile, they were building data to establish the flaws and efficacy of the disinfection system. Finally, if a patient died, his or her life insurance policy would pay off—relieving a bit of Cade Graham's cash flow problems and, of course, helping him with *Oscuro*.

Cade had taken hedging to a whole new level. Many patients died. But, as far as Enos, Ethan, Nilsson, and even Cade viewed it now, they died for the greater good.

Chapter Twenty-Three

Phase III—Replication (Flashback, Fall of 2018).

The implementation of Phase II and Project Ember went well for a few months. The disinfection system worked beautifully, thus supplying more trial data to suggest that the system was ready for market. There was also a steady stream of patients to The Grotto from *Isla Valladolid* who had been infected. The antiviral they were given showed great promise. Most patients fared well. Only a few died, and, of course, life insurance was collected for those who did not get well.

But things were not moving fast enough. Clinical trials require extremely large amounts of data, produced in phases over time. While the disinfection system and the permafrost antiviral were hardly in their nascent stages—they had been the subject of extensive trials and data collection, even for months before *Isla Valladolid* entered the picture (including through an online system to enroll volunteers)—these products were still not ready for prime time, as Dmitry and

Nilsson frequently told Cade and Ethan. When Cade reported this to Enos, he was not at all happy.

"We need to replicate what we are doing at other facilities. You know I can get the paperwork and approvals you need. Give me some more facilities and patients to work with."

"Enos, how am I supposed to do that?" asked Cade.

"You own other properties. We replicate the *Isla Valladolid* system at some of your other properties. Make it happen, Cade. Didn't you tell me you have a property near Acapulco?"

"Yeah, but it is not worth screwing with. The occupancy is way down. And there is more law enforcement presence because of the tourism."

"I don't care. Let's do it."

Over the next hour, Cade, Ethan and Enos sat in Hussong's, the altar boy keeping watch at the door, discussing a "replication plan." Although Cade had more properties at which to replicate the plan, it was not going to be enough to meet the timetable that Enos had in mind. Enos was now very much calling the shots.

"I have an idea to present to Dr. Nilsson. I have mules that transport immigrants to the border by the hundreds every week."

"You smuggle immigrants into the U.S.? Didn't see that one on your website."

"I told you, Cade, I am a master hedger just like you. Got to diversify your portfolio."

Ethan looked at Enos with amazement. He had not been involved in too many conversations with Enos at this point. Ethan, although almost thirty-years-old, had a callow face with a naïve expression. He bore a strong resemblance to his father but had olive skin and large almond-shaped eyes like his Brazilian mother. He wondered how the father whom he admired so much had gotten involved with Enos. He had never asked.

"What do you have in mind this time, Enos?"

"I'm thinking we offer the would-be immigrants an alternative to me charging my usual fee. They can participate in a clinical drug trial in exchange for free passage into the U.S. when the trial is finished."

"And where are we going to do these trials?"

"I've got that covered. We can use a couple of my warehouses. One at *Juarez* and another at *El Bajio*. Actually, another at *Anapra*. They were stash houses that we aren't using anymore. Shall I talk to Dr. Nilsson directly about getting the equipment and staffing in place?"

And with that, Phase III had begun. The clinical trials would be complete soon.

Chapter Twenty-Four

Back to BASA Trial (Present Day, July 2019).

It was Thursday and Judge Avery Lassiter was ready to reconvene the BASA trial. It had only been three days of "cool breezing it," but it had been a blissful reprieve.

When Avery walked into her chambers that morning, one of the interns, Spence, was lightly playing bossa nova music on his blue tooth in his office. "Get it Judge Lassiter, bossa for BASA?"

"Ugh. Stick to your day job."

"Ugh, says the queen of lame jokes," Annalise said and smiled as she scurried over to the Keurig. "At least he is not wearing a Metallica t-shirt and flipflops, Judge."

"Spence, are you ever going to get that draft opinion to me from the Goodman trial? How long is it now? Seventy-something pages? I am going to start calling you Faulkner, Jr.?"

"It's close, Judge. I'm doing one last cite check."

Sarah, the empathetic intern, plopped on the sofa in Judge Lassiter's office with a notepad, tossing her blond ringlets over her shoulder. "What do you think we are going to hear this morning, Judge? I can't wait to learn more. I feel like a giant Size thirteen shoe is about to drop, don't you?"

Avery loved hearing the youthful, enthusiastic effusions from her interns and law clerks. It made her heart swell. There was a period, after the Matt Braden incident, when Avery feared she would never trust or bond with interns or law clerks again. But that phase had now passed. Avery knew that Matt Braden was a one-off—a disturbed young man who had fallen through the cracks. She wouldn't let that nightmare ruin her passion for mentoring these brilliant, young legal minds. She remembered, forever ago, when she used to always be cheerful and eager before a day of court. She just felt jaded and tired right now, bracing herself for whatever new trajectory this tough case was going to take today. But the interns and Millicent kept her focused.

"Folks, I have no predictions on this one."

Millicent chimed in. "Trust me. This is rare for the judge not to have predictions. We often place bets on whether this or that is going to happen—not monetary bets, of course. Well, sometimes we do bet bottles of wine. Judge likes Spanish dry red wine, just in case you ever need to know that. Or Cloudy Bay Sauvignon Blanc if you can't find Spanish."

"Millicent, please do not encourage the interns to buy me wine. How would that look? Anyway, think about the gravity of all of this. For months, we have been thinking that we had a Ponzi scheme on our hands. We have very bright lawyers and investors involved in this case who, apparently after much digging, had concluded that BASA was a massive Ponzi scheme. We have a company founder, Dmitry Basayev, who has not been around to explain his side of the story, and no one has been able to find him to serve a subpoena on him. It sure has been a case with all of the hallmarks of a Ponzi scheme. But now we hear about all the diverted money to one of Basayev's side businesses? What has this to do with a helicopter company? Why in the heck does this side business have a ground lease on the super collider site in Ellis County? These sure seem like strange developments for a Ponzi scheme. Usually with a Ponzi scheme you just have a big nothing burger. A whole lot of nothing."

Avery went to her closet to grab her robe. As she did, her colleague Judge Hall walked into her chambers.

"Good morning, Lassiter Chambers. It sounds like a party down here. I hear that you have had a three-day break from BASA. Is that why you all look so chipper?"

"We don't look chipper. What on Earth makes you say we look chipper? We are anything but chipper. We are girding for battle. Everything in this case is a stinking, epic battle."

"Wow. Someone is cranky."

"I'm sorry, friend. I didn't mean to be. Yes, we have had a break from the BASA trial but unfortunately that break is over. We are about to get started again and, hopefully, we will get some more information regarding some very strange revelations that were unveiled last Monday."

"Yeah, I heard that there might be some connection to one of my cases, DRI-MED Helicopter?"

"Word travels at the speed of light around here. Did you overhear the law clerks gossiping in the hallway or what?"

"No, actually, I have an emergency motion that was filed yesterday in my DRI-MED case by your BASA Trustee. He is wanting to take discovery from DRI-MED personnel regarding a contract that DRI-MED apparently had or has with a company called DB Biocontainment, LLC—which I understand is owned by the same fellow that owns BASA. The motion also states that a bunch of BASA money was paid over to DRI-MED, indirectly through or for DB Biocontainment."

"Yep, we heard about some of that last Monday. That's why we took a break from the trial for seventy-two hours—to let the lawyers investigate these recent findings. Apparently, they think there might be more going on here than a Ponzi scheme. Crazy, huh, that there might be some overlap with your case?"

"Well as long as it doesn't mean more work for me!" Judge Hall chuckled as he walked out the door. Judge Hall liked to poke fun at himself, pretending as though he didn't like to work hard. The truth was that he was the first one in the building every day, by a couple of hours, and usually turned out the lights at night.

"I'll update you after my hearing." Avery smiled.

"All rise. Court is now in session. The Honorable Avery Lassiter presiding."

"Good morning. Please be seated."

Avery looked out over the courtroom. All the usual faces looked solemn. Avery noticed that Dr. Astrid Nilsson was once again in the back of the courtroom, wearing another stylish hat as if to disguise herself. It just made her more conspicuous. Surely, she must realize that.

"For the record, we are back today to resume the BASA trial. I note that present today are counsel for the Plaintiff, Mr. Chertoff, counsel for the Defendants, Messrs. Wesson, Thompson and Gray, and numerous other interested parties, including Mr. O'Malley, for the labor union investors—whom I might add dropped a bombshell on us last Monday. Hopefully, everyone has signed the court reporter's appearance sheet. I'd like to hear from the Plaintiff's counsel first this morning." Judge Lassiter looked toward the Robot. "Mr. Chertoff?" Avery had hesitated before saying the Plaintiff's attorney, Austin Chertoff's, name because sometimes she slipped and used nicknames that her staff and other lawyers used for the lawyer cast of characters.

The Robot came to attention and walked with a cadence

of confidence to the podium. He was strident and delivered his words as though savoring every syllable.

"Your Honor, it has been an odd and eventful three days for us. I know that Your Honor plays by the book, and strictly follows the rules, and prefers that everything in court be out in the open, on the record with everyone allowed to hear. I greatly respect that. But we have some very sensitive information that we believe should only be shared *in camera* with only a few parties present."

Everyone remained strangely silent.

Avery looked befuddled. "Okay, you can cut the cloak and dagger. You are correct that I like everything on the record. That's the way it's supposed to be. Not my rules. The federal rules. The courts are public places and, frankly, this is a very public matter where so many millions of dollars have gone missing. So many lives have been affected."

"Your Honor, I urge you to give us some latitude on this one. I ask that you permit me, Messrs. Wesson, Thompson, Gray, O'Malley, and the U.S. Trustee to speak to you in chambers to share a few things and discuss our likely next steps. If you become uncomfortable, we could all come back out and restate everything that we discuss in chambers on the record. I don't make this request lightly. This is highly unusual."

Judge Lassiter looked around the courtroom. It was quite full. Most in the crowded courtroom were lawyers or parties who were stakeholders in this case in some form or fashion. Others were probably just curious observers. There were possibly some journalists in the courtroom. The Robot may have been concerned about them. Perhaps it was Dr. Astrid Nilsson whose presence worried him.

"Okay. I will indulge you, counsel. The six of you, ring the doorbell to my chambers in five minutes. I need to warn my assistant Annalise that you all are coming back to visit. She'll probably want to tidy up a bit. For the record, we are taking a thirty-minute break for a chambers conference with counsel for the Plaintiff, counsel for all Defendants, also Mr.

O'Malley, and the U.S. Trustee."

"All rise."

Avery rushed back into her chambers.

"Annalise, did you hear all of that?"

"Yes, Judge, I did. I wish you had given me more than five minutes to clean up all of our messes back here. I already cleared off your desk and shoved all the paperwork in a banker's box and put it in your robe closet."

"Annalise, it's all fine. It's just a bunch of lawyers, not the Queen of England."

After five minutes of Mach 3, hair-on-fire, scurrying to make Judge Lassiter's chambers "presentable," Annalise ushered in the team of lawyers. She directed them to the red wing-backed chairs in the conference room adjacent to Judge Lassiter's office. She dutifully offered them water or coffee, which she was glad they declined. She was hoping this was a sign that they would not stay very long.

"Okay, let's get to it, counsel. What the heck is going on here?" Avery sipped on her third cup of coffee of the day.

The Robot was the first to respond. "Judge Lassiter, first, we are going to be presenting an agreed motion to abate the trial for sixty days. Mr. O'Malley has, indeed, stumbled on something here that, frankly, we are absolutely stunned that our financial advisors had not uncovered sooner."

Muttonchop Man smiled a bit superciliously.

"I'm all ears, Mr. Chertoff."

"We believe that it is absolutely the case that there is more going on here than a Ponzi scheme. There is, indeed, a second entity that Dmitry Basayev has been involved with called DB Biocontainment, LLC. It appears to have been (or maybe still is) an operating company of some kind—not merely a research and development company. We have filed an emergency motion in the DRI-MED Helicopter Chapter 11 bankruptcy case that's going on down the hall in Judge Hall's court, to take depositions and written discovery of some of the personnel at DRI-MED regarding its contract or dealings with DB Biocontainment and to see if they can tell us what "Project Grotto" is. We want to find out what DRI-MED has done for DB Biocontainment, what do they know about the company, and who dealt with whom at the company. Meanwhile we have other investigations underway regarding the identity of the entity that owns the super collider property and apparently leases it to DB Biocontainment.

Finally, we would like to get a court order allowing us to take a field trip out to the property and inspect it and see what this facility is all about. All one can see there is a large surface area with about Seventeen steel and glass domes scattered about. Again, we are trying to track down the landlord, but it is proving to be a significant challenge. The landlord's name is Ellis County Acquisition One, Ltd., but it's a Cayman Island entity and there are several levels of Cayman entities that are general partners and limited partners in it, and those entities have still more Cayman entities in the ownership chain, and so on and so on. It's a byzantine legal structure that will take weeks to sort out. Bottom line, there is something going on here that needs to be evaluated for the benefit of the parties who invested in BASA. Maybe there is a different way her to recover their money. We think this needs more focus than the trial right now—especially a trial that may be based on some wrong assumptions."

Judge Lassiter sat in silence for a moment. "Okay. I think you have certainly made a valid argument for abatement of this trial. It will be granted. But I ask again, why the cloak and dagger? Why did you ask to come back in chambers as opposed to just asking for this in open court? And you used the words '*in camera*' suggesting that there were some sensitive documents that you wanted me to inspect."

"Well Judge, it has to do with a woman whom you may have noticed sitting in the back of the courtroom during these proceedings. Have you noticed the hat-wearing woman?"

"Yes. I was telling my staff that I thought it looked like Dr. Astrid Nilsson, but I could be wrong."

"That's amazing, Judge. You are right. We had no clue who it was. We thought it might be a reporter. But we got curious. We asked one of the court security officers who checks the IDs of people bringing in cell phones if he had caught her name. He told us Astrid Nilsson. Then, to make matters more curious, we have had a private investigator watching the Ellis County site for comings and goings from a distance and snapping some pictures. Here's what we wanted you to look at *in camera*. Pictures of Dr. Nilsson coming and going at the site on a regular basis."

Avery looked at a stack of color, glossy, eight by eleven-inch pictures that were taken from a distance with a zoom lens. They were very good quality.

"It certainly appears to be her. I recognize the hat she is wearing in this one." Avery pointed to a picture of a turquoise, disc-shaped hat with yellow and lilac flowers atop it, fitting for the Kentucky Derby. "What do you think that means?"

"Well, she obviously has something to do with whatever is going on out there. I mean she is a world-renowned microbiologist and all."

"Okay, and?"

"We'd like to serve a subpoena on her and take her deposition. We wanted your permission to serve it on her today in court. We know that normally that would be sort of bad form, to spring a subpoena on someone in court like this—at least some judges think so. We were hoping to get your approval. Meanwhile, as I said earlier, we will be going to Judge Hall to seek permission to take discovery from the DRI-MED folks. Finally, we'd like your blessing on sending a process server out to the Ellis County site, to try to find someone to serve out there, so we can take an examination of a representative of DB Biocontainment, LLC."

Avery sighed. She looked over at the Whale and the twin-like bald lawyers, Paul Gray and Paul Thompson. "What do you all have to say about any of this?" The twin Pauls looked with their owlish eyes to the Whale for guidance.

The Whale turned his taurine head, cleared his throat, and looked at Avery with his brown droopy eyes. They were rather blood shot today. "As it turns out, Your Honor, there are some internal investigations underway at Toro Capital, trying to ascertain if there are any documents that might exist to shed further light on this. On the one hand, we feel rather emboldened at the new theory the plaintiff has that this was not a Ponzi scheme after all. My client always fervently believed that it was raising money for a legitimate endeavor. On the other hand, I will tell you in all candor that I and my legal team have never heard of DB Biocontainment. Early on in this case, we hired an e-discovery vendor and gave it key word search terms that we thought were very broad, but certainly those terms did not include 'DB Biocontainment,' or 'Grotto,' or 'Ellis County,' or any other term that might have hit on this new underground project. Mr. Chertoff and I are working cooperatively to craft appropriate, additional key search terms to see what additional, relevant electronically stored documents might turn up. Also, I have learned that a couple of the Toro Capital fund managers that worked on this BASA deal, but are no longer employed there, have been located. They, unfortunately, now work in Indonesia and have been hard to track down. We are going to be talking to them to see what, if anything, they might have ever heard about DB Biocontainment, LLC while they were raising capital for BASA."

"Messrs. Thompson and Gray? Anything to add?"

The twin Pauls stood. Thompson spoke. "Your Honor, we have both spoken to our clients. We can assure you that they were as shocked as you to learn about any of this. That's all I have." Mr. Gray nervously nodded, apparently signaling that he had nothing else to say.

"All right, Mr. Chertoff, you have my blessing to serve the subpoena on Dr. Nilsson. I also have no problem with you sending a process server out to Ellis County. We'll see what it turns up. I wish you all good luck in getting to the bottom of all of this. Are we done?"

"I think so. We appreciate Your Honor being willing to do this off the record."

"Okay. Well, let's all go back out in the courtroom, and I want to make a record that the trial will be continued for sixty days—subject to further orders if that's not going to be enough time. I will also put on the record that you all will be pursuing certain discovery aimed at learning more about DB Biocontainment."

With that, the chambers meeting was concluded.

Five minutes later, Judge Lassiter entered the courtroom.

"All rise."

"Please be seated."

As Judge Lassiter started to announce into the record the game plan for continuing the trial and letting the parties engage in discovery efforts, she looked toward the back of the courtroom and noticed that Dr. Nilsson was gone.

Chapter Twenty-Five

Max Finally Calls Back.

Late Thursday afternoon, after the bizarre revelations from the BASA case attorneys, Avery headed over to the Four Seasons Fitness Center to decompress with a quiet workout. She felt guilty, going alone. She loved to work out with her buddy Judge Maria Ramos at the courthouse gym. But today, she needed some alone time to process what might be happening in BASA. She was glad that the U.S. Trustee had been involved in the off-the-record discussion. It was entirely possible that a criminal referral was going to be necessary, if transactions between BASA and an insider entity had not been disclosed. Who knows what else Dmitry Basayev might have concealed from his investors? Hopefully, the lawyers were going to find out soon. This all felt so bizarre.

Avery climbed onto her favorite treadmill located at the end of a row of treadmills in the fitness center, where she could look out of a window at lush, manicured greenery and magnolias. She fiddled with the video screen on the treadmill and selected a walking trail video that would take the user through *Marienplatz* in Munich during Oktoberfest. It seemed like a good distraction. In a few moments, before Avery had even broken a sweat, one of the attendants walked by with a tray full of neatly rolled, cold, cherry water-infused, plush hand towels and, with silver tongs, handed a hand towel to her. Avery loved the service at this place. In a few moments, she would walk over to the refreshment bar and choose between cold water, room temperature water, water with lemon, or electrolyte-infused water. Maybe grab an orange, an apple, or an energy bar. Then she would go out to one of the three pristine swimming pools, where one should never even dream of going to retrieve a towel for oneself—it is the cabana man's job to rush a couple of thick towels, embossed with the Four Seasons logo, to you within seconds of your arrival poolside. Of course, then you are quickly offered an alcoholic beverage. Maybe later, Avery would hang out in the sauna or see if she could reserve some time in the spa. This was one of Avery's most ridiculous indulgences in her harried life. But it was not her demon. Her work was her demon. She never could quite pull herself away from it.

As Avery treadmilled through *Marienplatz*, passing happy revelers partaking in Bavarian beer, pretzels, and oompah bands, she heard her cell phone ring. She had forgotten to put it on the do-not-disturb mode. She could see that it was Max finally calling back. She stopped the treadmill and answered the phone.

"Max, you know that I could absolutely scream at you right now for going silent on me again, except that I am at the Four Seasons Fitness Center working out, and I don't want the people around me to think that I am a self-absorbed cell phone nerd."

An older man on the treadmill next to Avery looked at her as though she might, indeed, be a self-absorbed cell phone nerd.

"Avery, it's only been like two-and-a-half days!"

"Is that all?"

"I think. Weren't we talking on Tuesday morning?"

"Yes, I guess so."

"Well do you want to get to a quiet spot so we can chat?"

"I am walking out to the pool right now. I'll find a quiet spot. Go ahead and talk. Are you still in Hidalgo?"

"No, I am now in the Cancun area."

"Cabo. Hidalgo. The Yucatan Peninsula. It's like the Max Lassiter Tour de Mexico. I still don't get all of this."

"Well, I am about to explain in a little more detail what's been going on with my investigation down here. And then we will talk about the voicemail you got from Malta."

"Ah ha, so, you agree that it was someone calling from Malta? Richard Braden? You think he is alive? He's living over there and called me?"

"Yes, I'm afraid I do think that."

"Oh God. I'm not sure I am ready for this."

"Maybe you should order a glass of Cloudy Bay from one of the attendants."

"Oh, you better believe I am. I am waving one down right now."

"Okay, good. By the way, everything good with Heath and Julia?"

"Yep. They're just up to their usual activities. Nothing new. Julia says Heath has a girlfriend back at school, but he's saying nothing to me. Jake and Finley are enjoying the good life, spoiled as ever. Finley got stuck in the dog door again this morning, but he's getting more adept at slivering out."

"Okay. Well, I'll text the kids later."

"Okay. My wine just arrived. Tell me what's going on down there and your Malta theories."

"Well, the two topics are more interrelated than you might think."

"Your investigation of Cade Graham and Malta are

more interrelated than I might think? I don't think they are interrelated at all. What does that mean?"

"Well, remember how I was sharing with you on Tuesday how Cade Graham was into this life insurance settlements business, through one of his hedge funds? And a lot of the individuals who were the insureds on those life insurance policies had started dying suddenly? And many of them lived at a retirement community on the Yucatan Peninsula that Graham and a Mexican crime cartel essentially co-own, through an elaborate offshore business structure?"

"Yep. I remember all of that. How could I forget, Max?"

"Well, as it turns out, there is this fellow in Mexico that goes by the name of Enos that seems to have a connection to all of this. Down here, Enos is referred to as a spikey-haired gringo—probably in his early thirties. We have lots of videos from CCTVs of a fellow fitting that description, some of which were pulled from the retirement community cameras. Enos has also been seen on video cameras outside various businesses when Cade Graham was seen, and it just so happens that there is a site on the Dark Web called Enos.onion that advertises lots of illegal services including pseudocide. The site advertises every black-market service imaginable, including hit men for hire, hackers for hire, deep fakes, money and bitcoin laundering, shady investment opportunities, insider trading tips. Basically, any illicit thing that one could think of is advertised on Enos.onion."

"So you think this fellow Enos was hired to stage Cade Graham's death or what?"

"Well, yes, but it might go much, much deeper than that. Like I said earlier, we believe Enos is into all kinds of bad stuff."

"I'm trying to understand where this is headed, Max."

"Well let me cut to the chase. This Enos dude is connected to the *Los Chupas* cartel."

"That's not the name of the cartel you mentioned the

other day that has a connection to *Isla Valladolid*. You said something like the *Uhura* cartel the other day." Avery sipped her wine

"*Oscuro* not *Uhura*. *Uhura* was a female character in *Star Trek*."

"Oh, yeah. Whatever. Did I ever tell you I once met the actress who played Uhura? It was in a ladies' restroom at a black-tie political event out in Sacramento when I was practicing law?"

"You met Zoe Saldana?"

"No, no. I meant the original actress from the original series. I forget her name. She was very beautiful and polite."

"Why are we talking about this, Avery?"

"I don't know. Go on."

"There appear to be two crime cartels involved in all of this, Avery. *Oscuro,* which owns a controlling interest in the REIT that owns *Isla Valladolid*. It's headed up by a guy named Mateo Guerrero. And then there is the *Los Chupas* cartel that is headed up by a guy named Nicolas Samaniego. We are trying to figure out now whether Graham is or was playing ball with both rival gangs, without either one of them knowing it. We think he probably has been. The two gangs are rivals. There is no way that they would tolerate Graham doing business with both at the same time."

"This is nuts. Do you think maybe Graham really is dead? Maybe one of the cartels got wind of his two-timing ways and killed him?"

"Not sure. Maybe. But I need to tell you something about this dude Enos."

"Okay. What?"

"I think Enos is Marcus Braden."

Avery gasped and almost dropped her glass of Cloudy Bay. She cautiously put her drink down on the table beside her lawn chair.

"Max, what is going on? This cannot possibly be a coincidence! How is it that your investigation for Premier Mutual just happened to lead you to Marcus Braden? And what do you mean you *think* Enos is Marcus Braden?"

"Avery, please do not get mad at me but, the truth is, I have been spending a lot of time the past two years doing internet research, looking for the Braden boys. Regarding Richard in Malta, it's been nothing but dead ends so far. But, regarding Marcus, I have gone from having some strong leads and suspicions, to having near certainty that this guy Enos is Marcus.

"There is a group of retired law enforcement officers that have been working with me, using a gallery of pictures that we assembled of Marcus from the bombing in Austin, from his mug shot, and from all the pictures the FBI retrieved from Matt Braden's computer when executing the search warrant at his Pluto Street house in Austin. We have been using this gallery of photos to scan data bases of CCTV videos and social media and whatnot in Mexico, using facial recognition programs. I have a couple of friends in the DEA working down here with connections to the Mexican intelligence agency, and they have been tapping into its facial recognition platform regularly as well. Eventually, this blond, spikey haired, thirty-something-year-old guy, who looked as though he might be Caucasian, kept popping up as a possible match to Marcus Braden's photos. He has shown up in a dozen or so CCTV photos in Baja and, more recently, Yucatan, including at *Isla Valladolid*. We have seen the guy getting into cars and have captured the license plates on them and have discovered that all of the vehicles are owned by the same individual, Nicolas Samaniego— who happens to be the leader of the up-and-coming *Los Chupas* cartel. One thing led to another after that. My DEA buddy told me that DEA and local Mexican authorities were monitoring a site on the Dark Web called Enos.onion. They thought it might be a hub for *Los Chupas*. And word on the street was that there was a blond gringo who had some prominent role in *Los Chupas*. They call him the CFO. The further rumors were that this blond gringo was spearheading *Los Chupas*'s foray into the gasoline pipeline puncturing business. That's why I was in Hidalgo the other day. DEA and Mexican intelligence got a tip that *Los Chupas* might be hitting a pipeline in the area. I was trying to find Enos—Marcus."

"You were there when that explosion happened, and all those people were killed? You think Marcus Braden did that? Oh my God!"

"Yes, I'm afraid so. Dave Carrillo and I both were there."

"Max, I am not sure that I am connecting all the dots here and understanding how this has ended up intersecting with Cade Graham and Premier Mutual?"

"Well, my buddy Joe Meno at Premier Mutual has been aware all along of my internet and video searches for Marcus Braden. He had heard my working theories about this Enos dude. He knew that I was working an angle that Enos might have some sort of a connection to or relationship to someone at *Isla Valladolid* down in Yucatan because our facial recognition platforms had found several hits to Enos there and at nearby businesses."

"So, I guess your fishing trips down there in recent months weren't really fishing trips?"

"Well, I did fish some. Deep sea fishing and Enos fishing, too."

"Good God."

"So, Joe Meno calls me one afternoon last January and says, 'Max, you aren't going to believe this. I've been asked to put together a team to investigate what Premier Mutual thinks is a pseudocide of this supposedly dead hedge fund manager, Cade Graham, and Graham happens to own properties in Mexico, including being the controlling owner of *Isla Valladolid.*' Meno knew I believed I had been spotting Marcus Braden there. Moreover, Premier Mutual thought there was some funny business going on regarding residents who sold life insurance policies to Graham's hedge fund and then died soon after they did. Meno was like, 'what are the odds? This assignment has your name written all over it.'"

"Holy Mother of God. So, basically, you are down there looking for Cade Graham and also looking for Marcus Braden at the same time, and you think there might be a connection between the two?"

"Yep."

"I mean, you definitely think there is a connection between them. Maybe Enos just happens to know someone staying at *Isla Valladolid*? Maybe Marcus has tracked down that New Jersey priest who supposedly molested him, Father Iggy. Maybe he is staying there now. Didn't that priest supposedly go down to Mexico after being defrocked, to be a hermit?"

"Well, now that's an interesting idea, but we don't have any Father Iggy connection. We are pretty certain that somehow Enos and Cade Graham have connected with each other. We have seen videos of them both going into a cantina in Ensenada on two different days, around the same time, and then each leaving within a couple of minutes of each other. We are pretty sure that they were meeting there together. Maybe Cade hired Enos to stage a pseudocide for him and then it turned into something else. That's our working theory right now."

"Max, what are you going to do if you find Enos and it does turn out to be Marcus Braden?"

"Why are you asking? Are you worried that I won't show appropriate restraint?"

"Should I be, *Mad Max*?"

"Hey, I've got the Swiss Army Knife working on this project with me. It's probably him that you should worry about exercising appropriate restraint."

"Okay, we haven't talked about the phone voicemail. You agree it sounded like Malta in the background?"

"Yep. I recognized the word 'bongu' and the church bells and cat meows. That's Balluta Bay at St. Julian's, Malta, all right."

"You think Richard Braden is alive and living there?

Tweaking with me every now and then?"

"Afraid I do. But my buddies and I have not had the same luck tracking him down as we have with Marcus. Malta is a whole different ball game. But my gut tells me that Marcus—Enos—who advertises money laundering and Bitcoin transactions as among his specialties—is laundering money using Richard as a helper. As much as you love Malta, financial crimes like money laundering and Bitcoin shenanigans run rampant over there. If we can get to Enos, we will get to Richard. I promise."

Avery and Max wrapped up the call, and Avery sat in her lawn chair motionless for a moment. Was this really happening? When Avery became a judge, her new catch phrase had become "less drama, more momma." Her days of being a big firm lawyer had worn her out—always a client in the midst of a financial catastrophe who needed talking off a ledge; phone calls late at night; emails in the middle of the night; someone wanting a TRO first thing in the morning; someone needing you to fly to the east coast or the west coast or overseas even. A child looking at you with a forlorn, abandoned look on his or her face as you pulled out of the driveway—not knowing if you would make it home for the track meet or dance recital. Life as a judge was going to be a pleasant return to some normalcy. Hah!

Chapter Twenty-Six

The Tangled Web Gets More Tangled.

Avery left the Four Seasons about a half hour after her phone call with Max in a somber mood. What were the odds that Max's search for Cade Graham had intersected with Marcus Braden? How could Max have been secretly searching for Marcus all these months on the internet without telling Avery? Should she be upset with him? Avery's head was abuzz.

When she got home, her Cavalier puppies, Baxter Squared, were the only ones there. They greeted her with happy, panting exuberance, as usual. Baba Jo had gone with Julia shopping at a nearby mall and Heath was at a movie with friends. Avery was relieved to have some alone time. But even when Avery was alone in their house, she never felt alone. Thanks to Mad Max's overzealous approach to home security, the home felt like it had been taken over by the HAL 9000. The house beeped, chimed, and sang different codes constantly—not just when doors and windows opened and closed, but when laundry was finished, meals were done, when it was time to feed the pets, depart to activities, *etc.* Alexa was ubiquitous—upstairs, downstairs, in the basement and in the garage. Avery tolerated the over-the-top "smart house" because it made Max feel like the family was safer.

Avery decided to shower and then jump onto her computer and do some work. She was too anxious to settle down for a while. After showering, she made herself a plate of sourdough bread and sliced tomatoes, mozzarella, balsamic vinaigrette, and olive oil, and a cup of chamomile tea, spiked with a shot of gin and honey. Avery had gotten her favorite bone china out for her snack—the sage green, gold, and white set that her father had brought her mother back from Japan when he had been deployed there while in the Navy. It made no sense that she would—she just felt like pampering herself that way at the moment. The china had as much of a calming effect on her as the chamomile.

Avery went with her snack, tea, and laptop out on the back patio with Jake and Finley following close behind her. She told Alexa to play some Sting music. She then decided to jump on the court's PACER system and see if anything new had been filed on the BASA docket. Maybe it would show proof of service by now for the subpoenas that the Robot had announced he would be serving on Dr. Nilsson and possibly on other folks at the Ellis County tunnel. Maybe there'd even be responses to the subpoenas. Nothing showed up. Avery then decided to go back and look at the original bankruptcy paperwork for the BASA case to see if there was any mention of Dr. Nilsson anywhere. Avery remained highly curious as to what Nilsson's connection to BASA or to DB Biocontainment might be. Nothing turned up anywhere. Avery then started scrolling through the list of creditors and investors shown in the case records. Suddenly, Avery's eyes hit upon something. On the list of unsecured creditors of BASA were the names *"Mateo Guerrero Family Trust #1," "Mateo Guerrero Family Trust #2,"* and *"Mateo Guerrero Family Trust #3"*—all showing an address in Mexico City and reflecting that these trusts were owed millions of dollars by BASA, based on claims arising out of credit default swaps. Wasn't Mateo Guerrero the name Max mentioned as the leader of *Oscuro*?

Avery grabbed her cell phone and began texting Max. "Are you up? What did you say is the name of the leader of the *Oscuro* cartel that is involved with Cade Graham's *Isla Valladolid* property?"

Max replied in a couple of minutes. "Mateo Guerrero. Why do you ask?"

"Do you think that's a common name in Mexico?"

"Idk. Why these questions?"

"I discovered in one of my cases that there are some Mateo Guerrero family trusts listed as investors. These trusts are owed millions of dollars."

"Hmmm. Well, how many Mateo Guerreros would be rich enough to invest millions of dollars into a U.S. company?"

"Exactly."

"Well, maybe Cade Graham has gotten Guerrero involved in investing in all kinds of other things, not just *Isla Valladolid*. I guess it wouldn't be that much of a stretch to think he might have steered Guerrero or his family members to other investments. Graham was a hedge fund manager, after all. Or the investment might have no connection to Graham. Guerrero and his family are probably well diversified. Even crime families know to diversify their investments, I guess. LOL."

"I suppose... Well, anyway, it doesn't make me feel warm and fuzzy that a Mexican drug cartel is somehow connected to my Ponzi scheme case—or maybe it's not a Ponzi scheme case. Long story."

"????"

Avery sipped her hot toddy concoction and swirled her bread around in the vinaigrette. She kept scrolling through the list of investors. She didn't see Cade Graham—she thought she would double check that angle for grins.

Nothing. In fact, she saw no other names that surprised her.

Avery's cell phone pinged again. "Hello? Anything else?"

"Oh sorry. No, I guess that's it for now. Ttyl."

Avery had given up finding anything else noteworthy on the BASA court docket. Just as she was about to shut her laptop down for the night, she decided to look on the docket of Judge Hall's DRI-MED Chapter 11 case. She first found a reference to a contract with DB Biocontainment, LLC—Project Grotto; probably the one that Muttonchop Man and the other lawyers had mentioned to her in court recently. Avery decided to dig deeper and looked at the list of DRI-MAED's assets. To her surprise, she found another reference to DB Biocontainment in the listing of accounts receivable owing to DRI-MED. To Avery's shock, an entry read as follows: *Account Debtor: DB Biocontainment, LLC (re: Isla Valladolid). Contact: Dr. Astrid Nilsson,* followed by a P.O Box address in Ellis County, Texas. The account receivable was for $500,000.

Just then, the patio door abruptly opened, and Heath came bounding out in his swim trunks followed by three of his old friends he had reconnected with while home for the summer.

"Hey, Mom. You don't mind if we swim do you?"

Avery darted a glance at her son. She looked pallid and shaken.

"You okay, Mom?"

"Sure. Why, Heath?"

"You have that look in your eyes like you sometimes get?"

"What look?"

"Like that look you sometimes get right before you say, 'quick, someone bring me a hot towel for my neck and some cucumbers for my eyes.'"

"OMG, Heath! I don't ever say that! I mean... I don't think I do... Do I?"

Heath laughed. "I just mean you look really stressed,

Mom. Almost scared."

"I'm okay, Sweetheart. Sure, y'all can swim. Just don't make too much noise. It's getting late. I don't want the neighbors to complain."

Avery grabbed her laptop, phone, cup, and plate and walked inside the house. The dogs stayed outside with Heath and the impromptu swim party. They would enjoy having all the petting and attention that Heath's friends would give them.

Avery went into the kitchen, loaded up the dishwasher, then crawled into bed, and texted Max.

"The plot thickens. You're not going to believe what I just ran across from a case pending in Judge Hall's court. Call me if you can. It's too involved to text it."

"On the phone with Joe Meno right now. Can I call you back?"

Avery sighed. "I guess it can wait until tomorrow. Going to bed."

"Sweet dreams."

"Hah. My dreams are like something out of a Stanley Kubrick movie these days."

"What?"

"Nothing. Just being weird, I guess. Good night."

Chapter Twenty-Seven

The Best and Worst of Video Court.

"OMG Judge! Are you going to say anything about the cat?" Millicent reached across the bench and handed Judge Lassiter a sheet of paper with that burning question messily scribbled on it.

On Friday morning, after the previous day's series of bombshells—first in court from the BASA lawyers, then Max's phone revelations about his search for Marcus Braden in Mexico, then Avery's late night PACER discoveries in both the BASA and DRI-MED cases—Avery was having a hearing in a routine business case. Actually, it was "routine" case but rather annoying. Avery referred to it as her "colonoscopy case" with Millicent and Annalise. That meant that it was one of those cases where Avery would rather go have a colonoscopy than to sit through the parties' constant bickering. Avery didn't really mean that, but she had gotten that expression from her favorite mentor judge who recently passed away.

The hearing today was virtual with all the lawyers and witnesses appearing by *Zoom* video, rather than physically in the courtroom. Judge Lassiter, Millicent, and the court reporter were the only human beings that were present in the courtroom. While video court was more and more common these days—at least in civil business matters—Judge Lassiter preferred to do her video hearings with her staff physically in the courtroom, instead of from home, for fear that her dogs Jake and Finley might decide to bark at inappropriate times or make surprise appearances—which would obviously detract from the dignity of it being a court proceeding. She had taken Jake and Finley up to the courthouse before, but they could not behave quite as well as good old Baxter. Thus, she certainly didn't trust them to behave if she tried conducting court from home.

On the contrary, certain lawyers did not worry so much about their pets making cameo appearances during video court hearings. Millicent's note was a reference to a certain lawyer, Sue More (aptly named), whose black and white tuxedo cat was a few feet behind the lawyer, scratching noisily on a tall burlap-covered post. Ms. More had been a sex therapist before going to law school—something that Millicent thought absolutely hysterical and loved to share with everyone who did not know, frequently asking whether it might have been good practice for ultimately being a lawyer (whatever that meant). On this day, Ms. More was making a brilliant argument, but it was hard to pay attention to anything else as she spoke, except for the furiously scratching cat.

Ever since the courts had embraced *Zoom*, Millicent and Judge Lassiter had begun playing an irresistibly fun game of commenting on the often-unusual backgrounds that they would regularly see behind lawyers who were working from home. Today the scratching cat was taking the lead for the most entertaining background so far. The cat narrowly edged ahead of another lawyer, Frank Neiman, who chose to do the video hearing today from his laundry room, complete with a stack of folded towels and underwear behind him. What do people think when they make a choice like this?

Avery scribbled a note back to Millicent. "Millicent, you know that I am an animal lover. So, no, I am not going to say anything to Sue More about her cat. I'm sort of enjoying it. It's like a skinny version of my daughter's cat, Brimley. And it's far better than looking at Mr. Mannheim's background. He looks like he is in a Russian hostage video." The lawyer to whom Judge Lassiter referred, Artie Mannheim (the super-dork with the *Metallica* ring tone on his cell phone), sat near a chalky gray wall. His tie hung askew, and his hair looked uncombed.

"What about Jonathan Tate? With that bright sunny window behind him his face is all dark and shadowed, like he is in a witness protection program. Why don't people practice before they do their video participation? Geez." Millicent handed this message up to Avery.

Suddenly a second cat—an orange tabby—entered the background of the first lawyer, Sue More, and began competing for space on the scratching post. The cats soon began doing what cats do—hissing and meowing and batting at each other. The burlap scratching post was careening back and forth about to topple. Finally, Judge Lassiter said something.

"Ms. More, perhaps you should usher your cats to another room. It's starting to become distracting."

"Your Honor, it's okay. I've basically finished my argument. I'll yield the floor to Mr. Mannheim now." With that, Ms. More, with a satisfied expression on her face, scooped up the orange cat and put it in her lap.

Artie Mannheim's most used tactic was to make *ad hominem* attacks on his opponents when he sensed he was losing. And today he was most definitely losing. Despite his overall awkwardness, he had a pleasant, velvety voice that made his verbal barbs somehow more tolerable. Avery wondered if the Mannheim Steamroller (Avery's own nickname for the lawyer) would concoct an argument that Ms. More's cats were part of a diversionary tactic or perhaps an attempt to curry favor with the judge.

The matter at issue today involved a multi-party dispute over whom was the owner of certain crude oil stored in some storage tanks near the Gulf of Mexico, near Port Arthur, Texas. Mr. Mannheim cleared his throat when it was his turn to talk and softly announced he had a problem.

"Here we go," Millicent whispered.

Mr. Mannheim's problem was an unexpected one. His problem was that he had decided he needed to call his client representative as an impeachment witness today, but his client had just become indisposed. Specifically, his client— Henry Hiller, the CEO of a large energy equipment company—had just learned that one of his offshore jackup barges, with thirty men onboard, had been hijacked overnight by Somali pirates near the horn of Africa. The client was on the phone with the U.S. State Department and the families of the men and would probably be tied up for an unknown length of time. Mr. Mannheim asked for a brief continuance.

"I object, Your Honor. This is an outrage. An utter fabrication. I don't believe a word of this. I can't see any smoke rising around Mr. Mannheim, but I do believe that his pants must be on fire. Moreover, I do not know what Mr. Mannheim's client could possibly say that is relevant to this dispute today." These words were spoken by Mr. Neiman, the lawyer *Zooming* from his laundry room. As Mr. Neiman spoke, he backed his chair into the washing machine behind him and, in the process, knocked over a large mug of coffee.

"Clean up on Aisle five," Millicent whispered under her breath.

The Mannheim Steamroller's pale face turned bright red. He retorted, "Your Honor, I am highly offended by Mr. Neiman's scurrilous accusation that I or my client have lied. I urge you all to do a *Google* search right now of 'Somali pirates and Hiller Energy Equipment' and this will be corroborated. It's all over the news right now. May God have mercy on your soul, Mr. Neiman, for suggesting that I would fabricate such a story—considering that thirty men's lives are hanging in the balance right now as I speak."

Judge Lassiter tried not to roll her eyes. The Mannheim Steamroller's propensity for histrionics and hyperbole was now on full display. While she understood his reaction to being called a liar, and certainly felt bad for the hijacked men and their nervous boss, she doubted that the capturing by Somali pirates was going to last very long on a boat with thirty Texas oil rig workers onboard. The rig workers, no doubt, would all have packed their own firearms, whether or not firearms were allowed in international waters. The hijacking incident would probably be over in less than 20 minutes.

Ms. More spoke up, now with the previously-scratching cats on the credenza right beside her, silently glaring into the camera, as if they were now fully engaged in the hearing. "Judge, I just did a *Google* search. Mr. Mannheim is telling the truth. It's all over the news. I just saw an interview with Mr. Hiller on CNN. I agree to the continuance."

Ms. More's temporary fit of reasonableness was not shared by Mr. Neiman. "Your Honor, I still don't understand why Mr. Hiller's testimony is relevant and I will not agree to any continuance." Mr. Neiman chimed.

Mr. Mannheim's temples bulged, and his nostrils flared. "Your Honor, my client's testimony is relevant and necessary because Mr. Neiman's client impugned his character earlier. He said that my client has ulterior motives in this dispute—that what he really wants is to buy your client's company out of bankruptcy, and that he is litigating this dispute over the stored oil just to drive up litigation fees, so that your client will be forced to liquidate his company. In fact, my client has made no secret that he is interested in buying the company, but your client is breaching his fiduciary duties and hiding my client's generous offers from the creditor body in this case, against their best interests."

"What?" Ms. More—who represented a big bank in the case who was owed millions—cried out loudly, causing her cats to scatter in opposite directions.

Judge Lassiter sensed the hearing was on the verge of descending into chaos. "Look, let's cool breeze this. My afternoon is free if you all want to come back—assuming that Mr. Hiller's pirate crisis is under control by then. I sort of suspect it will be."

The lawyers looked at Judge Lassiter incredulously. She did not know why. Texas oil barge workers versus Somali pirates? It rarely lasted very long, and it usually did not go well for the pirates. "Why don't y'all come back at 2:30 and, meanwhile, you all should talk. Mr. Mannheim, please call my courtroom deputy and the other lawyers if Mr. Hiller cannot patch in to testify by 2:30. We are adjourned."

"All rise."

Avery exited the courtroom.

When Avery walked back in chambers, Annalise was standing at her desk waiting.

"Well, that hearing took a shambolic turn, wouldn't you say." Avery grinned at Annalise.

Annalise looked curiously back at her.

"Annalise, is something wrong?"

"I don't know. The FBI is here to see you. I seated them in your office. They said it was regarding a 'situation' they are investigating that might have a tie to one of your cases."

"Hmmm. One of my criminal referrals, you think?"

"Well, if it is, I don't know why they didn't just say so—you know, tell us the case name. I would have dug up any relevant case files for you if they had just told me."

"Well, no big deal. I'll find out soon enough. I mean, I guess I will. They are always cryptic when you talk to them. 'Need to know' basis and all that schtick."

"Well, better get in there."

Chapter Twenty-Eight

The FBI and Arkady Basayev.

Avery walked into her office and two FBI special agents both stood to attention and held out their hands to introduce themselves. They both flashed their badges and handed Avery their business cards. One of the agents was a bespeckled, bald white male with a giraffe-like stature and the other was an attractive black female with a layered pixie haircut who oozed professionalism. Both seemed more mature and seasoned than the ones who had worked on Avery's death threats a few years back.

"What brings you here, agents?"

The male agent spoke up. "Well, we are terribly sorry to show up here unannounced, but this is a fairly urgent matter, and we hope you can help."

"It involves one of my cases?"

"Maybe. We are not at all sure, but it is a theory that we want to run down."

"Okay. What can I tell you? Which case?"

"Well, let us first tell you what exactly we are investigating. It is the apparent homicide of an elderly man whose body was found in the park across the street from the courthouse a few days ago."

"That homeless man?"

"Well, it wasn't a homeless man. His name was Arkady Basayev. A seventy-five-year-old immigrant from Chechnya. A former well-known journalist in that country. Ever heard of him?"

"Did you say 'Basayev'? 'B... A... S... A... Y... E... V'?" Avery slowly spelled it out.

"Yes."

"Is he related to Dmitry Basayev from my BASA case?"

"Yes. He was his father. He came over to the U.S. apparently to be with Dmitry a few years ago. His last known address was in Atlanta, at an address the son used while he was a grad student at Emory. We aren't sure where he has been living the past few years or why his body would turn up here in Dallas—although we know Dmitry has obviously been in the Dallas area in recent times, since his company was apparently based just south of Dallas until recently. There are no public records turning up for Arkady Basayev here in Texas."

"Oh my God. This is so disturbing. I don't know what to make of it. Why is the FBI investigating this murder, by the way, instead of the Dallas PD?"

"We can't answer that question, Judge. I'm sorry."

"How was he killed?"

Both agents sat quietly and looked at each other. The female agent finally said, "That's still being investigated, Judge. There were some signs of trauma to various parts of his body, but that doesn't seem to have been what killed him?"

"Then how do you know he was murdered?"

"There are indications of poisoning, a tactic that could suggest a Russian connection, particularly when a Chechen is involved."

"Poisoning?"

The agents again sat in momentary silence and looked back at Avery without expression. "Judge, it's just one working theory. Initial toxicology reports turned up some polonium-210 in the old man's system. It's been used by the Russians on others. At any rate, it's not exactly something a normal person can put his or her hands on."

"Agents, I'm trying to process all this. Just so you are clear, Dmitry Basayev has essentially been missing himself, since putting his company, BASA, into bankruptcy a couple of years ago. The BASA Chapter 11 case was basically what we sometimes call a 'drive by filing'—meaning he put his company in bankruptcy, paid the court filing fee, and provided the necessary bankruptcy paperwork, and exited stage left—so that a bankruptcy trustee had to step in and take over the mess he left. There are plenty of angry creditors and investors of the company. Does the FBI also think Dmitry is dead? Because we have had some very strange developments recently in the BASA case—that to my knowledge have nothing to do with Russia—and Dmitry has been MIA for months?"

"What kind of strange developments?"

Avery hesitated. She didn't know whether to start with the publicly available information, the recent *in camera* chambers discussion, or her startling discovery on her laptop last night about the Mexican cartel connection.

"Well, where shall I begin?" With the Ponzi scheme that probably was not really a Ponzi scheme? Or Dmitry's secret company that apparently is doing some sort of business at the former super collider tunnel in Ellis County, Texas? Or the Mexican crime cartel that apparently is owed millions of dollars by Basayev's company?"

"You can't be serious."

"Oh, I'm serious as a heart attack. You better get your notepads or better yet, an audio recorder."

"Well, why don't you start with giving us the 30,000-

foot view, and then we will figure out where we should go from there."

For the next hour, Avery recapped the highlights of the BASA case. How, the young Chechen, Dmitry Basayev, the brilliant, handsome molecular biologist and computer scientist, had purported to the world that he invented some game-changing disinfectant technology that could be used in medical facilities and public spaces to rid them of super germs and all manner of infectious viruses and bacteria. How he raised almost a billion dollars from investors. How the disinfection invention had never quite come to fruition, and the investors were beginning to become suspicious that it was all a massive Ponzi scheme. How certain prominent, former directors of the company and one of the world's largest hedge funds (Toro Capital) were being sued over the debacle. How a labor union lawyer whose clients had invested in BASA had recently uncovered a secret company called DB Biocontainment, that was also owned by Dmitry Basayev, and it was apparently doing business of some sort as a tenant at the underground site formerly used by the U.S. government for the long-defunct super collider. How Judge Lassiter recently abated her trial against the former directors and Toro Capital, while the bankruptcy trustee and lawyers investigated what was going on with DB Biocontainment. How an eccentric, Nobel prize winning scientist, Dr. Astrid Nilsson, might be connected with all of this somehow. And, finally, Avery just realized last night that Mateo Guerrero, apparently associated with a Mexican crime cartel, is owed millions of dollars by BASA—although no lawyer in the case happened to mention that fact thus far.

The FBI agents stared blankly at Avery. Avery assumed that her rambling narrative might have drawn more of a reaction, even from two staid and sober feds.

"Well, you have given us plenty to think about. Until now, we thought that this was more than likely a Russian hit, but now it's suddenly more complicated."

A Russian hit? Avery was thinking silently to herself

that this would not be the first time that she had seen the FBI barking up the wrong tree, but they surely wouldn't pluck something like a Russian connection out of thin air. Or would they?

"Look, Judge, we can't say much, but just so you know, Arkady Basayev was a rather well-known Chechen journalist who often criticized the pro-Russian regime there. He chronicled human rights abuses and the Second Chechen War. He was most well-known for writing about an alleged mass poisoning of Chechen school children. He even won a Pulitzer Prize for his reporting. He immigrated to the U.S. shortly after that, after numerous acts of intimidation against him. Several of his fellow journalists there were murdered, likely at the direction of the Russian government."

"So, you're telling me that Putin ordered a hit against Dmitry Basayev's father? And it just so happens that they decided to execute the hit right in front of the Dallas federal courthouse?"

"We are not telling you that, Judge. It's just interesting—to say the least—that this fellow fled from his homeland for fear of retribution for exposing Russian and Chechen corruption, and now a decade or so later, he ends up murdered in the U.S. It is certainly an angle we must explore. But frankly your strange case puts an entirely new spin on this."

"Well, I remember precisely the morning they discovered the body. It was the day after it had been announced in court in my BASA case that the lawyers—the union lawyer in particular, a fellow named Harvey O'Malley—were starting to expect that there was something very weird going on with BASA. Something other than a Ponzi scheme. They had just discovered the secret company DB Biocontainment and the Ellis County tunnel thing. I don't know if that timing is somehow relevant to your investigation. I mean it was a bombshell really. And financial reporters were covering it all. It made the *Wall Street Journal* and *Bloomberg*."

The FBI agents stood. "Well, we have taken enough of your time, Judge. Thank you for all of this information. We will likely be in further touch."

Avery suspected that the FBI agents would not really be in touch with her. Avery stood and began escorting the agents towards the door.

"Oh wait. There's one more thing." One of the agents turned around and faced Avery. "There was a note folded up in Mr. Basayev's pocket. It had a Spanish name and an address. I wonder if this means anything to you. It said *Isla Valladolid* and then contained an address that was somewhere down in Yucatan. Also, there was something scribbled that looked like 'project ember.' Does that mean anything to you?"

"Oh God. Maybe. Can I get back with you? I need to do a little more research. There may be a connection to BASA."

"Sure. Take your time. This isn't going to be solved overnight."

The two agents quietly left.

Annalise and Millicent walked into Avery's office cautiously a few minutes after the agents left.

Millicent spoke up first, "Are we allowed to ask what that was all about? Was it about one of our cases?"

"I really have no idea. It was allegedly about the dead body found across the street recently. It was Dmitry Basayev's father."

Chapter Twenty-Nine

Can we talk, Judge Hall?

"Knock, knock?"

Avery had just strolled down to Judge Hall's chambers. The lawyers from her morning video hearing had called Avery's courtroom deputy and reported that they could not resume the hearing at 2:30 because Mr. Hiller, the CEO whose jack-up rigs were hijacked by Somali pirates, was still preoccupied. Apparently, the incident had swiftly ended, just as Avery predicted, with a swarm of rig workers taking out the Somali pirates with a hail of amazingly accurate gunfire. More than one hundred shots were fired against the four Somali pirates from a dozen different weapons. Government officials had more than a few questions. But all of Mr. Hiller's men and equipment were safe.

"Come on in. How is my favorite colleague?"

"That's what you call all of us!"

"Oh, only a few of you."

"Well, I am content to be in your club of favorites."

"It's a small club."

"It's a large club. You find good in all of us, whether we deserve it or not."

"Are you feeling down? You look a little stressed."

"Different from my usual stress?"

"Hah. Maybe."

"Well, I want to talk to you about the overlap in two of our cases. Remember, we were starting to talk about it the other day?"

"Sure. Do you think we should?"

"Well, I hesitated a lot. Trust me. But I am starting to think this is an exceptionally weird set of facts and we should talk and probably tell the lawyers in both cases that we talked."

"Hmm. You have me very curious."

"Oh, just wait. This is really weird."

"Most of your cases are really weird. We manipulate the computers in the Clerk's Office to make sure that you draw all the weird ones."

"You're hilarious. Seriously, I need your advice."

Judge Hall looked at Avery with a warm, friendly smile. Avery always said that Judge Hall had two facial expressions: his warm, friendly smile expression and his blank expression. His face did not ever express anger or other negative emotions. Avery envied his ability to keep his composure no matter what. Avery's genteel, late mother always tried to teach Avery a thing or two about hiding emotions. Some of that had rubbed off enough to make Avery a decent judge—although not nearly as decent as Judge Hall. Avery's mother once said to her, "It's quite a gift to suffer ignorance and politely smile back at what you are witnessing." Judge Hall had that gift.

"Well, here goes. Hold onto your seat." Avery started in cautiously. "Not only is there overlap in our two cases, BASA, Inc. and DRI-MED, but I am concerned that there might be overlap with something that Max is investigating down in Mexico?"

"Max? I thought he was in Mexico investigating the death of that playboy hedge fund manager, Cade Graham?"

"He is. And that investigation has grown extremely complicated. And now I am afraid that it might be converging with one or both of our cases. I am literally feeling like I might be heading for ethical thin ice."

"Okay. What are you saying? You sometimes get a little over-exercised with worry. No offense."

"Well, listen and decide."

"That's my job."

"So, for two years now, the lawyers, parties, and I have all been convinced that BASA was nothing more than a billion-dollar Ponzi scheme. The 'mother of all Ponzi schemes' we sometimes called it. Recall that Dmitry Basayev mysteriously disappeared shortly after the case was filed. Never a good sign for creditors when the perpetrator goes off the grid after running a Ponzi scheme. And the case has been mostly about suing people who might bear some responsibility for the fraud—the investment company, Toro Capital, that raised the majority of funds from investors, and two former directors who lent their *gravitas* to the company and should have known it was a fraud. But then the lawyers discover that Basayev had a side business, DB Biocontainment, LLC, that has significant assets and a ground lease at the former super collider site in Ellis County. DB Biocontainment seems to be a real operating company of some sort. And as you heard, some BASA funds were funneled through DB Biocontainment and were paid to DRI-MED, which is in Chapter 11 in your court."

"And the lawyers are trying to get to the bottom of that in my case, by taking discovery from DRI-MED to find out about those payments and what the contract called "Project Grotto" was."

"Right, I know. And you're probably going to tell me we should just be patient and wait for that process to play out."

"Now see. You don't need my advice. You always

know what I am going to say before I say it."

"Well, the plot thickens, Chief. Last night, I was up late looking at some of the original Bankruptcy Schedules filed in both of our two cases. In BASA, I happened to discover that some family trusts of Mateo Guerrero are owed money—millions of dollars—by BASA. Do you know who Mateo Guerrero is?"

"No. Tell me."

"He is the head of the *Oscuro* crime cartel in Mexico."

"Eww. That's kind of scary. Wonder how a Mexican crime cartel gets interested in investing in a Chechen scientist's Ponzi scheme?"

"Exactly. But there is more."

"Go on."

"In your DRI-MED case, I found a listing of accounts receivable, and it showed that DB Biocontainment owes DRI-MED $500,000 and the entry reads: *Account Debtor: DB Biocontainment, LLC (re: Isla Valladolid). Contact: Dr. Astrid Nilsson,* followed by a P.O Box address in Ellis County, Texas.

"I have heard of Dr. Nilsson, but I can't place it."

"Well, she is an eccentric Nobel Prize winning molecular biologist, originally from Sweden, who got fired from Emory University a while back, for being sort of whackadoodle in some of her theories. But more pertinent to this conversation, she has been showing up and sitting in the back of my courtroom in many of my BASA hearings and the lawyers think she has some sort of connection to Dmitry and the Ellis County tunnel. So, this would appear to confirm that."

"Okay. Well clearly there is some sort of overlap in our two cases that is either going to be a big deal or not. I'd say we just remain calm and see how this all plays out over the next few weeks, after the discovery has been completed."

"There is still more. The *Isla Valladolid* part is where this gets really weird."

"Okay. What do you think *Isla Valladolid* is a reference

to?"

"Well, I would have had no clue until the past few days. It turns out that *Isla Valladolid* is a bougie senior living retirement community near Cancun. Max has been investigating it as part of his search in the Cade Graham case. Cade Graham essentially co-owns *Isla Valladolid* with, guess who? Mateo Guerrero and other members of his *Oscuro* cartel."

"Holy cow. Now I understand why you are so stressed. So, you think that both my DRI-MED case and your BASA case not only have some overlap with Dmitry Basayev, but both cases might also have some Mexican crime cartel connection? And a connection to Cade Graham, too? Have you talked to Max about these discoveries?"

"Not too much. I have only just started to. I texted him last night about my Guerrero discovery. I thought might just be a strange coincidence and even wondered if it could be a different Mateo Guerrero. But I haven't told him about the reference to *Isla Valladolid* in your DRI-MED case. Do you think I should tell him? Are the ethical lines getting blurry here?"

"Well, I don't think they are yet. I still just think we should wait and see what we learn from the lawyers' discovery. And if you start hearing some extra-judicial information from Max that you think is relevant to your or my case, I guess we will have to bring in the lawyers and tell them what you and I have inadvertently learned from outside sources."

"Okay. Well, I know you have court in a few minutes. I'll let you get ready. Thanks."

"Never a dull moment around here, huh?"

"Sometimes I long for a dull day. Sometimes I want to go back to being the kid doing research in the library."

"That kid doesn't exist anymore."

Chapter Thirty

Max and Dave Go to Hussong's Cantina.

"Time to talk?"

After her visit with Judge Hall, Avery was sitting in her chambers and realized that she had never finished her text conversation with Max from the previous night. And, of course, now she wanted to tell him about the FBI visit this morning.

Max texted back in about five minutes. "Sorry, Avery. Dave and I are doing some intelligence gathering. Can I call you later? Or just text me if you need to."

"Where are y'all intelligence gathering?"

"Well, actually at a bar. LOL."

"It's starting to seem like you and Dave spend a lot of time in bars."

"We are at Hussong's Cantina in Ensenada in Baja. Does that ring a bell with you?"

"Uh, yeah. The Rosarito Bike Ride, circa 1999. As I recall, you and your riding buddies apparently had a little too much tequila there after the ride. I am surprised that they will let you back inside."

"Very funny. I guess enough time has passed. Either that, or I look like a harmless old man now. Anyway, we are tracking down a lead. There have been a few CCTV facial recognition hits here for Cade Graham and Enos. Going to see if anybody will tell us anything."

"Okay. Well, I wanted to tell you about what I discovered last night when going through the files in Judge Hall's Chapter 11 case of a company called DRI-MED. I found a listing for a $500,000 account receivable owed by a company related to one of my companies in bankruptcy (long story) and it was described like this: "*Account Debtor: DB Biocontainment, LLC (re: Isla Valladolid). Contact: Dr. Astrid Nilsson,*" followed by a P.O Box address in Ellis County, Texas."

"Hmm. *Isla Valladolid*?"

"Yes. DRI-MED is a helicopter company that does medical evacuations, among other things."

"So you think that this DRI-MED company has evacuated some patients maybe from the same *Isla Valladolid* that I am investigating down here? I mean can you tell for sure it's the same *Isla Valladolid*?"

"Well, first, last night you told me that maybe the Mateo Guerrero that is owed money in my BASA case might not be the same guy that heads up *Oscuro*."

"True. It could be a common name in Mexico."

"Well, now you are asking me if I think it is the same *Isla Valladolid* in Judge Hall's case as the one you are investigating that, by the way, *Oscuro* happens to partially own? And Judge Hall and I have already recently learned that there are some unrelated connections between my BASA case and his DRI-MED case that the lawyers are investigating."

"Well, I agree that maybe this is all too crazy to be a coincidence. But of everything you said, here's what really caught my attention. $500,000 worth of medical evacuations out of *Isla Valladolid*? That's a lot of helicopter trips, don't you think?"

"Yes. And?"

"We really should stop texting about this. I can't believe I let it go on this long. I mean, our communications on our phones should be secure but..."

"Okay. Well, I had something else weird to tell you about—a visit I got from the FBI today, but it can wait. But please call when you can."

"Will do. Love to you and the kids."

Max looked at Dave and then took a sip of his drink. "Remind me later, Dave, to show you the text conversation that I just had with my wife. I think something really weird is happening in one of her cases that actually might have some connection with *Isla Valladolid* and might even be relevant to all the recent sick and dying people there in recent months. I want to brainstorm with you about it, but right now we have people to interrogate."

"Max, I've got news for you. Nobody here wants to talk to us. We have already showed Cade's and Enos's picture to everybody who works here, and no one says they recognize them."

"But we haven't asked anyone about the kid. The one who is always showing up in so many pictures with Enos. The one they call the altar boy."

"*Monaguillo*."

"God, I love it when you speak Spanish."

Max had pulled up on his cell phone the clearest picture he could find of the young, well dressed teenaged boy that had shown up so often on CCTV accompanying Enos. He texted the picture to Dave. "Why don't you go up to the bar and ask the bartender and some of the regulars if they have seen him around here and maybe know who he is. Come on. Your Spanish is so much better than mine, Dave. You're the Swiss Army Knife. I know you can do it."

Dave muttered something in Spanish and headed toward the bar. He was gone several minutes, talking to different workers and patrons. As he did, Max texted Avery again.

"Refresh my memory on something. Remember the priest who molested the Braden brothers—his name was Father Iggy; right? You mentioned him recently when we were talking about why Enos might have been going in and out of *Isla Valladolid*. You said maybe Father Iggy or someone else that Marcus knows might live there. I am not sure if you were cracking a joke or not. Anyway, didn't we hear that maybe the Catholic Diocese in New Jersey had sent him down to Mexico after his pedophilia was exposed? To take refuge in a monastery maybe, where he would be a monk or hermit?"

A few moments passed. Max knew Avery would have the answer. She had an unnervingly accurate memory.

"Yes, his name was Father Iggy, and that's my exact memory of what we heard happened. Give me a minute. I'll think of the name of the monastery. I think it was in Guadalajara maybe."

"Ugh. Guadalajara is nowhere close to where we are right now." As Max waited for Avery to text back, Max began *Googling* different Catholic parishes, dioceses, schools, monasteries, and hermitages in surrounding areas. It was a very large list. None of them rang a bell with him.

Avery texted back in a few moments. "I am having trouble remembering. In fact, I actually don't know if we ever heard the exact place. Do you want me to see if I can find out? Not sure where I would begin."

"Well, don't worry about it for now."

"Why do you ask?"

"Just a hunch I am considering. I'll get back with you on it. Gtg."

Dave was approaching the table with a big grin on his face.

"Why are you grinning? Did a pretty woman try to pick

you up?"

"Nope. You know I don't have time for that. Besides, pretty women trying to pick me up is a daily event in my life. Not sure if it's my rugged good looks or my smoldering, yet restrained, personality."

"Good God. Whatever. Did you learn anything, Jose Sauve?"

"Yep. Three people told me that they see the altar boy around now and then. Most of them said they don't know his name, but they know people call him *Monaguillo;* and they say he seems to be an errand boy for a gringo with blond spikey hair. They didn't really want to say anything else. They say *Los Chupas* is very bad news. Worse than the *Zetas*. But they say the boy is a sweet kid and shouldn't be getting mixed up with *Los Chupas*."

"What did you mean that *most* of them said they don't know his name?"

"Well, one of the waitresses overheard me talking to the bartender and said she thinks the altar boy was the only child of a couple named Eduardo and Valeria Flores, who, unfortunately, died in a car wreck a couple of years ago. She said she had seen him and heard this story about him being an altar boy at a parish a few miles south of here called *Santa Teresa of Los Andes*. He apparently lived in an orphanage adjacent to the parish for a while."

"Holy shit. That sounds familiar."

"What sounds familiar?"

"Marcus Braden's father was killed in a car wreck. His mother committed suicide a few years later. He was raised in a Catholic orphanage after that."

"Wow. And now Marcus is hanging out with a kid with an almost identical life story? What are the odds of that happening?"

"I want to go down there. Tonight. Right now."

"Go down where?"

"*Santa Teresa of Los Andes*."

"Slow down. What do you think that's going to

accomplish?"

"I don't know. I just have a gut feel on this one. A very strong hunch. Work with me."

"Okay. Let's roll. Two cars or one?"

"Let's go together in that wonderful Isuzu Trooper that Premier Mutual has provided to me."

"Ugh. I hope you have cleaned it out since the last time I rode with you."

Chapter Thirty-One

Santa Teresa of Los Andes.

It was a somewhat cool and dry night for July. There was a calm, hard, radiant moon, whose beauty betrayed what was about to unfold.

Max and Dave had collaborated on a good story to use with the priest in charge at the parish, which was roughly forty miles south of Ensenada. First, Dave had called some of his local law enforcement buddies with DEA and asked them to check with some of their Mexican law enforcement contacts and see if they could retrieve any information about a deadly car accident in the last two-three years that had involved a couple named Eduardo and Valeria Flores. They hit the jackpot and learned that there was such a wreck in Rosarito some twenty-seven months prior, and the couple had been driving a Suzuki Aerio 2015 model. Dave and Max, with their Premier Mutual Insurance Company business cards in hand, would tell personnel at *Santa Teresa* that lawyers and engineers had discovered that the Suzuki

Aerio 2015 model had a dangerous manufacturing defect, and the manufacturer and its insurers had entered a legal settlement in connection with a class action lawsuit, of which victims of any accidents involving the vehicle were entitled to a damages award. Max and Dave would say that they were trying to track down the Flores child because he was entitled to a handsome legal settlement.

Max and Dave arrived at *Santa Teresa* at around 9:00 p.m., just after an evening mass had concluded and the parishioners had mostly cleared out. They walked into the modest but beautiful stucco sanctuary, and there were only a handful of lingerers, a couple of nuns visiting with each other, and a couple of altar boys straightening up at the front. Neither of the altar boys were the Flores kid.

Max and Dave decided to approach the altar boys. They had sweet innocent faces and looked like they were not yet teenaged.

Dave began speaking to them in Spanish. Max tried, but he could not follow along, so he paced around the sanctuary. Max began strolling through the front area of the sanctuary where there were portraits of some of the staff members and past priests. Suddenly a portrait and name caught Max's attention: Padre Ignatius Adamik ("Padre Iggy"). Max almost gasped but pulled out his cell phone quickly and snapped a picture of the portrait showing the name plate beneath. The portrait was in the section of portraits that appeared to be current staff.

Max quickly began texting Avery.

"Question. Was Father Iggy's full name Father Ignatius Adamik?"

No cell phone reception.

Max bolted up to the front of the sanctuary. He showed Dave the picture he had just taken on his cell phone. "Ask the boys the name of the priest whom they serve? Is his name Padre Iggy? Did he come here from the U.S.? New Jersey? And how long ago?"

"Slow down, Max. They are twelve years old. You're

going to scare them."

Dave took Max's phone over to the young altar boys and began speaking to them in Spanish again. The conversation was going on for quite a while, and Max's heart began to race, realizing that the conversation wouldn't be going on very long if the boys had simply said no, they didn't know who Father Iggy was. At that moment, a priest walked in and interrupted their conversation.

"Good evening. Is there something I can help you with?"

"You speak English, Padre?"

"Yes, and I overheard you and your friend speaking English to one another." The Padre nodded over toward Max standing a few yards away. Max slowly walked up to join the conversation. "Are you gentlemen visitors here from the U.S.?"

"Yes, are you the priest here?"

"Yes, my name is Father Jose Zurita."

Max's heart sank a bit, hearing that his name was not Father Iggy. "We are looking for a teenaged boy we heard used to be an altar boy here. He was the son of Eduardo and Valeria Flores. They were killed in a car wreck a few years ago."

"I know of whom you speak. We call him Eddie. Eduardo Flores, Jr. Why are you looking for him, if I may ask?"

Max and Dave exchanged glances, trying to decide who would answer. The priest interpreted their hesitation as a sign that they might be uncomfortable conversing in front of the young altar boys. Father Zurita uttered some instructions to the boys in Spanish, and they scurried off.

Dave then began the rehearsed ruse, handing the priest one of his Premier Mutual business cards.

"Padre, as it turns out, lawyers and engineers back in the U.S. have discovered that the model of car that the Flores family was driving when they had their accident, the Suzuki Aerio 2015, had a dangerous manufacturing defect, and the manufacturer and its insurers have entered into a legal settlement with victim representatives in connection with a class action lawsuit. The victims of any accidents involving the vehicle are entitled to a damages award. We have been trying to track down Eddie Flores because he is entitled to a significant sum of money."

Padre Zurita hesitated a few moments. "Well, I am glad that Eddie may be entitled to a sum of money to help him in life. But I am afraid Eddie does not come around here much anymore. I worry about him. He lived here at our orphanage for a while after his parents' accident. He was an altar boy. He was a very good child. Very kind. He was a favorite of *las monjas*, our nuns. But he left here when he turned eighteen years old, just a few months ago. I am afraid he is not keeping very good company these days. There was an odd man who befriended him—a man who began attending mass here a couple of years ago—who reached out to him, gave him gifts, and took him under his wing. He now apparently keeps company with that man all the time—works for him as an errand boy. The rumors are that the man he works for is a criminal. Part of *Los Chupas* that are very evil men."

Max chimed into the conversation. "Padre, the man that Eddie works for, is he a white man, from the U.S., with short, spikey blond hair?"

"Yes, he is the one. He calls himself Enos."

"Father, we really need to find Eddie. The sum of money to which he is entitled would be enough for him to start a whole new life, away from this bad fellow. Eddie would be set for life. Is there any way you can help us track him down?"

"Eddie sometimes comes in for Sunday mass. Not always but maybe once a month. If I see him, I will give him Mr. Carrillo's business card and tell him that we spoke and that he might be entitled to a large sum of money. Sir, do you have a business card as well?"

Max hesitated. What if Enos came around with Eddie

and saw Max's name on his business card?

"Father, I have run out of all my business cards, I am afraid. Please call the number on Dave's card. We travel together and will reply immediately if you or Eddie contacts us. We are going to be in the country for a while longer, reaching out to other victims. There are several we are trying to reach."

"Very well. Goodnight gentlemen. I hope I can help you contact Eddie."

"Oh, Padre, one more thing. I saw a portrait out in the foyer of a priest named Padre Ignatius Adamik. Padre Iggy. I have a brother in the U.S. who lives in Princeton, New Jersey. He and his family are parishioners at St. Paul's up there, and they used to know a Father Iggy at a nearby parish. He sometimes visited their parish, and they were very fond of him. I am wondering if that is the same Father Iggy that is here now? My brother heard he came down to a monastery in Mexico many years ago. If it is the same one, I would love to see him sometime and send him their love and prayers. My brother would never forgive me if I didn't."

Max was suddenly feeling some guilt. He had just lied to a priest twice in the last five minutes. Was it a sin if it was all geared toward rectifying criminal behavior? If it was in the name of pursuing justice? If it was for the greater good?

Padre Zurita hesitated for a long while. "Yes, Padre Iggy is here in our rectory, and he moved here from New Jersey. He is quite disabled and infirm now. I am not sure you could have a very meaningful conversation with him at this point. I am afraid that the end is likely very near for Padre Iggy."

"I am sorry to hear that." Max had just told another lie. He was not even remotely sorry if Father Iggy was about to die. He told himself that it was for the greater good.

"I guess Father Iggy would have to be quite old by now. It was twenty years ago or so when my brother spoke of him. I would still love to visit him. Is he up right now? Can you ask him if he is willing to see visitors from the U.S. who are fond of him?"

Padre Zurita paused for a long while once again. "When I said Padre Iggy was disabled, perhaps I was not clear. Padre Iggy was the victim of a terrible crime a few months ago. He lost both his eyes and his hands, among other things. He was savagely assaulted and mutilated in the rectory one night by someone who broke in. The *policia* never arrested anyone. I will take you to him, but he will not be able to see you. And you may be shocked at his appearance now."

Dave and Max looked at each other in silence. "Please take us back. I would like to send him good wishes from my brother in New Jersey. Perhaps it will cheer his spirits."

"Very well."

Padre Zurita walked Max and Dave through the side door of the sanctuary, uttering some instructions in Spanish to the young altar boys who were gathered outside the door. There was a long breezeway that connected the sanctuary to a rather large rectory with multiple units. Behind the rectory was an orphanage and school. Padre Zurita escorted Max and Dave to the farthest unit and rapped gently on a large wooden door a few times. The sounds of Schubert's melancholy *Winterreise* could be heard loudly playing on an old phonograph record player behind the door. Padre Zurita shouted something in Spanish and then took out his ring of keys and found the right one. He opened the door, rapping on it again as he did. It was very dark inside, but Padre Zurita flipped on a light switch. The light revealed a frail old man seated in a worn recliner. He was wearing sunglasses to hide his gouged-out eye sockets. His hands were bandaged stubs, as all of his ten fingers had been sliced off. His feet were bandaged stubs, as they had been cut off at the ankles. These were just the visible injuries that Max and Dave could see. They suspected there were more. Max and Dave both had little doubt who had done this and why.

After some small talk about who they were, and their pretend greetings and well wishes from New Jersey, Max asked Father Iggy, "Father, who attacked you? Was it

Marcus Braden from New Jersey? I am looking for him, Father. Marcus also did very terrible things to others. He killed many people, and he tried to kill my wife. Please tell me. Was it him? Does he now call himself Enos and wear bright blond short hair?"

Father Iggy had apparently drifted off to sleep. It was hard to tell for sure that he was asleep, because he had no eyes. But there was little doubt what his answer would have been.

Chapter Thirty-Two

Two Months Later (September 2019)—BASA and DRI-MED Joint Hearing.

Attorney Samantha Seigel was the lawyer that Judge Avery Lassiter most would have wanted to "grow up to be" if Avery had remained a lawyer and not gone onto the bench at age forty-two. Samantha Seigel was not only Ivy League educated and wicked smart, but was grace personified in a lawyer. She was beautiful with alabaster skin, long silky brown locks, and kind green eyes. Her long elegant neck was always adorned with pearls and *Hermes* scarves. She wore classic St. John suits and Christian Louboutin shoes. Her voice was calm and low with a warm, mellow vibe of a public radio personality. Her words were measured and always perfect for the occasion. She was maternal and strong at the same time. Some of the male lawyers in the local bar thought she was aloof with a cat-like temperament, but those were men who had never had the opportunity to work with her. She was a quiet, confident genius who knew how to calmly and efficiently maneuver through legal chaos.

It was early September, and the sixty-day abatement of the BASA trial was now at its end. The lawyers had apparently been knee-deep in their investigations in both the BASA case and the DRI-MED case. Samantha Seigel had recently filed a notice of appearance on behalf of Dmitry Basayev and DB Biocontainment, LLC in both the BASA and DRI-MED cases. This seemed like a very positive development. Dmitry Basayev must be alive if he had engaged counsel. And he had selected one of the best lawyers available to help him with the hot mess that he had apparently created. Samantha Seigel was brilliant in the law but also a pragmatist who knew how to convince a client to come clean and negotiate a deal (or even a surrender) when the situation required it. The parties—inclusive of the BASA Bankruptcy Trustee (represented by the Robot, Mr. Chertoff), DRI-MED (represented by Wade Scott), and Ms. Seigel, on behalf of Dmitry Basayev and DB Biocontainment—had asked for a joint status conference before both Judge Lassiter and Judge Hall to update both as to what their investigations and discovery had revealed.

"Get your popcorn ready," Millicent gleefully announced to Judge Lassiter and the interns. "This is going to be good."

Avery looked back at Millicent as if she were bracing herself for a development that may not necessarily be good.

"Was that statement in bad taste, Judge?" Millicent said with her chin lowered.

"Maybe a little bit."

Annalise spoke up, "Well, I was going to say something maybe in worse taste, Millicent. Like 'Judge, get your shepherd hook ready.' All these lawyers are big talkers who don't always like to stop or yield the floor to others. You'll be in court until midnight if you don't bring out the shepherd hook occasionally."

"If only." Avery sighed. "Someone needs to buy me one of those one day. Seriously."

"All rise. The honorable court is now in session. The Honorable Avery Lassiter and Henley Hall, jointly presiding."

"Please be seated," Judges Lassiter and Hall said simultaneously, looking awkwardly at each other.

As the judges sat, Judge Hall whispered to Avery sarcastically, "Why did David announce your name first? I am the senior judge here!"

"Maybe David was thinking ladies first? I don't know!" Avery whispered back.

"Let's walk back out. I want a do-over!"

The judges both quietly chuckled, and some of the lawyers in the courtroom looked puzzled.

Judge Hall cleared his throat. "We will now take appearances from the lawyers for the record."

The courtroom was packed. The lawyers lined up behind the podium one-by-one to make their formal appearances. The atmosphere suddenly felt heavy and ominous. Maybe it was Avery's imagination. Maybe she just felt extra uncomfortable that her former law partner, Wade Scott, was in the courtroom appearing as Chapter 11 counsel for DRI-MED. She and Wade had generally agreed that he would not appear in matters before her because of their long years of being in practice together and close friendship (not to mention the bond of both living through the Matt Braden suicide bombing disaster). However, there was technically no ethical rule against Wade appearing before her, all these years later. Of course, Wade had been handling the DRI-MED case before Judge Hall, not her, and this turn of events of there now being a joint hearing between DRI-MED and BASA had not been anticipated. In any event, Avery felt some sense of comfort that Samantha Seigel was now on the scene. This had to be a very good development. There are certain lawyers who judges innately know are going to be instrumental in solving messy problems. They have a "fixer" quality about them. A certain sagaciousness. Samantha Seigel was one of those lawyers. And of course, so was Wade Scott. And the two of them also both had the legal and life skill of civility. Civility had occasionally been lacking in the BASA case over the months. Hopefully. the match up of Samantha and Wade would prove to be a match made in Heaven.

After formal appearances by twenty or so lawyers, Wade Scott returned to the podium, placing a yellow note pad on it, filled with handwritten notes that he would likely never use. He took out a Montblanc ballpoint pen and put it next to the notepad, then removed his Jaeger-LeCoultre wristwatch and lay it down next to the pen. Wade tapped his Tulane ring on the wooden podium a couple of times—a nervous habit in which Avery had seen him engage hundreds of times. It wasn't so much a nervous habit as it was a superstitious good luck ritual he performed before launching into a usually perfect opening statement.

"Good morning, Your Honors. For the record, Wade Scott for DRI-MED Helicopter Company. It seems that all of the counsel involved in this tangled matter you are about to hear about drew straws as to who would start out today's joint status conference, and I am afraid that I drew the short straw."

This was, of course, Wade Scott's usual modesty. The lawyers probably unanimously urged him to start off the conference this morning. No one would bring the credibility and *gravitas* to the situation quite like he would—even in a cast of very fine lawyers. Today, Avery thought, Wade's face looked especially inscrutable. He seemed confident and ill at ease at the same time.

"A few weeks ago, I was approached by lawyers in the BASA case that, of course, has been pending before Judge Lassiter for more than two years. I was highly curious what on earth we would have to talk about. My client, DRI-MED, is an operating company that owns a large fleet of helicopters used in connection with offshore oil drilling in the Gulf of Mexico and the North Sea. DRI-MED also has a medi-vac business. My client resorted to filing Chapter 11 simply because of the downturn in offshore drilling activities. When offshore drilling scaled back a few months ago, this portion of our revenue plummeted. But things have remained fairly normal with my client's medical evacuation business."

"So, what did the BASA lawyers want to talk to DRI-MED and me about? It seemed very curious to us. We knew nothing about BASA except for what we had read in the newspapers. We had heard that it was an apparent Ponzi scheme of a young Chechen immigrant, a scientist, who represented to investors that he had invented some sort of state-of-the-art disinfection system."

"Well, the BASA lawyers wanted to talk about a contract, an account receivable on DRI-MED's books, and some payments that DRI-MED had received in the months leading up to its Chapter 11 case. The contract was with Ms. Seigel's client, DB Biocontainment, and my client nicknamed it the "Project Grotto" contract. It turns out that DRI-MED received various large payments for a couple of helicopters that DRI-MED retrofitted to transport highly infectious patients and for medical evacuation services it provided to DB Biocontainment in the months before DRI-MED filed bankruptcy. In fact, DRI-MED is still owed about $500,000 from DB Biocontainment. To put this into further context, DRI-MED has hundreds of contracts, hundreds of accounts receivable, hundreds of customers, and received thousands of payments from scores of customers in the year or so before it filed bankruptcy. DRI-MED is a huge international corporation. Thus, this contract and payment situation with DB Biocontainment was not on my or any of the DRI-MED lawyers' radar screens. DB Biocontainment was just one of an extremely large number of customers for whom DRI-MED provided medical evacuation services. And as for my clients, they were not aware that there was any connection between DB Biocontainment and Dmitry

Basayev or BASA. Why? Because the human being that DRI-MED always dealt with at DB Biocontainment was Dr. Astrid Nilsson. As far as anyone knew, Dr. Nilsson was the point person and control person for DB Biocontainment. She was the one who signed the contract with DRI-MED, who requested evacuation services, and to whom DRI-MED sent invoices and dealt with on all issues.

"Now, what did the reference to 'Project Grotto' mean? Well, the lawyers certainly had no reason to focus on that question until recently. As both Your Honors are aware, lawyers in the BASA case and the DRI-MED case have been engaging in discovery and informal information sharing the past several weeks. It didn't take long to find the human beings at DRI-MED who knew what the 'Grotto" was. It is an extremely sophisticated underground medical facility and lab in Ellis County, Texas at the former super collider site. Apparently, everyone associated with the project has nicknamed it the 'Grotto.' It is legit. It is operated by DB Biocontainment, LLC. My client has on many occasions evacuated sick patients from faraway locations such as Prudhoe Bay, Alaska and Cancun, Mexico and brought them to the Grotto for treatment. Again, all my client's services were ordered by Dr. Nilsson. My client had no reason to know that Dmitry Basayev had anything to do with the Grotto nor any reason to know that anything was amiss. After all, Dr. Nilsson is a Nobel Prize winning molecular biologist.

"Well, we have all come to learn that Dmitry Basayev is very much involved with the Grotto and, in fact, is the sole equity member of DB Biocontainment, LLC, or at least was when it was formed and when it obtained its substantial financing. Luckily, we had a very positive development happen in the last couple of weeks. As the lawyers for both BASA and DRI-MED began serving discovery on DB Biocontainment and trying to serve subpoenas out at the Grotto, Dmitry Basayev and DB Biocontainment had the good sense to hire one of the best lawyers he could have.

Samantha Seigel. Ms. Seigel and her clients immediately began cooperating with all the parties in both the BASA and DRI-MED cases. They know that Your Honors both expect an 'open kimono' approach in corporate bankruptcies, and secretiveness was absolutely not going to work here. So, with that, I am going to yield the podium to Ms. Seigel, and she has a unique presentation to make at this time."

Avery was thinking to herself that Millicent had been absolutely correct that they should have all had their popcorn ready. This was about to get really good.

Samantha Seigel approached the podium. One could have heard a pin drop. She had a thumb drive in her right hand. Avery was distracted by the beautiful Asscher cut emerald ring that Samantha wore on her graceful right hand. Avery was distracted by everything about Ms. Seigel, especially the extraordinarily perfect Promenade de Longchamp silk green scarf she was wearing. It seemed as calming and elegant as Ms. Seigel herself. Samantha Seigel was a legal goddess who garnered respect with a capital "R" everywhere she stepped foot. Avery was almost embarrassed at how much she admired her. Avery knew she had to be objective and not affected by that admiration.

"Your Honors, good morning. Samantha Seigel appearing for both DB Biocontainment and its owner, Mr. Dmitry Basayev. As you very well know, Mr. Basayev is also the owner of BASA. It is my privilege and honor to appear before you both this morning. I know that I am very late to the party, but I have been working mightily to get up to speed, and I hope I can be constructive in coming up with some solutions in this very messy situation that has unfolded in recent weeks.

"Mr. Basayev approached me about four weeks ago. He invited me to the Grotto. I have to say this was one of the most unusual client meeting locations that has ever been suggested to me as a rendezvous point. But I trusted my instincts that I should accept his invitation and see if I could help Mr. Basayev and DB Biocontainment."

"Your Honors, what I have come to learn is that there is something going on at the Grotto that has been kept very much under wraps but is absolutely extraordinary. The Grotto is a multi-unit underground hospital and BSL-4 research laboratory. The property has been entirely reinvented from a physics project to a medical science facility. Mr. Basayev has been very hard at work in the facility, literally day and night, trying to perfect his superbug disinfectant system and related products there. The BASA disinfection system invention is very real—not the fiction of a Ponzi scheme. It is, in essence, a state-of-the-art disinfection infrastructure for healthcare facilities, including such features as ceiling and wall panels that emanate UV light, an air purification ventilation system, a collection of i-Robot type roving machines that constantly disinfect floor surfaces with a combination of laser and environmentally friendly chemical products, bio-booths to scan people coming and going from healthcare facilities, and a cleaning system for catheters and medical tools that has superior qualities to other products on the market. In fact, the product is light years ahead of similar products on the market. It is proving to be infallible, really. It might even eventually be introduced into other public spaces besides medical facilities.

"But the Grotto is more than simply a lab for perfecting the BASA disinfection invention. Mr. Basayev is also using the underground facility to treat patients with atypical and hard to treat viruses and bacterial infections in a safe, secluded, subterranean environment, where the patients can be treated with minimal risk (taking advantage of the BASA disinfectant system in the process). He is experimenting with anti-viral therapies and vaccines there. He is conducting robust clinical trials. Some of these clinical trials relate to an antiviral for a gruesome super-flu that has been discovered in the permafrost in Alaska recently and has infected numerous people—particularly oil field workers at Prudhoe Bay and their friends and families both there and in Texas—

and has the potential to become a lethal pandemic. Mr. Basayev believes he has the ability to keep that permafrost virus in check before it wreaks havoc across the world. As far as the BSL-4 facility, the only thing remotely comparable to it is a room nicknamed the Slammer at an Army research lab in Maryland and certain *Doctors Without Borders* facilities which are far smaller in size and scope. The underground facility was completed in early 2016.

"Your Honors, we all know that a picture paints a thousand words, so I have a proposal at this point that I have run by Messrs. Chertoff and Scott and various of the other lawyers here. I have in my hand a thumb drive with a video of the Grotto. The video is essentially a tour of the Grotto conducted by Dmitry Basayev himself. The video is about two hours in length, and, I have to say, it is fascinating. It's a little long…I know, but all counsel believe that it would be helpful to you both to see it. I am going to make a proposal to you when the video is finished that is sort of a grand solution for all of the constituencies in these cases, and I think that the best way for you to assess the bona fides of my grand solution is for you to see the Grotto and hear from Dmitry Basayev himself. And, before you start to wonder, I have Mr. Basayev standing by, available to connect into this hearing by video conferencing from the Grotto, if Your Honors or any counsel want to question him afterward. Also, I have made Mr. Basayev aware that he will likely need to appear in person in this courthouse soon. It's just that he is afraid for his life. Mr. Basayev's father recently died under suspicious circumstances, and Mr. Basayev is afraid that his enemies might have been responsible for his father's death."

Judges Lassiter and Hall took a long, silent look at each other. They both then nodded. Judge Hall whispered, "This seems to have more significance to your case than mine, so why don't you take the lead. I defer to you."

Judge Lassiter cleared her throat. "Does any other counsel wish to say anything at this point? Does everyone, in fact, agree that Judge Hall and I should see this video?"

There was silence and nodding of heads.

"Okay. Let's see the video."

For the next two hours, there was silence in the courtroom as everyone sat in rapt attention to the video screens. Dmitry Basayev began the video with charming greetings. He didn't seem like a Ponzi scheme fraudster. Of course, so many times Ponzi scheme fraudsters don't seem like Ponzi scheme fraudsters. Avery was struck by his vivid, light blue eyes. They were almost spellbinding. He began by telling his life story, including how he grew up in Chechnya, raised mostly by his father journalist, after his mother died when he was very young. He described a loving father who encouraged Dmitry to pursue scientific endeavors, as well as a hard childhood of moving around frequently within Chechnya to escape those in the government who wanted his father dead. He told about his travels to the U.S., where he attended college at the University of Rochester, New York, then on to graduate school at Emory, where he did research at the CDC and also worked at Emory's Serious Communicable Diseases Unit. Since leaving there, he had been working with a team he had assembled that had invented the BASA super-intensive, ultraviolet light-infused disinfectant system and other products that kill some of the most lethal super germs. Through DB Biocontainment, he and his team had separately been perfecting therapies and working on certain vaccines.

Then after the introductions, the tour began of the subterranean vault. There was a break in the video after the introduction, and then Dmitry appeared above ground at the facility, at what he said was the southern-most end of the tunnel, where there was an isolated, communicable infectious disease unit. Dmitry and his videographer then went into a separate entrance through what he described as one of the seventeen shafts from the surface. At a certain point, their elevator stopped, and they were directed into a room where they were required to shower and then gear up into bio-hazard clothing. Then they went back into another elevator in which they went further downward into a fully equipped negative pressure isolation ward designed to deal with biosafety level-4 pathogens. Residing in this isolated, quarantined patient unit were patients in very bad shape with lethal infectious diseases—patients with very "high viral load"—and they were undergoing various forms of experimental treatment and therapies. This was referred to as Chamber 1 or, by its nickname, the "Wildfire Chamber" (which, Dmitry, joked was a reference to the underground facility in the book the *Andromeda Strain*). Some of these patients had been transported from Alaska at various times over the last six months or had otherwise been exposed to a mysterious disease that originated in Alaska and was brought back to Texas by infected oil pipeline workers.

The video went on to show the dedicated clinical laboratory next to the quarantine unit, just down the tunnel, for analyzing blood and bodily fluids from patients in the Wildfire Chamber, by simply taking samples down the tunnel without having to go into any separate environments. Everything in theory was all self-contained. There was a constant buzz of nurses, physicians, pathologists, virologists, and lab tech staff in the so-called Wildfire Laboratory.

The tour then took the viewers into the center Decontamination Unit, within the isolation unit, made of stainless steel and other highly durable materials, for contaminated waste to be brought and decontaminated with harsh chlorine bleach solutions and then burned—not sent through pipes and drains into the other areas of the tunnel or the public water system.

Further down, there was the so-called "Spa," which was another sterilization unit for personnel to shower and bring their own laundry before entering and exiting the facility—with, once again, egress through an exclusive shaft to the surface for this portion of the tunnel.

After another brief break in the video, Dmitry and his videographer were once again on the above-ground surface and then took a different elevator down a shaft to another unit for patients who were not suffering from any type of communicable disease but were feared to be having an adverse reaction after exposure to the BASA, Inc. experimental super-germ disinfectant system. This unit, referred to as Chamber-2 or the Nebula Chamber, was currently empty, because Dmitry explained that there had been no adverse reactions in months now, and he believed the BASA disinfection system had been through sufficient clinical trials and was now ready to go to market.

Finally, Dmitry walked the viewers further down toward the other direction of the tunnel from all of the aforementioned units, where there were laboratories and offices devoted to other research endeavors—mostly research aimed at perfecting the disinfectant system, but other research pertaining to pathogens and drugs. This was Laboratory-2 or the Nebula Laboratory. And, of course, at the very opposite end of the tunnel, far away from the patients and laboratory units, there were the fully furnished, resplendent living quarters and conference facilities. Judges Lassiter and Hall were astounded. They felt as though they were touring an underground castellated abbey. It was high tech meets medieval. In addition to scientists and state-of-the-art medical equipment, the Grotto was a place of art and beauty. Science and healing converging with esthetics. Dmitry Basayev obviously was as meticulous and eccentric with decorating as in his scientific endeavors. The walls of the corridors were lined with tapestries and fine art. It was surreal. There was a recreational facility with a gym, pool, and rock-climbing wall. Dmitry explained that he and many scientists literally never left the Grotto. Avery wondered what life would be like if one never saw the sun.

After the video was over, Judges Lassiter and Hall called a short recess.

"All rise."

After bathroom breaks and coffee refills, Judges Lassiter and Hall and their law clerks and interns congregated. They were all quite flabbergasted, to say the least.

"I feel partly relieved, to know my Ponzi-scheme-from-Hell trial is never going to resume again. But I am also a little concerned. Is this just stage two of another hoax?"

"But how could that multibillion-dollar facility be a hoax?" Judge Hall chimed in.

"I don't know. I am just being on my guard, I guess. Do you think it is strange that Dr. Nilsson did not show up in that video and Dmitry never mentioned her?"

"I was thinking that, too." Millicent smirked.

"Well, do you think anyone is going to ask to examine Dmitry by video next? And, if they don't, do you think we should ask some questions, Judge Hall?

"Don't know. I'm once again going to defer to you. I still think this has a lot more to do with your BASA case than mine."

"True. I suppose DRI-MED is mostly just trying to clear its good name here today, and show it was not somehow complicit in accepting fraudulent transfers or dealing with a potential crook."

"All rise."

"Please be seated."

Avery began. "We are back on the record in this joint status conference in the BASA, Inc. and DRI-MED cases. Ms. Seigel, I will ask at this point is your presentation concluded? Do you or any lawyers here wish to bring Mr. Basayev into the courtroom through live video transmission and ask him more questions on the record?"

"Your Honor, I do not have any more evidence to present, whether by video tape or live video. However, unless the other lawyers or you want to question Mr. Basayev, the next thing that I would like to do is to present to you my grand solution for this legal mess."

Avery turned to the other lawyers. "Does anyone want

to bring Mr. Basayev into this proceeding by live video and ask him follow up questions at this point?"

All the lawyers looked exhausted, as though they had been working around the clock. They, no doubt, had. Lawyers—like scientists working in a Grotto—sometimes never see sunlight.

The Robot stood up. "Your Honor, we have been engaged in extensive discovery. At this point, we have asked Mr. Basayev just about every question we can think of in depositions, and frankly, he has been very forthcoming. We are convinced that the disinfection system is not only very real, but also ready to go to market. Several of us have even gone out to the facility. It's legitimate. I brought experts down with me from U.T. Southwestern, the Mayo Clinic, and Baylor. They were stunned at what they saw. Mr. Basayev has real virologists and microbiologists working on real therapies. My experts not only toured the facilities, but they also talked to the staff, extensively, and looked at some of their data and clinical trial records. I think at this point we would defer to Ms. Seigel to outline her grand solution."

Avery hesitated. "I have a question, and I am not sure if it matters, but I am going to ask. I was curious why we didn't see Dr. Astrid Nilsson in the video. Mr. Scott mentioned that DRI-MED only dealt with her. I have seen her in the back of our courtroom on occasion. I have seen her give news interviews over the years. I am guessing Dr. Nilsson has been significantly involved with all of this and that she and Mr. Basayev met while he attended Emory. Can you say something to shed light on this?"

Samantha Seigel took a sip of her bottled water. "Your Honor, it is true that Dr. Nilsson has been very involved with these companies. Dr. Nilsson was a mentor to Dmitry when he was at Emory. He admired her and occasionally helped her on research projects. At some point, shortly before the BASA bankruptcy was filed, and after Dmitry got the Grotto up and running, he called on Dr. Nilsson for advice. For one thing, Dr. Nilsson has written extensively on permafrost issues—specifically, bacteria and viruses and various diseases that may lie dormant in the earth's permafrost layer. When the opportunity presented itself to Dmitry to treat certain patients working for a pipeline company called Tex-Core, who had developed a mysterious and very lethal disease up in Alaska, and it appeared that it might bear some relation to something that emanated out of the melting permafrost, Dmitry decided to call upon Dr. Nilsson for input. Additionally, Dmitry was generally beginning to feel like he was getting in over his head. He was a bit overwhelmed by trying to get the disinfection system cleared through regulatory hurdles and out in the marketplace, and also get his therapies developed. Dr. Nilsson eventually began helping Dmitry full time and even living down at the Grotto with other scientists who were working around the clock. She subsequently became the face of DB Biocontainment to the outside world, so to speak. She dealt with vendors, and she was in charge of the mechanics and procedures for the clinical trials. As you probably know, clinical trials are highly regulated and typically take many years to complete. Dr. Nilsson is very familiar with the system. She coordinated the paperwork and approvals needed for the clinical trials—many of which were outside the underground facility—and Dmitry basically was in the labs 24/7. He is the scientist, and she has more experience and more marketing and business savvy. The Grotto and the disinfection system were both his babies. The scientists were under his guidance. Dr. Nilsson arranged to find the patients who would be treated at the facility and participate in the clinical trials. Apparently, the clinical trials that got the disinfection system and certain therapies across the finish line, so to speak, were going on down in Yucatan, at certain facilities with large U.S. ex-pats in residence, and at various other Mexican facilities."

Avery sat in silence, trying her best to remain expressionless.

The truth was that Dmitry had become the tool, and Dr.

Nilsson was the oracle. She had come in like a thief in the night and taken over his conception. In Dr. Nilsson's mind, it was for the greater good.

"Well, it has already been a very long day. How about for now we just hear about your grand solution and then figure out where we go from here—as far as bringing in Mr. Basayev or other next steps."

"Very well, Your Honor. First, we want to start by making very clear that Mr. Basayev better understands his fiduciary duties now and is wholly committed to being more engaged in the BASA case and assisting and cooperating entirely with the Chapter 11 Trustee in that case. Second, Mr. Basayev has decided that he will put DB Biocontainment into its own Chapter 11 case. I will represent DB Biocontainment and have advised Mr. Basayev to retain his own separate personal counsel from this point forward, to avoid the perception of any conflicts of interest on my part. It is our intention, after DB Biocontainment is put into Chapter 11, to engage in an auction process for the assets of both BASA (to which the Trustee of BASA consents and will participate) and DB Biocontainment. In both cases, we believe the most valuable assets are the patents for the disinfection system and some of the therapies that DB Biocontainment has perfected—especially the antiviral for the permafrost flu that we believe poses a global threat in coming years. Regarding the latter, we have some folks in the courtroom—some employees of the pipeline company Tex-Core and their families—who were infected with the permafrost flu while working in Prudhoe Bay, Alaska, who were treated with the antiviral that DB Biocontainment has been perfecting, and they are alive now to attest to the efficacies of that drug."

There were twenty or so people in the back of the courtroom that Samantha Seigel pointed toward. Avery couldn't help but notice, even from thirty feet away, that they all had *almost glowing light blue eyes*. The same eyes as Dmitry Basayev had. Avery slipped Judge Hall a note. "Is it just me or do all those permafrost flu survivors have crazy, unnatural blue eyes?"

Judge Hall wrote back. "Do you think this is a reprise of *Village of the Damned*? Maybe they are telepathic too!"

Judge Lassiter quickly scrawled back, "Seriously, why don't you ask about them?"

They both resisted the urge to ask.

Meanwhile the law clerks and interns were also furiously passing notes. "OMG. Somebody call the *X-Files* people. Is Ms. Seigel going to explain those peoples' eyes?"

"I am honestly kind of afraid. It's like there are aliens among us. Do you think we should bolt out of here right now? LOL."

Millicent slipped a note to Judge Hall's career law clerk. "I bet both of our Judges are thinking of that Night King character from *Game of Thrones*. They both loved those books and the TV series. I dare you to slip your Judge a note asking him if he is noticing those peoples' eyes."

Oblivious to any of this behind-the-bench note shuffling, Samantha Seigel continued. "With regard to the Grotto facility, the assets of DB Biocontainment are actually a ground lease and all of the equipment and finish out inside of the Grotto. It may be that someone is interested in buying all of this in a bankruptcy asset sale or may simply be interested in being a new investor. It is our thought that we will consolidate the two companies for more efficient administration and marketing. This is probably the fairest and most appropriate thing to do since the lines are very blurred between BASA and DB Biocontainment."

Judge Lassiter weighed in at this point. "Well, this all sounds good, but who are the creditors of DB Biocontainment and what are they going to say about this consolidation strategy? And what are the separate creditors of BASA going to say about this strategy? Is the consolidation strategy prejudicial to one group of creditors versus another? Have they been consulted?"

"Your Honor, we have been working very hard to reach

out to the known major creditors. For BASA, it has been much easier. All of the creditors are listed on the Schedules in its bankruptcy case, and it's, of course, public record. The creditors are entirely private, accredited investors—what we sometimes call "angel investors"—since BASA, Inc. was not in its operating, revenue phase yet and did not have vendors or traditional financial institutions lending money to it yet. Toro Capital has been instrumental in helping us reach out to those private investors—many of them were brought to the BASA investment opportunity by Toro Capital.

"As for DB Biocontainment, this has been a little more challenging. As it turns out, most of the investors in DB Biocontainment were parties affiliated with Cade Graham— the well-known Dallas hedge fund manager with whom you are probably familiar, who happens to be missing and believed dead, although there is some controversy about that."

Avery almost gasped audibly. She tried her hardest to keep an unemotional poker face with that comment.

"We have been in communication with Cade Graham's estate representative, a fellow named Ethan Alves. He has all the necessary probate court documents giving him authority to speak for the Cade Graham controlled entities, and he is also an officer of Cade Graham's hedge fund, Ranger Capital, which brought most of the DB Biocontainment investors to the company. Mr. Alves thinks that all of the investors of DB Biocontainment, with whom he is in regular contact, are very supportive of this grand solution."

"So, what is your timing on all of this?"

"We will be ready to put DB Biocontainment in a Chapter 11 case in the next few days. We have an excellent investment banker ready, if the court approves him, to start a marketing process. He has prepared excellent marketing materials, a data room, a confidentiality agreement for interested bidders to sign, and has a list of hundreds of both strategic buyers and financial buyers who he will solicit if the court gives the green light for him to move forward. He thinks that it could be a very robust auction process. Regarding DB Biocontainment, the allure will likely be not just the underground facility and its unique concept, but the permafrost antiviral may also be of great interest to Big Pharma."

"Well, this all sounds very promising. It's amazing really. I have a couple of additional questions, and then we will adjourn and wait for the DB Biocontainment case to be filed and see how this all plays out."

Judge Hall slipped Judge Lassiter a note. "I think I know where you are headed. Stay in your lane." Avery smiled. She wrote a note back. "Stay calm. I am going to be careful."

Judge Lassiter looked up at the lawyers. "One night recently I was looking at the DRI-MED Bankruptcy Schedules. It was a few days after we abated the Ponzi scheme trial, and the lawyers had announced in BASA that there were some odd transactions with DRI-MED. I was just curious to confirm what I was hearing. Anyway, I saw one reference to an account receivable owed to DRI-MED by DB Biocontainment that referred to something called *Isla Valladolid*. Is that one of the facilities on the Yucatan Peninsula at which there were residents who participated in clinical trials?"

Samantha Seigel stood up. "Your Honor, I am not really sure I remember. I just remember Yucatan Peninsula."

Ward Scott next stood up. "Your Honor, my client just whispered in my ear that, yes, *Isla Valladolid* is the main facility that DRI-MED transported patients from in Mexico. DRI-MED would take patients from there to the Cancun airport, where a DB Biocontainment specially configured plane would then transport the patients to Dallas. Then, a DRI-MED helicopter would sometimes take the patients from the airport in Dallas out to the Grotto."

"Okay. My last question is this. I noticed that there were some large investors listed in the BASA Schedules that were described as Mateo Guerrero family trusts. Can someone tell me who that is?"

There was silence. Then, the Whale, who was Toro Capital's lawyers, slowly stood. "Your Honor, it is my understanding that Mateo Guerrero is a wealthy Mexican national who purchased some credit default swaps on BASA, Inc. debt that had originally been held by Cade Graham. Ethan Alves, whom you heard Ms. Seigel mention, has a line of connection to Mr. Guerrero and Mr. Alves reports that Mr. Guerrero is supportive of the grand solution that Ms. Seigel has outlined."

"So, Cade Graham was connected with financing both BASA and DB Biocontainment originally? And now he is dead supposedly, but people, of course, think he is not really dead?"

"Correct."

"Actually, I have one more hypothetical question." Avery sat hesitating more. "What if these therapies and the disinfection system are not as far along as Dmitry thinks or represents? Or say, hypothetically, there is a flaw with some of the clinical trials or something crazy like that. What do you think that might do to the auction process you envision?"

"Well, Your Honor, we anticipate having very sophisticated bidders who will do their due diligence thoroughly. If Dmitry and his team have not really gotten these products ready to go to market—if more clinical trials are needed or whatever—maybe they just need to transfer all of the intellectual property and trade secrets, if you will, to some third party who can make it happen—bring it all across the finish line at this point. As you know, there are plenty of people out there who make their livings taking pre-revenue enterprises like this from the R&D stage to global licensing companies or can otherwise figure out a way to complete and monetize their products."

"Thank you. We stand adjourned."

"All rise."

Judges Lassiter and Hall quietly exited the courtroom. The lawyers all stood in silence waiting for everything to sink in. Some of the lawyers quietly wondered why Judge Lassiter had asked those two last questions.

Chapter Thirty-Three

Market Frenzy.

A few days after the joint status conference in the BASA and DRI-MED case, DB Biocontainment filed its own new Chapter 11 case, as Samantha Seigel had indicated would happen. The court computer randomly assigned the case to Judge Lassiter. She had hoped that would not happen.

Avery was feeling turmoil and angst over whether she needed to recuse herself in both the BASA case and now the DB Biocontainment case, too. The reality was that Avery had extra-judicial knowledge about facts relevant to both cases. But were the facts material or not? Were they facts that might affect her decision-making? She knew things about Cade Graham because of Max's investigations of his alleged death down in Mexico. She knew that Max had serious suspicions that something highly improper was going on down at *Isla Valladolid* involving Cade Graham and probably Marcus Braden. And now she was going to be presiding over a case in which Cade Graham was the main holder of debt (albeit indirectly, and maybe posthumously). It felt like she had to step aside—although there was certainly no clear ethics rule here.

Should Avery disclose to the lawyers and parties that her husband was down in Mexico looking for Cade Graham and thought that he was still alive? Was that necessary and would that compromise Max's own investigation? Should she tell the parties that she happened to know that Mateo Guerrero was the head of *Oscuro* and that it and Cade Graham might be involved in something sinister at *Isla Valladolid*—she just was not quite sure what? Was whatever they were doing at *Isla Valladolid* something that might affect the perceived value of both BASA and DB Biocontainment, if people knew? Were the clinical trials that happened in connection with *Isla Valladolid* perhaps tainted somehow? When Avery had asked her follow up questions at the joint status conference, was she truly trying to give herself a better feel for the case, to allow herself to make better decisions, or was she subconsciously trying to obtain information to help Max with his investigation?

Avery was engaged in deep self-introspection during the first few days of the DB Biocontainment case. She would probably need to talk to Judge Hall as a sounding board.

Almost immediately after DB Biocontainment filed Chapter 11, it filed the expected paperwork to consolidate the case with the BASA case and also paperwork to engage in a marketing and sale process—aimed at finding either a buyer or new investor for the assets of both companies.

In the days that followed, two significant things happened. First, the debt of both BASA and DB Biocontainment began trading heavily (it was not traded on any public trading markets; it was simply trading from private holder to private holder and at sky-high prices). The debt in both companies had been considered almost worthless a few weeks earlier. Now, prices of the debt of both companies were soaring and trading at eighty percent of face value and higher.

One of the axioms of bankruptcy is that fortunes can be made in moments of desperation. There are parties that specialize in ferreting out and buying undervalued companies, securities, and debt instruments. They are experts in the business of failure and speculate on who can emerge from setbacks to live another day. They can search out opportunities, broker deals, and reap the rewards. Parties soon began filing something referred to as "Rule 3001e Notice of Transfer of Claims" in both cases, reflecting new holders of the BASA and DB Biocontainment debt. Avery noticed, to her relief, that the Mateo Guerrero family trust had apparently sold all their debt holdings in BASA to various third parties that looked like traditional Wall Street investors. Something similar had happened regarding the DB Biocontainment debt. All the original holders of debt seemed to be transferring their debt to some of the "usual" claims-purchasers (sometimes referred to as "vultures") who buy up distressed debt. In fact, it appeared as though all the original debt holders, that might have been entities owned by Cade Graham, were out of the picture now. Even the landlord on the ground lease at Ellis County (which had been a Cayman Island entity in a byzantine structure of Cayman Island entities controlled by Cade Graham) had apparently flipped the property to some third-party investor whose name was completely unfamiliar to Avery.

Avery felt still more angst. If Cade Graham and Mateo Guerrero were no longer parties in interest in this whole Dmitry Basayev saga, did this mean her ethical quandary was solved?

The second significant thing that happened in the days that followed the DB Biocontainment Chapter 11 filing involved pharmaceutical stocks. Apparently, journalists and other interested parties had listened in on the joint status conference among BASA and DRI-MED. Once word got out into the public domain that the BASA disinfection system was legitimate and might, indeed, be a game-changer in the healthcare space, and also that Dmitry Basayev was alive and had created an almost one-of-a-kind underground BSL-4 laboratory that had revolutionary therapies ready to go to market, every Big Pharma publicly traded stock skyrocketed. The big market players speculated that one of the large pharmaceuticals would likely be the winning bidder in the Chapter 11 auction and would score big from acquiring the disinfection system and therapies. Most of the Big Pharma stock prices more than doubled in price in the days following the joint status conference.

It didn't hurt that Enos, and Cade Graham were doing a few things behind the scenes, on the Dark Web and otherwise, to make sure things played out this way.

Chapter Thirty-Four

Should I Recuse? Worlds Colliding.

It was late September now and Avery had a new crop of interns. She had two young men this semester, one from SMU Law School and one from UNT Dallas Law School. One was named Mason and the other Mitch. Avery called them, along with Millicent, her career law clerk, the "M&Ms." She never could resist playful nicknames.

"M&Ms, come into my office."

The three dutifully queued into Avery's office. Millicent was displaying her usual effervescent vitality. The interns were somewhat quiet, notepads in hand, ready to take copious notes.

"Did you ever watch the TV show *Seinfeld*?"

The M&Ms all nodded affirmatively.

"Do you all remember when the character George Costanza felt like his 'worlds were colliding,' and he went apoplectic?"

The M&Ms all stared blankly. They had likely never

watched the show and were just trying to please her by nodding familiarity.

"Oh, never mind. I want to talk recusal and conflicts. I am afraid that it might be time for me to recuse in both the BASA and DB cases."

Millicent looked shocked and disappointed. She had worked so hard for so many months on the BASA case.

"Everyone, please keep this in the vault. My problem here is my spouse. As Millicent knows, he happens to be a retired cop, and he is now working as a private investigator for an insurance company. For several months, he has been investigating the death or disappearance of Cade Graham, the hedge fund manager that you heard the lawyers mention in the joint status conference recently."

"No way." Millicent looked shocked.

"Yes way. As we heard the other day at the status conference, Cade Graham apparently was a large investor in DB Biocontainment. And apparently also, at one time, in BASA. Meanwhile, I have heard some things about him from my husband—just small talk during my husband's investigation that now doesn't seem so small. I am trying to decide if this extrajudicial knowledge that I have might affect my judgments in the cases. And it gets more complicated or less complicated, because it looks like from the docket that Cade Graham may have recently divested himself from all of his holdings in the DB Biocontainment case."

Millicent spoke up. "Well, Cade Graham couldn't have done that if he is dead."

"Well, his estate representative, Ethan Alves, probably did it."

One of the interns, Mason, spoke up. "Judge, the internet is going wild, by the way, saying Ethan Alves is Cade Graham's son." The young intern felt very proud to have contributed something to the conversation.

Millicent chimed in, "Interns, no! Don't look at the internet during one of our cases. We have to be careful about obtaining extrajudicial knowledge."

The intern looked confused and embarrassed.

Judge Lassiter explained. "Mason don't feel bad. We can't live our lives with our heads stuck in the sand. We are going to see and hear things about our cases sometimes on the internet or TV or out in public. We just must remember that the internet is easy. And what I mean is, people can say whatever they want on the internet without evidence. The courtroom is hard. You have to back-up what you say. My point is who knows what is true or not on the internet. We have to be extra careful about what we see and how it might influence us."

"Anyway, Judge, as far as this ethical conflict you were describing, if you want to know what my sense is on all this..."

"No! Millicent what have I told you about your 'sense'?"

Millicent looked dispirited. "Ugh. Sorry. You have told me a hundred times that if you want somebody's '*sense*,' you will go to a fortune teller or a psychic. And that what you want from your law clerks and interns is their assessment of the evidence and the law, not their 'sense.'"

"Bingo."

Millicent sighed. "Okay, let me rephrase. I don't think the evidence thus far, or the law, give you a clear answer on what you should do, Judge. The judicial canons sure don't address this one."

"I agree."

The interns looked totally confused. These two didn't have much to add, based on their one week on the job. Understandable.

"Mason and Mitch, this is all about my ability to examine the evidence dispassionately. The trier of fact (me, in this case, not a jury) must exercise dispassionate neutrality. That's a fancy way of saying that I cannot let anything I have heard or seen outside the courtroom affect my judgment. I have to stick to the evidence and argument I hear during the proceedings. This gets dicey if you have heard things about people or the facts, even inadvertently, outside the courtroom."

Mitch and Mason were wide eyed and taking notes.

"Millicent, can you tell me anything to allay my concerns? Is there any reported case or any advisory opinion or judicial canon out there that you think remotely gives us some guidance in this situation?"

"Not really. I think it boils down to one of those possible 'appearance of impropriety' things, where, if the parties knew that you have some background information about Cade Graham and strange activity at *Isla Valladolid* where, it just so happens, clinical trials have been taking place, the parties and lawyers might be bothered."

The Judge scratched her head. "And the public might be bothered also, looking at it all objectively. Mason and Mitch, there is actually a federal law that describes clear-cut grounds for a judge's recusal and more gray areas that speak in terms of, might the judge's 'impartiality be reasonably questioned.'"

Millicent joined in. "True. However, we really don't know what we don't know here. Maybe none of what you know will really matter at all in your decision-making process in these cases. Maybe you are just going to be hearing about auction results and approving the highest and best bid for the assets of BASA and DB Biocontainment. Things might not get hairier than that."

"That's what makes this so hard, Millicent. I'd like to supervise these two cases to their conclusion. Perhaps I am worrying way too much. I mean I am not ever supposed to withdraw simply as a matter of convenience or simply to avoid controversy. That's not how it works. I have an obligation to the system to be sure I really need to recuse. But I have the double concern here that I am going to feel tempted to tell Max anything I learn that might be relevant to his investigation of the disappearance of Cade Graham, and maybe that's not ethical either, ya know?"

"Yeah. This is all crazy."

"Yep. That's the word. Crazy. Anyway, I'll talk to Judge Hall about my decision to recuse. I will tell him that we have found no hard and fast answer in the case law, canons, or advisory opinions, but I am recusing based on the *Seinfeld* 'worlds colliding' theory."

Again, the M&Ms both looked at Avery strangely.

"You guys, please *Google* the *Seinfeld* episode 'worlds colliding.' The great and poetic sage George Constanza said it upsets your universe when your worlds collide, or something like that. Anyway, whichever judge gets reassigned these two cases will not be too burdened getting up to speed with things. I suppose none of the Ponzi-scheme phase of the BASA case really matters at all at this point, since it all turned out to be a wrong premise. So whatever learning curve that I may have built up doesn't matter as much as it might otherwise have in different circumstances."

"Poor Judge Hall."

"Well, maybe the new judge will be randomly assigned to the cases."

"Poor Judge Lacey, if that happens."

"It will be fine."

Chapter Thirty-Five

The Auction.

Both the BASA and DB Biocontainment cases were reassigned by the computer to Judge Hall, after Judge Lassiter recused herself. Judge Lassiter never explained her recusal—it is not required. She thought it would be for the best to keep the reasons private—even if it did result in gossip and speculation.

The auction of the BASA and DB Biocontainment was wildly successful. There were many bidders from all over the worlds. Germans, Japanese, Indonesians. Ultimately a U.S. bio-tech venture capitalist bought all rights associated with the BASA disinfection system, with the goal of pitching the company to yet a bigger player after perhaps a road show to all of the major bio-tech players. Ironically, the company that was once maligned as "the mother of all Ponzi schemes" was now (again?) the hottest company on Wall Street. The venture capitalist purchaser soon entered into a lucrative contract with Dmitry Basayev to keep him on as a consultant.

As for DB Biocontainment, a joint venture of a well-known, clinical stage biopharmaceutical company and a publicly held company in the therapeutics space purchased all its property, including the ground lease on the Grotto, also keeping Dmitry Basayev on as a consultant.

It appeared to be a win-win for everyone. The auction process brought enough sale proceeds to pay all creditors of both BASA and DB Biocontainment in full plus interest. A rarity in the world of bankrupt companies.

As for DRI-MED, it received payment in full on the monies owed to it by DB Biocontainment and was out from any PR cloud. It also had a customer for the future, since the new owners of DB Biocontainment wanted continued access to the retrofitted bio-safe helicopters for future transports into and out of the Grotto.

After fist pumps, back slapping, and congratulations across the board, the BASA and DB Biocontainment cases were history. The cases were closed. Both Judges Hall and Lassiter were quite glad to have it all behind them.

Avery decided to text Max late at night the day after the closure of the two cases.

"You awake?"

"Hey. Yes. How's it going?"

"Just hadn't heard from you in a few days. Was getting a little worried."

"All is well. We are just having a dry spell making any progress down here. No new leads in quite a while. The Premier Mutual folks are probably getting a little frustrated with us."

"Sorry to hear that. So, I don't know if you remember us talking a few weeks ago about my BASA case where I discovered that some family trusts of Mateo Guerrero were investors and a case of Judge Hall's called DRI-MED that happened to have some references in its bankruptcy paperwork to '*Isla Valladolid*'?"

"Yeah, I remember."

"Well long story short. I ended up recusing myself because of you."

"Because of *me*? What does that mean?"

"It turns out that there was a third company involved besides BASA and DRI-MED. It is called DB Biocontainment. And CADE GRAHAM was an investor in it."

"What???"

"DB Biocontainment has an underground medical research facility at the old super-collider site. A fellow named Ethan Alves who is apparently Cade Graham's estate executor is acting for Graham. Long story short, there was an auction here where the assets of both BASA and DB Biocontainment (the underground facility) were pooled, and there was an auction and Big Pharma came in and scooped it all up. Graham's estate and all the investors came out big-time winners. But I recused myself from all of it because it felt wrong—because of your involvement in searching for Cade Graham."

"Avery, I barely understand any of this!"

"Well, call if you want to understand it better. I'm just saying that we had these three cases pending before me and Judge Hall that seem to have a strangely coincidental overlap with what you are doing: BASA, which was working on a state-of-the-art disinfection system (in which Guerrero invested); DB Biocontainment, which was owned by the same guy as BASA (in which Graham invested); DRI-MED, which had a contract with DB Biocontainment involving *Isla Valladolid*, in which both Graham and Guerrero have ownership and you've told me that Marcus Braden happens to have been spotted on CCTV there."

"Wow. I admit this is crazy all right. Sorry you had to recuse—I guess. I mean, I barely get this. It sounds incredibly coincidental and all, but you have a lot of hedge funds and corporate bigwigs in your court, so I guess it's not totally shocking that Cade Graham would be involved in one of your cases, is it?"

"I don't know. Let's just drop it for now. It's done. The cases are over. Hope things get moving in your investigation soon. I know you must be frustrated."

"That's the right word. Thanks. Ttyl."

Chapter Thirty-Six

El Monaguillo, The Alter Boy Surfaces.

It was early October. Max and Dave had grown exasperated. They had paid many visits to *Santa Teresa of Los Andes* in Rosarito. They had continued to regularly remind Padre Zurita that they had a potential large insurance settlement to award to Eddie Flores. Still nothing. Padre Zurita told Max and Dave that Eddie had come to mass one Sunday shortly after Max and Dave had first visited *Santa Teresa*, and the Padre gave Dave's business card to Eddie and informed him that he might be entitled to some money, but the Padre had not seen Eddie since.

Max and Dave were starting to feel some pressure from their boss at Premier Mutual. They had been in Mexico for several months. They had lots of leads but still no Cade Graham, nor any definitive proof that Cade Graham was alive. They all believed that facial recognition hits had picked up Cade Graham (and, of course, Enos), but that was not enough to resolve the issues with Premier. This case had morphed into much more than proving Cade Graham was alive so that Premier could avoid paying the death benefit on his life insurance. Now this was about investigating whether the suspicious deaths of all those residents at *Isla Valladolid*, during 2017-2018, that resulted in so many life insurance policy payoffs, were not accidental or natural—and perhaps were orchestrated by Cade Graham and those working in concert with him. Max and Dave were insistent that if they found the altar boy, Eddie Flores, they would find both Enos and Cade Graham, and the answers to what happened at *Isla Valladolid.*

One morning, Dave and Max were having breakfast in a café in Los Cabos. As they both sat in silence scrolling through the daily news on their cell phones, Dave's phone pinged. He looked at his phone, and his face suddenly lit up with excitement.

"Holy shit! It's him!"

"Him who?"

"The altar boy! He says he got my card from Padre Zurita and he'd like to talk to me!"

"Let's do it! Now! Where is he?"

"Hang on. He's texting me. He says he cannot talk right now, but can we talk at *Santa Teresa*'s maybe later today."

"Yes. Tell him yes."

"Of course, I am going to tell him yes. Calm down, Mad Max."

Five hours later, Dave and Max were sitting in the back pew of *Santa Teresa*'s, the designated meeting spot.

"He's late. You think he will show?"

"It's only 2:02 p.m. He's two minutes late. It's not time to panic."

"I don't panic, Dave. I'm a little OCD, but I don't ever panic. I'm a planner."

"Well, Mexican cartel members aren't like trains as far as being on time. Especially 18-year-old cartel members. I figure..."

Mid-sentence Dave stopped. His phone had just vibrated in his pocket. He pulled it out and read a text message.

"He's outside. He's sitting out at one of the picnic tables in the children's courtyard. He wants us to meet him there."

Dave and Max got up, fist pounded each other, and walked out of the back of the sanctuary toward the children's courtyard area. They saw Eddie sitting alone. No one else was around. It was perfect.

When they approached Eddie, Dave and Max both held out their hands to greet him. He acted shy and recoiled a bit. "Show me some proof of who you are!"

Both Dave and Max took out their business cards, flashed them, and showed Eddie their U.S. Passports.

"Okay. Thanks. I just had to be sure."

Dave broke the ice. "Your English is quite good. I speak Spanish. Do you prefer to speak in Spanish?"

"No. I am very comfortable speaking English. My parents taught me, and one of the Padres here taught me more."

"Was that Padre Iggy, by chance?" Max interjected and Dave shot him a worried look.

"Why do you ask about Padre Iggy?"

"We just know a few things about him. Some good and some bad."

Dave stopped Max from hijacking the conversation and taking it in a wrong direction.

"Eddie, as Padre Zurita may have told you, we may be able to arrange for you to receive a large sum of money, but it's not exactly about your parents' car wreck."

Eddie looked strangely at Dave. "I don't know exactly what you mean. Padre Zurita said the car that my father was driving was defective or something, and the car company and insurance company had a big money settlement for me."

"Well, we do work for an insurance company. But we

are looking for two men. Both American. If you can help us find them, there will be a large sum of money for you and even a plane ticket to the U.S. if you would like, and a lawyer who could arrange for you to stay in the U.S. if you would like."

Eddie looked confused.

"We are looking for a man who calls himself Enos. We know that you spend a lot of time with him. We know he works with *Los Chupas*. We are also looking for an older American man named Cade Graham, who might be doing business with Enos."

Eddie now looked terrified. "This was a trick. Why did you trick me?"

"Actually, Eddie we are trying to help you in part. Enos is very bad news. Cade Graham has gotten tangled up with him, and they both are going to have U.S. and Mexican law enforcement officers coming after them soon."

"Law enforcement does not scare Enos. He has worse problems. The *Zetas, Sinaloas, Oscuro, Los Chupas*—they all want to kill him right now. He will probably disappear soon, with millions of dollars. And they will never find him. No one will ever find him."

"Well, if Enos disappears, what happens to you Eddie?"

"Well, if you all have money for me, why do I have to worry about that?"

"Is that why you agreed to meet us? Because Enos has been supporting you? You have been working for him, and now he is about to leave, and you will be left with nothing? Or worse, one of the cartels' henchmen will come and get you? Kill you?"

Max was starting to feel a little bad. The kid looked scared to death.

Max interrupted. "Dave, let me start from the beginning. Let's tell Eddie everything, from the very beginning. And, Eddie, you do not need to be afraid. We are not going to hurt you. We are not going to turn you over to the *Policia* or the cartels. I have two kids close to your age.

I would never hurt a kid."

Max looked at Dave reassuringly. Dave guessed that this might be turning into one of those "good cop, bad cop" routines. Max continued.

"Eddie, here's the deal. Enos used to live in the U.S. You probably know that much. His real name is Marcus Braden, a.k.a. Marcus Smith. He and his twin brother killed numerous people in New Jersey and Texas. His brother blew himself up with a bomb trying. Marcus happens to be on the U.S. FBI's 'Most Wanted List,' and the U.S. Marshals are on his trail, too. It's only a matter of time until he is taken in, and maybe killed in the process. Trust me, the U.S. Marshals don't mess around. If they do not get a one hundred percent surrender, they shoot and not at the knee cap. Meanwhile, Dave and I are also looking for an American businessman named Cade Graham. We have seen pictures of him with Enos. We believe that they have been involved in some bad things, and Cade is going to go down with Enos. If you can help us find them, we will make sure you are safe and get paid handsomely. As Dave said, we can even get you into the U.S. and get you a lawyer to help you stay there if you want."

"How do I know I can trust you? You tricked me to get me here!"

Max and Dave hesitated. Max replied. "We feel bad about it, but we didn't know how else we could get through to you." Max then pulled out his iPad. He began showing Eddie grainy photo after grainy photo of Enos coming and going all around Mexico, including in and out of *Hussong's* and *Isla Valladolid*. Some of these pictures had Eddie in the background. He then showed several pictures of the pipeline explosion in *Hidalgo*.

"Eddie, we know that Enos is part of *Los Chupas*. And he is not just any member. They call him the CFO. He handles all the money. We know about him getting involved in the *Huachicoleros* business and that the *Zetas* are furious about it. We know that Enos has a band of *sicarios,* and he has put out hits on people all over Mexico. We know that some of those hits have been on residents at *Isla Valladolid* and that *Los Chupas* has been making money on those hits—which *Oscuro* has probably figured out by now, because *Oscuro* owns *Isla Valladolid*. So Enos has two cartels very pissed off at him, which is not a good thing. They feel like he is encroaching on their turf—taking away business opportunities of their own."

"You don't know what you are talking about. Yes, the *Zetas* are pissed off with Enos. But he has made money for both *Oscuro* and *Los Chupas*. Lots of money. But they do not think it is enough. They feel like he had been playing them both. But what he has done has allowed them both to make millions of dollars."

Max and Dave realized they had just gotten Eddie to inadvertently admit that he was very much aware of what Enos was doing.

"I don't understand. Are you defending Enos? What would your parents and Padre Zurita think if they knew you were hanging out with—being the errand boy—of a killer?"

"It's for the greater good. That's what Enos always says. He only kills bad people. And people who were soon going to die anyway."

Max and Dave fell quiet. The conversation was growing more disturbing by the minute.

"Eddie, how did you get mixed up with Enos anyway? Did you meet him here at *Santa Teresa's*?"

"Yeah."

"Did he hurt you?"

"No. He never hurt me. He protected me."

"From what? Why would you need protection here?"

Eddie was silent. He almost looked like tears were welling up in his callow, brown eyes.

Max couldn't help himself. "Was it Padre Iggy? Did Padre Iggy hurt you? Did Enos know?"

"I don't want to talk about Padre Iggy. Why are we talking about Padre Iggy now? I just want to talk about the money you promised me."

"Eddie, let's take this in steps." Max pulled out a wad of $100 bills. Dave looked at Max with some concern. "First, tell us this. Do you know who Cade Graham is, and can you tell us he is alive and does he do business with Enos. If you give me reliable information, right here and now, this cash in my hand is yours."

Max pulled up several clear pictures of Cade Graham on his iPad and showed them to Eddie.

Eddie spoke cautiously. "I know that man. Yes, his name is Cade Graham, although his nickname that Enos calls him sometimes is St. Jude. He is alive. He first hired Enos to fake his death. Cade had bad financial troubles and he wanted people to think he was dead. But then they started doing business together. Cade Graham owns *Isla Valladolid* along with *Oscuro*. He is a very wealthy man, but a lot of people were mad at him, and he was losing all his money. He wanted people to think he was dead and then he would just disappear. He had money hidden all over the world. Just like Enos."

Max handed Eddie a big wad of money. "There is more. Much more if you help us." Dave was cringing a bit.

Eddie flipped through the bills. Ten hundreds.

"Eddie, what kind of business are Enos and Cade doing together? We know it involves *Isla Valladolid*, but what exactly?" Max pulled out more bills.

"It has to do with life insurance money and medical experiments. The people who live at *Isla Valladolid*, when they die, they all have life insurance policies. Cade Graham and *Oscuro* somehow bought those policies from the old people. So, when they die, Cade and *Oscuro* collect all the money. Well, most of the money. Enos gets a small cut, too."

Dave interrupted. "And why does Enos get a small cut?" Dave was pretty sure that he knew the answer to this question but had to hear it.

"For his role in the deaths. They were going to die soon anyway. Enos just speeded it along. For the greater good. It was to help with the medical experiments. To help get disinfectants and drugs perfected or something like that."

Dave continued with the questioning for a bit. "I am not sure that I understand completely."

"Well, Cade Graham first hired Enos to put out hits on some of the old people at *Isla Valladolid* so he and *Oscuro* could start collecting money on their life insurance. But then they grew the business. They started doing medical experiments on the sickest people in the nursing home. They brought in a bunch of sterilizing equipment that Cade had invested in, to get it working right to start selling it in the U.S. and all over the world. And they also started injecting the residents with viruses and shit to see how the sterilizing equipment worked and if the drugs that Cade's other company was inventing would cure them. They called it a win-win situation. If people died, Cade and *Oscuro* collected life insurance money. If people lived, then Cade's other companies would have proof that their sterilization equipment and drugs were a success. Cade could make millions."

Max just handed Eddie another wad of money. "Eddie, how do you know all this?"

"I watch. I listen. I'm with Enos almost all the time."

Dave didn't know whether to be morally offended or impressed beyond belief with the way Max was casually handing out one hundred-dollar bills to the kid and getting him to talk. Dave just assumed that this was standard operating procedure back from Max's days dealing with informants on the police force. There didn't seem to be any real rules for what they were doing now.

"What other companies are you talking about, Eddie, that invented the sterilization equipment and drugs?"

"Companies that Cade Graham owns in Texas. I don't know the names."

"Where is Cade now, Eddie?"

"He's with Enos. Living in Enos's villa outside of *Rosarito*. It's back in the hills. Real secluded. There are bodyguards everywhere."

"What did you mean earlier when you said Enos was leaving soon?"

"Well, Enos and Cade just made a lot of money from their investment in the sterilization equipment and the drug company back in Texas. The companies were sold for lots of money, and lots of it went to Enos and Cade."

Max connected all the dots. Eddie was talking about the case Avery had been telling him about last month. It had to be BASA and DB Biocontainment.

"Eddie, you said earlier you didn't remember the name of the companies that Cade Graham owns in Texas. Were they by chance BASA and DB Biocontainment?"

"Yeah. Yeah. That was them."

"Holy shit." Max was pale as a ghost. Dave looked at Max baffled.

"Go on, Eddie." Max had refocused on the task at hand.

"Well, anyway, Enos and Cade bought stocks in pharmaceutical companies that are going to buy the drugs that are made by Cade's company, and they made a lot of money on those stocks. Like millions and millions. Enos says he is set for life and that maybe he will leave. *Oscuro* feels like they were cut out of the big money. *Los Chupas* will too, when and if they figure out what happened. They only half understand what happened back in Texas, but they feel like maybe they were cheated out of a big payoff. And of course, the *Zetas* have been after Enos for months."

"Where will Enos go?"

"Maybe to live with his brother in Malta."

Max felt his knees buckle a bit.

The three of them sat in silence.

"Eddie, will Enos take you to Malta? Has he said anything about that? Will he leave you with money? Will he protect you from the cartels? I mean, they probably all know that you hang out with Enos?"

"I do more than just hang out with Enos. I know a lot about the money. I might be the next CFO. He has taught me a lot about handling money. He said I was good with math and was a natural to take over one day."

Max proceeded cautiously. "Eddie, do you know what immunity means?"

Eddie stared back. "I don't think I know what you mean."

"You give us a little more information, and we will make sure you cannot get charged with any crime, and, as I said earlier, we will make sure you get a very large sum of money—much more than I have paid you today—and a free plane ticket to the U.S. You can trust me on this. This is not just about money. You are going to need to get far away from the cartels. They are going to associate you with Enos and all of his shenanigans. They will kill you, Eddie."

"Well, I like money. But I don't know if your plan is worth it. I know how to get into some of Enos's accounts. Accounts in the Cayman Islands, in Malta, Switzerland. There is both fiat money and bitcoin. Enos has taught me about it all. I am his Assistant CFO. If I wanted to trick Enos and all of *Los Chupas* I could drain those accounts today. I would be set. It would be much more money than you are probably going to offer me."

"Yes, but you would soon be dead. We can keep you alive and safe and rich."

"Tell me what you want me to do."

Chapter Thirty-Seven

Operation Hedgehog—Planning the Takedown.

After the meeting with Eddie, things moved swiftly. It was now late October.

Max and Dave first were required to provide some rather lengthy explanations to officials at Premier Mutual. Among other things, they had to explain Max's recent large expenditure of his "petty cash." Then they had to talk to the necessary contacts within the justice departments in Mexico and the U.S. to arrange for immunity and other accommodations for Eddie Flores. Max and Dave convincingly assured both justice departments that they had a lock on bringing in: (a) a most-wanted fugitive—Marcus Braden, who had murdered two U.S. federal judges, among others (and was now brazenly committing crimes all over Mexico); and (b) a missing billionaire Texas hedge fund manager—Cade Graham—who had faked his own death and engaged in a massive insurance fraud (involving the murder of numerous elderly U.S. ex-pats). But the most difficult obstacle was determining the proper "takedown" of Enos and Cade Graham—timing was a conundrum. Were they both about to disappear? Was there extensive documentary evidence that might establish their crimes, and would it disappear with them?

Dave and Max set up another meeting with Eddie in a few days, once again at *Santa Teresa's*. Eddie pulled into the parish's children's courtyard on a motor scooter, Max was struck once again at how young and innocent Eddie looked. Max couldn't help but think of his own son, Heath, and how different a life this kid had experienced—the loss of his parents at a young age, likely followed by molestation by Father Iggy here at *Santa Teresa's*. This had to be what drew Enos to this kid in the first place. They probably had this common, hideous bond. Enos likely tracked down Father Iggy to take out revenge on him. Then he likely befriended Eddie—knowing intuitively that Father Iggy had to be abusing Eddie just like Father Iggy had abused Marcus. Enos then maimed and tortured Father Iggy—refraining from killing him either because he couldn't bring himself to kill a priest, or perhaps he thought that removing most of Father Iggy's body parts would be a harsher, more fitting punishment.

"Good morning, Eddie. How has your week been so far?"

Eddie shrugged. "Enos is going to be out of here soon. Not sure where he is going, but he is definitely going somewhere. Any day now."

"How do you know for sure?"

"He is packing, making plans. Moving money. Talking to his brother a lot."

"Let me ask you a question, Eddie. When you get your big sum of money from us, do you have a place to keep it? A safe place? I mean you shouldn't just carry around the kind of money that we are talking about. Do you have a bank account or know how to set one up? You said that Enos has taught you a lot of things about money?"

The Altar Boy laughed. "Yeah, of course. I have been planning this all out since the Padre gave me Mr. Carrillo's business card and told me that I would get some money."

"How have you been planning it all out?"

"I have a Wyoming LLC with a bank account."

"You have a what?"

"I have my own Wyoming LLC. A limited liability shell company. I have seen Enos set them up a hundred times. Wyoming is a U.S. state where you can set up a limited liability company and you don't have to disclose who owns or manages the company. There is an address that you can use on Thomas Avenue in Cheyenne, Wyoming that houses more than 2,000 shell companies formed with Wyoming Corporate Services. Enos has a few hundred of them. I think he learned about them from Cade Graham. And I created one when I heard from the Padre that I might be getting some of my own money."

"Good God. This wasn't necessarily the answer that I was expecting to get. Does Enos know you did that?"

"No. I have my own laptop and that's where I set up a bank account, under the Wyoming LLC's name. That's where I will transfer my money."

Dave and Max were astounded at the sophistication of this young boy. An eighteen-year-old Mexican kid sounded like one of the "estate planning" lawyers exposed in the Panama Papers.

"Well, I am starting to think that this is going to be a lot easier than I thought. Eddie, do you have the ability to get access to any of Enos's bank accounts?"

"Yeah. Well, most of them."

"Most of them?"

"Well, all of them in Mexico, for sure, and probably several of the ones that are offshore, too. Even a couple of the accounts that he shares with his brother in Malta."

"Holy shit."

"Okay. Does Enos have separate accounts for his various businesses? Like, if he does assassinations for the cartel, the fees for those would go into a separate account? Or the fees for the gasoline pipe puncturing would go into a separate account? Or the fees he has gotten relating to *Isla Valladolid*? Or the clinical trial testing and so on?"

"Yes, separate accounts for all of that. Those are the operating accounts. Those are all here at Mexican banks. Then Enos has opened sweep accounts that he weekly sweeps those funds into, mostly in the Cayman Islands. From there, he invests the funds into different legit businesses to launder the money. A lot of those businesses are in Malta and they are owned by his brother. A restaurant. A scooter dealership. A marina. A hotel. Then he pays the funds out to the cartel leadership when he is ordered to. But also, he has Bitcoin stored in Bitcoin wallets and exchanges."

Once again, Max and Dave were astounded by what they were hearing from this eighteen-year-old Mexican child. He practically sounded like a wolf of Wall Street. Marcus Braden Smith was a self-taught financial whiz, and he had tutored Eddie in his ways.

"And, again, you are telling me that you have access to every one of Enos's accounts?"

"Most of them. Enos said if anything ever happened to him, the money needed to go to his brother Richard in Malta. But I feel like Enos probably has a few secret accounts that he hasn't shown to me."

Max and Dave sat in silence for a few moments.

"Eddie, let me make sure I understand all of Enos's businesses. He has hit men working for him. The *sicarios*. He collects fees for that assassination business and has a separate operating account for those fees?"

"Yes. A *Los Chupas* operating account."

"He has the *Huachicoleros* business. He makes money I guess by selling to third parties the gasoline or diesel that he steals and puts that money in a separate account?"

"Yes. Another *Los Chupas* bank account."

"Then he has his fake death business and a separate

account for that?"

"Yes. But that's his side business. He has his own personal account for that business. Not *Los Chupas* accounts."

"Okay. What am I missing? Anything else?"

Eddie laughed. "Enos has lots of other businesses. There is the life insurance settlements business."

"And clarify again what that is all about."

"That is the assassinations of people just for Cade Graham's companies. Old people at *Isla Valladolid*. And some other nursing homes with old people."

"And there is a separate bank account for that?"

"Well, yes. That one is complicated. Cade wires Enos the life insurance proceeds, and then we take a cut, and the rest goes to the *Oscuro* people."

"Do you mean Enos personally takes a cut or *Los Chupas* does?"

"Well actually just Enos does. He was worried about the *Los Chupas* boys hearing about *Oscuro's* involvement at *Isla Valladolid*. *Los Chupas* would think Enos is double-crossing them—working for *Oscuro* on the side. Cade Graham got involved with *Oscuro* before even meeting Enos, and he just pulled Enos in with him, but *Los Chupas* still might not believe that."

Dave and Max had their doubts about who pulled in whom in connection with the *Isla Valladolid* criminal enterprise.

"Anything else?"

"*Los Chupas* has warehouses in certain border towns: *Ciudad Juarez*, *El Bajio* and at *Anapra*. They were stash houses at one time for heroin and fentanyl for *Los Chupas's* drug trafficking. But *Los Chupas* had to stop this because that was *Zeta* and *Sinaloa* territory. Lately, Enos has been using the warehouses for clinical drug trials for Cade Graham's businesses. Enos brings people to the warehouses who want to immigrate to the U.S. They have drugs tested on them in exchange for passage into the U.S. by Enos's mules."

"And how does Enos get paid for that?"

"By one of Cade Graham's companies called DB Biocontainment. It goes to Enos personally, not *Los Chupas*."

"Would the *Los Chupas* boys be upset if they knew about that?"

"I don't know. Maybe. The warehouses belong to *Los Chupas* so probably, I guess. But Enos has always personally pocketed the money that he makes for his mule services. It's actually a lot of money. So, I think he just considered this an extension of the mule business."

"Did you say Cade Graham's company is called DB Biocontainment?"

"Yes."

"I thought the other day you said you didn't remember the name of the businesses?"

"I didn't. But I found some wire transfer information from them and remembered that this was the Cade Graham business that Enos was doing work for."

"What do you know about DB Biocontainment?"

"Just that it's in Texas. Near Dallas. It is in an underground facility. It's some secret lab."

"An underground facility?"

"Yes."

"Any other business we haven't covered?"

"Some fentanyl trafficking still. That's down to a pretty small amount, because of pressure from other cartels. That money goes into a separate *Los Chupas* account. He also sells some drug he calls GHBs."

"Georgia Homeboys? Roofies? Separate account for that?"

"Yeah. And also, there is a miscellaneous account for a few of Enos's side businesses like his Deep Fakes business."

"What type of Deep Fakes is Enos doing?"

"We use artificial intelligence sometimes to create fake photo images or voiceovers to blackmail government officials and sometimes PEMEX officials. Actually, I pretty much do all of that work. I should get all that money, but it goes into an Enos personal account."

The three of them sat in silence.

"Enos has a lot of investment accounts. He calls that his play money. He used one of them recently to buy a bunch of stocks of U.S. pharmaceutical companies. He said he made several millions of dollars just from that. I am pretty sure that's why he is about to leave. It was a big score. Plus, I know right now he fears for his life. The *Zetas* have been after him for months. Besides the *Huachicoleros* business that he has cut in on, they think he is using the border warehouses where the medical tests are happening to stash dope, in competition with them. I think he also figures the *Los Chupas* boys are going to kill him if they ever get wind of all his personal side businesses that he's cut them out of."

"Well, can you tell me this. Right now, which Mexican bank account has the most money in it? Have they all been swept recently?"

"The one relating to the *Huachicoleros*—Enos just got prepaid on a job that he is about to execute in a few days. Every once in a while, someone will prepay him. I don't know why. Anyway, I figure this is the last job he is going to do, and then he is gone."

"Where is that job going to happen?"

"Near a PEMEX terminal outside of Mexicali."

"Are you supposed to be involved?"

"Nah. I'll stay back at the villa. Lately, Enos likes me to stay there and keep an eye on Cade when Enos isn't around. I guess he doesn't completely trust him."

"What time is the pipeline rupture supposed to happen?"

Eddie hesitated. "I have told you a lot today. What about my money?"

Max handed Eddie another wad of U.S. hundreds.

"The job is going to happen at 11:00 a.m. this Friday."

"Eddie, what about documents? Paper or computer

records? Are you able to get to records that prove some of this?"

"Well, maybe. Enos has told me before that he has a plan to cover his tracks if he ever needs to. He has forensic shredding software on his main laptop that he uses. He has encryption on another computer—something like BitLocker that you have to have a decryption key for. And he regularly removes his SIM cards from his cell phones."

Max and Dave looked like they just had the air let out of their sails after hearing this news.

"Eddie, here's what I need you to do. Send Dave a text after Enos has left for Mexicali on Friday morning. Dave and I are going to meet you at the villa. Write down on this card the location of the villa." Max handed Eddie one of his business cards and a pen. "Meanwhile, I want you to transfer all the money in the *Huachicoleros* bank account to your Wyoming LLC bank account."

"Enos will kill me if he finds out I did that! It's like $100,000 U.S. dollars."

"Just do it. We are going to protect you."

Eddie sat silently a few moments. Then he wrote down the address of the villa.

"See you Friday morning. Eddie, don't be scared. You are doing the right thing, and you are going to be set up for life."

Dave looked at Max incredulously. He had no idea what Max was plotting.

Chapter Thirty-Eight

An October Surprise.

It was the day that Max had long been awaiting. Marcus Braden—Enos—was about to be outwitted and probably pay the ultimate price. And Max was going to capture Cade Graham all in the same process.

Max had hatched an elaborate plan. Dave was quite impressed. A little bit scared but impressed.

Max had tipped off PEMEX and law enforcement far and wide that another pipeline would be punctured at 11:00 a.m. on Friday October 25th. It would be executed by the blond gringo Enos, who was a member of *Los Chupas*.

Meanwhile, Max had arranged for various DEA officers, and their Mexican counterparts, to tip off *Los Chupas* members that Enos was skimming their profits and cheating them in all kinds of ways. *Los Chupas's* leadership was told to check the *Huachicoleros* operating bank account, and they would find it was empty. They should also check out their warehouses in *Ciudad Juarez*, *El Bajio* and at

Anapra. Enos had started some secret activity there on which he was making a killing, and not cutting *Los Chupas* in on it. It involved a partnership of some kind that he had going on with the American hedge fund manager, Cade Graham, who everyone in the U.S. has assumed is dead. The activity might even involve the *Zetas*—Enos might be double crossing *Los Chupas* (this part was a lie, of course). In any event, there might be something big going down there soon—likely Friday morning before the pipeline rupture.

And, if this were not enough, Max had also arranged for the *Zetas* to be tipped off about Enos and the pipeline puncture on Friday morning. The *Zetas* were also tipped off that there was something big going on at the *Los Chupas* labs/stash houses in *Ciudad Juarez*, *El Bajio* and at *Anapra* and perhaps they should send people out there earlier on Friday morning—after all, Enos had promised the *Zetas* months ago that *Los Chupas* would shut down its drug operations at those locations. Clearly, he had not kept that promise.

If this all played out just right, it was going to be a shit show of epic proportions.

Chapter Thirty-Nine

Blue Eyes.

Avery was sitting at her desk on Friday morning October 25, researching on her personal iPad whether there were diseases or medications that could cause a person's irises to turn light blue. She didn't have any court that day. Avery couldn't shake her reaction to the twenty or so people in her courtroom the previous month who had bright icy blue eyes. Was it the permafrost flu that had caused these survivors to have unnaturally blue eyes or was it one of Dmitry Basayev's therapies? Dmitry had the same eyes. Avery could not find anything in any of the recent news stories about DB Biocontainment and Dmitry Basayev that mentioned the eyes. Her curiosity over this was driving her crazy. Avery's phone suddenly rang, interrupting her research. It was Max.

"Hey, Avery. What are you doing? Preparing for court?"

"Nope. I don't have any court today. I am actually

doing some research on what sort of diseases or medications have been known to turn people's irises bright, light blue?"

"Uh. Okay. That sounds random."

"Okay. I know it actually sounds crazy, but I can explain."

Max braced himself for what he feared was about to be a long explanation. He looked at his watch.

"In our BASA and DB Biocontainment cases, we had twenty people sitting in the back of the court room one day who had all been exposed to some strange new virus that came out of the permafrost in Alaska—they were all Tex-Core pipeline workers and family members—and they had supposedly been saved by the therapies that DB Biocontainment invented. But all of them had these crazy bright, blue eyes. Unnatural in color. And no one ever explained it. I'm trying to find an explanation in any resource I can find."

"Are you sure this doesn't have something to do with your synesthesia, Avery?"

"No, Max. You know my synesthesia doesn't work that way!"

"Honestly, I don't know how it works after all these years."

"Besides, Judge Hall saw their eyes too, and so did our law clerks and interns. It was like characters from a horror movie, but kind of beautiful at the same time."

"Oh my God. This sounds nuts. No offense."

"None taken. What's up with you, Mad Max?"

"Well, we have made real progress recently. It has been a long time coming, but I think this is D-Day. We have a location on both Cade Graham and Marcus Braden. There is going to be a takedown in just a few minutes. Just wanted to talk to you before it happens. Just in case."

"Just in case what?"

"Avery, you know how these things can go. You never know."

"Max, you are a private investigator for crying out loud.

You are not a cop anymore. You retired from that. Dave is no longer a Marshal. You find people and other people handle the dirty work now!"

"I know. You are right. But this is Mexico. Anything can happen. You don't always know who to trust or who you can rely on to have your back. The corruption works like a well-oiled machine here. I hate to say it, but there are people on the take everywhere."

"Good Lord. What exactly is going to happen today?"

"You know I can't tell you. But I think our job will finally be done in a few hours. Say a prayer for me."

"I always do."

Chapter Forty

Cartel War and Plan B.

It was 10:30 a.m., thirty minutes before the expected PEMEX pipeline puncture. Undercover Mexican federal law enforcement officers were sprinkled around the scene. Hopefully, as soon as Enos/Marcus Braden arrived, there would be a quick arrest. After his arrest, a diplomatic turf war would likely ensue between the Departments of Justice in the U.S. and Mexico. The U.S. DOJ would want a hand-over to the U.S. Marshals for extradition back to the U.S., to prosecute Braden for the murders of two federal judges and numerous others in the U.S. Undoubtedly, he would get the death penalty. But Mexico would want to prosecute the America ex-pat who had escalated their country's cartel violence to a heinous new level.

The covert *federales* blended in well with the locals--wearing cowboy hats, overalls and work shirts, puffing on cigarettes, and carrying buckets and pails, looking on expectantly from afar, as though they were waiting for the opportunity to grab some free gasoline. Word always got out, far and wide, whenever the *Huachicoleros* were expected to arrive. Max and Dave had a hand in making sure word got out this time. There were several dozen men, women, and children standing around, awaiting free gas and maybe some sort of additional free gifts, which the *Huachicoleros* frequently brought to establish good will and cooperation among the rural folk.

Then, shortly after 10:30 a.m., the first signs of an impending clash between cartels emerged. The *Zetas* suddenly appeared in spectacular fashion, in their Mexican version of the Somali "technical"—an armored Toyota pickup with six-barreled Gatling guns that can fire up to a hundred rounds per second. Others had similar M-134s rotary machine guns. The trucks were carrying huge military-style batteries with heavy-duty electric cable. Who knows how the *Zetas* were getting this type of weaponry (possibly stolen from the Mexican military, or maybe smuggled through the black market into Mexico by American gunrunners), but just one of these "miniguns" could probably take out everyone on site with one push of the trigger. A mass casualty weapon, to be sure. All of the *Zeta* personnel wore camouflage (although that hardly seemed necessary) and tactical gear (vests, gloves, belts with knives, hand grenades, and other gadgets, elbow pads and knee pads). Some of them were carrying .50-caliber Barrett sniper rifles, which have a range of more than a mile and are powerful enough to shoot through a wall of concrete block as though it were nothing. Some were carrying AR-15s, AK-47s, and other fire power that was almost beyond comprehension.

And, as for *Los Chupas*, it seems that, just as Max and Dave had contemplated, *Los Chupas* had discovered the missing money from the *Huachicoleros* operating bank account. They also, based on carefully placed law enforcement tips, had visited, earlier that morning, their warehouses in *Ciudad Juarez*, *El Bajio* and at *Anapra*. The

Los Chupas leaders, upon checking out those houses, had no idea what was going on there now—what with the giant refrigeration units and hospital beds and medical equipment. They assumed it was some sort of new drug manufacturing facility that Enos had secretly gotten started. Or maybe Enos had teamed up with the *Zetas*. So *Los Chupas* did what drug cartels do when they feel that they have been double-crossed. They blew each of the three facilities to smithereens, not bothering to provide any warnings or clear out any humans who were on site. They destroyed the houses with a massive punch, using one of their new weapons of choice that, ironically, Enos had encouraged *Los Chupas* to adopt: small quadcopter-type drones carrying improvised explosive devices, Tupperware containers filled with C4 charges and ball bearings, designed to act as shrapnel. "Bomblets." Not only were several people on site when the bomblets were dropped, but refrigeration units full of valuable drug therapies were lost. Moreover, numerous vials of the permafrost flu virus were either obliterated in the blast or dispersed into the dry desert air of Mexico. Time would tell on that one.

Los Chupas was furious with Enos. They now knew that he had been skimming their profits and cheating them in all kinds of ways. Meanwhile, the *Zetas* were furious with Enos and with all of *Los Chupas*. Not only had Enos invaded their turf with the pipeline puncturing, but the *Zetas* believed that *Los Chupas* were the ones that reopened the stash houses in *Ciudad Juarez*, *El Bajio* and *Anapra* that Enos promised to shut down. Coincidentally, just after dawn, when numerous *Zetas* foot soldiers had arrived at *Ciudad Juarez*, *El Bajio,* and *Anapra* to investigate activity there themselves, *Los Chupas* had dropped their drone bomblets killing some, but not all the *Zetas* personnel on the scene. The *Zetas* naturally thought the timing was intentional. This was war now. It was time for Enos and *Los Chupas* to pay a big price to the *Zetas*.

Dave Carrillo was positioned on the perimeter of the

Mexicali pipeline area. He was getting antsy because Eddie was supposed to text Dave as soon as Enos left the villa to head toward Mexicali. Eddie should have texted Dave by now because the villa was more than an hour's drive. But when Dave saw the various armored vehicles arriving, he became far more agitated, realizing who they were: the "special forces" contingent within the *Zetas'* overall force structure. These "special forces" would not merely confront Enos and kidnap or assassinate him only. They were obviously planning a major battle with *Los Chupas*. No doubt *Los Chupas* had gotten wind of this and their "special forces" contingent would be showing up next. If word had gotten to Enos—and it very well could have, given his resources and uncanny ability to stay one step ahead of trouble—he might not even show up at all today.

Dave texted Max. "We have a situation developing here."

Max texted back. "Situation?"

"No sign of Enos and no text from Eddie yet. I should have heard from Eddie by now. But now we've got *Zetas* special forces arriving with automatic weapons like you wouldn't believe. Lots of them. It's crazier than anything I have ever seen. There is going to be a shit show. Strike that. It's going to be apocalyptic. Holy MF. *Los Chupas* is now arriving, also in armored SUVs. Not good."

Max was approximately an hour away from Mexicali, about one mile down the highway from the private road that led to Enos's villa, posing as an agricultural worker with a flat tire on his dusty old Isuzu pickup. "Well, hell. Maybe that explains why I haven't seen any vehicles coming out of the villa yet. I was hoping Enos got an earlier start and I just somehow missed him."

"Nope. Doesn't look that way."

"Shit. It's almost an hour drive from there. He definitely should have left by now."

"I've got a bad feeling about this."

"Well, what do you propose to do Han Solo?"

"I'm heading your way, Max. Enos isn't coming to Mexicali. He's bugging out. He's starting his getaway. I feel it in my gut."

"Hold on a second, Dave. Quiet a second."

There was a moment or two of silence, followed by the roar of several loud and large vehicles passing by Max.

Max got back on the phone. "Holy shit. Four narco trucks just came out of the road that leads to the villa and passed me hauling ass. There were literally a half dozen guys in each truck with Barrett .50 calibers and loads of cannisters of I don't know what. Truck beds all replaced with open-topped high-walled cargo bodies. It looked like the military."

"Okay. It's beginning to look a lot like fuck-this. I am heading there—as much as I might enjoy watching this spectacle unfold. It sounds like all Enos's protective detail has been dispatched to Mexicali to help deal with the *Zeta* special forces. We both know Enos is not going to be anywhere near this shit in Mexicali. That's probably why the kid hasn't texted me. Enos's game plan has changed. Enos is for sure still there, and the kid can't find a way to secretly text us."

"All right, I bet you're right. Get here quick. Roadblocks are likely in and out of Mexicali, unless you get here pronto."

"Roger that."

Chapter Forty-One

The Motto of the U.S. Marshals— "Let No Guilty Man Escape."

Dave texted Eddie Flores as he sped down the highway to connect with Max.

"What's going on, Eddie?"

No response.

Max had repaired his flat tire and was plotting Plan B as he waited on Dave. The original plan had, of course, been for Mexican law enforcement officers to nab Enos in Mexicali when Enos was there to execute the pipeline puncture. Dave would be there onsite to confirm the capture (or, quite likely, the kill). And Max would go into the villa after Enos had left, and Eddie would lead Max to Cade Graham and whatever digital or physical documents that Enos left behind, to hopefully be used as evidence of some of the cartel's (and Enos's and Cade Graham's) crimes. Dave would join up with Max at the villa later. But obviously things had changed now.

Max had Dave's reconnaissance drone in his pickup.

Should he take a chance and deploy it? It was a very sophisticated and expensive piece of equipment that Premier had paid for, fitted with FLIR thermal imaging surveillance equipment, to detect human movements. It was risky—it might be seen—but it was riskier not to know how many humans were in and around the villa. Max decided to wait a few minutes and consult with Dave on this. Dave was the drone expert anyway. Max was greening up with tactical gear. He had some flash bangs as well as other gadgets that he and Dave had put together, since they did not have all the weaponry with them in Mexico that they might have liked to have.

Eventually Dave's truck showed up on the horizon, careening at about ninety miles per hour.

"What took you so long, man?"

"I had to give a beautiful *senorita* hitchhiker a ride to the strip club where she works. I still got here in thirty minutes. What's the game plan, Mad Max?"

"My guess is that Enos, Cade, and Eddie are all still in the villa. The question is who else is there and what is the situation. Do you think we should use the FLIR?"

"We have no choice. Got to." Dave grabbed the drone and started readying it and the remote-control device for a deployment. He got it up and headed toward the villa in moments.

"We are outmanned even if it is just the three of them. For all we know the kid will turn on us. Enos may have taught him to use an automatic weapon. He's taught him all kinds of other fine things."

"Nope, I never allow myself to be outmanned, Mad Max. You should know me that well by now."

"What do you mean?"

"I've got some of my DEA buddies and some of their Mexican counterparts headed this way."

And, indeed, he did. The cavalry showed up momentarily. Approximately thirty men, armed for battle.

Mad Max grinned at the Swiss Army Knife. "You're

not a Swiss Army Knife, Dave. You just have friends in all the right places."

"Have I disappointed you, Max?"

"Yes. But only because I may not get to use all our make-shift weaponry here after all."

"Hah. More like you are disappointed because you were hoping for an opportunity to take out Enos personally."

"Me? Do you think I am motivated by revenge? I am a kind and gentle guy, Dave."

"Mad Max, I am reminded of an old Rolling Stones song right now. You know the one?"

"Hmm. No, Dave. I have no idea."

Dave started singing "you can't always get what you want, but if you try sometimes, you just might find, you get what you need."

"You sing terrible."

In a few moments, the drone returned. The video it captured showed just three human images and a couple of dogs within the entire compound. Serendipity.

"Should we warn, Eddie?"

"You know the answer to that, Max. We can't."

"I know. I just hate it that the kid could get killed in the crossfire."

"Max, stand down. Let the *federales* and DEA do it their way."

Max kept thinking of poor Eddie. He kept thinking of his own son Heath.

And so, Plan B had begun. The cavalry charged through the heavy iron gates toward Enos's compound. Max and Dave stayed outside the gates. They had push-to-talks where they could communicate with personnel within the villa if need be. One couldn't be sure if other cartel members might show up, although there were some *federales* positioned down the road as a first line of defense.

After the *federales* and DEA went toward the villa, it was eerily quiet for a while. Max and Dave were somewhat surprised. They were not sure what was going on, and they were not going to hit the push-to-talks and make any noise. Suddenly, a whispery voice came over one of the push-to-talks. "Holy shit. This guy has his own helicopter and helicopter pad. The helicopter is mounted with a Dillon Aero minigun. There is a middle-aged man sitting inside, looks like he is about to start it up. He's starting it up. Shit! Is that Cade Graham?"

Max and Dave in unison replied, "Yes! Don't let him get away!"

Suddenly, a group of law enforcement personnel swarmed out of nearby brush and charged the helicopter, guns drawn. As they did, Cade Graham looked up startled from his clip board and flight plan. He put his hands up in the air instinctively. It was over for Cade Graham. He immediately knew it.

But it wasn't over for Enos. He had heard the commotion. He was quickly grabbing some stashed weapons from his arsenal and activating shredding software on the one and only laptop that he had not already cleaned.

"Eddie, let's go."

"What's going on, Enos?"

"I'm leaving. You're coming, too."

"Since when, Enos? You told me I was staying here for a while, and you would come back for me later."

"Plans have changed."

Enos grabbed Eddie by the arm. "Let's go."

Enos walked slowly out of the massive Teflon-coated doors of the villa onto the front porch. He had Eddie close by his side. Enos put his handgun up at Eddie's head. Eddie was now his hostage.

There were approximately twenty law enforcement officers surrounding the villa. The others were with Cade Graham and had disabled the helicopter.

One of the Mexican officers picked up a bullhorn and began speaking into it. "Marcus Braden Smith. Drop the gun. Let go of the kid. Put your hands up. You aren't going anywhere."

"Are you really going to make a kid die today? I'll blow this kid's brains all over you. And I have boobie traps set up all over this place. Do you think I am alone? I have bodyguards inside. I have told them to stand down for now."

"That's some pretty strong BS you're spinning there, Marcus Braden. We know they are all gone. Fighting your war for you up in Mexicali. Probably all dead by now actually."

Max and Dave had by this point silently crept up in the brush about fifty yards from all the action and were looking on with binoculars. They had on them the only weapons that they had been allowed to obtain while in Mexico: two M24 sniper rifles. They were not authorized to use them. They were just carrying them for the ultimate disaster scenario.

"Dave, how good are you—what are your chances of getting a head shot from here with that weapon?"

"I'm pretty sure I could do it. What about you? You think you could do it?"

"Hell, I *know* I could do it."

"You're so full of shit."

At that precise moment, Enos whipped out an automatic weapon that been hidden behind Eddie. As Enos began to point the weapon toward the *federales*, Eddie whipped out a knife from a holder on his lower leg and stabbed Enos in the thigh and jumped away. It appeared that Eddie—whether by design or not—had hit Enos's femoral artery and Enos was bleeding profusely but was still twisting and moving. This gave the *federales* the opening they needed. The *federales* lit him up, with a hail of massive gunfire. Enos was instantly shot with more than a dozen rounds. He was lying still on the ground and likely dead.

Max and Dave stared at each other in silence. It was over.

"Max, you remember what the motto of the U.S. Marshals is, don't you?"

Max rolled his eyes. "No. Remind, me Dave."

"Let no guilty man escape."

"Well, mission accomplished, I guess."

"Yep, it doesn't matter who does the hit or the capture, as long as the guilty man does not escape."

"What are you saying? Do you think I am upset because the *federales* got to do the dirty work here? Do you think I am a glory hog who wanted to take credit for the take down? Those days are long gone, Dave."

"Yeah, right."

"Let's go down and check on Eddie. He looks Okay. We have a promise to keep with him."

"Don't you think we should check in with Premier Mutual first? They have been waiting a long time for this day."

"Eddie first."

Max and Dave walked down near the villa. Eddie was shaken but fine. He was sitting on the front steps of the villa, petting one of the dogs and drinking a root beer that one of the *federales* had given him.

"Eddie, we keep our promises. We are going to get you out of here. We've got you more money than that $100,000 that you wired to Wyoming. Premier Mutual has agreed to fund you an account and pay for you to go to college."

Eddie looked up at Max and Dave without much of an expression. He was in shock. The kid who had seen plenty of death and destruction in his short life was actually trembling. Max awkwardly put his arm around Eddie and sat with him a few moments.

Max and Dave next walked over to Enos's body which was surrounded by EMTs.

"Looks losick," Max said. "Is he going to make it?"

Dave had an exchange in Spanish with an EMT.

They said he'll bleed out in less than two minutes.

Max leaned down and whispered into Enos's ear. "Hey, Marcus. You piece of shit. This is Max Lassiter. Avery sends her regards. For the greater good."

Dave had a slow sip of tequila.

"Max, so how are we going to deal with Richard?

"Wow, that was fast. And I thought I was restless and antsy! We finally found Cade Graham and got to watch Marcus Braden get snuffed out, what, five hours ago? Now you're ready to move onto the next fugitive. Gotta love it. No wonder you were a legend in the Marshals Service."

The two of them were back at one of their newest haunts, Hussong's Cantina, decompressing after the explosive events at Braden's villa. Irony, since so many of Braden's and Graham's plans had been hatched there over the last few months. They had ordered a bottle of tequila, but strangely were not much in the mood for drinking. They were a bit solemn, in fact. The day's events had been overwhelming, even for these two. Max earlier had a long phone conversation with Avery. She had uncontrollably wept when she learned that Marcus Braden had been killed. Max could barely talk to her. She said she would have to call him back later. He wasn't sure if this was a normal catharsis, or she had moral reservations about the way the events had all unfolded. She frequently left him guessing.

"Well, you said a few weeks ago, we were going to have to go to Malta soon. What'd you have in mind?"

"I've got some ideas."

"I can't imagine what. We have zero contacts or resources we can tap in Malta. It's a whole different ball game than Mexico."

"Okay. First, it's a major break-through that we now know what alias Richard is using: Rasmus Aavik from Estonia. We can thank Eddie for that. We'll have a lock on Richard's location pretty soon. And, also, thanks to Eddie, we are going to have a solid money laundering case against Richard, even though there is almost no chance we can nail him for sending threatening letters to my wife or being involved with his brothers' murdering spree."

"Max, do you have a degree in forensic accounting or what? Eddie's word, while pretty compelling, is the word of a teenager. How are you really going to prove the money laundering scheme? The web and layers of offshore accounts and shell companies will be a nightmare to sort through. Money laundering cases usually take years for the FBI to put together. It takes teams of people, and the folks at the offshore banks are almost always uncooperative—it's not them it's their privacy laws. The FBI is not going to screw with all of this for a Maltese money launderer, even if he can likely be tied to some U.S. crimes. And, again, the only U.S. crime you can likely pin on Richard, besides sending threatening letters to a U.S. judge, is altering New Jersey governmental records to fake his death back in the late 1990s when he was a teenager. Good luck getting the FBI to spend more than ten minutes with you. Now, find a terrorist tie to him of some sort? Then maybe you'll get their attention. Maybe."

Max sighed. He had already thought through this a million times. "Well maybe you're right. But I'm not sure it's going to be as hard as you think. We have several bank account numbers and some account statements, and Eddie is a pretty smart kid. If I must spend all day and all night for a year, putting together the money trail, I will. And maybe we can get some of the gang members here to provide testimony if the *Federales* offer them some sort of deal to turn State's evidence."

"Isn't it pretty to think so?"

"Huh? Did you just quote Hemingway?"

"Huh?"

"Nothing."

Both sat in silence for a few minutes.

"Max, I am just saying that you're dreaming. You and I both know that Richard is a bad person. Likely just as bad as his brothers. But some criminals cannot be brought to justice through the legal system."

"So I should just give up? Drop it?"

"That's not what I am saying."

"Then what are you saying?"

"I'm saying you can either give this a rest—celebrate the victory that Marcus Braden is no longer breathing on this planet—or you can maybe do something off the grid to deal with Richard. I mean really off the grid. Not like what happened here in Mexico."

"I'm not sure where you are going, Dave. Sounds like some sort of vigilante justice idea. Dave and Max go all-out *Star Chamber*?"

Dave did not respond. He suddenly seemed more interested in his tequila.

"Well, whatever. I'm not throwing in the towel, Dave. And I'm not going *Rambo* vigilante at this stage of my life. It took me a very long time to bring justice to Marcus Braden. There were people who thought that it would never happen."

"Again, I repeat, Malta is not Mexico. Not only do you not have the contacts, but they play by completely different rules. You may have to change your way of thinking a bit. Adjust your moral or ethical code for a moment. You know, for the greater good."

"Weren't we both taught to live by the motto that the Rule of Law is the Rule of Law? That following the Rule of Law *is* for the greater good?"

"Wow I can't believe we are having this philosophical conversation after the day that we've just had."

"You know, I remember Avery used to lecture me some when I was a cop, whenever she felt like I was obsessing a little too much about the 'one who got away.' Whenever I would get angry about someone getting off on a technicality. Whenever I would rant about some defense lawyer who went way out of his way to assist some menace to society and to give the cops a black eye in the process. Avery would always say 'it's better that a thousand guilty men go free than one innocent man be convicted.' She said that I had to accept that sometimes the bad guys would win but that was the price of having an ethical compass and remaining civilized. A necessary price."

"I'm not sure I buy into that. Sounds great in theory. But folks in our jobs—or our former jobs—we get weary of seeing all the guilty ones go free. Sometimes it feels like more than that thousand-to-one ratio of Avery's."

"Yeah." Max took a slow drink. "We'll get Richard."

"Maybe we will, Max. Gotta admire your enthusiasm."

"Enthusiasm? I'm not sure that's what you should call it."

Chapter Forty-Two

The Siege at Malta. Forty-Two Days Later (December 9, 2019).

Avery texted Max. "You are never going to believe what happened today?"

"What?"

Max was distracted, looking through a pair of high-powered binoculars out over the smooth blue Mediterranean waters. It was going to be an especially nice day for fishing.

"Dr. Astrid Nilsson was arrested."

"No kidding? For what?"

"The murder of Arkady Basayev."

"What? The old guy found across the street from the court in Belo Gardens? Dmitry's father?"

"Yep. There was a press release today. A grand jury believed that there was enough evidence to conclude that she poisoned Arkady with some polonium-210 in some green tea she served him. Grand jury came back pretty fast, all things considered. I heard that there may have been some recordings that the old guy had of her discussing some bad stuff regarding the clinical trials and she was afraid he was about to go public with them. Knocked him off to stop him. I know that the FBI has to be in complete shock that it wasn't Russians."

"Lol."

"Arkady apparently had enough strength after she poisoned him to come to downtown Dallas before he dropped dead in Belo Gardens. The FBI assumes he was about to come into our building to talk to someone, to rat out the unethical clinical trials that she was cooperating in with Enos."

"Rat out her 'unethical clinical trials'? It was a little worse than that, don't you think?"

"You know what I meant."

"Well, glad they are getting to the bottom of it."

"Yep. And Big Pharma stocks have been plummeting. The market is now expecting a big setback in bringing the Basayev disinfection system to market as well as the Basayev therapies. The FDA and its EU counterpart are re-examining everything. All the data that they have been presented thus far is now suspect. It's a shame."

"It's a shame? Why would it be a shame that they are taking a closer look? Isn't that a good thing, all things considered?"

"Okay. That sounded wrong. It's just that there have been news reports in the last couple of days that a virus has broken out in parts of rural Mexico that looks like that permafrost flu. No one is sure how and why it got into rural Mexico—was it from the stash houses or *Isla Valladolid* or elsewhere? Would be nice to have Dmitry's therapies available down there if they truly are effective."

"Wonder if people are turning up with bright blue eyes in Mexico? Maybe you will finally learn whether it's the flu or the drugs that causes it."

"Ugh. You're terrible. So how are things looking in Malta, or do I want to know?"

"Well, it's a nice day for sailing around Malta—up to Gozo. At least that's what Richard Braden thinks. He goes out about this time every day. Should be pulling out of Balluta Bay any time now."

"OMG, Max. Y'all have found Richard Braden? Is Malta law enforcement cooperating?"

"Yes and no."

"Huh?"

"Yes, we have found him. He has been using the name Rasmus Aavik for several years now. He tells people that he used to be a sailor in Estonia. He has a lot of small businesses including a restaurant here in St. Julian's. Dave and I are watching him right now."

"What did you mean yes and no?"

"Well, yes we have found him but, no, Malta law enforcement is not cooperating in the least."

"Why not?"

"We're not sure what exactly is going on. We have given them a truckload of info. Proof of years of money laundering for both the Mexican cartels and the mob over here. Bitcoin hacks. Cyberattacks. Enough to put him away for a long time."

"What gives?"

"Don't know. So, we just sit and wait. I think Richard knows who we are. He definitely knows we're watching him. Doesn't seem worried in the least. Don't know if he has paid off the locals or what."

"Where are you watching him?"

"Well, right now we are sitting outside at the *Pjazza tal-Balluta* restaurant on the bay, having a beer. Our afternoon routine lately. It's within eye shot of his restaurant, and we also have a good view of his sailboat."

"The rough and boring life of covert surveillance. Oh...except you're not technically on surveillance... you're not on duty for any agency or employer. Y'all are rogue. Lol."

"We're on a mission from God? Lol."

"Good grief."

"Wait. Let me get back with you in a bit. Gtg."

Dave had just gotten a text from one of his local contacts. Dave abruptly handed Max his cellphone to read the text.

"Mr. Carrillo, I think you are going to see something happen very soon with Rasmus Aavik."

Dave replied. "???"

"Trust me on this. We have convinced the right people that we have a big corruption case against him that even goes far beyond what you have shared with us. But it's been complicated. Others may go down with him. This has been a big problem."

"Thanks for the update."

Max and Dave finished off their beers. "What do you think the text means? Wonder who the so-called *others* are?"

"Don't know. Let's go fishing. What better way to wait this one out, eh?"

Max and Dave had rented a small fishing boat that day—the type of boat the Maltese fishermen call a *luzza*. *Luzzas* are brightly painted vessels—blue, yellow, red, and green, and are always painted or engraved with a pair of eyes on the front of the boat (the *Eye of Orisis*). The eyes are a superstitious tradition, dating back to the Phoenicians, to supposedly protect the fishermen from any harm while at sea. Max and Dave often went out this time of day because this was when Richard always went sailing. On this day, Dave and Max would head out further. It was a beautiful day. The sky was blue with spinning, curling, friendly white clouds. And Dave and Max had new optimism that maybe Richard Braden's days as a free man were coming to a close.

"You are going to love Gozo, Dave. Steep cliffs. Caves and lagoons. Calm, crystalline waters. Not many people. Great fishing. Maybe we can fish around Comino today as well."

"Sightseeing later, Max. Business first."

"Business? What do you mean?"

"I want to watch Richard for a while."

Dave pointed to the spot in the harbor where Richard always kept his sixty-five-foot Jeanneau '64 sailboat, which had its name painted on the side: *Ad Maius Bonum*. It was a spectacular vessel. Probably cost $1.5 million USD brand new. Richard was just pulling out into the bay.

Max was impatient. He just wanted to relax and fish today.

"I see him, Dave. He's right on schedule. What's the point? We have told the locals everything we know. Do you think from that text you got that there is going to be some sort of dramatic high seas take down of him today or what?"

"Hah. I don't know. I just feel like watching him a bit."

Richard Braden had pulled out quickly and was moving at a brisk pace. He was alone, as usual, in his luxurious craft. He was living the sweet life for sure. He got out a bottle of his favorite wine and some *Bragioli* and *'hobz bizzejt* that he had packed in his ice chest. Later he planned to snack on some pastries with carob-flavored honey. He would eventually position himself in one of his favorite spots—near either *Gzira* or *Birzebbuga*—and set up his gear just as he liked it. Two rods at the back and two at the front. Hopefully, it wasn't too late in the season to catch some Lampuki or dolphin. He nestled back in his chair with a copy of the *Malta Times*. He put on some Sinatra music. He missed his brother. But life was still good for him.

Suddenly two drones flew over his sailboat. Richard looked up and cursed at them. "Stupid amateur hobbyists." He had been seeing them a lot lately on the beaches there. He hated them. The drones kept circling and circling the Jeanneau.

Dave and Max were not far behind in their colorful *luzza*. They noticed the drones.

"Hey, drone expert. Do you think that is by chance cops hovering over Richard for surveillance or just some amateurs playing around?"

Dave pulled out some binoculars. Max did as well.

Neither of them said a word. They kept watching curiously.

Dave finally spoke up. "Those are DJI M600s. Professional grade drones, not amateurish. I've got a bad feeling about this. We might ought to pull back a little."

Max looked at Dave with concern. Suddenly one of the drones stopped circling. It hovered in the air directly above it and then dropped an explosive payload—a ZMG-1 grenade—on Richard Braden's million-dollar sailboat. There was a blast radius of about fifty meters. Then the second drone dove and crashed into what was left of the sailboat creating a brilliant blast of flames and smoke. The sailboat was obliterated. Braden and his boat were gone. Nothing left but some debris in the water.

"Holy shit! What just happened?" Max began looking around frantically. They were quite a distance from the harbor or any shoreline at this point. No other humans were visible, although the blast of flames and smoke had to be noticeable for miles away.

"*That* just happened. You are not dreaming, Captain Max."

Max looked at Dave with a perplexed face. Dave said nothing.

"I suspect the first dump was a grenade, and then the second was loaded with a kilogram of C-4 explosives. That's all it takes. Straight out of ISIS's playbook."

Max continued to sit in startled silence. He was having difficulty processing what had just happened.

"Let's go up to Gozo now. Let me see what all the fuss is about in Gozo. Lead the way, Captain Max."

"Are you kidding?" For Christ's sake. We just witnessed Richard Braden's assassination! At the very least, we need to call it in and give witness statements to the police."

"C'mon, Max. Let's go."

"Dave, what the hell do you mean, 'let's go'? What's going on? Why are you being so nonchalant. We just watched the man we have spent hours tracking down and trying to get arrested get blown to smithereens!"

"Max, let me behind the wheel. I'll drive. Tell me if I go the wrong way."

The two of them rode in silence for thirty minutes. The hum of the small motor and lapping water were the only audible sounds. Finally, Max broke the silence.

"Dave, did you know that was going to happen? Who did it? Mob or corrupt cops? It wasn't you manning the drones—I know that much. No remote control on our boat, obviously."

Dave sat in silence. Max was growing impatient. Finally, Dave responded.

"Max let's just say that there are some things that should remain a mystery. I have a different background than you, man. You and I are alike, but we are also different."

"What are you saying? Spell it out."

"Max, there were things I did back when I was in Marine Special Ops that, some would say, were ethically or morally questionable. Others would say they were heroic. Missions in Yemen, Somalia, Algeria. All kinds of crazy mercenary shit. And, if I had the chance, I would do it all over again. I know what I did made the world a safer place."

Max continued to stare at Dave in silence.

"Max, we had a job to do here in Malta, just like I had a job to do back in those days. I may have rounded some corners here. I may have made sure some really bad people were plenty mad at Richard. I may have made a few suggestions about how those bad people might deal with the situation. That's not you. That's not your background, Max. It's not your nature—even if people do call you Mad Max. I couldn't let you become the kind of person you are not. Especially knowing how you felt about what happened to Avery and the New Jersey judges."

"Are you telling me you did something—or suggested something to someone—that you thought was for the greater good? Hah. Irony."

"You are on a need-to-know basis, Mad Max."

Max slid over and grabbed a Cisk Lager from their ice chest. Max handed Dave the beer and then got one for himself.

"You know, when I was a cop, I used to tell Avery that there was no easy or nice way to arrest someone who doesn't want to be arrested. She used to grimace a little. She used to remind me that I had to be careful talking or thinking that way. I knew she was right to lecture me. But I knew there were some things she just didn't understand."

Dave did not respond. He sipped his beer. He clearly didn't seem to want to engage any more on this topic.

"What do you think of the Maltese beer? My favorite is the Farson's Blue Label." Max was awkwardly trying to change the conversation. He suddenly become very uncomfortable.

"You don't have to change the conversation, Max. When and what are you going to tell Avery?"

"Hmm. I guess I will tell her that there was a coincidental mob hit on Richard, just as we were starting to close in on him? How does that sound?"

Dave shrugged and said nothing.

"I'll call her in a bit. You know her. She'll have lots of questions."

"Yep. Cross-examination is her stock in trade."

There was more awkward silence as the men started getting out their fishing gear.

"Max, that whole *greater good* concept. That's a Biblical concept, right? For the greater good?"

"Well, what do you know! I have found something outside the Swiss Army Knife's area of expertise: theology and philosophy. No, Dave, it's not Biblical!"

"I think it is. You're wrong man."

"For the greater good is an Aristotle thing, man. Or some Greek philosopher originally said it. Maybe it was Plato."

"Well, those guys probably plagiarized it from the Bible."

"Nope. I really don't think so. Think about it. For the greater good is kind of a sliding scale type thing—it's about picking the lesser of two evils. Or rationalizing that the end always justifies the means. It's an ethics thing, more than a moral thing. You can engage in a bad action if the outcome is good for the most people. The Bible, on the other hand, teaches that goodness comes from God—it is divinely established—and is not relative according to outcomes. But, come to think of it, the Bible does teach that God takes bad things and turns them into something good. So, I suppose."

"Okay. This got heavy fast."

"You're the one who asked, Dave."

"I'm going to pull into this little cove. It looks like a great spot to fish don't you think?" Max agreed. They pulled the *luzza* into a quiet spot, turned off the motor and started situating their gear to cast.

"Ya know, Dave. You were right about how we are different. But it's our training and background more than anything else that is the difference. In policing, you are told to be careful about the whole greater good thing. You sometimes know that you are dealing with a terrible criminal, but you must follow rules. Due process and the Constitution and all that. You are a protector but you're not God. I guess with war and the Marshals—what you've been trained for—it's sort of more ambiguous. Y'all are the last resort sometimes after all the rules have been followed, and the bad guy has gotten away."

"Let's talk about beer. You asked me earlier what I thought of the Maltese beer. I think their beer is a hellava lot better than some of their so-called gourmet delicacies. I don't know what the fuss is about rabbit stew. Give me a good American burger any day."

"Yeah, I agree. Next subject. What's next for the Swiss Army Knife? Are you going to take any more assignments from Premier Mutual?"

"I doubt it. I don't know. I'm thinking about going back to my old stomping grounds."

"You mean Gunnison? Colorado?"

"Yep. Maybe I'll run for Sheriff there."

"Good God. You, a politician? I didn't see that one coming!"

"Wanna come be my deputy, Max? You always said you were my Huckleberry."

"I never said I was your Huckleberry. Did I?"

Epilogue

The Apostle Paul's Ship Goes Ashore on Malta

"Once safely on shore, we found out that the island was called Malta. The islanders showed us unusual kindness. They built a fire and welcomed us... Paul gathered a pile of brushwood and, as he put it on the fire, a viper, driven out by the heat, fastened itself on his hand. When the islanders saw the snake hanging from his hand, they said to each other, 'This man must be a murderer; for though he escaped from the sea, the goddess Justice has not allowed him to live.' But Paul shook the snake off into the fire and suffered no ill effects."

The Book of Acts 28:2-7, Bible, New Testament (New International Version).